Lobster *for* Breakfast

Charlene Burck

To Carol –
Well, the class of '65 is
still on the move. I hope you
enjoy the book.
All my best,
Charlene Burck

Print ISBN: 978-1-48357-306-9

eBook ISBN: 978-1-48357-307-6

Acknowledgements

Writing a novel is a solitary pursuit. You can't be sure that what you've written will interest anyone but yourself until you swallow your pride, let other people read it and ask for their comments.

My manuscript readers—and you know who you are—have been sensitive, thoughtful and encouraging. I paid attention to every one of your suggestions and the book is better because of you. I consider it a true kindness that no one—not even the readers of my early rough drafts—advised me to abandon the effort and go out and get a real job. My sincere thanks to all of you.

A special shout out to my late parents, Charles and Celeste Johnson, whose spirit animates these pages. When Dad was still alive and I told him the father in the novel was loosely patterned on him, he said, "Oh good. Make me sexy." So Dad, that passage toward the end of the novel, the one with the racy love letters? That's for you and Mom.

Mille grazie to my husband Paul. Not only does the man know his spelling, grammar and punctuation, he's also the sentimental old fool who read the manuscript twice and got just as caught up in the story the second time around. Thank you, Paul, for your optimism and tireless assistance. I couldn't have done it without you.

Finally, to the legions of relatives and friends who've been secretly wondering if I'd ever get the book published: Thanks for sticking with me. Here's hoping you'll find it was worth the wait.

Prologue

When the mood was on him Henry Streator would drive the fifteen miles from his suburban home to the Minneapolis/St. Paul airport, park his car and board the next outbound plane with an open seat. The destination hardly mattered to him.

One sultry evening in August of 2002 he stepped off a plane in Cincinnati. Catching a bus into town he disembarked in an inner city neighborhood where he knew he'd find a VFW hall. He'd been there before. A sign out front read: BINGO TONIGHT. LOWER LEVEL. WATCH YOUR STEP.

He descended the stairs and entered the bingo parlor. His gaze swept the room and settled on a woman sitting alone at the second table from the back. He'd hoped she would be there. He didn't know her name; he only knew she looked as lost as he felt.

Summoning his courage he slipped into the empty seat on her right. Over the course of the evening he spoke to her of a place where a person could play bingo seven days a week.

The woman was Cora Matthews. She was mentally ill. She did not tell the man of her condition. In fact she was unaware of it herself.

Early the next morning, when Henry Streator boarded the redeye flight from Cincinnati to Minneapolis, Cora Matthews was at his side.

Chapter 1

June 6, 2005

Just getting out of the house that Monday morning was proving a challenge. Unruly hair and misplaced glasses had me running late for my first day of work at Procter & Gamble. My dad, who would be dropping me off in downtown Cincinnati on the way to his own job on the east side, was already idling the car in the driveway when I scrambled into the business suit I'd borrowed from my sister.

Katie owned just one suit and it was fire engine red. My mother had insisted Katie's suit would make a better first impression than anything hanging in my closet. She'd been wrong. Marriage and two kids must have layered a few extra pounds onto my sister. I was swimming in that suit: The jacket hung like a sack on my slender frame and the too-long skirt turned my calves into toothpicks. As for what the scarlet hue did to my pale skin? I've seen corpses with better complexions.

With no time to rethink my wardrobe I raced out the door to the car. As I buckled myself into the passenger seat my dad said, "Tell me this won't happen every day, Carrie."

"Never again," I vowed.

I flipped down the visor and stared at myself in the mirror, taking in the bushy blond hair, the gawky glasses and the over-sized suit. "I look like a homeless person."

My dad leaned toward me and sniffed. "You don't smell too bad."

I flipped the visor back up. "I bet you say that to all the girls."

He laughed. "At least I got you to smile."

Twenty minutes later he pulled to the curb in front of P&G headquarters, its massive twin towers thrusting skyward into the morning sun. I took a deep breath and turned to my dad.

He said, "You look fine, little one."

I didn't, but it was nice of him to say it. I got out of the car, threaded my way across the plaza and stepped through the doors of the building that was to become as familiar to me as the face of a friend.

That first day though, I was a stranger in a strange land. Who was this dispirited girl filling out intake paperwork, dragging through orientation, and learning the ins and outs of becoming an administrative assistant? This was not the me I was supposed to be. This was not the future I'd mapped out for myself.

For a kid growing up in a blue-collar neighborhood on Cincinnati's west side my aspirations had been lofty. In my all-girl high school I'd been a scholar, not much to look at, but one of those students expected by her teachers to set the world on fire.

The September after graduating from high school, full of hope and high ideals, I'd joined the masses converging upon the University of Cincinnati. My goal was to be the first member of my family to earn a four-year degree. From there I would go on to grad school. In my wildest dreams I pictured myself with let-ters behind my name and a career that meant something.

Six months into my freshman year at UC reality struck like a brick to the head when three bad things happened. Due to a slump in new home construction my dad and his coworkers at Queen City Fastener were offered a choice: take a twenty percent cut in pay or face layoffs. On the fifteenth of February they voted to accept the pay cut. That night an irregular heartbeat sent my mom to the emergency room, an expense only partially covered by my dad's health insurance. A week later our only car, a twelve-year-old Ford Escort with over two hundred thousand miles on it, broke down.

My parents, who'd barely been scraping by, found themselves in dire financial straits. My older sister and brother offered to help, but Katie had a family and mortgage payments of her own and Tommy was squirreling away every spare penny to move out of his mouse-infested apartment into something better. There simply wasn't enough money to go around.

I knew what I had to do. When spring semester ended I needed to put aside my books and find a full-time job. The extra income would allow my folks to buy a reliable car and pay down my mother's medical bills while keeping up the mortgage payments on the single-story home that was my parents' pride and joy. My extraordinary future would have to wait.

In March I informed my parents of my change in plans. My mother cried. My dad swallowed hard. They both looked relieved.

I pasted on a happy face and launched my job search.

Of all the companies I applied to, Procter & Gamble was the one I least expected to hear from. A Cincinnati institution and corporate giant—manufacturer of products like Bounty towels, Crest toothpaste and Tide laundry detergent—P&G could afford to be selective in its hiring. Knowing full well that a college dropout with a handful of liberal arts credits probably wouldn't make the cut I applied anyway.

Chalk one up for the eggheads: my good grades landed me an interview.

In mid-April with my expectation meter set on low I caught a bus to P&G headquarters, where I took an aptitude and skills test and answered a series of essay questions. When eventually I sat across the desk from my interviewer she was clearly impressed. Courtney informed me I'd aced my aptitude test and dazzled her with my answers to the essay questions. Even my lack of business and computer training was not the kiss of death I'd feared it would be.

"Ordinarily our support positions require a business background," she said. "However there are some settings where written communication skills like yours are in demand." Looking thoughtful she tapped her lip with a ballpoint pen. "Let me see what's available."

Three weeks later, just as UC's spring semester was wrapping up I'd received the call that would alter the course of my life. Courtney had secured me a position as an administrative assistant at Procter & Gamble headquarters. As clerical positions go it was a good job. With no other prospects and no excuse for turning it down I'd accepted the offer.

So there I was on the first Monday in June, resplendent in my sister's red suit, holed up with five other new hires in a windowless training room on the second floor of the east tower. Our indoctrination into all things P&G took most of the day. It was nearly four o'clock when a human resources employee named Joyce called my name and beckoned me into the hall.

"Ready to meet the people you'll be working with?" she asked.

I knew "absolutely" was the expected answer, so I mouthed it, although "ready to go home?" would have generated a more genuine response.

Joyce escorted me to the sixth floor, home of Paper Products Advertising. Exiting the elevator we walked down a corridor that opened into a carpeted space where men and women sat at desks arranged in clusters of three and four. On the far side of the room doorways to private offices lined the wall. Joyce led me across the space to the second doorway, ushered me into a medium-size office with a south-facing window and introduced me to C. Bradley Collins, Jr., brand manager of Cloud Soft toilet paper.

When C. Bradley Collins stood to greet me I went weak in the knees. I had just been assigned to work for the best-looking man in the company.

I have no idea what he said or what I said. Oh my god is what my insides were saying. When Joyce departed my movie-star boss emerged from behind his desk, took me in his arms and—

No, wait. That's not what happened. My new boss—Brad, he told me to call him—sat down and gestured for me to take the seat across the desk from him. After glancing at some paperwork Joyce had given him he focused his attention on me and said, "Carrie Matthews, welcome."

I had to fight the urge to snatch off my glasses, a habit I'd acquired at high school football games whenever a cute boy glanced my way. Tongue-tied I stammered, "Welcome," which was totally stupid.

Pretending not to notice my blunder he said, "First I'll tell you a little bit about what we do here. Then I'll introduce you to the other people you'll be working with."

I ordered myself to pay attention.

He held up his left hand—complete with wedding band—and raised his thumb. "Number one, don't expect glitz. We're in the advertising department, but we don't do advertising here. No actors. No cameras. We work with an ad agency in New York. They're the ones who produce the commercials, print ads, coupons, et cetera. We're the facilitators between the ad agency and various departments here at P&G—finance, legal, research and development, marketing and sales. The job's not glamorous, but it's necessary."

His eyes were impossibly blue; when he smiled they sparkled. And he had dimples. My god he had dimples. I tried to appear intelligent and interested as he ticked off points two through five on the remaining digits of his amazing left hand. Eventually his incredible mouth seemed to be describing the tasks I'd be performing.

I was in a daze when he took me out to meet the two associates whose administrative work I'd be doing. Dave and Nicole sat beside each other outside the door to Brad's office.

"Notice the open floor plan," Brad said, gesturing around the room, where two dozen men and women—representing other brands, I assumed—sat at desks arranged in similar configurations. "A few years back the department voted to get rid of individual cubicles in order to," he made quotation marks with his fingers, "foster a spirit of creativity and cooperation."

Dave piped up. "They call it synergy."

"How's that working for you, Dave?" Brad asked.

Dave raised his shoulders in a half-shrug. "Can't complain."

Brad showed me my desk, which was positioned so I'd be facing Dave and Nicole. Beside my desk was a support column.

"I'll synergize with the pole," I said. To my delight Brad smiled and flashed his dimples.

At that moment I set a new goal in life: make Brad Collins smile.

"You should see him, Mom. He's drop-dead gorgeous."

It was late Monday afternoon. As soon as my dad and I had gotten home from work I'd rushed to my bedroom and ditched my sister's suit. Now, comfortable in shorts and a T-shirt I was peeling potatoes at the kitchen sink. My mother stood at the adjoining counter chopping vegetables.

"Are we talking George Clooney gorgeous?" my mother asked.

I bobbed my head. "Even better." I put down a half-peeled potato and closed my eyes. "Picture a California surfer. Perfectly toned body, ocean blue eyes, sandy hair streaked with blond..." I faded off, willing my mom to see the amazing hunk of humanity in my mind's eye.

"I suppose he has that two-day stubble you like so much."

"I do and he does," I said. "Did I mention his dimples?"

My dad had entered the kitchen while we were talking. I'd already bent his ear about the same subject on the way home. He came up behind my mom and wrapped his arms around her waist. "Isn't it sweet, Joanie? Our little girl's in love."

"So I gather." She let him nuzzle her neck for a while before elbowing him away.

He took a drinking glass from the cupboard and filled it with tap water. "When's the wedding, Carrie?"

I sighed. "Unfortunately..."

"Don't tell me he's already taken," my dad said.

"Yeah, judging from the wedding band and the picture of the wife and kid on the desk."

My dad patted my shoulder in mock sympathy. "That's so unfair."

I sniffed. "It sucks."

"Hey, we're disappointed too," Dad said. "We have plans for your bedroom."

Mom laughed. "Tom, that's mean."

I wagged the potato peeler at my dad. "You make fun now, Dad, but when C. Bradley Collins falls madly in love with me and ditches his classy wife I'll be the one laughing."

My dad chuckled. "Just as long as we get your bedroom." He downed his water and went outside to work on the Escort.

In anticipation of collecting room and board money from me once I started working my parents had financed a late model used car. If Dad could get the old clunker running—and I had no doubt he would—I was slated to become its proud owner.

I started dicing the potatoes and tossing them into a saucepan.

My mom was sautéing onions and bell peppers in a skillet. "All kidding aside," she said, "you do know this man is off limits."

"Duh. Like he'd even notice me anyway."

My mother was nothing if not loyal. She waded right in to defend my ability to seduce another woman's husband. "You're appealing, Carrie. You're smart as a whip. You have a great—"

"Let me guess. I have a great personality."

"I was going to say sense of humor, but you do have a great personality."

"That's what they say about all ugly girls."

"You're not ugly, honey." She put down her spatula. I could feel her eyes on me. Finally she said, "Today's not your best day, but you looked nice at Mass on Sunday."

I cringed. I was like, seriously, Mom, is that even a compliment?

"If only you'd do something with your hair," she said.

My mother was always after me about my hair. She hated that I blow-dried the life out of it and wore it pushed back from my face, secured with clips and a stretchy headband. She of the poker-straight hair had no idea what it was like to wake up every day with a head full of yellow frizz.

"Katie and I were talking the other night, Carrie. We think you should try letting your hair dry naturally. The curls would frame your face."

That's just great, I thought. My mother and my sister have been discussing me behind my back. I suppose Dad and Tommy weighed in too. I pictured the four of them with their heads together pondering the burning question: Can this wreck be salvaged?

I administered a vicious chop to a potato. "I like straight hair. Why can't I have Katie's hair?"

"Katie has my hair. You have your dad's hair. That's life, Carrie. You need to make the most of what God gave you."

"Did God give me these frigging glasses?" For the hundredth time that day I shoved the black plastic frames up the bridge of my nose.

"Maybe you should try contacts again," my mother said.

"And get another eye infection?" I shook my head. "I'm holding out for Lasik."

"How do you plan to pay for that?"

"I'll save my money."

"I thought you were saving for college."

I rolled my eyes. My mother can be truly annoying when she states the obvious. Of course I was saving for college. That was the master plan. But couldn't I throw in a little eye surgery for good measure, preferably before tomorrow morning?

Chapter 2

I showed up for my first real day of work eager to see Brad Collins again. Would he be as irresistible as I remembered? His office was dark when I arrived and it stayed dark for an hour. It appeared I'd have to wait.

In the meantime Nicole helped me log on to the computer. Brad must have appointed her to be my mentor because she rolled her chair around to my side of the desk and ran through a checklist of things I needed to know. She was about to cram another factoid into my already brimming brain when I heard the voice that made me tingle.

"You came back."

I glanced up. Different suit, shirt and tie, but definitely the same guy standing on the other side of my desk. I would have to get over blushing every time C. Bradley Collins set eyes at me.

"Ready to dive in, Carrie?" Brad asked.

"S-s-sure, why not?" I said.

"At ten I have a conference call I want you to sit in on. You're going to take the minutes."

"Oh," I said, suddenly panicked.

"Don't worry, I won't let you drown. Grab a pad and pencil and come into my office at about quarter till. We'll go over what you need to know."

At 9:45 I entered Brad's office and took a seat across the desk from him. He'd taken off his jacket, loosened his tie and unbuttoned the top button of his white dress shirt. My breath caught in my throat; he looked even better that way.

"Every Tuesday morning I have a conference call with P&G marketing and Krause and Moser, our New York ad agency," Brad said. "The legal department will be involved today as well. It's our party, so we're the ones who write the report that goes out to everyone else."

He slid an open binder toward me. "Here's last week's report." He pointed with his pen. "We list the names of the people involved. Here are the discussion items and what everybody said. Here are the action items, current status and who agreed to do what. Dave and I have been doing the reports, but we'd like you to take over. It's not rocket science, but right now you won't be familiar with people's names or the terms we're throwing around, so I'll be your lifeguard."

I looked up from the binder. "Lifeguard?"

"You'll write up the report the best you can and send it to me. I'll dive in, do some editing and return it to you so you can see the changes I made." Brad shrugged. "There may be a lot of changes at first, but that's the way you learn. Eventually you'll do the whole thing yourself and we'll send it out as is."

At ten Brad dialed into the conference call and I started taking notes. I was so nervous my hands were sweating. That explains why a few minutes into the call a freaky thing happened that would have been funny if only it had happened to someone else. As I was trying to keep up with the rapid-fire delivery of an ad agency man with a New York accent my pencil flew out of my fingers, landed on the desk and rolled into Brad's lap.

Oh crap. My panicked glance flitted around the desk top, searching for something else to write with and finding nothing. Now what do I do?

Still attending to the conference call Brad retrieved my pencil and dangled it in front of me. I grabbed for it but he held on until I was forced to look him in the eye. His expression was amused and so steady I couldn't help but smile and relax as I took it from him. The exchange knocked the edge off my anxiety. I settled in and started making sense of the conversation rather than attempting to record every word.

I admit I was inexperienced and biased to boot, but I thought Brad was a master at conducting the meeting. He presented each agenda item in a logical context, kept everybody on topic and involved in the conversation, got people to make commitments and summarized the item before moving on. And there was something else, something in his easy manner and energetic style that said, "Isn't this fun? Don't you want to be part of making this work?"

When the call concluded, Brad said, "That wasn't so bad, was it?"

"Can I reserve judgment until I try typing it up?"

"You'll do fine. We chose you because you can put two words together. Not everybody can do that."

So I'd been chosen rather than assigned to Collins and company. I wondered if he would have chosen me if he'd seen me first.

I returned to my desk and started putting two words together, then two more, and two more after that. The report I eventually passed along to Brad wasn't flawless, but it didn't come back with as many changes as I'd feared.

My career as an administrative assistant was launched. I had not drowned; I was not even taking on water. I can do this, I thought.

Aside from the obvious draw of working for the best-looking man in the universe I discovered I enjoyed being an administrative assistant. Within a month I'd developed a productive working relationship with my colleagues and was beginning to anticipate and satisfy the administrative needs of the department. By the end of July the Cloud Soft advertising group was operating like a well-oiled machine.

In the process I'd acquired a new friend. Angie, administrative assistant for Puffs facial tissues, sat ten paces away from me in her own synergistic cluster. My first day in the department she'd invited me to have lunch with her in the company cafeteria. We'd hit it off so well we'd been brown bagging it together ever since.

Angie was three years older than me. Tall, porcelain-skinned and pencil thin, she looked like a model. I coveted what I called her Pantene hair, a glossy mahogany curtain that fell halfway down her back and rippled like satin when she turned her head. She'd worked in Paper Products Advertising for two years and knew everything about everybody.

As often as I could get away with it I steered my friend toward my favorite subject: Brad. From Angie I learned he had an MBA from Yale, he and his wife were Minnesota transplants and his son was seven years old. I learned that my boss, at twenty-nine, was the youngest brand manager in the department.

"He's got it all, Carrie," Angie had said at lunch one day, "looks, brains, personality and six hundred dollar Ferragamos." Noting my uncomprehending stare she said, "Italian shoes?"

Of course.

Neither Angie nor I had a real boyfriend to salivate over. For Angie it was by choice; she was too busy. She'd come to P&G with an associate degree and was studying fashion design in night school, which didn't surprise me since she had great taste in clothes.

Angie and I were the yin and yang of fashion. My stylish friend was none too subtle about what she thought of my wardrobe, which consisted of ensembles cobbled together at the thrift store. Once she discovered we both lived on the west side of town she was constantly prodding me to go shopping with her. I resisted, however; I was in the business of saving money, not spending it. In less than two months, even with paying room and board to my parents, I'd amassed the kingly sum of three thousand dollars.

That was about to change.

Chapter 3

On the twenty-sixth of July I turned nineteen. I came home from work that afternoon to find two pieces of mail waiting for me. One was a reminder from Dr. Wing, my eye doctor, that it was time for my annual checkup. Toward the bottom of the postcard was a handwritten note that read: *Let's talk about Lasik.*

The other piece of mail was an offer for a Visa card featuring a five thousand dollar credit limit and an interest rate of zero for the first six months.

I let out a whoop and punched the air. The next day, after ordering my new credit card I made an appointment with Dr. Wing for the following Saturday. "Let's talk about Lasik," I told the receptionist.

My eye surgery was scheduled for the third Friday in August. With Brad I'd arranged to take a sick day but hadn't said why. My plan was to surprise everyone by showing up at work the next Monday without my glasses. But when I joined Angie for lunch the day before my procedure I couldn't resist spilling the beans.

Angie, never given to the measured response, shrieked her approval. Eyes dancing she said, "Carrie, take off your glasses."

Mystified, I slipped them off.

She studied my face. "You are going to look fabulous." She slapped the table with both hands. "You know what would be awesome? You should get a complete makeover this weekend. New hairdo, new clothes, new makeup. When you come to work Monday you'll be a totally different person."

A different person—that did sound cool. I put my glasses back on. "I'm not supposed to wear eye makeup for three days after surgery."

"Screw that," Angie said. "We'll be careful; nothing bad will happen."

"We?"

"You're not blowing me off this time, girl. We have some serious shopping to do." She produced her cell phone and started pressing buttons. "I'll see if Sarah can cut your hair on Saturday. She's not cheap, but she's good." I listened in guilty silence as she wheedled her hairdresser sister into coming to work early on Saturday just for me.

By the time we finished lunch the Saturday arrangements had been made. I'd surrendered myself completely to Angie's will. She would be my combination chauffeur, makeup artist and clothing advisor.

"Trust me, Carrie, it'll be so much fun," Angie promised.

For once I was inclined to agree.

"I'm picturing a riot of shoulder-length curls," Angie said. "Layered, of course."

"Of course," said Sarah.

It was early Saturday morning. I was sitting before a mirror in the salon where Angie's sister worked. My eye surgery the day before had been cringe inducing but not painful. The minute it was over I could see without glasses, an amazing fact I was still getting used to.

I'd shampooed my hair at home and instead of blow-drying the curl out of it the way I usually did I'd let it do its corkscrew thing all over my head and down my back. It was divine having Sarah run her hands through my hair as she and Angie discussed their plans for turning me into a goddess. Sarah kept lifting the heavy top strands with one hand and raking the fingers of her other hand through the softer strands underneath. That underneath hair as it twined around Sarah's fingers was the color of blond you see on babies and can't resist touching. I felt prettier already.

Something about paying more than $7.99 for a haircut makes a girl feel pampered. With a sublime sense of entitlement I eased back in the chair and watched as Sarah picked up her scissors and made the first snip. I'd placed my fate in the hands of an expert. I would not be disappointed.

Thirty minutes later the floor was strewn with blond hair. Blond hair littered the arms of the chair and the plastic drape I was wearing. Strands of blond clung to Sarah's shirt and pants. There I was at the center of it all gazing at a new Carrie. Angie and Sarah stood on either side of me observing my expression in the mirror.

I stared at my reflection. The person staring back was not me. This was somebody else, somebody I'd give an arm and a leg to look like.

"Oh wow," I said.

"What do you think?" said Sarah.

"I feel like Cinderella."

Wiping imaginary sweat from her brow Angie said, "Whew! As the fairy godmother in charge of this transformation I'm happy you're happy."

I looked from one sister to the other. "I'm blown away."

Sarah grinned. "This was worth coming in early for," she said. From her workstation countertop she collected the headband and clips I'd worn to the salon. "You won't need these anymore. If you just let your hair air dry, the curls will frame your face."

I laughed. "Have you been talking to my mother? Face-framing curls is her mantra."

"Obviously your mom was on to something," Angie said. "Just look at you, Carrie. You're gorgeous."

I looked. And I was.

"Where to next?" I asked.

We were making our way through the parking lot, having just left the beauty salon. I'd been so entranced by my reflection in the mirror behind the cash register that I'd barely flinched when I'd paid my bill.

"My apartment," Angie said as we climbed into the car. "Did you bring your pitiful makeup collection?"

I dug in my purse and held up a plastic sandwich bag containing mascara, eye shadow and lipstick.

Angie eyed the contents and drove straight to the drugstore. In the cosmetics aisle she made the selections. "You won't need much of any one thing, just a few subtle touches to pull it all together and make your eyes pop."

"Popping eyes. Now that sounds attractive."

"You'll see."

I did see. Standing before a mirror in Angie's bathroom and following her instructions I turned my face from forgettable to fabulous in under ten minutes. By the time I brushed a hint of blush on my cheeks and feathered it in, my eyes were indeed popping.

I'd never been sure what color they were. Now I could see they were blue-gray with specks of amber. I stared into the mirror. "They're like, luminous."

Angie handed me my new cosmetics bag. "Gather up your goodies, girlfriend. We're off to the mall. Eyes like these demand a new wardrobe."

At Macy's we scoured the sales and clearance racks for good buys in my size. In Career Dressing I held up a black pantsuit with the price slashed to the bone.

Angie made a face. "Boring. Not your color. Not your style."

"Look at the price," I said, showing her the tag.

"If it doesn't flatter you, why buy it even if they're giving it away?"

"If they were giving it away, I wouldn't have to buy it."

Angie rolled her eyes. "Try it on, but I guarantee you won't want it."

By the time we'd commandeered the largest dressing room in the place Angie had collected an armload of possibilities for me to sample. She hung them on the hooks provided and selected a gray suit that featured a short fitted jacket and a pencil skirt.

"With your coloring," Angie said, "medium gray is the closest you should come to wearing black. Put on the black one you chose and then try this one. You'll see the difference."

I stripped down to my underwear and slipped into the black suit. I still thought it was okay. Sure, the black gave me the complexion of a cave dweller, the slacks had baggy legs, and the long jacket made me look like a middle-aged woman with something to hide. But the pants fit at the waist, the jacket fit at the shoulders and the price was right. Those had been the only items on my checklist before.

Once I donned the gray suit, however, I began revising my selection criteria. The pencil-slim skirt, which hit three inches above the knee, hugged my curves; the back slit was a little flirty. The tapered jacket emphasized my narrow waistline. And instead of washing me out, the gray perked up my color. I peeked at the price tag. Forty dollars more than the pantsuit, but I knew which one I'd be taking home.

Angie waved her arms. "You've been hiding that dynamite body under your clothes. I'd kill to have a figure like yours." She eyed me as I removed my new suit. "Dare I mention you could use different underwear?"

I sent her off to the lingerie department while I tried on another of her selections: a flared rayon skirt in a soft pine green and navy print, a matching green long-sleeve blouse with a stand-up collar, and a navy jacket. I did a little spin. The rayon swirled luxuriously around my legs.

Angie returned bearing not only bras and panties but stretchy tanks and camisole tops in a variety of colors. She dumped them onto a stool and looked me over. "So, am I two for two?"

For three hours Angie played hunter-gatherer, foraging the racks for fabulous finds while I stayed in the dressing room trying on one outfit after another. She had a knack for choosing clothing in colors and styles that flattered me. I was happy with nearly everything she picked out. Too happy, maybe, since my stack of must-haves dwarfed my stack of rejects.

Lunchtime came and went. Finally there was only one item left to try on, an elegantly simple sheath in pewter-colored silk. I'd been pushing it aside because I thought it was too dressy for work.

Angie lifted it off the hook. "I couldn't resist this. I know you're shopping for work clothes today, but this is an unbelievable buy. Should we give it a whirl?"

The dress went on like a dream. It had spaghetti straps and a scoop neck that allowed just the right amount of rounded breast to peek from the top.

Angie covered her mouth with both hands. "Oh my god. You...are...hot."

I stood on tiptoes in front of the mirror and surveyed myself from every angle. "My cousin Jenny's getting married in October. This'll be perfect."

Angie helped me out of the dress. "Let's buy this stuff and take it to the car. After lunch we'll hunt for shoes."

We had deposited our parcels in the trunk of Angie's car and were returning to the mall when my cell phone rang. It was Denny, my quasi boyfriend. We'd known each other for twelve years, having attended elementary school together before going off to our single-sex high schools.

"Jack and Jackie are fighting again," he said. "Jackie won't be coming to bowling tonight and she refuses to find a substitute."

Denny and I were on a Saturday night bowling league, which was wrapping up its summer season. Jack and Jackie comprised the other half of our team. Their tempestuous relationship made bowling an adventure; we never knew who would show up.

"Hold on a minute, Denny." I briefed Angie and asked if she'd like to substitute for Jackie.

Angie shrugged. "I'm not much of a bowler, but if everybody's okay with that, why not?"

I got back on the phone. "I have someone. I'll bring her with me."

"That was short and not terribly sweet," Angie said when I'd clicked off. "What's the story on Denny?"

"He's my backup date. I was going to ask him to my cousin's wedding so I wouldn't have to hang out with my parents, but now that I have the dress and my new look I'd rather go alone. Take my chances, you know?"

"You'll have every guy at the wedding, including the groom, falling all over you," Angie said.

I savored the thought. That had never happened to me before.

"I can't wait to see how your friends react to you at the bowling alley," Angie mused as we made our way to the food court.

"It's appropriate that my fairy godmother accompany me on my first—" I stopped dead in front of a women's clothing store. The mannequin in the window was displaying the most perfect combination of jeans and top I'd ever seen. I pointed. "I have to have that."

I tugged Angie into the store. We searched the racks but couldn't find that particular top or pair of jeans in my size anywhere. I climbed up behind the mannequin and located the labels. "She's wearing my clothes!"

We rounded up a sales clerk, who stripped the mannequin naked. We rushed into the dressing room and I tried on the outfit. I took in the skinny, low-waisted jeans and the form-fitting pullover top. "Oh, yeah. I know what I'm wearing tonight."

My parents weren't home when we got to my house. Angie and I hauled armloads of shopping bags into my bedroom. As I started putting things away I glanced at the clock on the nightstand and saw it was after four. Suddenly I was exhausted.

Angie must have been on the same wavelength. She said, "I'm going home to take a nap. I'll pick you up later."

When Angie departed I shut my bedroom door and stretched out on the bed for a fifteen-minute power nap. I woke to the murmur of my parents talking in the kitchen. My fifteen-minute nap had lasted an hour.

My mother had been saying something to my dad, but she stopped mid-sentence when I stepped into the kitchen. My dad, whose back had been to me, turned around, followed her gaze and came as close to doing a double take as I've ever seen anyone do in real life.

"Oh, Carrie, you're stunning," my mother said.

"This is Carrie?" my dad said. "I thought a movie star had wandered in off the street."

Mom took a step toward me and touched my hair. "Look at your curls."

"Feel free to say you told me so."

"I'm speechless," she said.

Dad laughed. "Not for long."

He was right. Mom and I both started chattering. I dragged her into the bedroom and showed her my cache of goodies. She gasped when she comprehended the magnitude of my purchases.

"I guess you can return some things," she said.

I grinned. "I could, but I won't."

When she left the room I dug out my new jeans and top and laid them on the bed. Excitement welled up in me. For once I'd be the one turning heads.

Chapter 4

To kids growing up in the western suburbs of Cincinnati, Mayfair Lanes—a decrepit den of inequity in the basement of a strip mall—was a place set apart. Leaving the quotidian world behind you'd descend the steps and pass through the glass double-doors into an alien universe of greasy nachos, cigarette smoke and stale beer. There was always a degenerate behind the counter to take your money and behind him cubbyholes stacked with ratty bowling shoes for rent. To the left of the counter ancient pinball machines featuring racecars and scantily clad women lined the walls. To the right a long curved bar led to a darkened room that was open on weekends for karaoke.

The forty or so lanes that occupied most of the space were set down two steps from the main floor. Molded plastic benches in a god-awful shade of maroon surrounded the scoring console and ball return. On the main floor a scattering of round tables and plastic chairs overlooked the lanes.

I'd always loved Mayfair Lanes. The oily gleam of the hardwood alleys; the crashing pins; the bar with its shady patrons hunched over their beers; the raucous, flashing pinball machines; the general grime, persistent as dirt under the fingernails: the whole seedy package carried a whiff of impropriety that made just being there feel daring and grown-up.

I don't know if it was the new me or the fairy godmother effect of Angie's presence, but our team was hot that night, racking up strikes and spares like pros. Denny and Jack were playing at the top of their games, and I was besting them. Even Angie was no slouch. Her slow ball, which clattered down the alley on the finger holes, had an uncanny habit of curving in at the last minute to cut an impressive swath through the pins.

We were mowing them down with such authority that going into the second game we were edging out our opponents—the league champions—by six pins. By that time the four of us were wound up to fever pitch, high-fiving each other no matter what we threw. Our opponents caught the spirit; we had to be the noisiest eight people in the place.

As we began our third and final game a friend of Denny's slipped into a chair at the table behind us. Kevin Steele had run in our crowd off and on until graduating from high school two years earlier. Home on leave from the Navy he'd dropped by the bowling alley to watch his old pal knock down some pins.

With his good looks and athletic ability Kevin possessed an easy grace and self-assurance that set him apart from the other boys. In pick-up softball games at the local park everyone wanted Kevin on their team. He could play any position, and when he came to the plate the outfield backed up. At parties he was the guy who sang and strummed guitar, spinning out classic rock songs in a sweet tenor voice.

I'd had a crush on Kevin since seventh grade, but he'd never given me a second look. That evening however, every time I glanced back to where he was sitting, his eyes were on me.

Angie cleared her throat and leaned close. "Hubba, hubba."

"I know."

"Go for it," she whispered.

I stalled until after I bowled the next frame. Then pumped on adrenalin from throwing a strike I bounded up the steps to the table where he was sitting and stood in front of him with my hands on my hips. "Hey Kevin, remember me, Carrie?"

He took his time looking me over. "You've grown up." With his foot he nudged a chair out from under the table. I sank onto the seat. We'd never been this close before. I took in his luscious brown eyes and dark lashes, hardly believing anybody this handsome could be interested in me.

"You're witnessing history in the making," I told him. "I'm tearing up the lanes tonight."

"I've been watching you from the bar." His smile was so intimate it made me shiver. On the table in front of him was a tall plastic tumbler filled with beer. He slid it toward me. I was underage, but a glance around told me no one was paying attention. I took a sip and slid the cup back to Kevin who slid it back to me. "You're thirstier than that."

I guessed I was and downed a more respectable slug.

We passed the cup back and forth until Denny called, "Carrie, you're up."

I stood and wiped the foam from my mouth and onto my jeans.

Kevin's gaze followed my every move. "Roll this one for me," he said.

I threw another strike. After a round of high-fives from my teammates I returned to Kevin's table. When I sat down and reached for the beer his hand closed over mine and held it there. He stared into my eyes. "What do you say?"

I didn't need to say anything. I just ran a slow tongue over my lips. He gave me a smoldering look and relinquished the tumbler. As the amber brew poured down my throat I felt his knee graze my thigh. Electricity surged through me.

I finished the game with a spare and a strike. My astounding score put us over the top against our opponents. Amid the flurry of congratulations I glanced at Kevin. He nodded his approval.

When our team crowded into the karaoke bar Kevin tagged along. Poor Denny saw he was outgunned and didn't complain when his old friend slid into the booth beside me. By the time Kevin mounted the stage and belted out an old Four Seasons song titled "Sherry"—substituting my name in a funny and somehow sexy falsetto—my sailor boy and I were a couple.

"Well?" Angie prompted.

It was noon on Monday, my first day back at work following my makeover. Angie and I had just sat down to lunch in the cafeteria. I was wearing my new green and blue ensemble, complete with strappy heels in muted navy.

"Well what?" I said.

"Duh, Carrie. Where did you and Kevin go after you left the bowling alley Saturday night?"

I flushed. "The park."

"What a surprise," Angie deadpanned.

"Oh god, Angie, he is so hot. I spent all day yesterday with him. We can't get enough of each other."

"So…did you…?" She wiggled her eyebrows at me.

"Not yet," I said, "but he doesn't go back until Sunday."

"You know where babies come from, don't you?"

"Even Catholic girls know that. Don't worry, it won't happen to me."

Angie unwrapped her sandwich. "What did your bosses say about your new look?"

I shrugged. "Nicole was all raves. Dave gave me a once-over and said he liked my hair. Brad didn't even notice."

"He's just playing it safe," Angie said. "Believe me, he noticed."

I'd returned to my desk after lunch when my cell phone vibrated. It was Kevin. I got up and headed for the hall.

"Kevin, hi."

"I missed you today, Carrie." The sound of his voice started my juices flowing. When he offered to pick me up from work I purred my acceptance.

The afternoon couldn't go by fast enough. I was feeling positively wanton by the time I entered Brad's office to deliver the mail.

I wonder if guys can smell wanton on a woman the way male moths smell pheromones on their females. Brad was at his desk. His eyes latched onto me the moment I stepped into the room. He leaned to one side in his chair, elbow on the armrest, chin propped on his hand. His gaze followed me to the side table where he kept his in-box.

Call me impertinent, but when I turned around to catch my handsome boss undressing me with his eyes I stared right back. "What?" I said, cocking my head.

That brought out the dimples. He laced his fingers across his stomach and swiveled his chair back and forth. He was reading me, an amused half-smile on his face. In a voice that would have been at home in a cocktail lounge he said, "I do believe Carrie's got something going."

My expression must have said it all, because Brad's gaze narrowed and his dimples deepened. He studied me a while longer, then nodded. "Oh yeah. Definitely something going on."

His eyes were still on me as I started to leave. I was halfway out the door when he called my name. I pivoted on my heels and poked my head back into his office.

"Everybody should have a sick day as productive as yours," he said.

Brad had read me right. I did have something going on. I had discovered sex. Well, foreplay, anyway.

During the week Kevin was home on leave he and I spent every evening together. We bicycled after work, went out with friends and had dinner with his parents one evening and with my parents another evening. What we really wanted, however, was to be alone with each other. That was tough, since I lived with my parents and Kevin stayed with his parents when he was home.

Saturday was our last day together. When he picked me up that afternoon he tossed a motel key card into my lap. Two hours later I was saying goodbye to my virginity in a street-level motel room in a motor court outside of town. For someone squeamish about inserting a tampon inserting Kevin was a major undertaking. It was bloody and momentarily painful, but a girl has to start somewhere. I left the motel that afternoon feeling different inside. I thought I might look different on the outside too, but nobody seemed to notice, not even my mother, who I was pretty sure had radar for that kind of thing.

Angie was the only person who guessed my secret, and even with her I shied away from discussing it. That was probably a mistake; I could have used her advice.

Since Kevin was stationed nearly eight hundred miles from Cincinnati at a submarine base in New London, Connecticut, I didn't see him often. His next visit home wasn't until October, when he escorted me to my cousin Jenny's wedding. It was a late afternoon ceremony on one of those brilliant fall Saturdays that makes your heart soar. In my pewter-colored sheath and matching high-heeled sandals I felt like a model. When Kevin came to pick me up he couldn't take his eyes off me.

Although it was stimulating being with Kevin again a tiny part of me was disappointed I hadn't gotten to play the field as I'd planned. There were a bunch of cute guys at the reception; I couldn't help but notice them noticing me.

One of my admirers turned out to be my cousin.

We'd just finished dinner. While Kevin was off in search of wedding cake a good-looking guy slipped into Kevin's chair and started bantering with me. We hadn't yet introduced ourselves when my brother stopped by and said, "Hey, Randy, I see you found my baby sister."

"Holy cow, you're Carrie," Randy said.

As soon as I saw the blush, so like mine, creeping up his neck and face all the way to his curly blond hair I knew who I'd been flirting with. Randy Matthews was my first cousin, the son of my dad's only brother, who had died of lung cancer. I hadn't seen Randy since his father's funeral six years earlier. Since I'd been thirteen at the time and Randy was my brother's age, it was no surprise we hadn't recognized each other.

When we'd recovered from our mutual embarrassment I asked how he knew Jenny. Since the bride was my mother's niece I wasn't sure how their paths would have crossed.

Turns out he was a friend of the groom. "Zach and I work together at the bank," he said. "I was surprised as heck to see your mom and dad here."

"Mom's already latched onto him," Tommy said. "She expects him to have dinner with us every Sunday for the rest of his life."

My newfound cousin laughed. "Sounds like a plan to me."

My parents had left the reception early and were in bed when I got home. I woke the next morning dreading to see my mother. No doubt she'd have a comment about the way Kevin and I had danced together. Let's face it: weddings are sexy. What red-blooded girl wouldn't engage in a little dirty dancing even with her mother watching?

Dad called my mom Joan of Arc and teased her about being more Catholic than the pope. Mom had been raised by conservative parents in a conservative parish, a parish to which we still belonged. She believed sexual intercourse outside of marriage was a mortal sin. She'd forbidden Katie and her husband Dean from moving in together until after they'd tied the knot. My thirty-year-old brother kept his lifestyle so opaque she had no opportunity to interfere.

As for me, when I was fifteen years old I'd taken a vow of chastity. The occasion was a daylong Catholic youth rally hosted by my parish. Whipped into a frenzy of religious fervor by a charismatic young priest I and a sanctuary full of crazed teenagers had pressed our hands to our hearts and promised to refrain from sexual activity until released from the vow by marriage.

Mom was banking on my four-year-old vow to keep me pure. I had no intention of setting her straight.

I thought I'd dodged a bullet because when I entered the kitchen that morning she was buzzing about something she'd heard at the reception. She was at the stove cooking breakfast while my long-suffering father sat at the kitchen table trying to read the Sunday paper and listen to my mother at the same time.

I made myself a bowl of cereal and joined my dad. "What's going on?"

My mother practically smacked her lips. This Joan of Arc was not shy about imparting juicy news. "Did Randy tell you about his mother?"

I shook my head. "What about her?"

"Well, three years ago, in the middle of the night, she simply hopped on a plane and flew to Minnesota with some man she'd never met before. She's still there."

While this information failed to shake me to my core I put on my oh-my-god-how-weird face to keep my mother off the subject of Kevin and me. I said, "I thought Aunt Cora's only interest in life was smoking cigarettes and watching TV."

"And playing bingo," my mom said. "Don't you remember she used to play bingo every Thursday night at the VFW? That's where she met this man she ran off with. He walked in and sat down next to her. Next thing you know she left with him."

I had to admit that was strange, even for my uncle's wife, who had always struck me as odd. I'd never admitted it to anyone, but I'd always been a tiny bit afraid of her.

My mom brought two plates of bacon, eggs and toast to the table. She slid one plate across the table to my dad and then sat down on my left with her own plate. "You know, Tom, I feel bad we didn't stay in touch with your brother's kids. Cora was hard to deal with, but we could have kept up with Randy and Debbie."

My dad, eyes still glued to the opinion section, grunted his agreement.

"What's Debbie up to now?" I asked my mom.

"She's married and lives in Louisville. She has two little boys. It's kind of a coincidence. Debbie and Katie are the same age and they each have two children. And Randy and Tommy are the same age and still single."

My dad folded the paper and laid it aside. "Those two sure hit it off last night. Turns out they're both runners." He looked at the clock on the microwave. "They're probably finishing up a run together right now. I told them to stop by later."

My parents dove into their food. I finished my cereal and was about to leave the table when the bullet I thought I'd dodged found its way to where it had been headed all along.

"Everybody raved about how pretty you looked last night, Carrie," my mother said. "And Kevin looked so handsome. Do you know what Ruthie asked me?" Ruthie was the mother of the bride and my mom's sister.

I shook my head.

"She was wondering if you were engaged. She thought you two looked awfully cozy on the dance floor." My mother pursed her lips in a way I dreaded. "Carrie, I know you're a good girl and Kevin's a good boy, but you have to think about the impression you're making on other people."

"We were just dancing, Mom."

"You were draped all over the boy." She laid a hand on my forearm. "How serious are you about Kevin?"

I shrugged. "I don't know."

"You're only nineteen, Carrie. Why tie yourself down when you have your whole life ahead of you?" With the pressure of her fingers she forced me to look at her. "You were going to make something of yourself, remember? You sat right here in this kitchen saying, 'Mom, don't let me do anything dumb.'"

Only after he returned to his submarine base did I admit to myself that my involvement with Kevin was the "anything dumb" I'd sought to avoid. My sailor had fallen hard for me. He called almost every night when his ship was in port. In his mind we were all but engaged, with marriage just around the corner. He could think of nothing more awesome than having me join him in New London.

I had no such plans. In the weeks following Jenny's wedding my ardor for Kevin had cooled. He and I didn't have much in common, a fact that became clearer to me with every phone call. I wanted to date other guys, but I felt bound to Kevin both by his devotion to me and the intimacy we'd shared. Although I didn't feel right calling it quits over the phone I promised myself that the next time he came home I'd make the break.

In theory it was a good plan.

Chapter 5

Kevin's submarine went out to sea over the Thanksgiving and Christmas holidays and Kevin didn't get back to Cincinnati until March. He picked me up on a Saturday morning and drove me to his parents' house. His younger twin brothers were out; his father, an automobile mechanic, was at work. While his mother cleared up the breakfast dishes Kevin and I sat at the kitchen table drinking coffee.

I'd intended to initiate our breakup conversation at the earliest opportunity. However, Kevin in the flesh is different from Kevin on the phone. The long-distance Kevin was a gung-ho sailor who hadn't read a book since high school. The real-life Kevin—with his fringe of dark lashes, the special smile reserved just for me and the hand roaming up my thigh every time his mother's back was turned—that Kevin was a different animal altogether. That Kevin made me decide to postpone our talk until the end of his visit.

When Mrs. Steele announced her intention to run up the street for a few things Kevin and I exchanged a glance. This meant we'd have time alone—twenty minutes at least. It might be the only time we'd have to ourselves in the vicinity of a bed all weekend. The moment we heard the garage door close we were all over each other and he was leading me down the stairs to his room on the ground floor of the house.

In no time at all I was lying on my back, naked and panting. Kevin grabbed his wallet off the dresser and began a frantic search through the compartments. Throwing that down he groped through his shaving kit.

"Shit."

I sat up. "What's wrong?"

"I don't have a condom."

"You'll have to go to the drug store."

"There's no time." He sat on the edge of the bed, lowered me onto the pillow and kissed me. He circled my nipples with his tongue. His hand slid between my thighs. His finger found just the right spot. How did he know that would feel so good?

I licked my lips.

He bent close. Need smoldered in his eyes. "Oh, Carrie, we have to..." He climbed on top of me. "I'll pull out before I come."

"We shouldn't," I protested. But once he slipped inside me my brain shut down. We were both moaning with pleasure before I recovered my senses and shoved him off me. He ejaculated on the bedspread between my legs.

While we were rushing to clean up our mess, throw our clothes back on, and return to the kitchen before his mom got home Kevin swore he hadn't spilled any seed inside me. I should have known better.

I never summoned the courage to break up with Kevin that weekend. He returned to the submarine base and I awaited my next period. When it was a week late in arriving I went to the drugstore and bought a home pregnancy test. The next morning I peed on the stick. I'd always been a good test taker; I passed this one with flying colors. I was pregnant.

I took up vigorous exercise and stomach pounding, hoping to shake something loose. I tried starving myself. After two weeks I wasted my money on another pregnancy test; I was just as pregnant the second time around. Although it flew in the face of everything I'd ever been taught, the idea of abortion entered my mind.

I kept the news of my pregnancy to myself. Whenever Kevin called it was all I could think of, but I didn't tell him and he didn't ask. I couldn't bring myself to admit to Angie, my closest confidant, how careless I'd been. She was no dummy and I'm sure she sensed a change in me. At first she asked some probing questions, but I deflected them and eventually she stopped asking. It helped that she was preoccupied with her schoolwork.

And my mother? I feared for my life if I told her. That Kevin and I were having sex was sinful enough. That I was pregnant and considering abortion would have sent her off the rails.

It was my boss who came closest to finding me out. Brad had been vacationing in Florida the week my period failed to arrive. By the time he returned I was operating on autopilot at work, displaying a cheerfulness I didn't feel.

To bring him up to speed on his first day back our team met in a conference room down the hall from Brad's office. To avoid engaging in chitchat I made sure to be the last one in the door. I took my seat as Dave was asking Brad about his trip to Orlando.

"You'll have to ask my mother-in-law how it went," Brad said. "After spending the week in a condo with her I have no opinion about anything, nor do I have the right to an opinion."

Nicole laughed. "That bad, huh?"

Brad made a dismissive gesture. "The good news is, mommy dearest has retreated to her lair in Minnesota, leaving me space and time to lick my wounds." He spread his hands on the table. "What've you got for me?"

While Dave and Nicole reported on what they'd been doing I wallowed in misery until I noticed Brad looking in my direction. Although I stared down at my notebook I still felt those blue eyes drilling into me.

As soon as our meeting adjourned Brad called me into his office and asked if everything was all right.

"Fine," I said.

He inclined his head to the door. "Those folks been treating you okay?"

"Of course."

"So it's personal."

I shrugged.

"I'm a good listener," Brad said.

"I'll remember that."

He'd given me a perfect opening. I'd been tempted to say more, but I was embarrassed. This was a situation of my own making. Comforting as it was to know he cared I shouldn't burden my boss with it. I was the one who needed to think it out and come to a decision on my own.

Thus after my parents went to bed each night I logged long hours on the Web reading and watching videos about abortion. Although I didn't approve of abortion as a birth control method I decided I would make an exception in this case. Sin or no sin, being a twenty-year-old mom was not the way I wanted my life to go. I would erase this one misstep and never take such a chance again. I was five weeks along when I set up a Saturday appointment at the local branch of Planned Parenthood.

The morning of my appointment Kevin showed up at my house unannounced. His parents had flown him home for a family party to celebrate his great-grandfather's ninetieth birthday. He hadn't told me he was coming because he'd wanted to surprise me.

When the doorbell rang I was getting ready to leave the house. My parents had just left to shop for a new washing machine. Although my Planned Parenthood appointment was in the afternoon my strategy was to leave while they were gone and stay out all day.

I opened the door. Kevin stood on the stoop wearing khaki shorts, a white T-shirt and a Cincinnati Reds ball cap turned backward. His bicycle was behind him on the sidewalk, a baseball glove hooked over the handle bar. It was the first week of May and he was already tan. His smile was blinding. He said, "Can Carrie come out and play?"

As he explained his unexpected presence my brain was racing. What should I tell him? How would I get away to keep my appointment?

I invited him into the house. When he learned my parents weren't home he got that smoldering look and suggested we play inside first.

Talk about a dual personality. At the same time I was resenting him for what he'd done to me my body was getting ready to try it again. Why not? The horse had already exited that particular barn.

As I led him down the hall to my bedroom he slipped a hand into the back pocket of his shorts and extracted a foil-wrapped condom. "This time I came prepared."

Ten minutes later we were finished.

"I should probably get going," Kevin said. "I was supposed to meet Denny at the park."

I rolled out of bed and gathered my clothes. "You mean he's been waiting for you?"

Kevin watched me dress. "It's okay, I have a good excuse. I got waylaid."

I glanced at him sidelong. "Is that what they call it now?"

Kevin grinned. "If it's way better than getting laid they call it waylaid." He sat up and swung his legs over the side of the bed. "Want to come with me?"

"I'll ride over on my bike but I can't stay. I have an appointment this afternoon."

Kevin stood and slipped into his shorts. "What kind of appointment?"

I hesitated. "A doctor's appointment."

"I bet I know what for."

My heart skipped a beat. "What do you mean?"

"I bet you're getting birth control pills." He pulled his T-shirt over his head. "That would be awesome."

"Why do you say that?"

"Well, you know the last time I was home? When we did it without a condom? You can't believe how much better that felt. I mean, today was great. But last time was unbelievable. That's why I almost forgot to pull out."

"You did forget."

Kevin looked sheepish. "No harm done, right?"

I bit my lip.

"Carrie?"

"Right, no harm done." I turned my back to him, opened my sock drawer and started rooting around.

"What the fuck," Kevin said. He'd come up behind me and was gripping my shoulders hard. He spun me around and bent his head down to stare into my eyes. "Are you lying to me?" His face had gone pale. I could feel the trembling in his arms.

I tried to twist away.

He took my face in his hands. "Tell me."

Tears sprang to my eyes. I let out a sob and pressed my fingers to my lips.

Kevin looked at me for a long moment, then pulled me into an embrace. "Jesus, Carrie, I'm sorry."

It took Kevin all of two minutes to get over the shock. Once he did he was thrilled I was carrying his baby. He began painting our future in such glowing colors I started to believe it might not be so bad. He would find a place for us to live and I would join him in New London. He had tons of friends with spouses and young families. I'd have plenty of company and support.

Out of his hearing I cancelled my appointment at Planned Parenthood, letting Kevin believe I'd postponed a prenatal checkup. It would hurt him to know I'd intended to terminate the pregnancy.

Kevin flew back to Connecticut the next day. I'd persuaded him not to share our news with anyone in Cincinnati. I certainly wasn't ready to inform my mother and I didn't want her to hear it any other way. In my mind abortion was still on the table. With Kevin gone the pretty pictures he'd conjured would start to fade and I might want to play the termination card. I could always tell Kevin I'd miscarried or that I'd been mistaken about being pregnant.

Inertia is a funny thing though. The longer I postponed taking action the less likely I was to do it. I never returned to the Planned Parenthood website, nor did I reschedule my appointment. It seems I'd decided to let the chips fall where they may.

Night after night Kevin called me brimming with excitement. Within a month he emailed me photos of a two-room apartment he'd rented on the second floor of an old house near the submarine base. The owner was a retired chief petty officer who had taken a liking to my young sailor. And why not? Instead of cruising around town with his friends Kevin was spending his spare time cleaning the apartment, refinishing cabinets and giving the rooms a fresh coat of paint.

I listened to him talk about the progress he was making, the nice yard we'd have and how convenient the apartment was to the submarine base. I tried to be interested, but it all seemed theoretical to me—something that might happen to somebody else in some distant future.

Meanwhile, life hadn't changed much for me. My morning sickness was manageable if I ate three saltines fifteen minutes before getting out of bed in the morning. My stomach, which I still pounded on every day, remained flat. We were busy at work, and I liked it that way. Brad hadn't asked any more questions about my personal affairs. Angie had given up as well. I could almost forget I had a life sentence hanging over my head.

"We're going out to sea the whole month of June," Kevin informed me on the phone one evening toward the end of May. "When I get back I'm coming to get you. The Fourth of July is on Saturday. I'll drive in on the third, spend Saturday in Cincinnati, and we'll drive back together on Sunday."

A feeling of dread clutched at my heart. This was too concrete. "There's no hurry," I said.

"Yes there is, Carrie. We're having a baby; we should be together."

"I'll just drive there sometime."

"In that piece of shit Escort? You can't drive that car here. It's not safe." He sighed. "Just give your notice at work and start packing."

I didn't answer, but I already knew I wasn't going to do what he said.

June flew by. When Kevin's ship returned to port at the end of the month he called me, sounding cheerful and excited. "I'm coming next weekend. Are you ready?"

"No."

"What do you mean?"

"I didn't give my notice at work."

"You had plenty of time."

"I'm not ready to leave yet."

The cheerfulness had fled from his voice. "Carrie, I'm driving to Cincinnati on the third and you're coming back with me on the fifth."

"You can come for a visit, but I'm not going back with you."

"You are," Kevin said. "You just don't know it yet."

Chapter 6

Kevin was wrong. He drove home that weekend, but I dug in my heels and refused to budge. To his credit and despite his evident disappointment he conceded defeat early on. Apparently he'd decided having a pleasant weekend was more important than having a fight he couldn't win.

We divided our time on the Fourth between my family and Kevin's. We began the day watching my brother and my cousin Randy compete in a 5K race, after which we adjourned to my sister's house for a picnic lunch.

Afternoon found us at Kevin's house, where a bewildering number of his relatives had descended upon the Steeles' back yard for the annual family reunion. For dinner we feasted on grilled burgers and hotdogs and an assortment of homemade favorites. We were still slurping watermelon when the first of the municipal fireworks spread its glittering canopy across the sky. Since Kevin's yard provided an ideal vantage point for watching, most everyone stayed to *ooh* and *ah* over the town-ship pyrotechnics.

Following the thunderous finale the aunts and uncles rounded up their children and said goodbye. Soon Kevin and I were sitting alone on the patio with his parents. The day's festivities, along with the previous day's drive, had taken their toll on Kevin; he was fading fast.

His mother stood and tugged her husband out of his chair. "C'mon, old man, we should let these people get some sleep. Kevin has a long drive tomorrow."

Kevin and I stood too. Mrs. Steele pulled her son into a warm hug. "It was great having you here today, honey." She planted a kiss on his cheek. "Don't stay up too late."

She put an arm around my waist. "Come over anytime, Carrie. You're always welcome here."

When his parents went inside, I turned to Kevin. "What was that all about?"

"I told them, Carrie."

I flushed. "You had no right."

"It's my baby too," he said.

I could feel my cheeks burning. His mother knows I'm pregnant, I thought. Everybody's going to know soon.

Kevin pulled me close. "It's okay," he whispered. He bent his head and kissed me, a lingering kiss unlike any we'd had a chance to share all day. I started to push him away, but his hands were caressing my breasts, teasing the nipples through the layers of summer-weight cotton I was wearing. His crotch was hot and insistent against mine. I pressed my body into his. He took my hand and led me through the patio door and across the family room toward his bedroom.

"What about your mom and dad?" I said.

"We have their blessing."

Knowing his parents were in their bedroom a floor above us we were as quiet as two lovers could be. Kevin was so tired he fell asleep still inside me.

I slipped out of bed and found my clothes. I padded to the bathroom, washed the semen from between my thighs and got dressed. Returning to the bedroom I gave Kevin a shake. "You have to take me home."

Kevin rolled onto his back. It took forever for him to answer. "Just stay here tonight. Please, Carrie?" He started to doze off again. I stood by the bed and jostled him. He grabbed my hand and held it. "I'll take you home in the morning."

"My parents will be worried."

I pulled out of his grip, walked to the bedroom door and switched on the overhead light.

Kevin threw his arm over his eyes. "Call them. Tell them you're staying here."

"I can't. They don't know about us."

There was a long silence. Kevin looked up at me. "You'll have to tell them sooner or later. Why not get it over with?"

"I'm not ready."

"God, Carrie, if I hear you say that again—"

"I'm not ready, I'm not ready, I'm not ready," I hissed. I put my hands on my hips and jutted out my chin. "What are you going to do about it?"

Kevin sighed. "Give me fifteen minutes. Then I'll take you home." He rolled away from me and clamped the pillow over his head.

I didn't like it but what else could I do? I turned out the light and crawled back into bed. For a few minutes I lay on my back staring at the ceiling. I could tell from his breathing Kevin had fallen back to sleep. I got up, took his keys from the dresser and stepped into the hall, closing the bedroom door behind me. I tiptoed through the darkened house and let myself out the front door.

Kevin's car was parked on the street. As I unlocked the door and climbed into the driver's seat the porch light came on. The front door opened and Kevin rushed out wearing only a pair of shorts. His feet were bare, his hair tousled.

He ran across the lawn to the car, came around to the driver's side and yanked open the door. "What the hell are you doing?"

"I'm going home."

"Do you have your driver's license?"

"Do you?"

He patted the back pocket of his shorts. "Right here."

He stood back. I got out of the car, walked to the passenger side and got in. Kevin slid behind the wheel and started the engine.

"I was going to bring your car back tomorrow morning," I said.

Kevin didn't answer. His face was grim as he drove the few miles to my house. When he pulled into the driveway he turned to me. "Carrie, I don't understand what's going on with you. I'm trying hard to make this work. I get that you're not coming back with me this time. But you can't put it off forever. Why don't you tell me what's wrong?"

How could I tell him I didn't want any of this? How could I say I felt smothered and trapped and that if someone offered me a way out I'd take it in a heartbeat? How could I tell him I wished we'd never met?

He reached out to touch my arm, but I shrank away against the door. Anger flared in his eyes. He pulled his hand back, slapped it onto the steering wheel and stared straight ahead.

I got out of the car and started up the sidewalk. With a squeal of tires Kevin pulled out of the driveway. As I opened the front door and looked back his car shot forward and peeled rubber halfway down the street.

I stepped into the living room.

"What's the problem, Carrie?"

I jumped. It was my mother's voice. She'd been sitting there in the dark waiting for me.

"We're having an argument," I said into the darkness. "Don't worry about it."

"Did Kevin try something?"

"It's nothing like that."

Mom clicked on the table lamp to the dimmest setting. She was in her favorite chair. "Come and sit down."

I sat on the sofa adjacent to her chair.

"We never talk anymore, Carrie. You don't seem happy."

"I'm deliriously happy." I placed my forefingers at the corners of my mouth and pulled my lips into a smile.

"Are you really?"

I dropped my hands into my lap. "Not all the time."

"Honey, your dad and I think you're too young to tie yourself to someone who lives so far away. You should be playing the field, enjoying your life."

I exhaled a long breath. "Kevin wants me to go to Connecticut with him."

My mother blinked. "Like get married and move away?"

"More like move away and then get married."

"What do you want?"

"I don't want to go."

"Then don't. Just tell him you don't want to go."

I licked my lips. "What if I don't have a choice?"

My mother looked stricken. "What are you saying, Carrie?"

I stared down at my lap. "I'm pregnant."

I could feel her eyes on me. When I looked up and met her gaze she covered her face with her hands and shook her head. "This isn't happening," she whispered. Eventually she sat back in the chair and gripped the armrests. "When? When did it happen?"

"March."

"March?" Her voice shot up fifty decibels. "And you're just now telling me?"

I heard the bed creak in my parents' bedroom. My dad would be joining us soon.

"We trusted you, Carrie. Have you been sneaking around behind our backs all along?"

"No, Mom, it was only that one time. We were alone at Kevin's house and we just...we got carried away."

"One time is all it takes. How often have I told you that?"

My dad entered the room in his pajamas. He put a hand on Mom's shoulder. She reached up and placed her hand on his. "Oh, Tom, did you hear that?"

He looked grim. "I got the gist of it."

"She had such potential," my mother said. "She was going to make something of herself." She looked at me and gave her head a long, slow shake. "You threw it all away for a moment's pleasure."

I bit my lip and blinked back tears.

"What are you going to do, Carrie?" my mother said. Her manner was cold, like she was interrogating a whore on the street corner.

"Kevin came home to get me this weekend, but I wasn't ready to go. That's what the argument was about."

"So you're going to stay here and do what?" she asked.

The disgust in her voice wounded me. I said, "Don't worry, I won't embarrass you with my big fat fornicating belly."

My parents' shocked faces told me I'd gone too far. I softened my tone. "The next time Kevin comes back I'll go with him. He already has a place for us to live."

My mother closed her eyes and gripped my dad's hand. I understood the war of emotions she was fighting. What I didn't know was which side would win. Would she find it in her heart to forgive me? I waited. I heard the sound of her labored breathing and worried she would have one of her attacks.

Eventually her breathing returned to normal. She opened her eyes and I saw sympathy there. That was my answer. She didn't approve of me, but she did love me.

I said, "I should've been ready to go with him this time, but I just couldn't admit it—to you or anybody else." I started to cry.

My mother rose from her chair, sat down beside me and took me in her arms.

Chapter 7

Not trusting myself to speak I tapped out my resignation on the computer, printed it and placed it in Brad's in-box toward the end of the day on the last Friday in July. When I looked up from my work a few minutes later Brad was standing in the doorway to his office. He crooked his finger at me and waited. I got up from my desk and walked toward him. He gestured me into his office, followed me inside and shut the door.

I took my customary seat, but instead of sitting across from me Brad propped himself beside me on the edge of the desk. He held up the two-sentence notice. "Care to explain?"

I glanced at the typed sheet then stared down at the floor. "I'm getting married."

"We let married people work here."

"I'm moving away."

"Where's the engagement ring? Where are the stars in your eyes?"

I raised my head. "I'm not happy about it."

Brad sighed. "When's the baby due?"

That got me. "Fuck," I muttered, as the tears started to roll.

"Yeah, that's usually what causes it," Brad said. He plucked a tissue from a box and handed it to me. "How far along are you?"

"Five months."

"Oh." He paused and I wondered if he was counting back to a day in March when he'd asked me some probing questions I'd avoided answering. "Too late to change your mind now."

"I don't want to be pregnant."

Brad looked thoughtful. "It's not just about what you want anymore. You're responsible for a new life. You made a choice—"

"But I didn't. He was supposed to—" I got flustered. Pull out sounded pornographic, so I said, "He was supposed to make sure it didn't happen."

"Carrie, if you examine it objectively you'll find that somewhere along the line you made a choice, or choices, that led to this situation. Your only choice now is to make the best of it."

He glanced at his watch. "I'm going home. Stay in here as long as you need to." He gave my shoulder a gentle squeeze. Except for a handshake it was the only time he'd ever touched me. If he'd kept his hand there for one second longer I probably would have done something that would have embarrassed us both.

My final two weeks in Cincinnati marked the beginning of my acting career. As word of my impending marriage spread among relatives and coworkers I soon realized it wouldn't do to display my true emotions. People seemed so happy for me I had to pretend to be happy too. I could have won an academy award for my performance.

With the human resources department I worked out that the company owed me two weeks of vacation. Calling it vacation allowed me to stay on the payroll for two weeks after I stopped working, thus continuing my health insurance until Kevin and I were married in Connecticut. Once we'd tied the knot—Kevin had arranged for a simple wedding ceremony the weekend after

I arrived—my medical care would be provided courtesy of the U. S. government.

My bosses moaned and groaned and wondered how they would get along without me, but we all knew they would. The plan was to hire a temporary assistant and eventually a permanent replacement. It was painful to see some of the work already bypassing me as they adjusted to my anticipated absence.

Angie was one of the few people at work who knew for sure I was pregnant. To her credit she didn't throw in my face the vow I'd made not to let it happen to me. The only reference she made to that long-ago conversation was on a card that accompanied a stylish little maternity dress she gave me. The card read: So you do know where babies come from.

My mother cried the first time she saw me in the dress. She and Mrs. Steele were taking me to lunch on Saturday, a week before I was to leave. Mom and I were getting ready in our separate bedrooms. I hadn't yet begun wearing maternity clothes, but since nothing else fit very well anymore I put on the dress and went to stand in the doorway to her room. She was sitting at her dresser applying makeup. When she caught sight of me in the mirror her hand began to tremble. She put down her eyebrow pencil, bent her head, and sobbed. I went to her, knelt on the floor beside her chair and pressed my forehead to her arm.

When we'd cried ourselves out Mom called Mrs. Steele and told her we'd be late. We dried our eyes, repaired our makeup and went to lunch. Although we'd had our differences in the past, from that time on until the day I left with Kevin my mother and I were gentle with each other.

Chapter 8

Whenever I recall the trip to Connecticut I think of it as the night of the frogs. Kevin arrived at my house early Sunday morning, hoping to get on the road by eight. He had spent all day Saturday driving in from New London. Now he was turning around and going right back.

Ever since I'd given my notice at P&G I'd been incapable of deciding how or what to pack. Nothing seemed to matter or make any sense. I was still dithering on Sunday morning, and the delay was making Kevin crazy. In the end he stalked into my bedroom and started stuffing clothes helter skelter into suitcases and bags and hauling them out to his car. At the front door I cried and clung to my parents while Kevin drummed his fingers on the steering wheel. It was after nine when we pulled out of the driveway.

Our trip from Cincinnati to New London would take thirteen hours. We traveled practically nonstop through Ohio, Pennsylvania, New Jersey and the southernmost tip of New York.

It was dark by the time we passed the sign that welcomed us to Connecticut. The evening had turned steamy. Ragged wisps of fog obscured the roadway. Approaching cars and trucks loomed out of the mist, each vehicle isolated in its own cocoon of light.

Water vapor collected on the car windows, making me feel closed in and wary.

"Ready for a pit stop?" Kevin asked.

I shrugged. I was so tired I wasn't sure I'd be able to get out of the car.

As soon as Kevin took the turnoff to the rest area we saw them: hundreds of frogs had descended upon the place. They leapt in front of the car, ghostly in the headlights, their tiny bodies spread-eagled like grotesque human fetuses. I heard them thumping against the doors and felt them being squashed under the tires.

Kevin pulled into a parking spot. When I emerged from the air-conditioned car the humidity settled on my skin like condensation on a cold glass. At my feet I saw frog guts smashed on the pavement and sidewalk. A reek like rotting fish assaulted my nostrils.

I gagged. "I don't have to go that bad," I said and got back into the car.

Kevin tiptoed his way to the restroom. When he returned he said, "Guy in there told me it happens once a year. He called it a phenomenon."

"Lucky us," I said as we drove away.

We were fifty miles from New London when I noticed Kevin nodding off behind the wheel. I called his name and he awoke with a start.

He pleaded for me to take over the driving, but I was even more tired than he was.

"Shouldn't we stop somewhere for the night?" I said.

"We can't. I have to be back on base early tomorrow morning."

Kevin remained behind the wheel. I managed to keep him awake by fondling him and promising sex when we reached our destination. More than once I fell asleep with my hand between his thighs.

"We're in New London," Kevin said, jiggling me awake. "The sub base is across the river. We'll be home in a few minutes."

I rubbed Kevin's crotch and mumbled, "Sex."

"Sex," he repeated, sounding beyond fatigued.

Kevin drove across the Gold Star Memorial Bridge and north on Highway 12. A few miles past the submarine base he made a left turn onto a side street and almost immediately turned right into a gravel driveway leading to a two-story clapboard house. I recognized it as my new home from the pictures he'd emailed. It was a single-family home that had been carved into three furnished apartments, a large one on the first floor and two smaller ones on the second floor.

Carrying only the essentials we'd need for the night we accessed the building through the front door, climbed the stairs and entered our apartment. We stowed a few things, brushed our teeth and fell into bed.

Kevin reached out and touched me. "Sex."

I woke in the wee hours of Monday morning with an ache in my abdomen. I spent time on the toilet but the cramps got worse. Kevin was still sound asleep. I knew he needed his rest since he had to work that day, so I sat on a kitchen chair and waited for him to wake up. While I waited I noticed the cramps were coming in waves. A frisson of fear swept over me.

I rushed into the bedroom and shook Kevin awake. "I'm having the baby."

Kevin bolted up like he'd been shot with adrenalin. "You can't be."

"But I am." I started to cry.

We scrambled into our clothes and I scooped a few things into a bag. We sped to the base and were waved through the gate by the Marine guard. Minutes later Kevin pulled up to the emergency room entrance.

I was rushed to the delivery room where I gave birth to a one pound two ounce boy. He lived eight hours. Because it was a live birth we had to give him a name. We named him Kevin, Jr. I left the hospital the next day with a birth certificate and a death certificate. The burial was at St. Mary's Cemetery in New London. A Navy chaplain officiated.

Kevin had been granted three days of bereavement leave from his submarine. He was a basket case, his face contorting and dissolving into tears at unexpected moments. I on the other hand was numb. We weren't allowed to have sex. Sex was what I knew how to do with Kevin. He wanted to be comforted and loved. Those were things I did not know how to do.

On Thursday Kevin returned to work, leaving me alone in the apartment. I'd talked to my mother every day on the phone. That morning she called me.

"How are you, honey?" she asked.

"I don't know what I'm doing here. I have no desire to unpack. I have no desire to become all domestic and start grocery shopping and cooking and learning how to get around on the base."

There was a long pause on the other end of the line. My mother said, "Do you want to come home?"

"Yes."

It was the first time I'd admitted it, even to myself. Once I did, there was no turning back.

By the time my mom and I clicked off, the gears in my brain were already whirring. I called Angie on her cell phone, hoping to catch her at lunch. I hadn't talked to her or anybody at P&G

since I'd left Cincinnati. As briefly and dispassionately as I could I told her I'd lost the baby.

I was unprepared for how shocked she was. She was so sympathetic she was practically crying. She started asking for details, but I cut her off. "Angie, I'm coming home."

"You're leaving Kevin?"

"Yes. I can't stay here. Did they hire somebody to take my place yet?"

"They have a temp." She sounded so vague and disoriented I wasn't sure I should have called her.

"I want to come back to work, Angie."

She huffed out a breath. "Carrie, give me a second to digest this."

"Should I call you later?"

"No, just a second." I heard a scraping noise and pictured Angie pushing back her chair and getting up from the table. A moment later she came back on the line. "I was eating lunch with some people, including the temp who's taking your place."

Taking my place, I thought, instantly envious.

Angie seemed to have climbed out of her fog. "Are you going to call Brad?"

"I don't know. I'm afraid I'll put him on the spot, like I just did to you."

Angie said, "Why don't I tell Brad what happened and say you'd like to come back. I'll leave it up to him to call you. I bet he will."

I waited two hours on pins and needles before the phone rang.

"Carrie, it's Brad."

His voice still had the power to make me shiver.

"I'm sorry to hear about your baby."

"Maybe it was for the best."

"For whom?"

Startled by the question I had to think a minute. "For me. And for the baby too. I wasn't ready to be a mother."

"You would have learned." When I didn't answer he said, "Have you told Kevin you're leaving?"

"Not yet."

"Are you sure you can do this to him?"

Again I had to stop and think. I hadn't expected an interrogation. "He'll be better off in the long run."

Brad's only comment was to clear his throat. After a pause he brightened his tone and said, "So you'd like to come back to work."

"If that's okay."

"Hey, we're lost without you. Your computer filing system has us mystified."

"You mean there's supposed to be a system?"

Brad laughed. "When are you coming back?"

We discussed the logistics of my return and I told him I'd be in touch. Before we clicked off, Brad said, "Carrie, be careful what you say to Kevin. There's no way not to hurt him, but don't say something you'll regret later."

It was late afternoon. From the front window of the apartment I saw Kevin pull into the driveway and emerge from the car. He was handsome in his navy dungarees and chambray work shirt. His waist and hips were slim, his arms sinewy. My heart gave a twinge when I saw how stooped and sad he looked. As if he knew I was watching he straightened up and squared his shoulders.

He took a grocery bag from the back seat. Poking out of the top was a bouquet of flowers wrapped in cellophane. When he started across the lawn toward the building I turned from the window, opened the door to our apartment and stood back.

I heard him climbing the stairs. He came through the door wearing a smile that didn't reach his eyes. When he saw my bags and suitcases lined up against the wall his smile disappeared.

"What's this?" he said.

Tears sprang to my eyes. "Oh, Kevin."

I saw his jaw tighten as he made sense of the situation. He stalked past me and dropped the grocery bag onto the kitchen table. The bag toppled over and the contents spilled out. A jar of spaghetti sauce rolled off the table, crashed to the floor and shattered. I cringed, but Kevin ignored it.

He turned to me. "You're leaving." I'd never heard his voice so flat and cold.

I nodded. "This was a mistake."

"What exactly was a mistake?" His look was steely, his words clipped and precise.

"Me coming here."

He gave an exasperated sigh. "You've only been here four days. You're not giving it a fair trial."

"I want to go home."

He looked around. I knew he was seeing the walls he'd painted and the cabinets he'd refinished in anticipation of my arrival. "This is your home." His look softened. He came forward and put his arms around me. "We're meant to be together, Carrie. We love each other."

I felt like a piece of wood in his arms. Don't say anything you'll regret later, I reminded myself.

Kevin released me and took a step back. "You do love me, don't you?"

I dipped my head. "I'm not sure."

"You're not sure? Carrie, don't you remember how we made love? How can you make love like that and not be *in* love?"

His eyes filled with tears. "We made a baby together."

I looked away. I didn't like seeing him like this, his emotions so raw, his pain like an open wound. This was a Kevin I didn't know.

He started pacing the room. Finally he stopped in front of me. "I bet that's it. You're feeling bad about the baby. We both are." He took me in his arms again and rocked me from side to side like a mother comforting a crying child. "Carrie, we can have another baby as soon as you're ready."

I pushed him away. "Oh god, Kevin, the last thing I want is another baby."

He froze. His eyes went cold. "Tell me you don't mean that."

Resentment boiled up in me. I was about to say something I would regret later. I could have stopped myself, but I didn't. I stabbed a finger at his chest. "You didn't have a condom. You said you'd pull out. You got me pregnant." I was feeling defiant now. I put my hands on my hips and spat out my words. "I didn't want to be pregnant. I spent five months pounding on my stomach, trying to dislodge the damn thing."

Kevin's eyes opened wide in shock. He drew in a sharp breath and staggered backward as if I'd hit him. "Well it worked," he roared. "The damn thing is dislodged. Are you happy now?"

"Yes," I screamed. "Yes, I'm happy. Now I can get the fuck out of here."

Kevin expelled his breath in an inhuman growl. The look of hate that flamed from his eyes seared my soul. Through gritted teeth he said, "I should beat the crap out of you."

He stared at me for a long moment. Then he wheeled around, crashed his fist against the wall and slammed out of the apartment.

I clamped my hands over my mouth. I had just done something so evil I didn't know myself.

Kevin was gone for five hours. I cleaned up the mess on the floor, put away the groceries and hid the sad flowers in the trash. I nibbled at a meal and finished my packing, then washed up and climbed into bed. Kevin returned an hour later. There was only one place to sleep in the apartment. The springs creaked as he climbed in.

It's strange to share a bed with someone you've just destroyed. We lay there with our backs to each other. Part of me ached to roll over and put an arm around him. Part of me wondered what I would do if he put his arm around me.

The next morning I pretended to be sleeping while Kevin got up and went to work. After he left I called a taxi to transport me and my hodgepodge of bags to the Greyhound bus station in New London. As we drove by the entrance to the submarine base a pang of guilt nearly caused me to lean forward and ask the driver to turn around. The moment passed, however, and before long I was standing in line to buy my bus ticket.

While I waited for the ten o'clock bus that would take me to my transfer stop in Philadelphia I made four calls on my cell phone. I called my mother, told her I'd be arriving in Cincinnati early the next morning and made arrangements for my dad to collect me.

Second, I called Brad to let him know I would return to work on Monday.

He sighed. "What's the rush? Why don't you to take some time to heal?"

"Are you kidding? My ancestors were out picking cotton the day after giving birth."

"Your ancestors?"

"Well, some people's ancestors."

"This is no joke, Carrie. My wife had two miscarriages after Chip was born. After the second one she hemorrhaged and ended up needing a hysterectomy. You don't want that to happen to you. I'm surprised you're allowed to travel already."

I didn't tell him I hadn't consulted a doctor.

"Let's do this," Brad said. "I'll cancel the temp and inform HR you're returning. If you wake up Monday morning raring to go, great. But if you need more time just let me know. We can manage without you for a few days."

I made my third call to the Navy chaplain, a soft-spoken Catholic priest who had officiated at the burial. He had been kind. I wanted him to know that Kevin was alone and might need his support.

My final call was to Kevin's parents. I got their voicemail and left essentially the same message I had given the chaplain. I made no excuses for my behavior and said I wouldn't blame them if they hated me. Before hanging up I said, "Kevin deserved a lot better."

I put away my phone, slid down in my molded plastic seat and wiped my wet cheeks with the back of my hand. I'd become one of those sad people you see in bus stations. Ten minutes later I boarded the bus and left New London forever.

It was 2006. I'd just turned twenty. Three years would pass before I saw Kevin again.

Chapter 9

I didn't return to work on Monday. The all-day bus trip—along with the week that preceded it—had taken its toll. When I dragged myself out of bed Monday morning I took one look at my gray face in the mirror and crawled back under the covers. My mother persuaded me to go to the doctor, who prescribed vitamins with iron, another day of rest and lots of water. My mother wanted to pamper me and I didn't resist.

Mom had always worked from home as a seamstress. She'd started out sewing custom-made draperies but over the years had added quilts, table runners and wall hangings to her repertoire. A pleasant result of Mom's homebound occupations was that she was always around when I came down with some miserable bug and had to stay home from school. There was nothing like having a mom who would run me a hot bath and while I was soaking put fresh sheets on my bed. On sunny winter days she'd make up a cozy spot for me on the sofa opposite the picture window in our south-facing living room.

Since returning from Connecticut I'd been spending most of my daylight hours stretched out on that sofa, racing through a novel called *Sister Carrie* by Theodore Dreiser. By Tuesday afternoon I was about three-quarters through when my mother came into the room carrying a glass of water, one of many she'd forced upon me since my visit to the doctor.

I glanced up, feeling mischievous, a sure sign I was on the mend. "Mom, why didn't you tell me I was named after a mistress?"

She set the water glass on a nearby tray table. "What are you talking about?"

I held up the book. "I found it on a shelf in the basement. You told me you read it when you were pregnant with me and that's why you decided to name me Carrie."

"I didn't exactly name you after her. I just liked the name."

"I always thought Sister Carrie was a nun, which was scary enough. Now I find out she was a mistress to two men."

"Carrie, if all you're getting out of the book is that she was a mistress you're missing the point."

"What is the point?"

My mother took the book from me and studied the faded dust jacket, which bore an illustration of a pretty woman dressed in early nineteenth century attire. "This book was on my parents' bookshelf for as long as I can remember. When I was pregnant with you and the doctor put me on bed rest it's one of the books my mother brought over for me. I read it right here in this room."

I made space for her on the sofa and she sat down with the book in her lap.

"What surprised me about this novel is how modern it felt," she said. "Carrie was as resourceful and independent as girls are today. She arrived in Chicago determined to make something of herself. She did what she had to do to survive."

My mother ran a finger over the young woman's elaborate hairdo of upswept curls. "She was beautiful and talented, and yes, she used that to her advantage. But she didn't lose her decency or compassion in the process." She shrugged. "That's what I got out of it."

"Maybe you did name me after her."

"Maybe I did." She stood, reopened the book to my page and handed it back to me.

I caught my mother's eye. "I didn't miss the point, Mom. I hope I can live up to the name."

"You will." She tucked a wayward curl behind my ear. "Don't emulate the mistress part though."

"No chance of that. I'm swearing off men at least until I get through college."

She gave me an appraising look. "Does that include the boss you're so crazy about?"

My heart did a flip-flop. "I'm not crazy about him."

"You bring him up often enough." She cleared her throat. "I heard you on the phone with him yesterday."

"So what? I had to let him know I wouldn't be coming in."

"I understand, but it was the way you spoke to him. You didn't sound like an employee talking to her boss. After you hung up you came into the kitchen and you were blushing."

Right on cue I felt the color rising in my cheeks. I couldn't look my mother in the eye.

"He's a married man, Carrie. I wonder if it's such a good idea for you to work for him."

"Mom, he has no interest in me. Zero. He's my boss and that's all."

"So you're nuts about him and he has no interest in you. Sounds self-defeating to me."

I rolled my eyes. "I have a tiny crush on Brad Collins. Every woman in the office has a crush on him. That doesn't mean they want to hop into bed with him."

"That goes for you too?"

"Absolutely."

After my mother left the room I uncrossed my fingers and made a mental note to stop discussing my boss at home.

It wasn't true what I'd told my mom about Brad having zero interest in me. His interest in me might not have been romantic, but he had taken an uncommon interest in my career. From my first days at Procter & Gamble he'd thought enough of my work and aptitude to give me far more responsibility than other assistants were given in their departments.

Turns out I had a knack for the advertising business. Early on, Brad had assigned me the task of reviewing the print ads produced by the advertising agency before he passed them along to the legal department for approval. Not only had I caught typographical errors, but more than once I'd suggested copy or artistic changes that everyone considered an improvement. It wasn't long before he began including me in planning and brainstorming sessions where my opinion held as much weight as the other members of the team.

Since I lacked the credentials for an actual promotion he referred to my expanded involvement as an internship. The arrangement assumed I'd stay in the department, get the appropriate schooling and climb the ladder into management.

Toward that end and with tuition assistance from P&G, the September after I returned from Connecticut I reentered the University of Cincinnati. My plan was to take as many evening and weekend classes as I could manage until I got my marketing degree. Thanks to advanced placement credits earned in high school, plus a year of college already under my belt, I figured I could do it in less than three years.

"I bet you appreciate that time management course you took in high school," Angie said to me at lunch one day.

It was mid-October. We were sitting together at our usual table in a quiet corner of the company cafeteria. Angie was putting the finishing touches on a sketch for her portfolio. I was poring over my macroeconomics book, cramming for a quiz that evening.

I looked up. "What time management course?"

"That's my point. My school didn't offer one either. But wouldn't it have been a good idea?"

In the past months Angie had become my best and just about only friend. After I returned from Connecticut none of my former pals had called me, not even Dennis. They'd probably heard about me dumping Kevin and didn't want anything to do with me. That was just as well. I'd been avoiding them too, along with any neighborhood haunts where I might run into a member of Kevin's family or even Kevin himself.

If you're stuck with just one friend, Angie is the one to be stuck with. Busy as we both were, Angie and I rode our bikes or played tennis together once a week and caught the occasional movie on a Friday night. Not only was she my clothing guru, she even found me a new car—a late model Toyota Corolla gently used by her grandmother—to replace my decrepit Escort.

Change was in the air, however. Angie had completed her coursework in fashion design at UC and had been shopping her portfolio far and wide. In December she was offered a coveted apprenticeship with a Manhattan firm that specialized in high-fashion apparel for women. She snapped it up in a heartbeat and would be moving to New York after the first of the year.

During the Christmas holidays I helped her pack. One closet in her apartment held her creations—handcrafted skirts, blouses, slacks and jackets. As I folded the one-of-a-kind items and placed them in cardboard cartons it hit me how much I was going to miss her. I put on a sorrowful face. "You can't leave,

Angie. Who's going to prevent me from buying the next black pantsuit calling my name from the clearance rack?"

Angie laughed. "Even the fashion-challenged need to try their wings eventually." She handed me a roll of packing tape. "You'll do fine, my little fledgling." While she held down the flaps on a bulging carton, I taped it shut.

"Speaking of leaving," she said, "have you thought maybe it's time for you to be moving on too?"

I hadn't been thinking that way at all. In fact I was about to take an advertising course that would dovetail with my work and legitimize the informal internship that Brad and I had arranged. I saw myself moving up in the department, not leaving it.

"I'm happy where I am," I said. "Why should I leave?"

Angie gave me a knowing look. "Carrie, this thing you have for Brad? It's not going anywhere. Why don't you give it up and get on with your life?"

Out of respect for Angie I spent the weeks after she left toying with the idea of transferring out of paper products advertising. I updated my résumé and perused the internal job postings, seeking headquarters jobs for which I qualified. Over lunch I sauntered through other departments and tried to picture myself working there.

In the end, however, I stayed put. Working for Brad *was* my life.

Chapter 10

In June I celebrated my second anniversary at P&G. To my surprise my boss marked the occasion with a gift. He and I were the first ones there that morning. When I poked my head into his office to say hello he waved me in, got up from his chair and shut the door.

He retrieved a plastic Home Depot bag from under his desk and handed it to me with an expectant smile. "It's symbolic, but it's also practical."

I reached into the bag and pulled out a gnarly-looking black tool belt with lots of pockets and loops for hanging things. Curious, I looked at him.

"Get it?" he said.

I thought for a minute and said, "It's symbolic because I'm the fixit person on the team."

"And?"

"It's practical because of the volunteer work I've been doing."

To fill the gap in my social life created by Angie's departure I had started volunteering with an organization that was doing rehab work on rundown houses in an area of Cincinnati called Over the Rhine. The group had committed to renovate a multi-block section and needed all the help they could get. I had precious little free time, but Brad was allowing me to take off one afternoon a week with pay to "go pound nails," as he put it. I loved the work and always came back to the office the next day brimming with tales of my home repair exploits.

"See if it fits," Brad said.

I buckled the belt around my waist. Contrasted with my watermelon-colored blouse and gray skirt it made quite a fashion statement. I spun around on one heel and stopped in front of him, hands on the side pockets like a gunslinger ready to draw my weapons. I grinned. "It's perfect."

My boss was looking at me with an expression that made me go weak in the knees. He said, "Marcy hates when I give her practical gifts. I hope you're not insulted."

"Are you kidding? We're all about practical in my family. Katie, Tommy and I just gave my parents two-by-fours and wallboard for their wedding anniversary."

Brad laughed. "What are they building?"

"Mom's been wanting a workout room in the basement. Last week we framed the walls and ran the electric. This weekend we're installing the wallboard." I unbuckled the belt. "Thank you. This'll come in handy."

I didn't get to break in my new tool belt on Saturday after all. A morning class at UC, followed by research at the college library, kept me on campus until mid-afternoon. By the time I drove home, went downstairs and poked my head into the new room, Dad and Tommy were collecting tools and debris and Mom was sweeping the floor.

Tommy made a face. "Look who walks in just as we're wrapping things up."

"Aw shucks, did I miss all the fun?"

"The day is still young, kiddo," my dad said. "We should have time to tape the seams and slap on the first coat of joint compound."

I gave my dad a wry smile. "When you say 'we' you mean me."

"You're the expert."

It was true. I was the expert-in-residence at finishing wallboard. I did a better job than anybody else at laying down the tape and mudding it over with joint compound so the seam didn't show once the wall was painted. I'd taken over the job from my dad on an earlier project and had been doing it ever since.

We assembled the equipment and I set to work while Tommy and my parents relaxed on folding chairs. I was in the groove, taping and plastering, when the doorbell rang. Tommy went upstairs to answer it and came back with my cousin Randy, who had become a regular around our house ever since Jenny's wedding two years earlier.

Randy surveyed the surroundings and grinned. "My new bedroom. Aunt Joan, you shouldn't have."

"Sorry, Randy. You're looking at our new exercise room," Mom said. "Your uncommonly patient uncle has waited thirty-five years for this."

While Tommy rounded up another chair and distributed cans of cold beer my cousin informed us he'd just returned from Minnesota. "Kind of sad news," he said. "The guy my mom lived with—Henry Streator? Last weekend he died of a heart attack."

"Oh, that *is* sad," my mother said. I hoped she didn't sound as insincere to Randy as she did to me.

"The autopsy showed he was dying of pancreatic cancer, so the heart attack may have been a blessing," Randy said. "He must have known he had cancer, but he hadn't told Mom. I flew up

Monday and we had his body cremated. No funeral service or anything."

"Did he have other family?" That question came from my dad.

"Apparently not. According to neighbors he was widowed several years ago. He was seventy years old, had no kids and no close relatives."

"How's your mother?" Mom said.

"She doesn't seem to be grieving, if that's what you mean. I never quite figured out their relationship."

"What will she do now?" Mom said.

Randy gave an exasperated sigh. "I wanted her to come home with me, but she insists on staying in Minnesota. Henry left her everything—house, car, furniture. All paid off, zero debt and forty thousand dollars in savings."

Tommy whistled. "Not bad."

"The lawyer we consulted thought there should have been a retirement account too—Henry was an airline pilot for over thirty years—but we haven't found it. Not that it matters. Mom has my dad's social security and pension to live on. Physically though, I don't see how she'll take care of the house. She's not all that well herself."

"Does she still smoke?" my dad asked.

"Like a chimney. And her diet is horrible. My sister's going to try to get her to move to Louisville with her, but I don't hold out a lot of hope for that."

"I have a dear friend who moved to the Twin Cities a few years ago," my mother said. "She's a nurse. I could ask her to look in on your mom."

I hid a smile. My mom had been devastated when her friend Sharon Weikel had moved away. Poor Mrs. Weikel, I thought, this is the way my mom is going to get back at you for leaving town. She's going to sic my crazy aunt Cora on you.

"That's too much to ask," Randy said. "Debbie and I will take turns running up there."

The conversation moved on to other topics and I continued working. Eventually I troweled wall mud onto the final seam and feathered it out with a deft hand. "Done," I announced.

My audience applauded.

As we were cleaning up, my cousin said, "How did you get so good at this, Carrie?"

"Practice, I suppose. I've done a fair amount of it."

"She's working on that big rehab project in Over the Rhine," my mother said. She made it sound like I was in charge.

I shrugged. "I put in a few hours a week. You should drive down sometime. The whole neighborhood's being transformed."

"I heard you were there on Tuesday when Troy Grove spoke," my brother said. "Did you like him?"

I bobbed my head. "I liked him so much I signed up to work on his campaign."

Chapter 11

Troy Grove was a candidate for the U.S. House of Representatives, the first Democrat in years who had a chance of winning in Hamilton County. I'd been so fired up by his visit to the worksite I'd joined a group called University Women for Grove, whose function it was to accompany the candidate to events, hand out literature and drum up support.

My work for Grove's groupies, the informal nickname we college-age volunteers had acquired, represented my fledgling foray into politics. As the summer progressed and I got to know the candidate personally I became ever more committed to helping him win the election. By September I was spending as much time stumping for Grove as I was on my college classes.

This was one volunteer activity I didn't discuss at work, since talking politics on the job was risky. You never knew who you might be alienating. Although I guessed some of the other administrative assistants were Democrats I made no such assumption about the managers. In a town as conservative as Cincinnati it was safe to assume nearly everyone in management was a Republican.

That's why encountering Brad on election night came as such a shock.

As usual on Tuesday nights I had driven directly from work to school. Since it was the first Tuesday in November, however, I ducked out of my marketing class early and drove downtown to the Westin Hotel, where Grove supporters were gathering in one of the ballrooms to watch election results.

The place was packed with exuberant folks in campaign hats milling about and waving Grove for Congress signs. Many of them held drinks purchased from a bar set up in the hallway just outside the ballroom's main entrance. At the far end of the room a woman stood on a platform bellowing something incomprehensible into a microphone. A screen mounted above the platform displayed ever-changing election results.

I spotted Rochelle, a fellow groupie, across the room. She and I had become friends working on the rehab project. I was making my way toward her when Brad stepped into my path, an ironic half-smile on his face. My breath caught in my throat.

"You look surprised," Brad said, his voice rising above the din.

"I assumed you were a Republican," I shouted.

"Do I look like a Republican?"

I thought for a second. "I guess not," I yelled. "You don't have horns."

Brad laughed. He put a hand on my shoulder and leaned in close. I could smell the alcohol on his breath. In a husky whisper barely loud enough for me to hear in the noisy room he said, "Do you know what you look like, Carrie?"

I shook my head. "What?"

After a second's hesitation he said, "Trouble."

At least that's what I thought he said, for just then a roar went up from the crowd as new numbers appeared on the screen showing Troy Grove taking a sizable lead in one of the highly contested suburbs. Bright lights came on and television cameras panned the room. Brad straightened up and dropped his hand from my shoulder.

When the hubbub subsided, a resonant baritone voice boomed Brad's name.

Brad and I pivoted toward the sound.

"Hey, Clayton. It's been a while," Brad said. He shook the hand of a tall black man with a Michael Jordan smile.

Brad introduced me to Clayton Shaw, assistant district attorney for Hamilton County.

The big man took my hand. "Call me Clay."

"Nice to meet you," I yelled.

"Let's get out of here," Clay said to Brad. "How about dinner?"

"Sounds good," Brad mouthed. "Carrie?"

Thinking this was my cue to leave I said, "I should get going. I saw a friend over there."

I started to back away, but my new acquaintance stopped me. "Wait, Carrie. You think I want to eat alone with this guy?"

Thus persuaded I found myself seated at a linen-covered table flanked by the two best-looking men in the hotel's upscale seafood restaurant. In their impeccably tailored suits both men exuded a kind of virile self-possession that I, from my working-class background, had never experienced before. I thanked my lucky stars I'd dressed for the occasion. In honor of Election Day I was wearing Angie's version of red, white and blue—a muted navy jacket with white pinstripes, a burgundy blouse and a flirty blue skirt that showed off my legs.

My companions couldn't have been more attentive and I couldn't have been more self-conscious, especially when I had to show my driver's license in order to be served wine.

While we ate our salads we discussed the man we hoped would become our next U.S. congressman. Troy Grove had cut his political teeth as a city council member in Cincinnati, where he'd gained a reputation as a thoughtful reformer. A charismatic populist with the gift of gab, his star had risen quickly. One of his singular talents was the ability to take complex issues and explain them in a way we lesser mortals could understand.

"Troy makes it look easy," Clay said. "He hits all the talking points, but he weaves them in so seamlessly you don't see the mechanics behind it."

"I've traveled with him on the campaign bus," I said. "He's totally relaxed, whether he's heading to a partisan rally or a candidate debate. Sometimes he doesn't use prepared notes."

Brad bobbed his head. "Then he steps up to the microphone and everything he says makes perfect sense."

"Exactly," I said. "He creates a vision of how things could be."

While the wait staff whisked away our salad plates Clay said, "So Carrie, aside from your obvious charms, what rated you a seat on the campaign bus?"

"University Women for Grove. I'm a volunteer."

Clay snapped his fingers and pointed at me. "No wonder you look familiar. I saw you handing out literature at the county fair. You looked very provocative in your little cheerleader skirt."

I rolled my eyes. "It was a golf skort."

"What the hell is a golf skort?" he said.

I laughed. "It's a skirt with shorts underneath. Women wear it when they play golf. It's supposed to be modest, not provocative."

"How about the T-shirt with Grove for Congress emblazoned across your chest?" He let his gaze drop to my chest, where it lingered for a moment before he smiled into my eyes. "I guess that's not supposed to be provocative either."

I was saved from having to respond by the arrival of our entrees, which for me featured Maine lobster. I'd never before ordered anything so expensive the price couldn't be listed on the menu. But when my dining companions learned I'd never tasted lobster, they'd insisted I try it. They'd even had me select my own victim from a salt-water tank in the restaurant lobby.

With a flourish the waiter placed an oval platter before me. Occupying center stage was my lobster, all rosy and fragrant. The waiter tied a bib around my neck and demonstrated the rudiments of dissection. Although I was tentative at first, once I got the hang of it I set about dismembering my hapless crustacean with gusto. The fruits of my labor were so succulent I had to restrain myself from moaning over each butter-drenched morsel that passed my lips. Thus occupied I was content to step out of the spotlight and enjoy my meal while the two men caught up on each other's lives.

I gathered that Brad and Clay had met as undergraduates at Yale before their paths had diverged: Clay's to Yale law school and Brad's to the MBA program. As luck would have it they'd both ended up in Cincinnati. I sensed they'd been better friends in college than they were now and that they probably didn't associate with one another unless circumstances like this evening's chance meeting threw them together.

Talk about the whereabouts of mutual acquaintances occupied much of the meal. The waiter was already hovering nearby, prepared to pounce on our almost empty plates, when the topic shifted to family matters.

"Tell me about Charles Bradley Collins the third," Clay boomed. "Big name for a little guy."

"He's not so little anymore," Brad said. He produced his cell phone and clicked through a series of photos of a slender boy with blond hair who looked a lot like his dad. "Everyone calls him Chip. He turned nine in September."

Clay whistled. "Nine years old already." He looked at me. "Carrie, your boss shocked the hell out of everybody when he tied the knot toward the end of senior year." Then with a sly smile he turned back to Brad and said, "What was it, Brad, nine months later when Chip was born?"

"Not quite," Brad said. He sat back to let the waiter take his plate.

"What's Marcy up to?" the assistant D.A. asked. "Still doing interior design?"

"She is, although she's never found her niche here in Cincinnati. She thinks she'd have better luck up north. Her parents have an architectural firm in Minneapolis."

Clay wagged a finger at Brad. "She'll drag you back there one of these days."

The waiter distributed our desserts and poured the coffee. I was savoring my coconut gelato when Clay turned his attention on me. "Did we bore you to tears, Carrie?"

I shook my head. "I'm experiencing a wine-induced sense of well-being."

"You're a cheap date," he said and looked at Brad. "One glass of chardonnay and our little cheerleader's under the table." He picked up the wine bottle and motioned as if to refill my glass. "Let's see where a second glass gets us."

Brad covered my glass with his hand. "She's good."

Clay observed the gesture with a smile, put down the bottle and said to me, "What will you do with your free time now that the campaign's over?"

I started telling him about my college courses when I got an idea. "I'm supposed to write an article about the election for my newswriting class. Could I interview you?"

Clay opened his palms in a gesture of submission. "Fire away," he said.

From my purse I produced a pencil and a narrow reporter's notebook.

Brad excused himself from the table while I plied Clay with questions about why he supported Grove and what he expected him to do once he got to Washington. Despite being rather full of himself, the assistant D.A. was articulate and passionate about what he hoped the Democrat, if elected, would accomplish. While we talked, the waiter cleared the table and presented the check, which Clay took care of paying.

I was still scribbling notes when Brad returned. "Let's go see who's winning," he said.

As we got up from the table I thanked Clay for dinner. He engulfed my hand with his big paw and said, "The pleasure was mine." With two fingers he fished a business card from his breast pocket and slipped it into my breast pocket. "Let's do it again sometime. Call me."

The festivities were in full swing when we returned to the ball-room. Rochelle waved and I went to join her.

By eleven o'clock all the news services had projected Troy Grove to win. Although he'd not yet arrived in the hall to give his acceptance speech I decided to go home. Brad saw me leaving and offered to walk me out. He was quiet as we made our way to the car. Eventually he cleared his throat and said, "I'm not sure I did you a favor by introducing you to Clayton Shaw. He's a love 'em and leave 'em kind of guy."

"I gathered that."

"Will you call him?"

I shook my head. "I can't imagine it."

"What if he asks me for your phone number?"

"Let's cross that bridge when we come to it. He'll probably forget all about me after tonight."

"No he won't," Brad said.

I found the car, unlocked the door and turned to Brad. I was conscious of how alone we were in the garage and how close to me he was standing.

"Can I ask you a question?" I said.

He shrugged. "Sure."

"Earlier this evening, why did you say I looked like trouble?"

"Oh, you heard that," Brad said. "That was the whiskey talking."

"What does it mean?"

Brad fixed me with a steady gaze. After a moment's hesitation he said, "It means you're one hot chick and I'm one married guy." He reached down and opened the car door. "Now be a good girl and go home."

My brother had given me a Word of the Day calendar the previous Christmas. I kept it in the office on the far corner of my desk where my fellow word nerds could stop and check it out.

Brad was the first to look at it the morning after the election. I was so conscious of him standing there I couldn't work.

"You still have yesterday's word on here," he said.

I glanced up from the report I was pretending to edit. "I guess I forgot to look at it."

He tore off the top sheet and laid it on the desk in front of me. "It's a keeper."

Brad watched me as I read. The word chosen for the previous day was *propinquity*. Beneath the definition, the word had been used in a sentence taken from *The New Oxford American Dictionary*, which read, *He kept his distance as though afraid propinquity might lead him into temptation.*

We looked at each other; neither of us said anything. Brad rapped his knuckles on my desk, then turned and walked into his office.

It was January before Clayton Shaw left Brad a message for me to call him. I keyed in his number on my work phone. When he came on the line, that rich baritone voice—warm and familiar and sounding so delighted to hear from me—brought a smile to my face. When he asked me out to dinner I was tempted, but in the end I told him how busy I was with school. Without saying it in so many words I tried to convey the impression I was seeing someone.

Clay laughed. "Okay, Carrie, message received. When you get over that crush you have on your boss why don't you let me know?" He didn't wait for my response before hanging up.

"Well?" Brad asked the next time we were alone in his office.

"Well nothing. I'm not going out with him."

Brad held my gaze. "Good."

Chapter 12

When does waiting become unbearable? Almost a year had passed since my election night dinner with Brad and Clayton Shaw. In that time I'd only become more besotted with my boss. There weren't enough anniversary tool belts and lobster dinners in the world to satisfy the longing I felt for him. I was close to the point where titillation without a payoff crosses over from pleasure to pain. Brad Collins was the itch I couldn't quite scratch.

That was the situation the day the power went off at work. It was mid-October and the Cloud Soft team was preparing to host a conference. In conjunction with our New York ad agency we were rolling out a new advertising campaign that we wanted everyone to embrace. Key sales personnel would be attending.

I welcomed events like this because Brad and I worked so closely together that we literally rubbed elbows in our haste and eagerness to get things organized. I knew from experience, however, that once the conference started I'd be back at my desk and he'd be otherwise engaged. At night if there was a dinner to go to, his wife would be the one invited, not me. I tried managing my expectations, but I always ended up disappointed.

This time would have been no different had fate not intervened.

On Wednesday afternoon, a day before the conference, a sudden thunderstorm swept through town, knocking out power to much of the city. We were finalizing our preparations when the lights blinked out and the computers went down. I had been about to send an important multi-page document to the printer.

Brad emerged from his office. "Did you get it printed?"

I shook my head.

"Damn," Brad said. "So we wait."

Auxiliary power provided adequate light to get around, but the silent machines made the place feel like a morgue. We waited for nearly an hour before the overhead lights flickered on and the machines whirred to life. Because the power outage had occurred toward the end of the day, the other administrative staff had been dismissed and I had the printer and copier to myself.

Brad found me in the copy room and asked if I could stay late in order to make any last-minute changes.

"I can stay, but I'll miss my ride."

"We'll get you home," he said.

Nicole and Dave stayed too. We set up the twelfth-floor conference room for eighteen people and laid out the materials at each place. Brad did a quick run-through of his presentation and pronounced it a wrap—no changes required.

In high spirits the four of us left the building together and headed for the nearby parking garage. The pavement was still wet, but the sky had cleared and the day had turned unseasonably warm. At half past six the sun rode low on the western horizon.

"I'll take you home," Brad said.

He led me to his car, a silver Audi sedan with a black convertible top, and let me in on the passenger side. After removing his suit jacket and tossing it into the back seat he slid behind the wheel and gave me a conspiratorial smile. "Should we put the top down?"

I grinned. "Sure." I rummaged in the bottom of my purse and found an elastic hair band. By the time Brad had lowered the convertible top I'd pulled my hair into a bushy ponytail and secured it with the band. I dropped my purse between my feet and buckled my seat belt.

When I glanced up Brad's eyes were on me.

"I suppose I look like a dork," I said.

He expelled a long breath and shook his head. "Not even close."

Riding in a convertible was a rare treat for me. Riding in an elegant convertible with the man of my dreams was an experience to be savored. I nestled into the leather seat and tilted my face to the sun. As we left town and picked up speed, the wind tugged at my hair, liberating the shorter strands from their binding and whipping them around.

I stole a glance at Brad. His eyes were on the road, his face bathed in a golden glow. Eric Clapton was on the car's sound system, warning a potential lover to take a look and walk away. Good advice, perhaps, but what red-blooded girl could walk away from the face I was looking at?

The sun had set in a blaze of crimson by the time we drove down my street. I pointed out my house and Brad pulled into the driveway. Through the living room window I saw my mom sitting in her favorite chair. She looked up and waved.

I was about to thank Brad for the ride when he thumped the steering wheel with his fists. "I shouldn't have brought you here."

I laughed. "Rough neighborhood, huh?" I reached down to unbuckle my seatbelt.

He stopped my hand. "Wait." His eyes locked on mine. "May I take you to dinner?"

"You don't have to. My mom'll have something for me to eat."

"I know I don't have to. I want to take you to dinner." He was still gripping my hand.

"Won't you be late?"

"Late for what?"

"Late getting home."

"I can be late this one time. Just say yes."

I looked toward the house. My mom would be mighty curious about why I was leaving. She wouldn't approve if she knew I was with Brad. I chewed my lip. "Let's go," I said.

Ten minutes later Brad steered into the crowded lot of Luiggi's Restaurant and Deli and backed the car into a secluded space at the rear. He pressed a button and the convertible top closed over our heads.

As I reached up to release my hair from its binding Brad said, "Let me do it."

Heart pounding I lowered my arms and shifted around so he could reach my ponytail. Ever so gently he removed the elastic band and dropped it into my lap. Starting at the nape of my neck he combed his fingers through my curls, untangling the knots with infinite care. The sensation as he lifted each tendril and let it fall was exquisite. Moments passed. Neither of us spoke.

When every inch of my scalp was tingling I turned to him.

His eyes scanned my face. Then he leaned forward and kissed me.

A little moan escaped my lips. When he drew back I touched a fingertip to his mouth and then to mine. "More," I whispered.

That made him smile. I could see his dimples in the half-light. Such a tantalizing smile, I needed to taste it. I took his lower lip between my teeth. The effect on Brad was electrifying.

He gripped my shoulders and pushed me against the seat with a kiss so hot it ignited a flash fire in my groin. When we surfaced for air we were both gasping.

"Jesus, Carrie, you don't fool around."

"Me? It was you."

"It was you," he teased and drew me into his arms. Our tongues probed each other's mouths. Soon he was caressing my breasts and between my legs. My hand found his crotch. The Audi was too confining. We were breathing hard, desperate to get closer to each other.

The sound of a child's chatter stopped us in our tracks. A family of four was approaching, heading for the vehicle parked on our left.

Brad and I sat back in our seats, panting.

I smoothed my skirt and gave Brad a sidelong glance. "I feel like a teenager."

He laughed. "We are *so* busted."

We waited while the kids were buckled into the mini-van. The father climbed in on the driver's side, but the mother paused outside the passenger door. When she said something about running back to the deli to buy cheese and olives, Brad groaned. "Let's go eat," he said.

"Carrie, I have some news."

Brad and I were sitting across from each other in a booth at Luiggi's. We'd placed our order and were waiting for our salads to arrive. A flameless votive candle flickered on the table between us.

Brad slid the candle aside and pressed his palms flat on the table. "I'm giving my notice at work Friday."

The breath went out of me. "Why?"

"Marcy's been wanting to move back to Minnesota. For the past year I've had my feelers out for jobs in the Twin Cities. Last week I accepted an offer. I start in three weeks."

I looked at Brad, at the face I couldn't wait to see on Monday mornings and regretted leaving on Friday afternoons. His eyes were on me, his lips slightly parted. A few minutes ago, I had tasted that mouth. My cheeks were still raw from the scrape of his beard. My groin still throbbed with want of him.

I swallowed hard. "So tonight is..."

"Our last night. Our first and last night."

In speech class I had learned the art of controlling my emotions through measured breathing. I folded my arms, stared down at my lap and held my breath until the sob that had been welling up inside me subsided into an ache at the pit of my stomach.

Our salads and drinks arrived. We were silent while the server placed them on the table.

When she'd gone I asked, "Is it a good job?"

He shrugged. "I don't know, Carrie. It's something you do to keep the peace."

Brad attacked his salad. I nibbled at mine.

"I hope I like it," Brad said between bites. "The company is called TrueMark Educational Systems. It's one of several new companies growing up around No Child Left Behind."

"What do they do?"

He considered a minute. "Think about it, Carrie. All those high stakes tests the kids take? The test materials have to come from somewhere. Then they have to go somewhere for scoring." He gestured with his fork. "The results need to be reported quickly. It all has to be secure, on time, accurate. TrueMark handles all that and more for several states across the country. They make the process as seamless and hassle-free as possible for school districts, and they make lots of money doing it."

"What's your role?" I asked.

He grinned. "I'm Doctor Feelgood. Official title, director of sales and marketing. I keep current clients happy and drum up new business from other states. I'll have a team of two sales people besides me. Sandy Madison is already on staff. She's very good, a former high school principal. The other one's Eric Brown. You know him."

"Guy you go to lunch with?"

Brad nodded. "I hired him away from P&G with promises of great wealth. Then there's Michael. He runs the website. He's talented, just needs better direction."

"You're starting to sound enthusiastic."

Our hoagies arrived. Brad must have been a lot hungrier than me. He wolfed down a quarter of his sandwich before answering. "I guess I *am* looking forward to the challenge. Maybe I was ready for a change."

This wounded me. I'd always thought he was as content as I was. Instead he'd been searching for an excuse to shake the dust of Cincinnati from his feet and move on.

The sky was dark by the time we left the restaurant. We got into the car and Brad took my hand. "Carrie, the thing I regret most is leaving you. I hope you know how special you are." He leaned over and kissed me. A soft, affectionate kiss. A kiss that said goodbye.

That's when I teared up.

"Hey, I'll be old news in a month," Brad said, cradling my face in his hands and wiping away my tears with his thumbs. "After all, you've got Clayton Shaw waiting in the wings."

He started the engine and retraced the route to my house. As he drove I memorized his profile, his left hand on the steering wheel, his right hand shifting gears. Our first and last night together, I thought. All these years I've wanted him and he waits until now to show me the feeling is mutual. If the power hadn't gone out at work this afternoon would he have left town without ever letting me know? Was he just playing with me now that he knew the coast was clear?

By the time Brad pulled into my driveway the lump of despair in my stomach had morphed into something like resentment. I was determined to make it into the house without revealing my true emotions. But after I said a tight-lipped goodbye and stepped out of the car I felt so lost I couldn't walk away. I needed more from Brad Collins. On impulse I turned around, ducked into the car head first and knelt on the seat, facing him.

"Forget something?" Brad said.

"Yeah." I threw my arms around his neck. My lips found his and I kissed him hard enough to rattle his teeth. It was a no holds barred full frontal assault packed with fury and passion. It said, *Fuck you for leaving me, and here's what you're giving up.*

I sensed Brad's surprise. His arms went around me. His kiss was deep and insistent. His need had the force of an open fire hose. When I'd drunk my fill I rocked onto my haunches and stared at my boss. His face was suffused with desire. "I want you," he breathed.

He reached for me, but I resisted and backed out of the car.

"Good," I said.

Chapter 13

My mother never emptied the dishwasher before I left for work, but the morning after I went to Luiggi's with Brad she started doing just that while I sat at the kitchen table eating my cereal. As she extracted the clean dishes and stacked them on the counter she said, "Nice car you came home in. Who was that driving?"

"Just somebody from work."

"Somebody named...?"

I wanted to tell her it was none of her business, but that would make it look like I had something to hide, so I said, "Brad."

"Brad Collins." She pounced on the name like a cat pouncing on a mouse. Clearly I'd confirmed her worst suspicions. "Where did you go when you left here?"

"Luiggi's."

"Do you think that was a good idea?"

I shrugged. "The salad was a little wilted."

She narrowed her eyes at me. "You know what I mean."

I gave her my innocent look. "Not a clue."

"Carrie, the car door was open. The light was on. I saw you kissing him."

Oh.

Like a criminal caught red-handed I made my argument. As in: *kissing isn't adultery* and *it's never happened before* and *it'll never happen again.* I stopped short of telling her the reason it would never happen again. Why should my mother have the satisfaction of knowing Brad was leaving?

By then I'd finished breakfast and had taken my bowl and juice glass to the sink. I attempted to beat a hasty retreat, but Mom blocked my way. "How old is this man, this married man?"

When I told her he was thirty-two she clucked her disapproval. "Ten years older than you. *And* he's your boss. There must be a rule against that kind of thing at a company like Procter & Gamble."

I stared at my mother and she stared back. If looks could kill, both of us would have dropped dead right there in front of the dishwasher. In my coldest possible voice I said, "Mom, if you make trouble for him I will never speak to you again."

When it came to staring contests my mother usually won. This time, however, she lowered her gaze before I did. Still, as I huffed off to the bathroom to brush my teeth I could hear her in the kitchen rattling the silverware and spluttering her disapproval.

Thanks to some judicious pedal to the metal I arrived at work before eight. I had just made it to my desk when Brad shot out of the copy room carrying a stack of papers.

"Carrie, when you have a chance I need you to get me off the hook here. I'll be in the small conference room. Bring your stapler."

I dropped my purse into a drawer, grabbed the stapler and caught up with him.

"I thought of one more handout I wanted for today," Brad said, "but when I ran the copies I forgot to select collate."

"Been there." I brandished my stapler. "I can handle this."

We entered the conference room and Brad placed the papers on the table. "Eighteen copies, five pages each."

Rushed as he'd seemed Brad didn't leave right away. He watched me as I began separating the stack into five piles, one for each page number. Out of the corner of my eye I saw him step into the hall and glance around. He reentered the room, shut the door and approached the table.

I put down the papers and turned to him. For the first time that morning I really looked at him. He was wearing his best suit and my favorite shirt and tie. God, he was beautiful. I had all I could do not to walk right into his arms.

Brad cleared his throat. "I should have had someone else take you home last night."

"Why didn't you?"

"I think we both know why."

"Are you sorry it happened?"

He chewed his lip, considering. Then he shook his head. "I'm not sorry. Not unless you are."

I took my time remembering what there was to be sorry about. I recalled how I'd nibbled his lower lip and how he'd reacted. I pictured his hands on my breasts and under my skirt. When I recalled where my hand had strayed I couldn't help it, I smiled.

"Do I look sorry?"

His eyes drank in every inch of me. "You look..." He ran a hand through his hair. "You don't make this easy, Carrie. I'm trying to tell you last night was a mistake, but all I can think is how much I want to be with you again."

"So what are you waiting for?"

"Do you truly want this?"

"I do."

He drummed his fingers on the table. Finally he said, "I'll work something out and let you know."

The day after the conference Brad announced his resignation. With just two weeks to wrap up his affairs he went into departure mode with a singled-mindedness of purpose that excluded every other consideration. He was all business—writing reports, paying final visits, making explanatory phone calls, tying up loose ends.

The first week, expecting to hear from him at any minute, I put my life on hold. Instead of carpooling with my dad I drove my own car every day even when I didn't have an evening class. I worked ahead on my school assignments and submitted them early. I turned down all invitations.

Day after day there was no message from Brad. Had he forgotten? Had he changed his mind? Had the message been so cryptic I'd missed it?

Finally on Friday when I delivered the afternoon mail to his office he said, "Next Tuesday at five," and pressed a folded slip of paper into my palm. I opened it at my desk. It read: *Kingsgate Marriott. Lobby.*

All weekend I savored my delicious secret. I wondered how much time we would have together. Would we go to dinner first? Probably not, since we couldn't chance being seen. No. We would go directly to the room. Our room. I planned what I was going to wear, down to the last stitch of clothing. Then I pictured Brad taking it all off, piece by piece.

The last time I'd been in a hotel room with a man I'd lost my virginity. This time I would lose my innocence.

I was about to have an affair.

On Monday morning everything changed. The department manager summoned the Cloud Soft team to a meeting. When we'd
assembled around the conference table he thanked Brad for his
service and introduced us to Nelson West, our new brand manager who'd been recruited from another department. My heart
sank when I learned Brad would be flying to New York to introduce Nelson to key people at the ad agency. They would depart
on Tuesday afternoon and return late Wednesday evening.

After the meeting Brad picked up his coffee mug and beckoned me to walk with him to the break room.

"They sprang it on me this morning," he said. "I didn't have a
chance to tell you."

"Could we make it Thursday night?" I asked.

He shook his head. "My brother's flying in from Minnesota
Thursday night. I have to pick him up at the airport. He and Chip
are going to drive back in the convertible so Marcy and I can
drive together in the SUV."

We entered the break room and Brad headed for the coffee pot. A woman came in behind us, coffee mug in hand. When
she struck up a conversation with Brad I filled a paper cup with
water from the dispenser and left.

On Friday afternoon, Brad's final day at P&G, I entered his office
and found him at his desk packing personal items into a cardboard box. Without the framed posters on the walls—one titled
"Minneapolis, City of Lakes" and the other of the Cincinnati sky-
line at night—his office looked forlorn. The overcast sky outside
his window mirrored my mood.

I placed a small square of white paper in front of him. It was
the Word of the Day calendar page from Election Day, a year earlier. I pointed to something I'd written beneath the definition for

propinquity. "That's my cell phone number in case you think of anything you need."

Brad picked up the scrap of paper and studied it. When he looked at me regret was written on his face. With a pang I realized it was unlikely he would ever punch in that number.

He handed the paper back to me. "You'd better keep this."

I palmed the scrap and left without a word.

At four o'clock Brad emerged from his office with the packing box in his arms. He said goodbye to Dave and Nicole. When he got to me he balanced his carton on the corner of my desk as we exchanged good wishes and shook hands.

We shook hands. That's how I said goodbye to the man I adored.

The only moment of intimacy came just before he walked away from my desk. When he reached down to pick up the box, his fingertips brushed my wrist. It lasted only a second and it may have been accidental, but I didn't think so. He locked eyes with me, hoisted his carton and turned to leave. In the blink of an eye he was gone.

I sat back down at my desk and for the next half hour pretended it didn't matter. I pretended the space where he'd stood didn't still vibrate with his presence. I pretended my wrist where he'd touched me was just my wrist.

At four-thirty I got up and left. As I rode the elevator to the first floor and crossed the lobby to the entrance I was remembering my first day of work. I'd been so resentful of the hand fate had dealt me that I'd spent all of the morning and most of the afternoon wishing I could be someplace else. Then I'd been ushered into Brad's office. He'd looked up from his desk and suddenly there was no place I'd rather be.

In all this time I hadn't changed my mind or my heart.

I drove to the university and muddled through a Spanish class, then headed home. The house was deserted, Mom and Dad having gone to a movie. I ran myself a hot bath and climbed into the tub. I slid down until the water came up to my neck.

In Spanish *to love* and *to want* are often expressed by the same verb, *querer*. In English we make a distinction. I'd never known how to label what I felt for Brad. He was my first thought in the morning and my last thought at night. At work I had a kind of radar that sensed where he was and what he was thinking. His scent, his voice, his looks—everything about him pleased me.

Love or want? I wasn't sure. Now he was gone and I'd never find out. I soaked in the tub until the cooling water gave me goose bumps. When I heard my parents arrive home I opened the drain.

There was a tap on the bathroom door. It was my mother informing me that my cousin Randy wouldn't be coming to dinner on Sunday as planned. Earlier in the week my aunt Cora had finally agreed to move to Louisville to live with her daughter. Before she had a chance to change her mind Randy had dropped everything to fly to Minnesota. Over the weekend he and his mom would be driving to Kentucky in the car she'd inherited from Henry Streator.

How ironic. The only thing I used to know about Minnesota was that it was cold. Now an inexplicable twist of fate had my loved ones shuttling to and fro like spaceships navigating a wormhole. This weekend alone, Randy would be heading in one direction and Brad in the other; they might even pass one another on the road.

"We postponed dinner until next Sunday," my mother said. "Katie and Dean are tied up, but Tommy's coming. Will you be home?"

"There's a dedication ceremony in Over the Rhine that afternoon," I said. "I might be a little late, but I'll be here."

Only two weeks had passed since our blowup over Brad, and already my mother's attitude toward me had softened. Although I hadn't told her Brad was leaving, no doubt she'd noticed my somber mood. She probably thought it was her fault my sparkle was gone and was trying to make it up to me.

I finished in the bathroom, then padded down the hall to my room and climbed into bed. Propping myself against the headboard I picked up my cell phone and called Angie. When she answered I said, "He left."

"Who left?"

"Brad. He's gone. This was his last day."

"I'm stunned. Where did he go?"

"He has a new job in Minnesota."

"How long have you known?"

"Two weeks."

"Why didn't you call me sooner?"

"I didn't want you to tell me it was for the best."

"Well it is," Angie said.

I sniffed. "I wonder if he'll ever think of me."

"I'm sure he will. But not in the way you want."

"What do I want?"

"You want him to want you. But he isn't that kind of guy. With his personality, his looks, his sense of style—my god, his wardrobe is to die for—he could have just about any woman he wants. But there's never been a whiff of anything like that with Brad. He's not the kind of man who cheats on his wife."

He kissed me. I thought it but I didn't say it. If I'd spoken them aloud those three words would have opened the floodgates and I'd have ended up telling her everything. I swallowed hard and resisted the urge to confide. What right did I have to destroy the image she had of Brad?

"Are you up for some good news?" Angie said. I could hear the excitement in her voice.

"I'm desperate for it."

"I'm leaving on Monday for Paris. I'll be there eight weeks as part of my internship. When I get back at the end of the year they've offered me a permanent position here in New York."

That was fabulous news indeed. The rest of our conversation revolved around Angie's job and what she would be doing in Paris. As we were about to hang up she said, "Life goes on, Carrie. It'll go on for you too."

I knew it would. It just wouldn't be worth living.

Chapter 14

By Monday morning Nelson West's name had replaced Brad's on the wall outside what I still thought of as Brad's office. Nelson was a competent manager, but suddenly everything I did felt routine. I went through the motions, but without Brad's enthusiasm to feed off of, the joy was gone. By Friday I decided I'd been at the job too long.

I should have used the weekend to update my résumé and begin my job search, but I couldn't summon the energy. Instead I did what I was used to doing on weekends: I studied, attended class, helped my parents rake leaves and treated my nieces to dinner and a movie on Saturday evening.

On Sunday I drove to an Over the Rhine neighborhood where an entire block of homes was ready for occupancy. The organizers had arranged a ceremony to show off the renovations and turn over the keys to the new occupants. Everyone who'd worked on the houses had been invited to attend the Sunday afternoon celebration.

I arrived early and met my friend Rochelle, who joined me in a tour of the latest house we'd worked on together. The final product was a charming two-story brick row house that had been substantially renovated but still retained its original character. The new owners, a single mom and her three children, showed us around with obvious pride.

The dedication ceremony was held on a cordoned off street where a platform—complete with microphone and loudspeakers—had been erected. The residents had been invited to sit on the platform behind the guest speaker, who was none other than U.S. Representative Troy Grove, the man Rochelle and I had helped to elect the previous November.

To my surprise one of the dignitaries in Grove's entourage was Clayton Shaw. He looked just as intriguing as the last time I'd seen him.

"I know him," I whispered to Rochelle as Troy Grove was being introduced. We were standing toward the back of a decent-sized crowd.

"Duh," Rochelle said. "We campaigned for him."

"I mean the black guy on the right, in the gray suit."

"He's hot."

Like the mature adult I pretended to be I spent a good portion of the congressman's speech fishing in my purse for the business card Clay Shaw had given me and wondering if I dared approach him. At the conclusion of the formal proceedings I showed the card to my friend.

"You want to meet him?" I asked.

Rochelle laughed. "Why not? You obviously want to see him again."

We worked our way to the front, where Representative Grove had descended from the platform and was mingling with the crowd in a reception line. Clay Shaw had stationed himself at the head of the line as a facilitator, it appeared, to keep people from crowding the congressman.

We were drawing near when a haughty-looking blond took her place beside the assistant D.A. and put a possessive hand on his sleeve.

"Uh oh, your boyfriend appears to be spoken for," Rochelle said.

"I'm changing my mind about going up there," I said.

"He's already spotted you. You can't just walk away."

Clay *had* looked down the line and recognized me. I'd waved, and he'd nodded and smiled. It wasn't the smile I remembered though; there was nothing intimate about this smile.

When we got to the front of the line, Clay's sleeve-grabbing companion moved in close, her defensive antennae aquiver. I introduced Clay to Rochelle and told him she'd campaigned for Grove too.

"Excellent," he boomed, and produced another phony smile. "Don't forget, ladies, it's only a two-year term. The congressman will need your help again next year."

He scanned the crowd and, seeing he had to detain us a bit longer before passing us along the reception line, he asked about Brad. "I haven't talked to your boss in months," he said.

When I told him Brad had moved back to Minnesota he was clearly surprised. He looked into my eyes and said the first and only thing to come out of his mouth that day that sounded genuine. "I'm sorry, Carrie. I know how much you enjoyed working with him."

A moment later Rochelle and I shuffled forward in the reception line.

On my way home I felt despair creeping in. Tomorrow I'd return to another week of joyless work. My personal life sucked. I adored my nieces, but spending every Saturday night with them wasn't healthy. I hadn't been out on a date in so long I wasn't sure how to go about getting one. I replayed the afternoon encounter with Clayton Shaw. I saw his impersonal smile and the woman clinging to his arm. So much for the guy waiting in the wings. I was yesterday's blond.

By the time I pulled into the driveway, depression had descended upon me like a pall. I climbed out of the car, conjured up a smile and went into the house.

My parents, my brother and my cousin were gathered around the kitchen table eating dinner. My mother had prepared one of Randy's favorite meals: smoked sausage, sauerkraut and mashed potatoes. Since I'd called ahead to say I'd be late, Mom had put my meal into a warm oven.

I'd walked in on a conversation about home renovation. At first I assumed they were discussing the Over the Rhine project, but as I served myself and took a seat beside Randy it became clear the subject was his mother's house.

"What's new?" I said.

My dad passed me a serving bowl of applesauce. "Randy's got a logistics problem."

Randy swallowed a mouthful and said, "Now that Mom's in Louisville with my sister, we're looking to sell the house in Minnesota. The realtor we contacted says it's going to require a lot of work if we want to get anything near what it's worth. So I have to figure out how to handle the repairs from down here in Cincinnati."

There it was again: the Cincinnati to Minnesota wormhole. Even as my cousin explained his predicament an idea began taking shape in my devious brain. Had an amazing opportunity just dropped into my lap?

"Whereabouts in Minnesota is your mom's house?" I said.

My cousin had just shoved another hunk of sausage into his mouth. He must have been starving himself for a week anticipating this meal. "Twin Cities," he said between chews.

Casually as I could I said, "Like, where in the Twin Cities?"

Randy gave me a curious look, clearly mystified by my sudden interest in the precise location of his mother's house. "Nowhere you ever heard of. A suburb south of Minneapolis called Lakeville." He shrugged. "Nice town about twenty minutes from the airport."

Lakeville. I seared the name into my memory.

By shirking kitchen cleanup duty I managed to slip away to the computer and Google up a map of the Twin Cities metropolitan area. Toward the bottom of the map was Lakeville. Its nearest neighbor to the north was Burnsville. That name rang a bell. I'd already visited the website of TrueMark, Brad's new company, several times in the past week. I pulled it up again and bit a knuckle to keep from crying out. My recollection had been right: TrueMark was in Burnsville. Brad's employer and Aunt Cora's house were practically neighbors.

By the time I returned to the kitchen the table had been cleared of dishes and the dominoes were out. Randy had introduced the family to a domino game called Mexican Train, which we played almost every time he visited. Usually it was fun. On this occasion, however, I couldn't wait for it to be over.

Whenever Randy and Tommy came for dinner the three of us had the habit of visiting for a while in the living room after my mom and dad retired. That evening was no different. When we'd settled into our customary positions, with Tommy sitting beside me on the sofa and Randy to my right in my mom's favorite chair, I broached the subject that had been on my mind all evening.

"I have a proposition for you, Randy," I said. I'd been sitting cross-legged on the sofa but now I straightened up and planted my feet on the floor. "I can solve the problem of what to do with your mom's house."

"I'm listening," he said.

"I'll find you a seasoned home rehabilitator who will move into the house, renovate it on a shoestring and turn it back to you to sell. Or she could even sell it herself."

"She?" Randy said. "And that person would be..."

I pointed at my chest. "Yours truly."

Randy and Tommy shared a laugh. They looked at me like I was insane.

"Why not me?" I asked.

"Carrie, you'd have to move," Tommy said. *Like, duh.*

"So what? Mom's about to kick me out anyway."

"Even if that were true, which it's not," Tommy said, "you can't just move to Minnesota. What about your job?"

I shrugged. "I'll find a job in Minnesota." I leaned toward Randy, tingling with excitement. "I can do this, Randy. I've repaired wallboard, stripped floors, replaced grout. Whatever needs to be done, I can do it."

"But why would you *want* to do it?"

"I think it would be cool to fix up a run-down house on my own and turn it into something people would pay good money to live in." All other considerations aside, now that I'd said it, I meant it.

My cousin looked doubtful. "That would be great if the house was down the street and you could run over there on weekends. I'd foot the bill for that. But I can't afford to send you to Minnesota. How would you live?"

"How much are you willing to pay to have somebody fix it up?"

Randy looked uncomfortable. "I'm embarrassed to admit it, but the house is in tough shape. My mom really let it go. The realtor said it would cost at least thirty thousand dollars just to make it livable. We plan to pay for it out of the money Mom inherited from Henry."

I made some quick mental calculations. "Well, if you give me thirty thousand, pay the taxes and let me stay there free for a year, I'll fix it up for you."

Tommy could hold his tongue no longer. "Carrie, you're nuts. Don't make these stupid promises without getting more information."

Randy signaled time out. "Relax, Tommy. I won't hold your baby sister to anything she says tonight. She's obviously on drugs." He turned to me. "On the other hand, Carrie, if you're even the least bit serious about this I won't dismiss the idea."

"I'm totally serious," I said. "I'd need to find a job up there, but it wouldn't have to pay all that well if I'm not paying rent. I'll check out the job market."

Randy looked intrigued. "It would be a huge relief to have somebody I trust living there fixing up the house while the market is in the doldrums. We wouldn't be in a hurry to sell if we knew the place was being taken care of." He paused a moment, then gave a decisive nod. "I'm driving down to see Mom in Louisville next weekend. Let's you and me mull over the idea and touch base before I leave."

I grinned and stuck out my right hand. "Deal," I said, and we shook on it.

Goodbye, sleep. Hello, computer. As soon as Randy and Tommy left, I jumped on the Internet and started searching Craigslist for jobs in the suburbs south of Minneapolis. An hour later I had fourteen possibilities. None of the jobs excited me much. Still, what would be the harm of brushing up my résumé and shooting off some applications?

I was about to turn off the computer when I succumbed to temptation. For the second time that evening I typed in TrueMark Educational Systems. When the home page came up I scrolled down the left side and clicked on Employment Opportunities.

A handful of jobs were listed, but the only one for which I qualified was customer service representative. Not exactly a choice position, but how much would it be worth to me to work at the same company where Brad was employed?

I gnawed a thumbnail. My application was certain to raise eyebrows at TrueMark. I'd have to craft a cover letter so persuasive it would leave no question the reason I was moving to Minnesota was to rescue a *favorite aunt* from financial ruin by renovating her house, something I'd *always dreamed* of doing. What a *fortunate coincidence* that my former boss had moved to Minnesota as well. Why wouldn't I apply to work at a company he'd spoken so highly of and where his endorsement of my credentials would carry weight?

I smiled. My pulse quickened. *Oh yeah, I can do this.*

Over the next few days I applied online to seven companies from the list of job possibilities I'd compiled on Sunday night. On Thursday evening I turned my attention to TrueMark. All week I'd been laboring over a cover letter that would snag me an interview with Brad's company without getting him in trouble. I reread it now with fresh eyes and gave myself a figurative pat on the back.

I filled out the online application and attached my résumé and cover letter. For the longest time my cursor hovered over the SEND key. Finally, I held my breath and clicked.

A few days later my cell phone sounded. It was late evening and I was sitting at the desk in my bedroom studying for a test.

The caller ID read Marriott. Inexplicable as that was I had a premonition about who was calling. In a company as small as TrueMark I had guessed the powers that be wouldn't waste time letting Brad know his name had been used as a reference.

Even before I answered, my heart was beating a wild tattoo. I put the phone to my ear and said, "This is Carrie."

"Guess who this is." I could hear a smile in that most familiar of voices.

"Mr. Marriott, I presume?"

Brad chuckled. "Speaking."

"How's your new job?"

"It's all right. Spending way too much time in hotel rooms. This week it's the Marriott Hotel in Indianapolis."

"What are you doing in Indianapolis?"

"Same thing I do everywhere. Pitching to the state board of education. Next week it'll be some other hotel in some other state capital." He paused, then said, "I got an interesting voice mail today from Denise Gavin in human resources. She received an application from someone who used to work for me. She wanted to know what I thought of her."

"What did you say?"

"As you can imagine, my first reaction was panic. I'm like, what the hell, Carrie, don't you know what people will think? Fortunately I checked my email before returning her call. She'd forwarded your application materials. I have to say, your cover letter was persuasive."

"Whew," I said. "You don't know how hard I worked to give it the right spin."

"You made that up about renovating your aunt's house, right?"

"Would I lie on a job application?" I spluttered, pretending to be insulted.

Brad laughed. "You have to admit the timing raises questions."

"I know it's a colossal coincidence, but I swear that's the way it went down. My cousin has been trying to get my aunt to move out of her house for over a year. A few weeks ago she finally gave in. All I did was take advantage of the situation."

"Which leads to my next question," Brad said. "Of all the contractors your cousin could have hired, how did he happen to choose you to do the renovations?"

I cleared my throat. "In the interest of full disclosure, Randy didn't so much choose me as let himself be persuaded."

"Ah Carrie, you're a born marketer."

"I'll take that as a compliment."

"Well, marketing is a big plus in this business," Brad said. "You've definitely piqued the interest of the folks at TrueMark."

I sucked in a breath. "Seriously?"

"Seriously. Your skill set has opened up a world of possibilities for them."

"How so?"

"Ever since I started interviewing with TrueMark they've been raving about how their customer service is superior to any of their competitors. I won't go into all that can go wrong in this business, but trust me you need a trained and educated customer service department to keep things from spiraling out of control. I want to feature it more in our marketing and advertising, but first we need somebody to develop marketing materials and Web content. When I talked to Denise this afternoon I told her you could do that."

I hopped up from my desk and did a little dance. "This is so much better than I expected."

"Hold on, Carrie, there's a caveat. The company isn't ready to create the position yet. What they'd like you to do is come in as a customer service rep, get familiar with the business and start assembling databases you can use later on.

"The other thing is, they can't know I've contacted you. Convincing as your cover letter is I want to avoid arousing suspicion about us. That's why I didn't use my cell phone and that's why there won't be any record of this phone call. So when you talk to Denise—"

"It'll all be new to me."

"Right. She probably won't tell you as much as I have about their future plans so keep that under your hat."

"Are you sure they're going to contact me?"

"As of right now I'm the fair-haired child at TrueMark. I gave you a solid endorsement and showed how hiring you can solve a problem for them. I'd probably have to resign if they *didn't* call you."

I laughed. This was vintage Brad. "Sounds like I hitched my wagon to a star."

"I wouldn't go that far," Brad said.

"But you *do* walk on water."

"Oh, little girl, I miss how you feed my ego."

"Oh yeah? Anything else you miss?"

"Maybe a few other things...so what are you wearing right now?"

"Do you want to hear about the baggy sweats I'm actually wearing or should I make something up?"

"Be creative."

I sat on my bed and thought for a minute. "All I have on is a tiny pair of bikini underpants and a white ribbed tank top," I purred. "It's almost indecent the way the top hugs my breasts. You know those fat pencils preschoolers use?"

"Yeah."

"Can you picture the pink erasers?"

Brad choked on whatever he must have been drinking. "You've done this before, Carrie."

"Only in my dreams."

"You're damn good."

"Then why are you critiquing my performance? You're supposed to be turned on."

"I *am* turned on, but with all these clients sitting around the conference table and you on speaker..."

I burst out laughing. "Way to destroy a mood."

He chuckled. "I couldn't resist. How about a rain check?"

"Any time," I said.

Brad cleared his throat. "Listen, Carrie. Just a heads up. I can't promise what's going to happen between us when you get here. It'll be different from P&G. Since we won't be working in the same department there's no legitimate reason for you to call me or come by my office. I'll have to contact you. It's not only the people at work we have to worry about. My family is even more important."

As he elaborated on the precautions we would need to take, the elation I'd been feeling began seeping away. This was grownup stuff—the serious side of having an affair. Brad had more to lose than I did. One false move and his marriage, his career, or both, could be destroyed.

After we said goodbye I sat there holding the phone in my hand. It wasn't too late to call the whole thing off. I hadn't quit my job and nothing had been firmed up with my cousin.

I put down the phone, stood and studied my reflection in the mirror over the dresser. My body was ripe and full of longing for this one man. I cupped my breasts and felt my chest rise and fall under my hands. I fingered the warm place between my legs. Even through the sweatpants it felt moist and swollen with desire.

I stared into my eyes. It's a funny thing about eyes. They don't change. No matter how old you get or how much makeup you apply they're still the same eyes you looked out of when you were five years old. You can't lie to your own eyes in the mirror.

I held my gaze until I blinked. Then I reached over and flipped off the light. I knew the course I was embarking on was risky and immoral. I also knew I wouldn't turn away. Right or wrong I wanted Brad. And despite the risk he wanted me. If TrueMark offered me the job I'd take it.

Chapter 15

December 31, 2009

I left Cincinnati in a cold drizzle. An hour before dawn on the last day of the year I climbed into my Corolla and started the engine. My parents stood in the driveway, huddled together under an umbrella. They'd argued long and hard against what Mom had branded my harebrained scheme. When I'd shown no signs of budging, however, they'd accepted my decision. They looked grim as I backed out of the driveway.

Refusing to let the lowering clouds bring me down I turned the heat on full blast and pumped up the rock and roll on my MP3 player. Along with my Google maps I'd placed a cardboard carton full of snacks within easy reach on the seat next to me. A thermos of steaming coffee and a bottle of water stood ready in the cup holders.

Soon I was on I-74, crossing the state line from Ohio into Indiana. My plan on this dreary Wednesday was to drive straight through to Minnesota, move into my aunt's house, spend the rest of the week cleaning and getting organized, and start my new job the following Monday.

Beyond that I wasn't sure what to expect. I'd heard from Brad only once after I'd accepted TrueMark's offer. When he'd called to congratulate me he'd sounded vague about the future of our relationship. "We'll have to play it by ear," he'd said, citing family and social obligations that consumed most of his free time. He didn't specify whose ear we'd be playing it by, but I was pretty sure it wasn't mine.

My immediate concern was the weather, which was deteriorating the farther northwest I traveled. I checked my dashboard for the outside temperature: still above freezing, but just barely. The pelting rain had already forced me to reduce my speed. If the rain turned to ice I was in for an adventure.

It was already past noon by the time I reached the turn north onto I-39 at Bloomington, Illinois. I was running two hours behind where I'd expected to be and I knew from radio reports I was heading into sleet. I'd had high hopes of making the trip in one day, but now it was clear I wouldn't arrive in Minnesota that night. In fact my chances of getting as far as Wisconsin were slim.

Resigned to my fate I began scanning the blue road signs looking for a likely place to stay. I considered spending New Year's Eve in the incongruously named Illinois town of El Paso just so I could call my mom and talk like a Texan. The El Paso exit came and went, however, and I was still on the road, having decided to put a few more miles behind me before calling it a day.

That was a mistake.

Twenty miles north of El Paso the temperature dropped below freezing. Within minutes a sloppy mix of snow and ice coated my windshield, clogged my wipers and slicked the roadway beneath my car. With the dashboard flashing bright orange skid warnings I pressed on; the next exit couldn't come soon enough.

I was emerging from a dry underpass when my front tires hit a patch of ice. A jolt of fear shot through me as my Corolla started skidding sideways. Heart in my throat I whipped the steering wheel back and forth in an effort to regain control. It was no use. I was headed for the ditch.

That's when I panicked and slammed on the brakes.

In an instant the rear of my vehicle lunged ahead of the front. I sucked in a breath as my car began to spin. A kaleidoscope of images whirled past my frantic eyes. For a split-second I caught sight of the orange and black eighteen-wheeler I'd passed a half-mile back. It was barreling toward me, the gap between us narrowing at a terrifying rate. Gripping the steering wheel for dear life I braced for the impact.

I don't know how many revolutions the Corolla made. One moment I was careening off course, sure I was about to die; a moment later the danger had passed and I was cruising along in the left lane with my faithful steed miraculously pointed north.

I started breathing again. My hands were slick on the steering wheel. As I turned my head to check on the traffic the orange and black rig rumbled past in the right lane. The driver, a grinning, gaunt-faced fellow with a scraggly beard and a ponytail, stuck his left hand out the window and saluted me with an upraised thumb.

Giddy with relief I blared my horn. I could have kissed that trucker, that paragon of virtue, my fellow traveler on planet earth. The hand of God had just reached down and plucked me from the jaws of death, and that angel of the asphalt had not only avoided plowing into me he'd also witnessed my deliverance. We were brothers.

I cowered in the slow lane after that, playing it safe and scouring the horizon for the next hotel. When I spotted a Best Western just off the freeway near Oglesby I took the exit and headed for the blue and yellow sign. With a sigh of relief I pulled into the parking lot and shut off the engine.

I snapped up the last available room, settled in and called my mom. Mothers only think they need to know everything their children are up to. I gave mine the edited version of my day, and she was better for it. Toward the end of our conversation she promised to call Sharon Weikel to tell her I'd be a day late.

Aside from my dad, Sharon Weikel was my mom's dearest friend. Even now, five years after Mr. Weikel's job transfer had moved the family to Minnesota, she and Mom remained close enough to impose upon each other. The Weikels had come through with an invitation to let me stay in a spare bedroom while I worked on Aunt Cora's house. A generous offer to be sure, but one I had no plans to take them up on.

"I'm not staying with the Weikels, remember?"

My mother sighed. "You need to keep your options open, Carrie. You heard what Randy said about the house. What if it's too filthy to live in?"

While we were talking I'd been pawing through my overnight bag for the bathing suit I knew was in there somewhere. The hotel boasted an indoor pool and hot tub, and I intended to get my money's worth. Triumphant, I pulled my suit from the bag and pictured myself sinking neck-deep into the steaming hot tub. The image alone was enough to put things into perspective.

I cut off my mom mid-argument by agreeing with her. Of course it made sense to have a contingency plan. And yes, she should notify Sharon Weikel I'd be a day late. By the time we hung up, Mom and I were great pals once again.

Day two on the road was blessedly uneventful. It was mid-afternoon when I crossed the storied Mississippi River on I-90 at LaCrosse, Wisconsin, and spotted the sign: MINNESOTA

WELCOMES YOU. Rugged yellow cliffs festooned with stalactites of blue-tinted ice rose to greet me as my car climbed out of the river valley.

Darkness had descended by the time I reached Lakeville. The map led me away from the downtown area to a neighborhood of neat-looking homes on wooded lots. What I was seeing was better than I'd dared hope.

I drove down my new street. The houses varied in style from one- and two-story to split-level. Most were decorated for the holidays, with outdoor lights ablaze and indoor light spilling from the windows onto fresh snow.

The only dark house on the street was a single-story structure bearing my aunt Cora's house number. I eased my car into a short driveway in front of a two-car garage. To the right of the garage and set back about ten feet was the attached residence. Ranged along the front of the house from left to right were a large window, the front door, and two smaller windows. Dense shrubs crowded the door and nearly obscured the windows.

Some considerate person had cleared the driveway and sidewalk of snow. I shut off the engine and got out of the car. Ambient light from the neighboring houses lit my way as I started up the walk, which curved from the driveway to the front door. The ragged shrubs made the place feel creepy, like there might be somebody lurking behind them or watching me from inside the house. I mounted the stoop. Fitting the key into the lock I opened the door and stepped inside.

The vile stench is the first thing that struck me. I once had a pet gerbil escape its cage and crawl under the stove, where it had died. That was the stomach-churning odor that predominated in this house.

I groped along the wall and found a switch that turned on an overhead light. I was standing in an entrance area with the living room to my left. Randy had not exaggerated: the place was in tough shape. The walls were gouged, the curtains torn, the wall-to-wall carpet stained and threadbare. Newspapers and junk mail were stacked high on the tables, and the sofa and chairs were soiled and lumpy. As I wandered from one unsavory room to another, unidentifiable items crunched and squished underfoot.

I took out my cell phone. Wait until Mom hears about this, I thought. When she answered I chirped, "Well, I made it." I was about to launch into a light-hearted description of the horrors surrounding me in my new home when she stopped me with one word.

"Carrie."

What's in a name? In this case disapproval on a grand scale. It was astonishing how much disapproval my mother could pack into a single word. Something had happened since the last time we'd spoken, and whatever it was must be my fault.

"Angie just left here," my mother said.

Oh crap. "We've been out of touch," I said. "I didn't know she was in Cincinnati."

"She's visiting her parents before she returns to New York. She brought you a scarf from Paris."

"That's cool," I said and waited for the other shoe to drop.

"When I told her you were on your way to Minnesota she said a curious thing."

I cringed. "She did?"

"She asked if you were going to be working for Brad Collins."

I swallowed hard. "Oh."

"Why didn't you tell me Brad Collins was in Minnesota?"

"I didn't think it was relevant."

"Of course you didn't. Will you be working for him?"

"Not really."

"What does that mean—not really?"

"I'll be working at the same company he works at, but not for him."

My mother sighed. "He's a married man, Carrie. He has a child. Is he the reason you quit a good job at Procter & Gamble—a job you loved—and suddenly you just had to become a customer service agent for a company you know nothing about?"

"I was tired of my job."

"You were moving up, taking on extra responsibility. You said yourself you were in line for a promotion."

"I wouldn't have gotten a promotion without a degree."

"You're only a year or two away from getting your degree," my mom said. She sounded so frustrated I thought she might start crying. "I've been puzzled about this for weeks, ever since you got the insane idea to move into Cora's house. I went along with it, but I didn't *get* it. Then Angie tells me this news about Brad Collins. I'll ask you again, Carrie, and this time I want the truth. Has something been going on between the two of you?"

"Nothing is going on, Mom."

I could hear my mother's skepticism in the silence on the line. When I judged the silence had stretched long enough, I brightened and said, "Do you want to hear about the house?"

She huffed out a breath. Even over the phone her effort to shift gears was tangible. "How is it?"

"It's horrible, disgusting, filthy—and it stinks. I don't think Aunt Cora ever threw anything away. Honest to god, Mom, I'm standing at the dining room table looking at a wooden crate of furry green balls that used to be tangerines, according to the label. Oh, and here's a dried-up flower arrangement that's still wrapped in cellophane." I read the attached card. "Oh my god, Mom, it's from Randy. It says 'Happy Mother's Day.' Can you believe this? It's been here since last May."

"Or maybe the May before that," she said, sounding more delighted than grossed out. "I'm not all that surprised. I was in Cora's house just the one time when your uncle Terry was so sick. The place was a pigsty."

Now we were on familiar ground. This version of Mom I could handle. We talked for another five minutes. For the umpteenth time she encouraged me to call Sharon Weikel to tell her I'd like to stay with her after all. I held my ground, insisting I'd tough it out in my sleeping bag.

We were about to hang up when my mother said, "It's a sin, you know."

I hoped she was talking about the state of Aunt Cora's house, but I knew better.

"It's a mortal sin, Carrie. People get hurt."

When I clicked off I saw I had a single-word text message from Angie: OOPS.

A half-hour later I was cleaning one of the two revolting toilets in the house, using a sponge and cleanser I'd found in a cabinet under the bathroom sink, when the doorbell rang. I jumped up and gave my hands a quick wash at the sink, then dried them on some wadded-up toilet paper. When I opened the door Sharon Weikel stood on the stoop. My mom had been busy.

"Mrs. Weikel. I was going to call you tomorrow."

"I saved you the effort." She was carrying a tin of what I assumed were Christmas cookies. "How are you, Carrie? You look wonderful."

"Thanks, I'm great." I opened the door wider. "Come in if you dare."

She stepped inside. With her first breath I saw her nose wrinkle. She clutched the cookie tin to her chest as if she was afraid it too would become contaminated. Her eyes swept the room. "Oh, honey, you can't stay here."

She was right of course. I'd just needed someone other than my mother to say it. At Mrs. Weikel's urging I called my mom, who had the good manners not to gloat when I told her of my change in plans.

Mrs. Weikel must have acclimated to the smell because when I got off the phone she wanted me to show her around. As we explored the rooms I began to see why my mother liked her so much.

Sharon—she asked me to call her that—was a bundle of enthusiasm. She could imagine Aunt Cora's house without all the crap. She raved about the convenient layout, how I could come in from the garage and turn left into the laundry room or walk back a short hall to the kitchen. She loved the breakfast nook with its bay window and view of the back yard, and the adjacent family room with the three-season porch at the rear. She adored the way the house wrapped around the deck on three sides.

We walked down the hall and I showed her the bathroom where I'd been attempting to muck out the toilet, and the two rooms whose windows could be seen from the street. One was an office, the other a guest room. Opposite the guest room was the master bedroom. I flipped on the feeble overhead light. The place was cavernous, dark and unspeakably filthy.

Waving toward a door on the left side of the room I said, "There's the master bath. We won't go in there. Trust me it's equally depressing."

"It might be depressing now, Carrie, but it can all be fixed. There's lots of potential here."

I turned out the light and we retraced our steps to the living room. As we prepared to leave the house Sharon said, "Here's what I've been thinking. Before you start cleaning and painting the first thing you need to do is throw out all the junk. If you rent a trash bin Walt and I will come down and give you a hand emptying the place."

"I can't ask you to do that."

She waved a dismissive hand. "Your parents helped us pack when we were moving up here. We'd like to return the favor."

I followed Sharon north on the freeway. We passed through Burnsville—home of my new employer—and drove across the Minnesota River to the Weikel home in Bloomington where Sharon's husband Walt, their daughter Jill and Jill's boyfriend Derek were waiting to greet me.

Mr. Weikel hadn't changed much, but Jill, two years my junior, was another story. When I'd last seen her in high school, she'd been a wholesome-looking and slightly chubby fifteen-year-old. In five years she'd changed as dramatically as I had. At twenty, she was striking: tall and slender, with stick-straight hair—jet black with streaks of magenta—halfway down her back, black nail polish and lots of eye liner and mascara. I would have pegged her as an art student and I'd have been close. A junior at the University of Minnesota, she was studying stage design. Her equally Goth-looking boyfriend, a U of M senior, was poised to get his degree in graphic arts.

The three of them were eager to hear about my aunt's house. As Sharon and I described the place I warmed to the possibilities. The excitement must have been catching because by the time we got to the part about renting a trash bin everybody wanted to sign up for duty.

"Can we do it this Saturday?" Jill asked. "The weather's supposed to be good."

"If I can get a dumpster you've got yourself a deal," I said.

Sharon showed me to my room, a basement bedroom vacated by Jill's older brother, who'd moved to Colorado. It was a typical boy's room, with a twin bed pushed against the wall, a closet, a desk, a chest of drawers and a nightstand.

Besides the bedroom the Weikel basement featured a bathroom, a family room and a laundry room. A door led from the basement into the two-car garage. In the garage Sharon pointed to a pedestrian door that led outside. "You'll be able to go in and out without even coming upstairs. I'll give you a key."

Derek and Jill helped me tote my belongings from my car to the bedroom and left me to get organized. After hanging my clothes in the closet and stowing a few things in drawers I washed up in the bathroom and climbed into bed. I stared at the unfamiliar ceiling of my borrowed bedroom and gave my head a slow shake. Nothing had gone as expected. My fantasy had been to move in to Aunt Cora's house, toss a few items, sweep a few floors and do a little laundry. Within a week I'd pictured myself inviting Brad over for a visit.

"Ha," I said to the darkness.

Chapter 16

There was no question about the first order of business when I entered my aunt's house the next morning. The smell had gotten worse. Without taking off my coat or gloves I steeled myself and followed my nose to the source of the odor: to the kitchen...to the sink...under the sink.

I held my breath and peeked into the wastebasket. In the bottom was a dead mouse in the bloat stage of decomposition. It had probably been running along the drainpipe when it had fallen into the empty container and been unable to climb back out.

Gingerly I extracted the wastebasket and carried it out through the sliding door and across the deck into the back yard. I trudged through the snow to a wooded area near what I judged to be the property line, where I dumped the hapless victim, pushed it down with my foot and kicked snow over the top. Mission accomplished, I retraced my steps to the house. I'd left the door open and already the place smelled better.

I headed for the laundry room where Sharon and I had discovered a cabinet full of cleaning supplies that probably hadn't been touched in years. For the rest of the morning I worked non-stop, tackling one room at a time. I started with the main bathroom, reasoning that if the Weikels were going to help me on Saturday, they deserved a clean bathroom.

The room in the best shape was the guest bedroom. Randy had told me his sister Debbie had brought in a new bed after Henry Streator had died so she would have a decent place to sleep when she visited her mom. The door must have been kept closed because the mattress didn't reek of smoke. I'd be hanging onto that bed.

I swept, straightened and cleaned with gay abandon, barely looking at the stuff I scooped out of drawers and tossed into trash bags. Most of it was junk. The linen closet in the hall held some treasures though: towels and bedding that were like new. Into the washing machine and dryer they went while I disinfected the closet shelves. In no time the closet was restocked, and fresh towels hung in the bathroom.

Before I'd left the Weikel house that morning I'd arranged for the delivery of a dumpster. It arrived around noon. After the driver parked it in the driveway and drove off I began dragging out bags of trash and tossing them into the bin.

I had just deposited my final bag of the morning and was returning to the house when a voice called, "Welcome, neighbor." I looked around. A trim woman with short-cropped pepper-and-salt hair was waving at me from the front porch of the house directly across the street. A wiry-looking man with wispy white hair came out the door behind her. Both of them were in their seventies, I guessed, probably ten years older than my parents.

They crossed the street and introduced themselves as Vic and Janet Lundgren and told me they'd been keeping an eye on the house for Randy. I learned Vic had been the angel who'd cleared the driveway prior to my arrival.

To be polite I invited them in. To my dismay they accepted.

"We haven't been inside the house for years," Janet said. "Why don't you give us a quick tour, then stop over at our house for lunch."

I held open the front door. "It's not ready for prime time yet."

It wasn't. Viewing the house through their eyes I was reminded how shabby the place looked. Aunt Cora had been a smoker and it showed. Everything, including the supposed-to-be-white ceiling, had a dingy yellow cast.

"I'll be tossing the carpeting and most of the furniture," I said.

Like Sharon, Janet chose to accentuate the positive. In the living room she indicated the ceiling to floor divided-light window that would have looked out onto the front yard were it not for the shrub that blocked the view. "Even though this is the north side of the house, if you get rid of that old yew you'll be surprised how much brighter this room will be."

Vic called me into the dining room. He ran his hand across the table and glanced at the matching chairs and buffet. "I'd hang onto this furniture," he said. "All it needs is refinishing." He wasn't as sanguine about the galley kitchen, with its dated vinyl floor tiles, laminate counter top and banged-up oak cabinets.

"Redo," I said, and Vic nodded.

We crossed into the adjoining breakfast nook.

"Just look how the light pours in through this bay window," Janet said. "You'll love this."

"Any use trying to salvage the dinette set?" I asked.

Vic looked doubtful and Janet said, "You know, Vic, she could have the table and chairs in our basement. It's a lot better than this. We'll show it to you when you come over, Carrie."

We wandered into the adjacent family room.

"Now this is nice," Vic said, ignoring the nasty furniture and carpet and taking in the stone fireplace and the vaulted, pine-paneled ceiling.

Janet made a beeline for the three-season porch and peered in. "I've always loved this porch and deck. Henry and Adriana used to have the best cookouts here."

"Adriana?"

"Henry's wife," Janet said. "Lovely woman. Wonderful cook."

"I didn't picture him as being married," I said.

Vic chuckled. "Join the crowd. We had him pegged as a confirmed bachelor until he showed up with Adriana." He explained that as a pilot for Northwest Airlines, Henry had regularly flown from Minneapolis to Mexico. "When he started spending every vacation there too we suspected something was up. One day he returned home married to this beautiful Mexican woman."

"What happened to her?" I asked.

Janet looked solemn. "She died of breast cancer about ten years ago."

Vic wagged his head. "The heart went out of Henry when Adriana died. He let the house go and kept to himself even after he brought Cora here."

"We didn't get to know your aunt," Janet said.

"I didn't know her well either," I said. "She was married to my dad's brother. We always thought she was a little crazy."

Vic and Janet exchanged a look.

I smiled. "I guess you have some stories."

"A few," Janet said, then glanced at her watch. "I left a casserole in the oven. The timer should be going off right about now." She hooked her arm in Vic's and led him to the front door. "Carrie, come over in ten minutes. We'll get you back to work in no time."

Janet was true to her word. Within thirty-five minutes my new neighbors had fed me a delicious meal in clean and comfortable surroundings and taken me to the basement to show me their old oak dinette set, which I snapped up in half a heart-beat. They promised to keep it for me until I was ready for it.

I was about to head out their front door when Janet waved me into the living room. The Lundgrens and my parents must have purchased their living room furniture in the same era, when faux Mediterranean was all the rage and everything came in matched sets. The pieces—sofa, chairs, tables and lamps—though dated, were in great shape. "I've been wanting to replace this furniture forever," she said. "If I do I'll let you know."

Vic grunted. "Carrie, you'll be the excuse for my wife to redecorate our entire house."

Chapter 17

"Heave ho," Mr. Weikel barked, and the living room sofa—with Walt hoisting one end and Derek the other—tumbled into the dumpster.

It was Saturday morning, another brilliant winter day. I'd arrived at the house by seven, with Sharon, Walt, Jill and Derek not far behind.

Our strategy was to dispose of the large items while the dumpster was nearly empty. Walt and Derek had already dragged out the queen-size mattress and box springs from the master bedroom and stood them in the dumpster. The family room sofa had been next on the chopping block.

Watching the ease with which that ungainly piece of furniture had been dispatched, I said, "God, I love men."

Sharon laughed. She and I were dragging the sofa cushions to the bin. "They do come in handy at times," she said. "But you don't have to take a back seat to anybody, Carrie. You performed a miracle here yesterday."

I lofted the cushions over the side. I *had* worked my rear end off the day before. Like a hurricane I'd swept through every room, collecting trash and tagging the few items I wanted to keep. I'd disassembled the dinette set and end tables so they'd take up less space in the bin. I'd pulled down damaged and out-dated window coverings, including the ponderously dark velvet curtains—burgundy-colored dust magnets—that had cast the master bedroom into a state of perpetual gloom.

By Friday evening I'd reached the smallest bedroom, which had been used as an office. Against one wall was a reasonably nice computer desk I intended to keep, along with its match-ing chair. On the desktop was a computer that didn't look too ancient. I couldn't afford a new computer, so I'd see if I could get that one working.

The other side of the room held cardboard boxes crammed with paperwork documenting what appeared to be every finan-cial transaction Henry Streator had ever made. When I'd shown the boxes to Sharon and Walt on Saturday morning they'd agreed I could probably toss most of the contents.

Jill volunteered to go through the cartons. She promised to let me know if she found anything more important than yel-lowing receipts and instruction manuals for items long ago dis-carded. When I checked on her later she was just finishing up. She pointed to a carton she'd set aside that bore a handwritten label: KEEPSAKES AND JOURNALS. "Might be something worth-while in there."

I riffled through the carton. Buried under the clutter of ticket stubs, programs and souvenir matchbooks was a stack of spi-ral-bound notebooks. I sighed. I was in an unsentimental, throw-the-junk-out kind of mood. I blew the hair out of my eyes. "I don't know. I'm inclined to toss it."

Jill looked dubious, but she nodded. "I guess I'm done in here then."

Only later, when I was yanking up the wall-to-wall carpeting in the family room, did I have second thoughts. I dropped what I was doing and hurried into the office. The boxes were gone.

Walt and Derek had already cleared the room. I rushed outside to the dumpster. A few boxes were stacked on the blacktop beside the dumpster. I searched for the one labeled KEEPSAKES AND JOURNALS. It wasn't there. I cursed.

Jill was coming down the sidewalk with two broken lamps. "What's the matter?"

I gave the dumpster a frustrated kick. "I changed my mind about that box you showed me, but it's gone."

Jill tossed the lamps into the bin and turned to me with a mischievous smile. She crooked a finger. "Come with me."

I followed her into the house and down the hall to the office.

She opened the closet door and there on the shelf was the box. "I thought if you didn't want it I'd take it. That kind of stuff fascinates me."

I gave her arm a grateful squeeze. "We'll go through it together sometime."

By the end of the day the trash bin was stacked high. Ragged rolls of carpet poked out of the top. After tossing in a final armload of carpet nailing strips I returned to the house smiling and satisfied. One of the luckiest finds of the day was discovering hardwood floors hiding under the carpet in the living room, dining room and hall. Just picturing the floors sanded clean and gleaming with a fresh coat of varnish lifted my spirits.

It was only dinnertime, but darkness had descended long ago. I washed my hands at the kitchen sink, then joined Sharon and Walt, who were sitting at the dining room table nibbling pretzels and sipping beer. I'd ordered a pizza, but it hadn't yet arrived.

Jill and Derek had departed earlier, dirty and exhausted. They both had part-time jobs as clerks at a local shopping center.

When I realized they'd spent most of their free time slaving away at my house I couldn't help but feel guilty. They hadn't seemed to mind though. In fact they'd offered to come back whenever I needed them.

Sharon glanced around. "Unbelievable," she said. Her face was smudged and her hair a mess, but she looked content. "Who would have guessed we'd accomplish so much in one day?"

Walt leaned back in his chair, stretched and winced. "I discovered a few muscles I haven't used for a while."

Sharon set down her beer. "I have an idea, Carrie. Let's call your mom. She'll be tickled to hear from us."

I pulled out my cell phone and dialed. When Mom answered I placed the phone in the center of the table, put it on speaker and told her Walt and Sharon were with me. She sounded pleased but more subdued than I would have expected. When we told her about our progress on the house her enthusiasm seemed forced. Sharon gave me a puzzled look and I shrugged my shoulders. Finally Sharon said, "Joan, are you all right?"

"I'm just mad at myself," my mom said. "I had a tachycardia spell last night. It leaves me feeling so weak I have to lie around all the next day. I can't even work on my quilt. I'll be good as new tomorrow."

Sharon picked up the phone, clicked off the speaker and put it to her ear. She rose from her chair and walked into the other room, where I could hear her talking in serious tones. As a cardiac care nurse Sharon understood my mother's condition better than Mom did.

The doorbell rang and I went to get the pizza. As I turned away from the door Sharon relieved me of the pizza box and handed me the phone.

Mom was still on the line; she assured me she was fine. "Go eat your supper," she ordered.

Sunday I worked alone at the house, combing through the kitchen, basement and garage for more stuff to toss out. I had the dumpster until the end of the week and I intended to get my money's worth. When I'd finished, the kitchen was organized, the basement was navigable and the two-car garage actually had room for two cars. As an added bonus, in a garage alcove I'd discovered a well-stocked workbench and a storage area for the lawnmower, snow blower and wheelbarrow.

I made it back to the Weikels in time to eat dinner with Walt and Sharon. Without Jill there it was a good opportunity to bring up my rental arrangement. They didn't ask for much and I was pleased to pay it. Sharon granted me the run of the house and said I was welcome to grab anything I wanted for breakfast and lunch. As for dinner I told her not to expect me unless we'd planned it in advance.

Once I headed downstairs to finish unpacking I started getting the jitters. In a few hours I'd be heading off to work at TrueMark. I hadn't heard from Brad in weeks. Why hadn't he called? What was he thinking? I had no idea.

Chapter 18

"She's here," Denise Gavin said into the phone.

Denise was the personnel manager at TrueMark. It was Monday morning, my first day of work. Denise had met me in the reception area of a low-slung brick building located in an industrial park on the west side of Burnsville. She'd ushered me into her office, where she'd gestured for me to take one of two chairs across the desk from her. I'd chosen the one closest to the window—the one, as it turned out, with a perfect view of Brad's Audi in the front row of the parking lot.

The first thing Denise had done was to pick up the phone.

In less than a minute Brad breezed into the room wearing a boyish grin and an aura of self-assurance you wouldn't expect an employee of two months to possess. It was as if he owned the place. I'd almost forgotten how good-looking he was.

He approached me with his hand extended. "You made it." We shook hands and he dropped into the chair next to mine.

Breathe, I told myself. He's just an old pal from Cincinnati.

"How was your trip?" he said.

"A little hairy, but I got here."

"All settled in?"

When I explained I was staying with the Weikels instead of at my aunt's house, I tried to read Brad's expression, but he wasn't giving anything away.

After a few minutes of chitchat Brad slapped the arms of his chair and levered himself out of the seat. "Listen, Carrie, I know you and Denise have a lot to talk about. I just wanted to welcome you to TrueMark. You're going to love it here." He pointed a playful finger at Denise. "And Denise, you're going to love Carrie. I promise."

Denise flushed. "I'm sure we will."

Before he went out the door Brad gave me an informal salute. "I'm off to Atlanta this afternoon. I'll probably see you around here next week. Good luck."

While my first day at Procter & Gamble could have been characterized as opening with a requiem that burst into the hallelujah chorus the moment I met Brad, my TrueMark debut began with hosannas and took a nosedive from there. Within eight hours Brad's promise that I was going to love it at TrueMark had become highly suspect.

After Denise had walked me through the HR orientation she'd turned me over to my new boss. Lindsey Latham was the accounts manager in charge of, well, managing the accounts, whatever that meant. She had interviewed me over the phone and we'd hit it off. Lindsey was the one I hoped would allude to the plans they had for me to develop marketing materials. But although she was warm and welcoming, she said nothing about the promotion I was already counting on. For the foreseeable future I was strictly a customer service representative.

As she described my duties I found myself thinking, Does anybody really want to be a customer service representative? What high school student goes to her guidance counselor and says, "I'd like a job where they fit me with a headset, chain me to my desk and make it so I can't take a leak without asking permission."

Lindsey wrapped up her presentation and showed me to my cubicle. She took me around and introduced me to my fellow CS reps: Amanda, Dawn and Tracy. Their cubicles were identical to mine. The four of us were clustered together in a secluded part of the building with no windows. Each desk featured a computer, and a telephone console with a bewildering number of buttons.

Tracy was introduced as the senior customer service representative. I recognized immediately she was going to be a problem. She was a doughy-figured woman—in her thirties, I guessed—with pouty lips and an excess of eye makeup. When we were introduced, resentment was evident in the set of her jaw and the coldness of her eyes.

Amanda and Dawn—closer to me in age—seemed friendlier. Amanda was girl-next-door pretty; she wore her brown hair in a thick braid that hung halfway down her back. Dawn was tiny and cute, with wispy blond hair that made her look like a pixie. Both glanced up briefly from their work to smile and say hello.

Unfortunately it was Tracy who would be providing my training. She had me sit in my chair, then she lifted the door on the storage cabinet over my desk and gestured. "Here are the manuals for every state we work with. Each state has different procedures. You have to learn them all."

She hauled down a fat black binder with MICHIGAN spelled out in bold letters on the spine and laid it on the desk in front of me. "Right now is a slow period. Toward the middle of the week though, Michigan and Louisiana will receive their testing materials from us. That's when the phone calls and emails will start. There are always school districts that didn't get what they expected. Maybe they didn't receive their Braille copies or materials for special education students. We have to find out what happened and arrange overnight delivery."

Again Tracy reached into the overhead compartment. She pulled out a volume the size of a phone book for a small town and dropped it onto the desk. "Here are the directions for the telephone system." Tracy's headset emitted a beep. "I have to take this call. Why don't you read through the materials until I get back."

Tracy returned to her cube, which was across the aisle from mine. I opened the telephone instruction manual. The table of contents alone was several pages long and incomprehensible. My heart sank. This was nothing like what I'd done at Procter & Gamble.

The phone sounded in the adjoining cubicle and I heard Amanda answer, sounding confident and professional. I strained to follow to the conversation, knowing that in a few days it would be me fielding calls. What if I told people the wrong thing? What if I sent test materials to the wrong place? With a sense of dread I wondered what I'd gotten myself into.

Tracy returned and suggested we take a break before getting down to business. After stopping in the restroom we headed to the lunchroom, a large room set up like a kitchen: with three refrigerators, plus a sink, microwave ovens and automatic coffeemakers lined up on an L-shaped counter. I dispensed a cup of coffee for myself and joined Tracy at one of several tables that filled the room.

"During slow periods two reps can go on break at the same time," Tracy said. "Once we get busy—later this week, for instance—we'll be staggering our breaks and lunches so there are always three people on the phones."

"What did you do before I came?"

"Simple. We hired temps during the busy times. It worked out fine until some big shot decided we needed a fourth full-time rep." The look on her face told me what she thought of that idea.

Just then Brad walked in with a colleague and acknowledged me with a brief wave. I waved back.

Tracy's eyebrows shot up. "You *know* him?"

"We used to work together in Cincinnati," I said, trying to sound offhand.

She pursed her lips and gave me an appraising look. "Oh," was all she said.

I'm a big picture person. I may be a small cog in a big wheel, but I like to know how the entire mechanism works, not just my part of it. In order to establish priorities and be enthusiastic about what I'm doing I need to understand how my job contributes to the whole. As my boss, Brad had recognized that about me and had taken the time to paint the big picture.

To Tracy I was a small cog. Period. She made it clear my job was to answer phones and emails and do what I was told. Whenever I asked questions that would broaden my scope of knowledge about the company she'd answer, "You don't need to know that," and turn my attention back to the manual we were studying.

I was so frustrated by the end of the day I wasn't sure I'd have the energy to carry out my evening agenda, which was to wash down the walls at the house. But what else was I going to do? Go back to the Weikels and sulk about my lot in life? How could I? I was the one who'd set the course. I had no one to blame but myself.

At five o'clock I pulled my purse from the desk drawer and put on my coat. I glanced into the cubicles of the other reps, but they were dark. Their shifts had ended earlier than mine and they'd left without saying goodbye. I wound my way to the lobby and out the front door into the parking lot. The spot where Brad's car had been parked was empty.

I felt abandoned; Brad was on his way to Atlanta and I was stuck with Tracy, who hated my guts. I climbed into my car and started the engine. As I backed out of the parking space I caught my reflection in the rearview mirror. I've looked better.

On Tuesday I found out why Tracy resented me.

Lindsey had scheduled an early morning meeting with all CS reps. Although I didn't understand half of what was said at the meeting I took diligent notes, hoping I could decipher them later with the help of Amanda and Dawn, who seemed to have warmed to me.

The big news as far as I was concerned came toward the end of the meeting. It was the announcement that I would be taking over from Tracy the responsibility for maintaining the customer comments database.

Lindsey explained the database to me. "One of the things all the reps do is keep track of why the customer called or emailed, what the service rep did about it, how the problem was solved, comments the customer made, et cetera. They forward the information to a database where it gets distilled and categorized. Anything we can use to improve our service and convince our customers we're doing a good job needs to go into that file."

I nodded, probably more eagerly than was wise, since out of the corner of my eye I caught a sour expression on Tracy's face. Brad had referred to the database as being a key element in developing marketing content for the company. For me it was confirmation that I was being tapped for a position that would use my sales and marketing training.

"Tracy's been doing a good job with it so far," Lindsey went on, "but she has so many other responsibilities she's willing to turn it over to you."

To my surprise Amanda and Dawn burst out laughing.

Lindsey got a twinkle in her eye. "Okay, Carrie, I admit it. This database was my idea and everybody else thinks it's a real pain. So Tracy's probably not too sorry to give it up, are you, Tracy?"

Tracy didn't look up from her notebook. She shrugged one shoulder. "Not really."

So that was it. Tracy felt she was being passed over in favor of me, a newcomer with no credentials.

Lindsey directed Tracy to show me the database after the meeting. "Look it over today, Carrie," Lindsey said. "It'll be a great way for you to see what kinds of questions we get and how we handle them. It'll help you on the phones tomorrow."

The customer database, which Tracy pulled up on my computer when we'd returned to our desks, was a massive spreadsheet with far too many columns to be useful. It was obvious Tracy had done little or nothing to organize the raw data input by her and the other reps.

I was glad she'd left it alone. What were the words Lindsey had used? Distill and categorize. I wanted to be the one to distill and categorize the data. It was my project, something I could sink my teeth into. Brad had been correct: This was right up my alley.

What a difference a day makes. With the database to study and Tracy leaving me to my own devices I started to relax. After perusing the database entries I realized handling customer requests wasn't rocket science. Chances are I'd muddle through as well as anyone else.

My first day on the phones was not as bad as I'd feared. The hold button—where I parked callers while I scrambled to find answers to their questions—became my best friend. I made my share of mistakes, but nobody died as a result.

Thursday and Friday went even better. Sometime on Thursday I ceased breaking out in a sweat every time the phone sounded. By Friday afternoon I was such an old hand that Amanda and Dawn made me an official member of the team by inviting me to join them for happy hour at Froggie's, the local watering hole.

For a split-second I hesitated. I had other things to do. Walt Weikel had offered to help me spray paint my ceilings on Saturday morning, for which I still needed to buy paint and supplies. On the other hand my new coworkers had come to my rescue more than once in the past few days and I was eager to cement my friendship with them.

"Sounds great," I said, feigning more excitement than I actually felt.

Froggie's was bustling when I arrived. Dawn and Amanda waved at me from a square table near the center of the room. A server wasted no time checking my ID and taking my drink order. I had just scored some appetizers from the buffet and gotten back to the table when Tracy arrived. I hadn't known she was going to be there. Judging from the annoyed expression that flitted across her face when she laid eyes on me, she hadn't expected to me to be there either.

Office gossip occupied my colleagues while we downed our appetizers. The three of them sliced and diced nearly everyone at TrueMark, from the mail clerk to the company president. After one nasty jab at someone unknown to me, I said, "Holy crap, you guys. I'm afraid to leave the table for fear of what you'll say about me."

They laughed. The alcohol had loosened everyone up, even Tracy.

"It's Friday," she said. "We're just blowing off steam."

Dawn wrinkled her brow. "Let's see, who can we say something nice about?"

"What about Lindsey?" I said. "She seems fun to work for."

The three exchanged a look.

"I give her an eight," Amanda said. "She's supportive and has great ideas, but she's not the most organized person in the world."

"Like that database she's got you working on, Carrie?" Dawn said. "She had to have it but she had no clue how to set it up. Tracy had to figure it out."

From across the table Tracy gave me a penetrating look. "I know somebody we can say nice things about. The new sales manager."

Amanda swooned and Dawn clutched my arm. "You have to see this guy, Carrie," Dawn said. "He's a god."

Before I could comment, Tracy said, "Carrie already knows him."

Three pairs of eyes locked on my face.

Dawn hooted. "How do you know Brad Collins?"

Taking pains to sound matter-of-fact I explained how I'd worked for Brad in Cincinnati. Even as I answered the first question I could see the next one forming on Amanda's lips.

I took a stab at changing the subject but Amanda held up her hand. Her eyes were dancing. "Wait a second. You don't get off that easy. You knew Brad Collins in Cincinnati, and now you're both here? What's that about?"

Dawn grinned and pummeled the table with her fists, jiggling the nearly empty beer glasses. "Tell all, Carrie. Your secret is safe with us."

"There's no secret," I said and trotted out the Aunt Cora Story, the same one I'd used in my cover letter to TrueMark. This time my enthusiasm for the renovation project was so genuine I had no trouble convincing my colleagues that the house was my sole reason for being in Minnesota. In fact, when I mentioned I needed supplies to paint ten ceilings the next day, they were more interested in giving me directions to Home Depot than they were in discovering what mischief I might be up to with the company heartthrob. By the time we'd parted company that evening I was reasonably sure even Tracy's suspicions had been put to rest.

Ten turned out to be an optimistic number of ceilings to paint in one day. I did manage it that weekend, however.

Bright and early Saturday morning Walt packed his sprayer equipment into his truck and followed me to my house. He helped me set everything up and taught me how to hold the sprayer and dispense the right amount of paint to where it needed to be.

Once I got the hang of it we were on such a roll that Walt seemed inclined to stay, even after the kitchen ceiling and breakfast nook had received two coats. When it was time to start on the dining room I sent him packing, however, having decided there's a limit to how long a girl should monopolize someone else's husband.

After Walt left, with no one to help move furniture, place the drop cloths and keep the paint gun supplied with paint, my progress slowed considerably. I was laying down drop cloths in the living room when Jill and Derek showed up. I met them at the door wearing safety goggles and a facemask, my hair tucked under a painter's cap. Rather than scaring them off, my getup only whetted their appetites.

They suited up and in the next four hours we tackled one room after another. At one point I ventured out to buy more paint and returned with sandwiches and drinks. We ate our lunch sitting on the floor in the breakfast nook. I showed them the paint chips and carpet samples I'd picked up at Home Depot the night before. With a lacquered fingernail Jill tapped the ones she liked.

Derek took Jill's hand and examined the polka dots of white ceiling paint that adorned her nails. "Looks good on you," he said. He leaned forward and kissed her on the mouth with such warmth I started wondering what extracurricular activity might have occurred while I was gone.

Chapter 19

My second full week in Minnesota proved the old saw about all work and no play. Laboring as a CS agent by day and a home renovator by night had turned me into a dull girl. My only other activities were eating, sleeping and making so many trips to Home Depot that the management was about to give me a reserved parking space.

All week I'd been looking forward to spending Friday happy hour with my coworkers. Turned out that was a once-in-a-while thing; they all had something else to do that night.

For me it was back to the old grind at the house, patching walls and sanding them down in preparation for weekend painting. By ten o'clock I was letting myself in through the Weikels' basement door. I could hear the TV on upstairs but I didn't feel comfortable barging in on Sharon and Walt. Jill, I assumed, was out for the night. Except for Brad, that was about it for my circle of Minnesota friends.

I washed up, grabbed a magazine from the family room and climbed into bed feeling sorry for myself. I'd been putting on a good show of appearing happy and confident, but in truth I was homesick. Cincinnati seemed so far away. I missed my own bedroom. I missed my family. I missed knowing a city like the back of my hand.

My relationship with Brad was non-existent. He hadn't called me from Atlanta the week before. This past week I'd spotted him in the break room and all he'd done was nod. Thursday he'd popped into a department meeting to have a word with Lindsey. As he'd stood in the doorway oozing sex appeal from every pore I'd willed him to look at me, but he hadn't.

To think I'd kissed those lips. I'd tasted that mouth. Those perfect hands had been on my breasts and between my—

There was a tap on my door. "Carrie, are you awake?" It was Jill's voice.

"I'm awake," I said. "Come on in."

Jill entered the room with her makeup smudged and her hair disheveled. "I saw your light on. I hope you don't mind."

I shook my head. "I was bored anyway."

She began wandering around the room fingering my possessions, behavior so uncharacteristic of her I suspected she'd had a drink or two.

I asked if she'd been out with Derek.

"Kind of. My class is building the set for the drama department's next play. Derek's in a competition to design the poster. He went with me to get ideas." She picked up a plastic dispenser from the dresser. I cringed. It contained my monthly supply of birth control pills. I didn't usually leave them sitting out, but there they were.

She turned to look at me. "Why do you take these?"

"Duh, why do you think?"

"Are you having sex?"

"Not at the moment, but it's good to be prepared."

Jill returned the dispenser to the dresser, walked across the room, flopped down on the foot of the bed and rolled onto her side to face me. She said, "Back in Cincinnati did you attend that Catholic youth rally at our church?"

I nodded. "How about you?"

"Yeah. I was, like, thirteen at the time. Did you take the vow of chastity?"

"I did, but I broke it."

"I took it too," Jill said. "I'm still a virgin, but just barely after tonight."

"What happened?"

She hesitated for a moment, then she said, "You can't get pregnant with your clothes on, can you?"

"I don't think so. Why?"

Jill twirled a magenta strand of hair around her finger. "After we left the theatre this evening we went to Derek's car. It was parked on a dark street. There was nobody around so we got into the back seat and were making out. We pulled our jeans down. Derek took my hand and put it...well, you know where. I usually avoid touching him there, but tonight I couldn't resist. One thing led to another. All of a sudden he was on top of me. We were rubbing together and he started moaning. Then something happened." She gave an embarrassed laugh. "Get the picture?"

"Oh yeah, in full color. You had your underwear on, right?"

"We both did."

"You'll be okay. If it happens again though..." I leaned over and opened the nightstand drawer. I fished out a three-pack of condoms and tossed it to her. "You need to have one of these handy."

Jill sat up, scooted her back against the wall and examined the package.

I caught her eye. "Use one every time. No exceptions."

She nodded. Looking thoughtful she laid the package in her lap and with a fingertip began tracing the geometric pattern of the comforter. My defensive radar told me she was about to bring up my pregnancy. Hurriedly I said, "Guess what I did this week. I ordered carpeting for the bedrooms, the office and the family room."

"Already?"

"Yeah, I'm having it installed the Monday after next." I slipped out of bed, grabbed the paint chips and carpet samples from the closet and spread them on the comforter.

"Awesome colors," Jill said.

"Thanks. I need to paint the walls before the carpet's installed. I repaired holes and cracks every night this week so I'll be ready to start painting tomorrow. Think I can paint four rooms in two weekends?"

Jill picked up one of the paint chips. "Mocha au lait," she read. She placed it on the square of family room carpet and gave an approving pat. "Derek has to design his poster this weekend, but I can help you."

"I won't turn you down," I said. "I should pay you for all your work."

"I wouldn't take anything, Carrie. Neither would Derek. It's good practice for when we get our own house."

"You're serious about this guy."

She grinned. "He's my soul mate."

There was a *whoosh* of water through the drainpipes as an upstairs toilet was flushed.

"That's probably Mom," Jill said. She scooted off the bed. As she went out the door she held up the package of condoms. "Thanks, Carrie."

Chapter 20

"So two times Henry flew off somewhere and returned with a woman," Jill said.

It was Saturday morning. Jill and I were painting walls in the family room. Jill was on the ladder cutting in the paint near the ceiling. I was painting around the windows, doorways and baseboards and telling her everything I knew about Henry Streator.

"Apparently his expedition to Mexico was more successful than the one with my aunt," I said. "According to my neighbors, Henry and his wife—her name was Adriana—were crazy about each other. Not so much with Aunt Cora."

Jill had stopped painting and was looking down at me from her perch on the stepladder. "Do you know about Adriana's garden?"

I shook my head. "What's that?"

"When I was going through the keepsakes box I came across a sheet of paper that looked like a will. It was handwritten, with Henry Streator's signature on it. At the bottom of the page there were a few lines that referred to Adriana's garden." She closed her eyes. "I can't remember the exact words, but it sounded like something you'd read in a fortune cookie."

"Adriana's garden," I said. "Now you've got me curious."

Jill reminded me of my offer to let her go through the keepsakes box with me.

"Once I move in and get organized," I promised, "going through that box will be my first order of business." To be truthful it was my second order of business, but Jill didn't need to know that.

Thanks to fast-drying paint Jill and I managed to apply two coats of *mocha au lait* to the family room walls before noon. We'd cleaned our brushes and were about to tackle the master bedroom when Sharon and Walt showed up with lunch. Sharon hadn't seen the house for two weeks. She was so complimentary about the progress I'd made and the colors I'd chosen that she had me beaming.

Fifteen minutes later I was positively glowing. My neighbors, Vic and Janet, must have noticed the activity and decided to put in an appearance. I brought them into the breakfast nook where the Weikels were camped out on the floor finishing the chili Sharon had brought.

After I introduced everyone Janet turned to me and said, "Guess what we just purchased?"

I held up crossed fingers. "New living room furniture?"

Janet grinned. "We ordered it this morning. So if you're still interested in the old stuff—"

"Sold!" I yelled and gave Janet an impulsive hug.

"My turn," Vic said, and I hugged him too.

Janet agreed to hang onto her old furniture until after my carpet was installed and Vic agreed to open the door for the carpet installers so I wouldn't have to miss any work.

"Meantime," Vic said, "why don't Jan and I bring over the kitchen table and chairs so you folks don't have to sit on the floor."

Walt and Sharon offered to lend a hand and off they all traipsed to the Lundgrens, returning ten minutes later with the gently used dinette set I'd seen in their basement. The round oak table and four captain's chairs fit perfectly in front of the bay window. The matching hutch, which they brought over on a second trip and placed against the wall, looked like it had always been there.

Things were starting to come together.

Before Jill abandoned me for her real job she generously cut in the paint around the ceiling in the master bedroom. As her reward she got to roll the walls while I stayed ahead of her, cutting in around the windows and baseboards.

After Jill left I painted the office, then stood back and inspected my handiwork. Although I loved the moss green color I'd chosen for the office and bedrooms I could still see traces of the previous wall color peeking through. I sighed. Despite the one-coat promise on the paint can the rooms would require a second coat.

I was done for the day though. It was already past eight o'clock and my entire body was aching. As I cleaned my paint equipment in the laundry room a thought occurred to me. Instead of driving to the Weikels to sleep, why not stay at the house? There was a bed in the guest room, the linen cabinet contained a supply of freshly washed sheets and towels, and I'd stocked the bathroom medicine cabinet with the necessary toiletries.

I called Sharon and told her my plans, then headed for the kitchen in search of dinner. Excitement bubbled up in me. My first night at home.

"Guess where I am right now?" I said. I was talking to my cousin Randy. It was Sunday morning and I'd reached him at his apartment in Cincinnati.

"Um, the Mall of America," he said. He sounded groggy, like maybe he was still in bed. I'd been up for so long, it hadn't occurred to me anybody on Eastern time would still be sleeping.

"Not open yet," I said.

"I give up. Where are you?"

"I'm enjoying a bowl of cereal in the breakfast nook at your mother's house. I stayed here for the first time last night."

"How was it?"

"Awesome. I slept like a baby." I told him about my progress on the house and all the help I'd received.

As I talked he emerged from his stupor. "At the rate you're going, Carrie, we'll be ready to put the house on the market in two months."

"You won't though, will you? I need a place to stay."

Randy laughed. "Don't worry. I promised you a year. The housing market still sucks anyway."

I heard a woman's voice in the background on his end of the line.

"I should have asked if you were busy," I said.

"That's okay. She was in the shower."

"I'll let you go," I said. But then a thought struck me. "Have you ever heard of Adriana's garden?"

"From Henry's will?" he said, sounding surprised.

"I guess," I said.

"We didn't know what it was so the judge who read the will decided to ignore it at least until more information came to light. What do you know about it?"

"Nothing yet, just the name. I'll be in touch if I find out more."

"Don't go to a lot of trouble," he said, and it sounded like a warning. "The will's already been settled. Sometimes it's best to let sleeping dogs lie."

Chapter 21

Much as I'd enjoyed staying overnight at Aunt Cora's house it only made sense for me to wait until the carpet was installed before I moved in. In the meantime I was a painting dynamo. By Tuesday night the office and the bedrooms had received a second coat of paint.

My Wednesday evening task was to apply semi-gloss paint to the woodwork. Laying down a smooth coat of paint on window frames, doorframes and baseboards is tedious work. I was attacking it with unusual gusto, however, because of something that had happened at TrueMark that morning.

I'd been sitting alone reading the newspaper in the break room when Brad and three other employees came in and seated themselves at a table near mine. After a few minutes one of the men—a heavy-set fellow with an impressive gut—extricated himself from the table, lumbered to the refrigerator and waddled back carrying a small oblong package wrapped in white butcher paper.

He came up behind Brad and laid the package on the table in front of him. Then he stood at Brad's shoulder grinning like a kid who's just presented his mom with a bouquet of dandelions.

Brad craned his neck to look at the guy. "What's this, Bill?"

"Open it," Bill said.

Brad folded back the paper. I couldn't see what was in the package, but Brad got such a curious look on his face I knew it had to be something weird.

The poor guy, reading Brad's incomprehension, said, "It's goetta. You know, pork necks, oat groats, pepper? My wife's from Cincinnati. We always bring back a supply when we drive down at Christmas."

I had all I could do to keep from laughing. I'm a true Cincinnatian. I know goetta. Brad doesn't know goetta. He was like, "Wow, Bill, you brought this for me? Thanks, we'll have some tonight."

Looking surprised Bill said, "Most people eat it for breakfast."

I'd been observing the exchange over the top of my newspaper. At that moment Brad glanced up and caught my eye, a wry smile playing on his lips. I ducked my head to hide my grin.

I was still chuckling that evening as I crawled around on the bedroom floor dragging my paintbrush over the baseboards. Sharing that episode with Brad had seemed like old times. No wonder I was feeling energetic. Maybe there was hope for us yet.

Being a customer service rep wasn't as physically confining as I'd feared. We weren't chained to our desks after all. As long as we made sure the phones were covered we could hop up and do other things without asking permission. It was a cooperative effort and the four of us worked well together.

Tracy's animus toward me had dwindled. She was still abrupt with me at times, but she treated others that way too. Sometimes when her mood was black, keeping her pacified was like walking on eggs. On those days Amanda, Dawn and I tiptoed around until Tracy left at three-thirty. Once she was out the door, however, we let our hair down.

That was the situation on Thursday afternoon when Brad showed up in customer service.

It was nearly four. My coworkers and I had scooted our desk chairs into the aisle outside our cubicles. I sat facing my colleagues; at my back was the hall that connected our department to other parts of the building.

I was entertaining my new friends with a graphic account of discovering the putrid mouse in the wastebasket when their gaze traveled up and past me. Two sets of eyes widened simultaneously. I stopped mid-sentence and swiveled around to look. Brad was standing three feet behind me. My heart leapt. Literally. It jolted in my chest. An involuntary "Brad" escaped my lips. Thank goodness my back was to my friends. No doubt my face would have revealed more than I wanted them to know.

Brad introduced himself to Amanda and Dawn. He took his time shaking their hands, then stepped back and said, "Did I interrupt some important business?"

My colleagues giggled.

Amanda found her voice. "Carrie was telling us about discovering a dead mouse under the kitchen sink."

"I hope you gave it a good sendoff," Brad said.

"I buried it in the snow."

He nodded. "That works—until spring."

My phone beeped, indicating a customer service call coming in on the toll free line. Customer calls rotated in order from one phone to another, depending on whose phone was busy and who had taken the last call. Although the call was on my line, with the press of a button it could be picked up on any CS phone.

"I'll get that, Carrie," Dawn volunteered, and scooted back to her desk. Amanda also took the cue and disappeared into her cube, leaving Brad and me alone.

He lowered his affable stranger mask for a beat and we locked eyes. A moment later he was play-acting again. "Lindsey told me about the database you're organizing. If you have a minute I'd like to take a look."

I sat at my desk and Brad rolled Tracy's chair into my cubicle and sat beside me. No doubt he was aware our conversation would be less than private.

I pulled up the database and showed him how I was compiling the information so it could be displayed in graphs, charts and PowerPoint presentations. As I clicked through the pages I'd assembled I could sense his enthusiasm building.

When I'd finished he said, "This is fantastic. We'll be able to run with this."

That's when he got to the real point of his visit. He'd invited the people in his department to go cross-country skiing that weekend at his family's lake cabin two hours north of the Twin Cities. "I know it's short notice but I was wondering if you'd like to join us."

I was stunned. "This weekend? Really?"

"You can't live in the land of ten thousand lakes without visiting lake country," he said. "We'll drive up Saturday morning and return Sunday afternoon."

I hesitated. The house wasn't quite ready for the carpeting, but how could I turn this down?

"It'll be a good group," Brad said and ticked off the names of his two account executives and their spouses. "Then there's Michael Holder, our amazing Web master. You've probably seen him around the office. Tall? African American?"

Although I hadn't known his name, I'd definitely noticed Michael, not only because he was one of the few people of color in the company, but also because he was especially good-looking.

"He's young and single, Carrie," Brad teased. "You'll like him." He picked up a pen and scribbled *NOT* on my note pad.

I batted my eyelashes and said, "I can't wait to meet him."

"I take it that's a yes then?"

"I wouldn't miss it."

I couldn't help but notice he hadn't mentioned his wife. I wanted to ask if Marcy would be there, but I hesitated to bring it up with other ears listening in.

"I don't suppose you have cross country skis," Brad said.

I shook my head.

"We can probably find skis and boots that come close to fitting you at the cabin. But if you could scare up something in advance, that might be better."

He filled me in on the particulars and we Googled a map to his house in Edina, where we were to meet at nine o'clock Saturday morning.

"We'll take two cars," Brad said. "It's going to be cold, so dress warm."

Dawn and Amanda waited a decent number of seconds after Brad left before they crowded through my doorway with grins on their faces.

"Some people have all the luck," Dawn hissed.

Later that afternoon I was shutting off my computer preparing to leave work when the desk phone sounded. It was Brad calling from the courtesy phone in the break room.

After making sure I was alone he explained why he'd sprung the invitation on me. All along he'd expected Marcy to be with him at the cabin. They'd arranged for Brad's parents to watch Chip and take him to a weekend basketball tournament. But when Brad's parents had come down with the flu Marcy had agreed to stay in town with Chip.

He lowered his voice and said, "I know I'm taking a chance, but I want to see you. When Marcy decided not to go, there were only going to be two women and four men. I'm going to say I invited you to round out the party."

"Does Marcy know I'll be there?"

"Not yet. I'll tell her tonight."

I rushed out after work and blew my budget on new clothes: ultra skinny jeans with a waistband so low the zipper was less than two inches long, a short white angora sweater with a scoop neck, an equally short white quilted jacket, and a sexy night-gown—just in case.

Jill turned out to be a lifesaver. She fitted me with her cross-country skis, boots and poles. Even better she promised to button things up at the house. She and Derek would finish painting the wood trim, clear the furniture out of the rooms and sweep the floors.

Pretty nice tradeoff for a three-pack of condoms.

Chapter 22

The six people milling about on the sidewalk in front of Brad's home when I drove up Saturday morning looked as if they'd spilled from a box of crayons. It hadn't occurred to me that I needed special clothing for cross-country skiing. These folks were decked out in fitted pants and jackets in eye-popping shades of grape, lime, lemon and orange—colors most people wouldn't be caught dead in anyplace else. Brad was resplendent in a sky-blue jacket with black and white insets that made his face look tan and his hair especially blond. And oh, his black ski pants—Gore-Tex never looked so good.

I parked my Corolla behind another car in Brad's driveway, opened my door and climbed out. The conversation stopped. Brad separated himself from the group and came toward me, a strained smile on his face. I'd seen that look before; he was annoyed.

"We were about to give up on you," he said.

"My car wouldn't start," I said. "I had to get a jump."

I hauled my overnight bag and my borrowed ski equipment from the trunk and Brad fit it into the rear storage area of a medium-size SUV. Three other pairs of skis were clamped onto a roof-mounted rack.

Brad beckoned to the others. "Let's move out. I'll make the introductions later. Sandy and Larry—into Michael's car. Cincinnati contingent—Eric, Susan, Carrie—you're with me."

Susan and I climbed into the back seat of Brad's SUV. Eric sat in front with Brad. As we got underway, Eric, who remembered me from P&G, introduced me to his wife and told me he wasn't surprised my car wouldn't start. "The temperature plunged last night," he said.

I didn't tell him my car had started just fine; I wasn't about to blame my lateness on uncooperative hair.

"If you think it's cold here wait until we get two hours north," Brad said. "The wind off the lake can be wicked."

We may have been the Cincinnati contingent but I turned out to be the only native Cincinnatian in the car. Susan and Eric hailed from western Wisconsin: as with Brad and his family it was Eric's employment at P&G that had landed the couple in my hometown. I gathered from the conversation that the two of them were happy to be back on familiar turf.

"What brought you to Minnesota, Carrie?" Susan asked. "Are you in sales too?"

"Customer service," I said.

Sounding a tad dismissive she said, "You mean like answering phones?"

I sensed Brad's unease with Susan's questions, but what could I do? Since I wasn't allowed to disclose the company's future plans for me I shrugged and said, "More or less."

Susan wrinkled her brow. "Why would you come all the way up here for—"

That's as far as she got before Eric broke in. "How was your drive up from Cincinnati, Carrie?"

Relieved to have the subject changed I took my time describing the dicey weather conditions I'd encountered my first day on the road. A vivid account of my spinout on I-39 north of El Paso had my audience hanging on my every word. By the time I described the truck driver's reaction even Brad was laughing.

By eleven o'clock we were nearing our destination, traveling on narrow roads cut through forests of pine and white birch. A layer of white carpeted the forest floor, and at road's edge the wind had whipped the snow into fantastic shapes. Aside from Brad's SUV and Michael's car there had been no other traffic for miles. Eventually Brad signaled and turned down a recently plowed driveway.

"I see my brother's been busy plowing," Brad said. "Most owners close up their cabins for winter, but we had the place winterized. Greg spends time up here year 'round. He'll have everything ready for us."

"What's he do for a living?" Susan asked.

"Greg's a computer whiz," Brad said. I could hear the admiration in his voice. "He performs cyber security for a number of businesses. He can do it from anywhere as long as he has a computer link."

We skirted a stand of birch trees and the cabin came into view—a sprawling single-story structure with a multi-gabled shake roof and cedar siding stained reddish brown. It wasn't the kind of beautiful that made your jaw drop to the floor, but it nestled into the landscape as if it had always been there. At the far end of the cabin a column of smoke spiraled from a stone chimney that extended above the tallest roof peak. Neat outbuildings were tucked into the surrounding woods. The property was so secluded you couldn't see the neighboring cabins.

Brad parked in a sheltered area behind the cabin. Michael pulled in beside us and we all emerged from our vehicles.

Brad pointed. "Kitchen door is around the corner. Grab your bags and go inside. We'll get the skis later."

I shouldered my overnight bag and followed the others. As I rounded the corner of the building a blast of wind tore at my clothing and snatched my breath away.

"God, it's frigid," Eric exclaimed as we hustled through the door.

The kitchen was warm and spacious, featuring a U-shaped counter with a window above the sink that overlooked the lake. In the center of the room was an island with a butcher-block top where someone, presumably Brad's brother, had laid out the beginnings of a buffet lunch.

We put down our bags and Brad made the introductions. Sandy, as she pumped my hand, came across as confident and energetic, born to sales. She was probably in her mid-forties, tending toward plump, a former school administrator. Her lawyer husband Larry, also on the hefty side, appeared more reserved than his wife. Michael was indeed the good-looking guy I'd spotted in the office. When Brad introduced me as his coworker from Cincinnati I tried reading expressions but I couldn't tell what they thought of me being there.

"I'll show you the rest of the cabin," Brad said.

We shouldered our bags and Brad led us through a wide doorway framed by heavy timbers into a space that glowed with the warmth of burnished wood. The dining and living areas were one large great room with exposed beams in the ceiling, pine-paneled walls and wide-plank floors. To our left the front door—flanked by a row of windows—opened onto a porch that ran the length of the house. Wide wooden steps led from the porch to a snowy pathway that sloped down to the lake. Sunlight filtered through the barren tree branches and splashed onto the porch floor.

At the far end of the great room a fire flickered in a massive stone fireplace with a raised hearth. In front of the fireplace was a rugged oak coffee table surrounded on three sides by leather sofas. Wooden shelves on one side of the fireplace held games. Books lined the shelves on the other side, before which an over-stuffed chair and a floor lamp created a reading nook. Under one of the front windows a jigsaw puzzle lay partially assembled on a drop-leaf table.

To our right, across the great room from the front door, was another timber-frame doorway. "The bedrooms are through here," Brad said and led us down a hallway along which were three bedrooms, a bathroom and an office loaded with flickering computer equipment.

Two of the bedrooms boasted queen-size beds. A playful toss of a coin found Eric and Susan claiming the master bedroom while Susan and Larry took the smaller room. Michael was assigned to the final bedroom containing two twin beds.

"Looks like my brother's staked out the other bed in here," Brad said. "I'll take one of the sofas in the great room."

I was beginning to wonder if he'd forgotten about me when he beckoned me back into the kitchen, through a doorway and into a short hall that led to three modest rooms. This was obviously the business end of the house—the servants' quarters, so to speak. The first room was a no-frills powder room. A second room held a washer and dryer, plus all the utilities that made the cabin livable.

The third room was to be my home away from home. It was a combination storage room and bedroom. To my right, outerwear for various seasons and weather conditions hung from hooks mounted shoulder-high on the wall. Above the hooks, wire bins containing gloves, socks, scarves and hats lined a plank shelf. Plastic storage bins were stacked along another wall. To my left, a set of bunk beds was snugged up against an inside wall. The nightstand was a small wooden table with a lamp on top. High above the table was a hexagonal window, the only window in the room.

"Greg and I loved staying in here when we were kids," Brad said. "We called it the bunkhouse. It's not much to look at but it's warm and private."

I ducked down and tossed my bag onto the lower bunk. "Nice."

The entire company had just reassembled in the kitchen when the abominable snowman stomped through the side door, accompanied by a gust of wind. His facemask, fur cap and knit scarf were encrusted with ice crystals, and his heavy jacket and padded overalls gave off the aroma of wood smoke and the great outdoors.

With the sweep of an arm Brad said, "Meet my baby brother Greg."

Greg acknowledged us with a wave. Standing on a throw rug by the door he began peeling off layers of clothing while he updated us on trail conditions. He'd been out on a snowmobile creating paths for us to follow on our skis. "The trails aren't professionally groomed," he said, "but at least you won't have to muscle your way through sixteen inches of snow. It's cold but beautiful out there. The air is full of diamonds."

When he'd stripped down to jeans, a flannel shirt and stocking feet Greg stepped off the snowy rug and grinned at Brad. The two enveloped each other in a warm embrace. I detected a family resemblance, but for the most part, the brothers were very different. Greg was shorter and stockier. His features were rugged, his beard bushy and reddish-brown. His shoulder-length brown hair was pulled into a ponytail. While Brad's movie star looks turned heads wherever he went Greg probably sailed through life without attracting much attention.

Again Brad went around the room, this time introducing his brother to the guests. I was last in line. When he introduced me as a former coworker from Cincinnati I saw Greg's attention sharpen. He shook my hand as he had with all the others, but he seemed wary. I sensed he was trying to figure out why I was there. An alarm bell sounded in my head. He was suspicious of Brad and me.

On the butcher block island Greg set out a tray of sliced beef, ham and cheese, baskets of bread and rolls, and jars of pickles and peppers. Brad had brought coffee cake, which he placed on the dining room table, along with a bowl of fresh fruit. We helped ourselves and when we'd eaten our fill we wandered around the cabin in stocking feet sipping steaming mugs of coffee.

Nobody seemed in a hurry to venture out into the bitter cold. From inside, the bright sun made the day seem deceptively benign, but the wind whistling around the corners of the cabin told another story.

By one o'clock the temperature outside had crept to ten degrees above zero.

"Double digits," Brad announced. "I call that downright balmy."

"I call it thirty below with the wind chill," Eric grumbled.

Brad prodded us to action. Everyone protested, but in the end we suited up and, buffeted by gusts of arctic air, straggled outside and gathered our equipment. Some people sat on the porch and waxed the bottoms of their skis. Greg took one look at my skis and told me they weren't the kind that required wax. I wasn't sure if that was good or bad.

Most of us carried our skis down the slope to the lake; Brad and Eric skied down. The fact that I needed help putting on my skis should have been a clue to everyone that I was out of my league. That and the low-rise jeans and short jacket that every time I bent over exposed a strip of bare skin around my waist.

As we were about to depart Brad's brother appeared beside me with a puffy jacket and a knit cap. "Put these on," he urged. "You're going to freeze."

I was already freezing. My eyes were tearing up, my nose was running and my hands and feet were chilled. I layered the dun-colored jacket over my white one and tugged the brown wool cap over the perfect hair I'd spent so much time styling.

With Greg leading the way on the snowmobile we headed across the lake toward a wooded area on the opposite side where there were no cabins. Within seconds the other skiers were ahead of me. When the gap between us grew noticeable Greg drove back, picked me up on the snowmobile and ferried me forward. This happened an embarrassing number of times before we made it across the lake.

I sensed from Brad's lack of attention to my predicament that once again I'd embarrassed him. Maybe he was hoping if he pretended I didn't exist no one would wonder why he'd planned a ski weekend and invited someone who couldn't ski.

Traversing the lake had been difficult enough but when we started up the hill into the woods I had no idea how to climb a slope with my feet clamped to boards. I kept slipping backward. Once more Greg came to the rescue and hauled me up the first hill.

As he deposited me back on the path he said, "Do you think you can make it from here? I'd like to drive ahead and clear the trails again."

What I wanted was to throw myself on the ground in front of his snowmobile and beg him to get me the hell out of there. Instead I told him I'd be fine.

After Greg departed it fell to Brad and my newfound friends to set me aright every time my forward progress was arrested. Poor Michael, who turned out to be athletic in a long-distance runner sort of way, assumed most of the burden. And I *was* a burden. In no more than fifteen minutes I had spent so much time on the ground that my jeans were soaked and snow had worked its way under my borrowed jacket and onto the bare skin at my waist. I could no longer feel my hands and feet.

We came to a point where the main trail continued straight ahead and a second trail led off to the right.

"Listen up, everybody," Brad said. "The trail on the right features steep hills and hairpin turns. Eventually it makes a loop and rejoins the main trail maybe a mile ahead. Are you up for it?"

Naturally everyone but me wanted to take the more challenging route. When I said I'd be fine by myself on the main trail Michael offered to stay with me.

"No, Michael, you should go," I insisted. "I'll just plug along here. Maybe I'll learn something."

It was agreed. I would go it alone and we would meet in about an hour where the two trails converged. If I wasn't at the meeting place they'd ski back and find me. Relieved of their responsibility they swung onto the trail and were out of sight in moments.

Although the pressure was off me to keep up with the others I was determined to move forward as quickly as possible if for no other reason than to keep the blood flowing in my veins. I had gone only a short distance when I took another tumble skiing down an almost non-existent slope. In trying to get back up I got my legs tangled. Now I was lying with my head downhill and one ski pointing north and the other pointing south. Try as I might I couldn't get the skis to point in the same direction.

I was indescribably cold now. I had read somewhere that if you start feeling sleepy you're in trouble. I fancied I needed a nap.

I tried to release the skis from my boots so I could stand, but my frozen fingers wouldn't cooperate. If that wasn't enough the straps of my poles had become twisted around my wrists. I stripped off my gloves and had just rid myself of the offending poles when Brad glided around a bend in the trail from the direction I had recently come.

I almost cried in relief.

I knew I looked ridiculous lying in a tangle on the ground. As he approached I called out, "I don't quite have the knack of this yet," but my face was so numb I could hardly form the words. It was like trying to talk with a mouth full of Novocain.

"I'm freezing," I admitted when he got closer.

Brad looked grim. "Carrie, we're fucked." Wordlessly he released my skis from my boots. He picked up my gloves from where I'd tossed them and dangled them in front of me. "These are driving gloves. No wonder you're freezing."

He stuffed my flimsy poor excuses for gloves into a pocket of his jacket, pulled off his own gloves and dropped them into my lap. Stiffly, painfully, I fumbled them onto my hands. My god they were hot, gloriously hot, from the heat of his body.

Brad's brother pulled alongside on his snowmobile.

"Would you mind taking her back to the cabin?" Brad said.

My borrowed equipment and I were loaded onto the snowmobile and whisked up and down a few hills and across the lake to the cabin. We climbed the steps to the porch and Greg ushered me through the front door into the great room. He instructed me to remove my wet clothes, cover myself with something warm and avoid rubbing or applying heat to the frozen areas. In short I was to allow myself to warm up naturally.

"Will you be okay?" he said. I could tell he wanted to return to the others.

I felt a sob rising in my chest. "I'm fine," I managed to say. "Here, take these back to Brad." I pulled off the gloves and shoved them at Greg, practically pushing him out the door onto the porch.

As he clomped down the steps I leaned against the closed door. The snowmobile roared to life. When the sound of the engine receded I heard myself whimpering. With frozen fingers I fumbled out of my ski boots. Shedding my borrowed outerwear I minced across the floor to a dining room chair. Like an invalid I lowered myself onto the seat.

Everything ached — my fingers, my toes, my cheeks, even my eyeballs. I pulled off my socks; two toes on each foot were deathly white, tinged with green. Several fingers were similarly hued.

I suspected my blood was the consistency of a slushy. I couldn't shake the image of a small shard of frozen plasma, having formed in one of my appendages, breaking free and traveling through my bloodstream to puncture my heart. The thought made me feel faint. I put my head between my knees and dropped to the floor. If I was going to pass out I might as well be at ground level.

I crawled across the plank floor to an open space in front of the fireplace. I wriggled out of my inappropriate jacket and my inappropriate jeans. My thighs were cold enough to chill a six-pack of beer. I dragged a wool blanket off the nearest sofa and wrapped it carefully around my legs and feet. Gingerly I settled my head on a throw pillow and lay still on my back.

The progress of my blood as it resumed its flow to my fingers and toes was excruciating. Even the ignominy of my disastrous skiing debut was forgotten as I bore the pain of moribund tissue coming back to life. My heart thudded in my chest. I was beyond crying, yet tears trickled from the outer corners of my eyes and into my ears. It felt like my eyeballs were melting. For ten minutes I lay there wondering if I might not be better off dead.

When the pain eventually subsided I stood and looked myself over. My entire body was lobster red. My fingers and toes felt arthritic and hot. Cautiously I stretched. Nothing seemed broken. I was reasonably sure I had survived without permanent damage to anything but my ego.

I tottered to the bunkroom and donned a dry pair of jeans from my overnight bag. I appropriated a pair of thick wool socks from one of the wire storage bins and tugged them on. Returning to the great room I placed a wooden chair in front of the fireplace and draped my wet jeans over it to dry. In the powder room I repaired my makeup and puffed up my squashed hair.

I smiled into the mirror. That's more like it, I thought. By the time Brad returns I'll be back in my sexy jeans. He'll take one look at me and forget his annoyance. The weekend is still salvageable as long as I don't have to go back out there again.

My spirits thus buoyed I padded to the kitchen for a drink of water. I took a glass from the cupboard and was filling it from the tap when Brad's wife and son came through the side door.

Chapter 23

Marcy and Chip had arrived carrying grocery bags. I recognized their faces from the photo in Brad's office. Marcy was just like her picture—cool, slim and attractive. With her sleek, dark hair and stylish clothes she looked every bit the interior designer. Chip was a blond ten-year-old, with his dad's good looks.

I introduced myself by name only, fearful that if I tried to explain why I was there I'd take a chance of contradicting whatever story Brad had concocted.

"Did you give up on the skiing?" Marcy asked. She was unloading onto the kitchen counter the items she'd brought. Chip had gone to get their duffel bags from the car.

"I was rotten at it. I came back to warm up."

Marcy gave me an appraising look. Something about the way her eyes swept over me made me feel low class. With one glance she'd pegged me as a clearance rack shopper, and she wanted me to know she hadn't been fooled.

"Chip could teach you a few things," she said, as he came through the door.

"Teach what?" Chip asked.

"Cross-country skiing," I said.

Marcy took the duffel bags and set them on a chair. "Carrie came up here for a ski weekend but she doesn't know how to ski." Imagine that, her tone implied.

Chip shrugged and gave me a shy smile. "I'm okay at it. I could teach you."

God, he was cute. "Thanks. Maybe later." I placed my water glass by the sink. "So what happened at the basketball tournament?"

"We got knocked out in the first round," he said cheerfully. "I'm over it already."

Marcy ruffled her son's hair. "Didn't I tell you a Blizzard heals all wounds?"

It took me a second to realize she was talking about an ice cream treat rather than a snowstorm.

Chip grinned and ducked away from his mom. "Wanna play a game?" he asked me.

"Sure," I said.

I followed him into the great room and across the floor to the shelves beside the fireplace. He started rooting through a stack of board games. Chip raised his voice. "Mom, you wanna play?"

"Only if we play Clue," Marcy called from the kitchen.

Chip groaned, but pulled out a battered Clue box. "She always wins."

We'd just finished our game when members of the ski party began straggling back. From my position on the floor I had a view of the front door. Brad was the first to arrive. I caught a fleeting expression of terror on his face when he stepped into the room and saw the three of us together. Marcy had gotten up to stoke the fire and had her back to him. By the time she turned around he'd composed himself.

Brad broke into a smile and came toward us. "This is a surprise."

Chip hopped up and ran to his dad. "Guess who won Clue, Dad."

"Your mother," Brad replied. The look of affection he directed at his wife made me feel like an outsider.

"Actually, Carrie took the honors," Marcy said. Her eyes flicked to my face and then back to Brad. I couldn't read her expression.

"How're you doing, Carrie?" Brad said as if noticing me for the first time. "Warmed up?"

"Toasty."

Brad nodded but immediately turned his attention to his son. He clamped an arm around Chip's shoulders. "What happened, buddy? I thought you'd still be pounding up and down the court."

As Chip launched into a detailed description of the fateful basketball game the two wandered off together. Marcy smiled at their retreating backs. I picked up the Clue box from the table and returned it to the shelf.

Marcy squinted toward the lake. "Here come the rest of them. Would you like to help me put out snacks?"

A half-hour later the returning skiers, wind-burned and pleasantly exhausted, had changed into après ski clothing and were gathered on the sofas that surrounded the fireplace. Chip had claimed the upholstered chair in the reading corner; wearing a headset and playing games on a hand-held electronic device he was oblivious to the rest of us. Greg, who had assembled pans of lasagna the previous night, slid them into the oven to bake, then joined us by the fireplace. Brad was in the kitchen filling drink orders.

Marcy passed around a tray of cheese and crackers. I followed behind with veggies and dip.

Michael caught my eye. "Are you okay now?"

Sandy gave me a sympathetic smile. "You looked cold out there, Carrie."

"I've never been so cold in my life," I said. "My fingers and toes were kind of green when I took off my gloves and socks."

Michael frowned. "That's not good. Let me look at your fingers."

I put the tray on the coffee table and sat next to Michael on the sofa. He took each hand in turn and examined my fingers.

"They're nice and pink now," he said, and released them. "Let me see your toes."

Slipping off my borrowed socks I asked, "What are you looking for?"

"I'm looking for tissue that appears white and lifeless, like the blood has stopped flowing to that area. It could indicate frostbite." He patted his lap. "Put 'em up here."

I shifted around on the sofa, leaned against the armrest and lifted my feet onto his lap.

"Who made you the doctor?" Eric teased.

Without taking his eyes off his task Michael said, "The U.S. army. I joined out of high school and they made me a medic. I've seen frostbite turn into gangrene if untreated."

With a feather touch he examined each toe. The sensation was so pleasant I didn't want him to stop. He put slightly more pressure on one toe. "Can you feel this?"

"Oh yeah," I said, a little breathless.

Everyone laughed.

Michael looked embarrassed. He patted my feet and slipped them off his lap. "You're healthy."

"Too healthy," Eric intoned, which got another laugh.

Brad came in with the drinks, and the evening really got started.

Brad was in his element, working the room, refilling drinks and snack trays. He shared an easy camaraderie with his team. In introducing them to Marcy he had a funny or affectionate anecdote to tell about each one. He charmed Eric's wife and coaxed a smile from Sandy's husband. I was the only one he ignored. I understood why, but still it hurt.

I stole a spare moment to slip into the powder room and put on my now dry jeans. Studying myself in the mirror I saw rosy cheeks, flashing eyes and a riot of honey blond curls. My angora sweater might have come from a clearance rack, but it hugged my curves just right. I'm not neat and chic like Marcy, I thought, but I *am* hot.

When I returned to the great room Brad was standing, drink in hand, his back to the fireplace, regaling the assembly with a golf story that involved himself and Eric, his frequent golf partner in Cincinnati. I crossed the floor and sat at the jigsaw puzzle table, which gave me a good view of everyone in the room.

"So we're on the green at eighteen," Brad told his audience. "Eric's like two feet from the cup, an easy par for him. I'm ahead by one stroke, but to win I need to sink a twenty foot downhill putt."

Brad placed his drink on the mantel. Pretending to hold a microphone to his mouth he announced in hushed tones, "Folks, if he can sink this putt for a birdie Brad Collins will win the round. This may be the biggest challenge of his professional career."

He gripped an imaginary putter and made an elaborate show of lining up his shot. Then he straightened up and took in his audience. "As most of you know I'm not at all competitive," he deadpanned, which set off hoots of protest. "But Eric, he's a bulldog. He's determined to win this thing by fair means or foul."

Brad re-adopted his putter's stance. "So I'm starting my backswing when Eric says, 'Brad, if you make this putt I'll suck your—'" At a warning cough from Marcy, Brad broke off and glanced at Chip. He lowered his voice and said, "If you make this putt I'll perform a certain obscene act on the first tee and give you half an hour to draw a crowd."

A burst of laughter from the folks gathered around the fireplace caused Chip to glance up from his game, a vague smile on his face. Aside from the laughter it was obvious he hadn't heard a thing.

Brad crinkled his eyes at Eric. "Well…with an incentive like that…" He mimed a ball rolling across the green and dropping into a hole. "It's probably the most inspired putt I've ever made. I look over at Eric. He's staring at the cup with his mouth open. He looks at me—"

"And you're giving me this shit-eating grin," Eric said.

Brad made a helpless gesture, as if to say, *What did you expect? Sympathy?*

"So Brad, did he pay up?" Michael asked.

Brad folded his arms and shook his head. "I'm still waiting."

Everyone laughed, all but Marcy, who was sitting on the sofa staring daggers at her delectable husband. The phrase, *we are not amused* popped into my head.

Later, after the spotlight was no longer on Brad he retrieved his drink from the mantel and walked over to his wife. He put a hand on her shoulder and said, "Sorry, Marcy, I forgot about Chip for a second. He wasn't listening anyway."

"Whether or not he was listening, it was a crude story," she said.

He grinned. "Crude but funny." He leaned down and kissed her cheek.

Marcy looked up at Brad and sighed. To my surprise the corners of her mouth tugged into a smile.

As the dinner hour approached Brad and Greg took over in the kitchen. Marcy rooted around in a china cabinet and came up with a tablecloth, two pewter candleholders and slender beeswax tapers. I helped her spread the tablecloth and put out the plates, napkins and silverware.

Secretly I thought it a shame to cover the rough-hewn boards of the dining room table with a cloth. It seemed to me placemats and chunky candles would have better suited the surroundings and the simple meal of lasagna, Italian bread and tossed salad.

Marcy was the designer, however, and the table did look elegant with the candles lit and the wine and water glasses gleaming. At the far end of the room the fire blazed yellow and red above the hearth. When the food had been set on the table and Brad called us to dinner Greg dimmed the electric lights and we gathered for our meal in the intimate glow of firelight.

Brad assigned our seats. He and Greg were at opposite ends of the long table. I was seated to Greg's left, followed by Larry, Sandy and Eric. To Greg's right sat Chip, Marcy, Michael and Susan. That I was about as far away from Brad as possible did not surprise me.

Across from me sat Chip, looking like an angel in the candlelight. I could hardly take my eyes off his spun-gold hair, blue eyes and pink cheeks. He appeared as fascinated with me as I was with him. Whenever I caught him looking, however, he would turn his attention to his food.

Around the table, talk flowed as freely as the wine in our glasses. Sometimes—when Brad made a toast for instance—everyone was involved in the same conversation. At other times multiple conversations created a pleasant din.

Sandwiched between Greg and Larry, whose meaty arms and shoulders restricted my view down the table, I found myself isolated. Greg appeared content to let his brother do the talking while he topped off wine glasses and kept the serving dishes filled and circulating. When he did speak, it was to Chip; the two were obviously great pals.

Marcy monopolized Larry by talking almost non-stop to him across the table. Not only was he an attorney and therefore worthy of her attention, she'd also discovered that, like her, Larry had grown up in Edina, which I gathered was an impressive place for Minnesotans to be from. Once she uncovered the Edina connection she hauled out a mental list of people they might have in common. After dropping one name after another and failing to uncover more than a smattering of mutual acquaintances she started mentioning places—the country club, the high school, prominent homes her architect parents had designed or renovated—that Larry at least had a nodding familiarity with.

I was hoping she'd wind down soon because I wanted to join the conversation at the other end of the table. They were discussing snow blowers. I hadn't been able to start the one in my garage. Even though my neighbor was more than willing to remove the snow from my driveway I wanted a working machine for times when Vic might not be around. I would have liked to ask for recommendations on whether I should get it fixed or buy a new one but decided it would be rude to talk over Marcy.

Chip, who I could tell had also tuned in to the snow blower conversation, was unhampered by the same constraint. Out of the blue he announced to the entire room, "The next time it snows my dad is going to let me run the snow blower."

That got Marcy's attention. In the blink of an eye lawyer Larry and the Edina connection were forgotten. She shot Brad an icy look. "Over my dead body."

The room went silent. Brad's jaw tightened but he didn't reply.

Chip looked crestfallen. He turned a pleading face to his mom. "But Dad said..."

Brad cut in. "Let's talk about it later, okay, Chip?" He gave his son a smile that dared to look a tad conspiratorial.

Chip shifted his focus to his dad. He dipped his head and looked soulful. "Okay," he mouthed.

A wordless communication passed between Brad and Marcy, but nothing more was said.

The ebullient Sandy wasted no time redirecting the conversation. "The way this winter is going we may not have to use our snow blowers again. Do you realize we've had almost no snow in the Twin Cities since the holidays?"

Michael caught my eye from across the table. "Isn't that when you got here, Carrie? Maybe you brought the mild weather with you."

"Carrie might dispute you on that," Susan said. She looked at me. "You should tell everybody your story about driving up here from Cincinnati."

The wine had me feeling mellow enough to think that sounded like a good idea. I put down my fork, leaned forward so I could see people's faces, and recounted the tale of my spectacular spinout, with a few embellishments to entertain my listeners. As in the morning telling I had my audience laughing by the end.

The topic of winter driving had touched a nerve. It seemed everyone had his or her own horror story to relate. As the conversation rolled around the table I began to relax and enjoy myself.

Chip had taken to staring openly at me; he had something on his mind. I winked at him. That was probably a mistake, because at the next lull in the conversation he took the opportunity to hit me with the kind of non sequitur only a child can get away with.

In the split-second of silence that sometimes occurs at even the liveliest of dinner parties Chip raised his high, clear voice and asked, "Carrie, did you know my dad in Cincinnati?"

Gulp. I'd been reaching for my wine glass, but I pulled my suddenly shaky hand back and shoved it into my lap. I nodded at Chip and kept my voice light. "Yep, we worked together."

"And he wanted you to come to Minnesota," he stated in that innocent way kids have.

The room went quiet. Was it my imagination, or were Marcy's eyes drilling into me? I was glad the lights were dim and my cheeks already wind-burned, because I felt a familiar flush creeping up my neck. Better make this good, I thought.

As if there was nobody else in the room I looked only at Chip and said, "Actually I'm here to fix up my aunt's old house."

I was about to launch into the cover story I'd used on my customer service colleagues when that lovely child took me off the hook. "Oh," he said, curiosity satisfied. Then, oblivious to the thunderous silence all around, he speared another forkful of lasagna and popped it into his mouth.

After what felt to me like an eternity Greg said, "You're renovating a house?"

Without missing a beat I turned to him and launched into a detailed description of the work I'd been doing to make Aunt Cora's house livable. As I'd hoped, our table companions lost interest and other conversations started up.

I could have kissed Greg. Had he overcome his initial suspicions about what I was doing there? I wasn't sure. I only knew my taciturn dinner partner had found his voice and asked precisely the right question to divert the attention from his brother and me. Furthermore, he seemed truly interested in learning about my plans for grout cleaning, floor stripping and table refinishing. He even offered to help me with a project or two.

"I thought you lived here at the lake," I said.

"I divide my time between the cabin and the cities. I have a townhome in Burnsville."

Under different circumstances I would have welcomed the offer. It was clear Greg was interested not just in my house but in me. He would have been quite a catch. Young, single, nice-looking, successful—just the kind of guy my mother would choose for me.

But he was Brad's brother, which put him off-limits. However, as the conversation wore on and against my better judgment he maneuvered me into a position where I ended up giving him my cell phone number.

He probably won't call, I told myself. And if he does I can always turn him down.

We adjourned to the living room for coffee and dessert. Afterward Marcy sent Chip to brush his teeth and change into his pajamas. When he returned he snuggled against his mother on one of the sofas and fell asleep. Brad tucked a blanket around him. In hushed tones the adults continued telling stories, getting to know one another, making each other laugh.

Because of Marcy and Chip's presence the beds had to be reassigned. I removed my overnight bag from the lower bunk, and Chip, half asleep, was led in and put there in my place. Eric and Susan insisted on giving up the master bedroom to Brad and Marcy. Brad protested; Marcy not so much. In the end Brad converted one of the leather sofas in the great room into a bed for Eric and Susan.

I had a choice. I could sleep on one of the other sofas in the great room or I could claim the upper bunk above Chip in the bunkhouse. It was a toss-up. Either way I was odd woman out—the one who shouldn't have been invited. I decided to give Eric and Susan their privacy and throw in my lot with Chip.

I lay awake for what seemed like hours, feeling foolish and forlorn. The sexy negligee spent the night buried in my bag. Instead I wore a serviceable set of men's long underwear borrowed from a wire basket in the bunkroom.

Although I'd have sworn I tossed and turned all night I must have fallen into a sound sleep at some point, because when I opened my eyes the next morning my black driving gloves—those symbols of disgrace that Brad had stuffed into his pocket on the trail—were beside me on my pillow. Seems my ex-boss had paid me a nocturnal visit after all.

I rolled onto my side. The pre-dawn light framed by the hexagonal window told me it was too early to get up. The faint sound of regular breathing floated up from the bunk below. Chip was still asleep. I ignored the signals my bladder was sending and closed my eyes.

When I opened them again the sky outside had brightened. I heard a noise in the room and looked around. Chip, still in his pajamas, was rooting through his duffel bag, which was atop one of the plastic storage bins stacked against the wall. His back was to me.

I shifted and the bed creaked. Chip stiffened and whirled around, obviously startled. When he spotted me he broke into a grin. "I didn't know *you* were in here."

I propped my head on my arm. "Sorry. I didn't mean to scare you."

"I wasn't scared." He came closer. "I usually sleep in the top bunk."

"I guess you were too heavy for your dad to lift up here last night."

"I weigh eighty-seven pounds," he said.

"Wow. That's a lot."

Chip shifted from one foot to the other. "I could teach you about skiing today."

I smiled. Just when I'd been wondering how I'd get through the morning, here was my eighty-seven pound savior. I pushed back the covers and sat up. "Let's do it."

The Sunday morning weather was a far sight better than the weather that had greeted us upon our arrival Saturday. The skies were still blue and nearly cloudless, but by eight o'clock the outside temperature had already climbed into the teens above zero. Most important, the wind no longer whistled around the corners of the cabin or spun the glittering crystals into drifts across the path.

A hearty breakfast and copious amounts of coffee had everyone primed to hit the trails for a repeat of Saturday's outing, this time with Greg on skis instead of operating the snowmobile. Chip and I suited up too, but our plan was to stay close to home so he could give me private lessons on the gentle slopes nearby. I sensed Marcy was reluctant to leave her son in my care, but eventually she was persuaded to join the others.

Chip was a perfect teacher, patient and encouraging, with a sense of fun. By the end of our first lesson I had learned the herringbone method of climbing a hill and the *yikes, here I come* method of descending a modest slope. What was most remarkable was how warm I felt compared to the day before. Once I got moving I generated so much heat I hardly needed my much-maligned driving gloves.

Chip was easy to be with. At times he and I would ski single file in companionable silence. At other times we'd ski side-by-side chattering like magpies. I suspected Chip had a tiny crush on me. I had a major crush on him.

When we ran out of slopes we descended onto the relatively smooth surface of the snow-covered lake. Chip skied beside me, demonstrating the kick and glide technique.

"How'd you get so good at this?" I asked.

"Grandpa Collins takes me skiing every Christmas," he said. "Did you know I'm named after him?"

I stopped in my tracks. "Really? Your grandfather's name is Chip?"

He rolled his eyes. "That's my nickname. My real name is Charles Bradley Collins the third."

"No kidding," I said. "Instead of Chip, you should be called Trip."

"Why?"

"You know, Trip, like triple. Because you're the third." With the tip of my ski pole I drew the Roman numeral for three in the snow. I pointed. "That could be your symbol."

"Cool. I never thought of that."

I shrugged. "I like Chip better though. Your dad says you're a chip off the old block."

He looked pleased. "My dad's the old block."

Judging from the position of the sun it must have been close to noon. Chip and I were tooling around on the far side of the lake. In the distance we saw the other skiers gliding in single file toward the cabin. We made a U-turn and were headed for home when we came across a patch of ice that was so smooth the wind had swept it free of snow. Chip wondered aloud if we might spot fish swimming beneath the crystal-clear surface; we decided it was something that needed investigating.

We had removed our skis and were lying opposite each other face down and peering into the depths when a piercing whistle reached our ears. Brad was at the top of the hill beside the cabin gesturing for us to come in.

I looked at Chip. "Should we pretend we didn't hear him?"

His eyes got big. "Should we?"

I shook my head. "Better not. We'd get in trouble."

We stood and brushed ourselves off. As I bent to collect my skis and poles a pile of snow landed on my head. I spun around. Chip was standing there grinning and dusting the evidence from his hands.

I scooped up an armload of the white stuff and chucked it at him. He ducked out of the way. I went for him again, missed and fell to my knees.

"You monster," I yelled, in mock anger.

Chip grinned. Eyes narrowed and teeth bared, he clawed the air and lurched toward me. "I'm Bigfoot," he growled.

I grabbed him around the waist and we rolled onto the snow, laughing. It was the most fun I'd had all weekend.

By mid-afternoon we were back in the Twin Cities. I drove to Lakeville and let myself into the house. Jill and Derek had come through for me. The bedrooms, office and family room were empty, the woodwork painted, the floors swept. The living room, which wasn't being carpeted, was jam-packed with the contents of the other rooms.

I entered the master bedroom. According to Janet Lundgren the original room had been dark and uninviting until Henry, at Adriana's urging, had hired a contractor to create a conservatory-like space by bumping out the bedroom's south wall ten feet and lining all three sides of the new construction with windows and a set of French doors that opened onto the deck. On this January afternoon the sun poured through the glass, making the moss green walls melt into the outside world.

The yard was wonderfully secluded. To the east and west dense hedges planted along the property lines shielded the view from the houses on either side. To the south the yard was deep, with a nondescript tangle of shrubs, grasses and trees at the rear. If there was a house back there I couldn't see it.

Such a lovely view, yet someone had chosen to block it by enshrouding the room in those awful burgundy drapes I'd tossed into the dumpster that first day. Behind the drapes I'd found aluminum mini-blinds that were so grimy I couldn't tell what color they were. My first instinct was to toss them too, but realizing I might want the privacy they would afford I'd stowed them in the basement.

It was only three o'clock. Although I didn't feel like it I changed into my paint clothes and dragged myself downstairs to clean the blinds. Among other things the basement featured a stationary tub and a floor drain. I would need both—plus lots of spray cleaner and elbow grease—to tackle the project.

Tackle it I did. And glad I was that I'd kept the blinds. Once liberated of their deposits of cigarette residue, grease and dust they turned out to be light brown and in decent condition. They would match the carpet and be perfect for shutting out the darkness and the stray Peeping Tom.

I shook the excess water off the blinds, brought them upstairs, remounted them and let them down to finish drying. Then I stood back and hugged myself, pleased. Nothing warms the cockles of my heart more than discovering I've just saved a chunk of change. A professional contractor would have trashed those blinds without blinking an eye. Aunt Cora was getting her money's worth out of me.

My cell phone rang, and for a split-second I had the insane hope I'd hear Brad's voice on the other end of the line.

It wasn't Brad. It was his brother, calling to ask if I'd left a set of long underwear in the bunkroom. I cringed and confessed to borrowing a pair of long johns from one of the bins and leaving them on the bed to be washed with the bed linens. "I meant to tell somebody. Sorry."

"Don't worry about it," Greg said. "I just thought if they were yours I'd return them."

"Nope, not mine," I said. Yeah, like I'd really own a pair of men's long underwear.

"Well...okay then," he said.

There was an awkward silence, after which we both started to talk—me to say goodbye and Greg to say, "You were going to show me your house sometime, remember?"

Crap. "Sure," I said, "why don't you give me a call the next time you're in town?"

"I'm here right now. I drove down after everybody left."

Damn.

"How about tomorrow after work?" Greg said. "Five-thirty, maybe?"

Realizing I wouldn't be able to evade my way out of the situation, I decided to get it over with. "I'm having carpeting installed tomorrow," I said. "You could help move furniture back into the rooms."

"I'll be there," he said, sounding pleased. I gave him the address, and all of a sudden it was easy to get him off the phone. He had what he wanted.

Chapter 24

What I wanted was to avoid running into Brad at work on Monday. I'd been jilted, and having to interact with the perpetrator so soon after suffering my ignominy filled me with dread. I gave myself one day to mourn and gather my wits.

I got my wish in an unexpected way. Tracy called in sick, leaving three CS reps to deal with a shipping crisis in Indiana. Test materials that should have arrived the previous Friday had not shown up at the schools due to a winter storm that had dumped fourteen inches of snow on the Hoosier state.

Administrators from every school district were calling us in a panic. Testing was scheduled to begin on Wednesday and they wanted to make sure the materials would arrive on time. To keep the phone queue from getting too long we were skipping our breaks and eating lunch at our desks.

It was late afternoon before the phones ceased ringing. Amanda, Dawn and I were taking a breather when Lindsey stopped by. "Great job today, ladies," she said. "Everything's back to normal."

"Have you heard from Tracy?" Amanda asked.

"She sounded awful," Lindsey said. "I told her to stay home tomorrow. Just a reminder, I'll be busy with visitors from the

Mississippi Department of Education for the next two days. I'll probably bring them over here sometime tomorrow morning."

Dawn grinned. "In other words, look sharp."

Lindsey laughed. "I'm not worried. You guys are plenty sharp."

When five o'clock rolled around I wasted no time leaving work and heading to the house. Janet had called toward the end of the day to report the carpeting was in and to say her grandsons were available that evening to help move the furniture from her living room to my family room.

"It's supposed to snow tomorrow," she said. "Vic thought we should take advantage of the dry pavement and good weather."

When I stepped from the garage into the house I wrinkled my nose. New carpet does not have the best smell in the world, although it beats the hell out of a dead mouse.

I went first to the family room. It looked fabulous. The brown Berber with its brick-red accents was perfect with the walls and the stone fireplace. I'd been worried the room might be too dark, but if it was it was the kind of dark that enticed you in to watch a movie or snuggle in front of the fireplace.

Before I made it to the other rooms Vic and Janet's teenage grandsons appeared on my doorstep lugging an armchair. A minute later Greg drove up and I put him to work too.

Within twenty minutes the Lundgren's living room furniture had become my family room furniture. It fit right in. The brown and red pinstripes on the sofa and chairs matched the carpet and the fabric's creamy background gave the room the brightness it needed.

"What else can I do?" Greg said after I'd slipped the boys a few bucks and walked them to the front door.

I inclined my head toward the mattress, box springs and frame that had been in the guest room but were now propped against the living room wall. "You could help me move that bed into the master bedroom."

We carried the frame down the hall. This was the first glimpse I'd had of the other carpeted rooms. Wow. What an improvement. In the master bedroom I flipped on the new overhead light I'd installed the week before. Darkness had already fallen. As I'd hoped, the closed blinds and the sea of plush brown carpet made the space feel cozy.

"Terrific room," Greg said. "Where do you want the bed?"

I thought for a minute. "Let's put it on the south wall with the windows all around."

After setting up the bedroom we carried the computer desk, computer equipment and bankers boxes to the office. Greg got the computer working. He pronounced the operating system ancient but still usable for games and word processing.

Next we moved the TV into the family room. Greg helped me arrange my newly acquired furniture to not only showcase the fireplace but also make the television viewable from the sofa and the two chairs.

While Greg was hooking up the DVD player I flopped down on the sofa and pretended to operate the TV remote from a prone position. "This is awesome."

Greg checked me out from behind the television set where he was kneeling and plugging in cables. "You look right at home."

I sat up. "I have to be careful not to love this place too much. In a year my cousin's going to sell it." I described the agreement I'd made with Randy to spend the year preparing the house for resale.

"Maybe *you'll* buy it," Greg said.

"Out of my price range I'm afraid."

Greg smiled. "Never say never."

My designated day of mourning had come and gone. Tuesday I decided to dress up for a change. At P&G my business attire had included suits, dresses with jackets, and high-heel shoes. At TrueMark, where business casual reigned supreme and the weather had been cold, my wardrobe had been limited to sturdy shoes, warm slacks and bulky sweaters. Nobody had even seen my legs.

Potential clients—members of the Department of Education from Jackson, Mississippi—would be visiting the company for meetings on Tuesday and Wednesday. That was as good an excuse as any to haul out the outfit that had never failed to draw attention before: the gray suit with its short, slim skirt and watermelon-colored blouse that I'd been wearing the day Brad gave me the tool belt.

When I arrived at TrueMark that morning there were no parking spaces close to the building, so I parked in the far corner of the lot. As I was mincing along in my heels trying to avoid puddles of slush I spotted a dark sedan creeping down one of the rows. There was a woman behind the wheel, another woman beside her in the front seat and a man in the back seat. I didn't recognize any of them. I waved them down. The car stopped and the driver opened her window.

"Are you from Mississippi?" I asked.

The driver appeared frazzled. She gave me a self-effacing smile. "Is it that obvious?"

I laughed. "You looked lost." I pointed toward the front door. "You missed the visitor parking. It's just around the corner from the door."

"Hop in," she said. "You can show us in person."

The four of us were old friends by the time Meryl—we'd exchanged names—maneuvered the car into the visitor's slot. She was not a great driver. Turned out she'd been unnerved upon leaving the airport to see tall banks of dirty snow on the sides of the road and a scattering of snowflakes falling from the sky. The fact that the roadways themselves were clear had done little to lessen her fear.

Meryl was so relieved to be out from behind the wheel that she was letting off steam by talking a mile a minute as the four of us came through the front doors into the reception area. Lindsey was waiting, and so was Brad. Their eyes opened wide when they saw me with their potential clients.

Brad stepped forward with his hand extended. "Meryl, Bob, Shauntell. Good to see you again."

Flustered—did I mention Brad had that effect on women?—Meryl handed me her briefcase so she could take his hand.

Brad's eyes flicked to me. "I see you met Carrie."

Meryl nodded. "She found us in the parking lot." She gave me a warm smile as she retrieved her briefcase. "Thank you, Carrie."

I smiled back. "My pleasure." There was an awkward pause. "I should get to work. I hope you have a productive two days."

Meryl seemed surprised to see me backing away. "Oh…sure," she said. It was clear now she'd assumed I was part of the sales team sent out to rescue her from the evil parking lot. "I hope we'll see you again."

"I hope so too," I said. As I headed back to the isolation ward that was customer service I was smiling. Nothing like making a grand entrance.

Later that morning I was picking up a report I'd sent to the printer when from some distance away I heard Lindsey say, "Over here is our customer service department." As I returned to my desk Lindsey, Brad and their three charges rounded the corner into our sanctum sanctorum.

Meryl, Bob and Shauntell greeted me like old friends.

"Carrie's in charge of our customer relations database," Lindsey said. "We track every customer contact we have with a view toward making your experience with us seamless and pain-free."

"I'm working on it right now," I said.

Meryl, who was the clear leader of her delegation, said, "Let's take a look."

Holy shit, that was unexpected.

All five of them crowded into my cubicle while I gave the Mississippians an overview. Amanda and Dawn poked their heads in too. Lindsey and I supplied the commentary. I pulled up charts and graphs that showed matters we'd dealt with and progress we'd made. From the questions the visitors asked I guessed dissatisfaction with the service at their current testing company was one of the reasons they were considering TrueMark. Any questions I couldn't field Amanda and Dawn were quick to answer. We did our best to dazzle them.

I knew we'd succeeded when, as the visitors filed out of my cube with Brad in the lead, Lindsey squeezed my shoulder and gave me a discrete thumbs up.

Although I wouldn't call it stalking I did manage to run into Brad and his charges several more times during their visit. On Wednesday afternoon I was filling in for the receptionist, who was on break, as the guests were preparing to leave for the airport. We were in the midst of our first true snowstorm since I'd arrived in Minnesota.

The southerners were in a tizzy. They'd rarely seen snow before and never in this abundance. Meryl, who I'd learned was the superintendent of education for the state, was so relieved when Brad offered to deliver them to the airport in their rental car that she relapsed into the babbling woman I'd encountered on Tuesday morning.

Before Brad went out the door he leaned over the desk and asked me to have Michael pick him up from the car rental lot at the airport. We shared an amused smile.

Later that day I was getting ready to go home when my phone sounded. I recognized the number; this time I knew it was Brad calling from the break room.

"So now who walks on water?" he said.

"You mean it's not you?"

"I'm yesterday's news," Brad said. "You're the new miracle worker around here. You impressed the hell out of the Mississippi folks. Lindsey thinks you may have won the contract for us."

"We got the contract?"

"Not signed and sealed yet, but looking good." He lowered his voice. "I want to see you."

I squeezed my eyes shut and took a deep breath. "I don't think so," I said.

"I know you're hurt but I can explain everything. Have you moved into your house yet?"

My heart started doing somersaults. "I'm in the process."

"Give me your address. Saturday morning I have an eight o'clock meeting in the office. I'll drive to your place at nine. Whether you've moved in or not just be there."

What I should have said was, *I thought we were fucked.* Instead I reeled off my address. He asked if I had a garage and if he could park in it and I said I'd have the garage door open. I hung up knowing I was making it way too easy for him. When you want someone so bad you're about to cry it's tough driving a hard bargain.

I'd been planning to stay with the Weikels until the weekend but Brad's call advanced the timetable. I rushed out of the office at five and drove to Bloomington intent on moving out that very night.

When I arrived I found Sharon, Walt and Jill sitting down to dinner at the kitchen table.

"So soon?" Sharon said when I told them my plans. She sounded disappointed.

Walt laughed. "If Sharon had her way she'd keep you here forever."

"It does seem sudden," Jill said. "Will you still need help on the house?"

"I'd welcome it if you have the time," I told her. "Not this Saturday though. I have to work. I'll call you next week and we'll set something up."

I don't know how I made it through Thursday and Friday without bouncing off the walls. Between the excitement of moving and the secret thrill of knowing what Saturday would bring I could barely contain myself.

On Thursday Lindsey gave me another reason to smile when she stopped me in the corridor and told me she'd been overjoyed with how I'd performed for Meryl and company.

"If we win the Mississippi contract consider yourself partially responsible, Carrie, not just for demonstrating the database, but for your professionalism and poise under pressure. Seven people crowded into your cubicle and looking over your shoulder. Now that's pressure."

She steered me into an empty conference room and closed the door. "I'm sure you remember what we discussed on the phone before you took the job."

I nodded. "Integrating my work with sales and marketing."

"I'm more convinced than ever we should do it but we need buy-in from upper management before a position can be created. I'm guessing that won't happen until the beginning of the fiscal year in July. I wanted you to know we haven't forgotten."

I thanked her and said I'd been jotting down ideas about how the new position would function. "Would it help if I put together a job description?"

She grinned. "Brad warned us you're always a step ahead of everybody else."

Chapter 25

My mom once tried a new recipe for pork roast "studded with garlic, double-wrapped in foil and slow roasted to perfection." She'd started the roast in the morning and all afternoon the tantalizing aroma had filled the kitchen. When at last she'd taken it from the oven and pealed back the wrapping the meat was so tender it was falling apart. I can still see my mother plucking a crusty morsel out of the foil and popping it into her mouth. Her eyes closed and she practically swooned. "Oh taste this, Carrie," she breathed. "This is unbelievable."

I did and it was. The fat, the garlic, the slow roasting had transformed a lowly pork shoulder into an object of carnal delight. Soon Mom and I were bellied up to the kitchen counter pulling the meat to shreds and slurping it into our mouths. By the time my dad got home from work and walked through the kitchen door we had garlicky grease dripping from our fingers and running down our chins.

That was as close to gluttony as I'd ever come until Saturday morning in my bedroom with Brad.

I'd been peeking out the living room window when a silver Audi with Cincinnati plates swung into the driveway and disappeared into the garage. Seconds later the garage door rumbled shut. Brad had a hand up to rap on the entry door when I opened it. He stood below me on the concrete stoop wearing jeans and a tweedy sweater over a blue dress shirt. Without a word he stepped into the hall and shut the door.

For an awkward moment we stared at each other, close enough to touch but not close enough to hug. Then with an uncertain smile Brad took a step toward me and ran an index finger along the deep scoop of my camisole top. He gazed into my eyes. "Now where were we?" he said.

All week I'd been promising myself that nothing was going to happen between Brad and me until he apologized for how he'd treated me at the cabin. But that one fingertip and those four words were the only apology I needed. I licked my lips and said, "Luiggi's parking lot."

Brad threw back his head and laughed. He drew me close and I wrapped my arms around his waist. The top of my head came to his chin. I buried my face in his sweater; it smelled faintly of cedar. I felt the rise and fall of his chest. His hands made slow circles on my back.

Remembering my manners I looked up and asked if he wanted coffee and breakfast rolls. He shook his head. "What I want is right here," he said.

I started to say something witty, but his mouth stopped mine with a kiss so deep and searching it turned me inside out. His fingers slid into the rear pockets of my jeans. He lifted me onto my tiptoes and pressed me tight against him. I molded my body to his.

We groped our way to the bedroom trailing waves of heat. In tantalizing slow motion we peeled away our wrappings. Zippers and buttons, snaps and clasps gave way to insistent fingers. Each item of clothing that dropped to the floor offered a new vista to explore, a hidden delight to caress. I was as succulent as a pork roast. I wanted to be slurped and savored. I wanted to slather Brad in my juices. My mouth, my tongue, my hands wanted to be all over his body at once.

And what a body it was. Kevin had been a boy, lithe and bony like a colt, wondrous in his own way. But Brad was a man—muscled, substantial, experienced. He lowered me onto the bed and watched my face. He knew what I needed and he gave it to me.

In the brief eternity the gods had set aside for our enjoyment nothing existed outside the universe of Brad and Carrie seeking and finding satisfaction in each other. We climaxed in waves, long and pulsing. When the last drops of pleasure had been wrung out we collapsed onto the mattress.

We were entwined in my bed running languid hands over naked flesh. Brad had already found the bathroom and disposed of the condom I'd barely noticed him putting on.

He lifted a tendril of hair off my face. "Well, little girl, after all the years of foreplay we finally made it to the main attraction."

I took in the smell and feel of him. "So what's the verdict?"

His teeth flashed white. "Mmm. Definitely not innocent."

The sound of my own laughter surprised me. It was a new laugh, deep and sensual, resonant with self-assurance. "Last weekend you told me we were fucked," I said. "Now we really are."

I'd meant it as a joke but Brad didn't laugh. He took my chin in his hand. His expression was tender. "Carrie, I'm sorry about the way I treated you at the cabin."

I affected a pout. "You *were* rather beastly."

He kissed away my pout. "And you were late getting to my house."

"Two minutes late," I protested.

He laughed. "All I know is everybody else was standing there when you pulled up. You got out of your car wearing those tight jeans and that little white jacket. No way did you look like a cross-country skier. I swear, Carrie, if you'd stepped out of a wet dream you couldn't have looked any sexier than you did that morning."

"Oops. My bad."

He fondled my breasts. "You're bad, all right. And you don't know the whole story."

"There's more?"

"There is, and it ain't pretty," Brad said. "The day before the ski trip my team and I were on our way out to lunch when we passed you in the lobby. You were talking to the receptionist and didn't see us. Soon as we got out the door Michael goes, 'Who's the blond?' Before I could answer, Eric goes, 'That's Brad's girl-friend. She followed him here from Cincinnati.'"

Brad sighed. "Eric's a kidder. We were friends before I was his boss, so he thinks he can get away with that kind of shit. I laughed it off, hoping that was the end of it. But after we got into my car he made another suggestive comment. He was sit-ting behind me in the back seat. I adjusted the rearview mirror so I was staring right at him. He was wearing a big old grin on his face. Cold as ice I said, 'Don't go there, Eric.' That shut him up real fast, but the damage had been done. He had me rattled and everybody knew it. It seemed an inappropriate time to tell them I'd invited you to the cabin."

"So they weren't expecting me."

"Right. Marcy was the only one I told. When you showed up at my house looking that way I felt like I had a scarlet letter sewn to my jacket."

"No wonder you were annoyed with me."

"It wasn't your fault. I screwed up. I'm sorry."

I shrugged. "It mattered more then than it does now." I tickled his chest hair and said, "Do you want to know the best thing about that trip?"

"What?" Brad said.

"Meeting Chip."

Brad chuckled. "You're his new best friend, Carrie. He thinks you should accompany us every time we go to the cabin."

"Now there's an idea. How did you get out of that?"

"I said you were too busy fixing up your house."

"Good answer. I really do have my work cut out for me for the next several months."

He rolled onto his back, laced his fingers behind his head and took in his surroundings. "Don't change anything in here. This room is fantastic. It's like making love outdoors."

He smiled at me and said, "So, little girl, what's *your* verdict about today?"

I tasted one of his nipples and then the other. "Indescribably delicious...but over too soon."

He pulled me on top of him. "Next time we'll take it slower."

We were generating such warmth I started thinking the next time was at hand until Brad's watch—the only thing he was wearing—gave a little *ping*. He sighed. "I told Marcy I needed two uninterrupted hours at work but I'd turn my phone back on by ten."

He rolled me off of him, sat up and swung his legs over the side of the bed. Retrieving his jeans from the floor, he tugged his cell phone out of a pocket and switched it on. Phone in hand, he headed for the bathroom. Within a minute the phone sounded and the real world started up again.

Chapter 26

So began my Saturday morning affair with Brad. I would open the garage door at eight-thirty. Brad would attend his eight o'clock meeting at TrueMark, show up at my place by nine and let himself in. Within minutes of his arrival we were heading for the bedroom or whatever location struck our fancy that week. One warm Saturday I ambushed him in his Audi.

The sex never failed to satisfy, but what I came to cherish just as much was the sweet interlude that followed lovemaking, when we lay in each other's arms and luxuriated in the intimacy of our surroundings. Although we never called it love, we shared an easy affection that could have passed for love.

On one occasion, I was sitting up against the headboard and Brad was lying on his side exploring my stomach creases. He probed my navel and said, "Can I ask you a personal question?"

"Okay, I guess."

"Try not to be offended," he said gravely, "but what the hell is goetta?"

I threw back my head and laughed. "I thought you found something gross in my belly button."

"Your belly button—like every other square inch of you—is exquisite." He kissed my navel and pulled me down beside him. "So tell me all about goetta."

"Well for one thing, you're pronouncing it wrong. It's pronounced *getta*, like get a job or get a life. I don't know exactly what it is but it's delicious. You slice it and fry it and eat it with eggs."

I tapped his chest. "Do you still have the goetta Bill Schmidt gave you?"

"I took it home and stuck it in the freezer. Marcy doesn't want anything to do with it."

"Bring it over here and we'll eat breakfast together some Saturday."

He snuggled against me. "Sure it won't interfere with anything else?"

"Not if you arrive at a reasonable time and we do the anything else first." I kissed him on the nose. "You wouldn't want to do it the other way around."

"Why not?"

"Well, after you eat goetta and fried eggs, your arteries will be too clogged to do anything else." I sat up and straddled him. "You know, Brad, giving a gift of goetta is an act of love in some parts. I suspect your friend Bill has a little crush on you."

"Carrie, how come you've never given me goetta?"

"And have you say, 'What the hell is it?' I couldn't handle the rejection."

A week later Brad brought the package of frozen goetta. The Saturday after that we had our Taste of Cincinnati breakfast. To save time I started frying the goetta before Brad arrived. I was at the stove when I heard him come in from the garage.

"Something smells good," Brad called. He followed his nose to the kitchen.

"You're in for a treat," I told him.

He approached me from behind, put his arms around me and cupped my breasts. He nuzzled my neck and pressed himself against me. "I'm up for a treat."

I leaned into him. "I can tell." I put down the spatula and turned off the burner.

There are one hundred sixty-eight hours in a week. My week was divided into one hundred sixty-seven hours without, and one hour with, Brad. Some weeks—like the Saturdays he returned to the family cabin with his family and the Saturday he took Chip to a basketball game—I saw him only at work. Throw in a handful of sizzling phone calls he placed from anonymous out-of-town hotel rooms and you'd have the sum total of my contact with my Saturday morning lover. The arrangement sounds pathetic, but somehow it worked. I was satisfied, for a while at least.

The balance of my life proceeded much as before. My customer service job at TrueMark was bearable. I prepared for my promotion by writing a job description that would require someone with my exact credentials to perform. To demonstrate my ability I mined the customer database for nuggets of marketing wisdom which I displayed on a mock website I created.

Having my own house to come home to was a constant joy. I began to furnish the painted and carpeted rooms and continued to make improvements to the rest of the house. Since the baseboards in the rooms with hardwood floors were too battered to salvage I tore them out. Once the walls were painted and the floors refinished I would replace them with new oak trim. I had never before cut and fitted trim, but I knew that somehow I'd figure it out. At times I sat back and marveled at my own moxie.

Jill and Derek were still eager to lend a hand with the remaining wall painting. I let it be known I was taking a yoga class on Saturday mornings and wasn't available until half past ten. Accordingly, during the months of February and March my helpers would show up in the late morning to lend a hand. Despite my promise to Jill that going through Henry Streator's keepsakes would be my first priority once I moved in we hadn't yet gotten around to the task.

Greg Collins had turned into a problem. He called nearly every week to see if I could use his help. I had to make excuses to prevent him from stopping by. The way I told it, not only did I have my Saturday morning yoga class to attend I also had tons of friends to do things with and multiple errands to run. As far as Greg knew I was a busy and popular girl who had all but abandoned her efforts at home improvement.

I was thankful Greg hadn't mentioned anything about me to Brad. I suspected Greg was like my brother Tommy, who was so closed-mouthed about his relationships with women he drove my mother crazy. Brad would have a fit if he knew Greg had been at the house. If Greg found out about Brad being there I couldn't bear to think what might happen.

No, giving Greg Collins my address had not been a good idea. Kind and helpful as he was, having him as my friend was a liability. If he didn't get the message soon I'd have to ditch him in a less subtle way.

Chapter 27

I never set an alarm for Saturday morning because I always woke in plenty of time to prepare for my assignation with Brad. Perhaps routine was already setting in by week number six, however, because I overslept that Saturday morning. In my defense I had gone to bed late, after hosting a dinner party to thank the Weikels and the Lundgrens for all the help they'd given me. The party had been a smashing success, judging from everyone's reluctance to leave. I'd held it on a Friday evening so Jill and Derek could attend. Those two ended up staying into the wee hours. It was two o'clock by the time I got to sleep.

I woke at twenty till nine. I'd opened the garage door and was rushing around getting ready when my cell phone rang. It was my sister informing me that my mother had suffered another tachycardia episode during the night.

"It stopped on its own," Katie said, "but it must have been worse than last time because she's actually agreed to go to the doctor next week."

I was promising Katie I'd call Mom later in the day when I heard Brad pull into the garage.

"How's everything going with you?" Katie said. "Is it cold up there?"

"It's still winter," I said.

The garage door rumbled shut and Brad stepped into the hall. I held up a finger and pointed to the phone. He nodded and headed for the kitchen. I wandered into the living room.

"We already have crocuses and daffodils popping up," Katie said.

"Lucky you."

"It's Aunt Carrie," I heard Katie saying. "Do you want to talk to her?"

A few seconds passed and a sweet voice said, "Hi, Aunt Carrie."

"Hello, Megan."

"It's Becca."

"Becca, you sounded so grown up I didn't recognize you."

We stumbled through a conversation consisting of my feeble questions and Becca's short answers. Finally Katie got back on the phone and started telling me what the kids were doing in school. While I listened I went in search of Brad. He was sitting at the table in the breakfast nook involved in a craft project. Spread before him were sheets of copier paper and a colorful assortment of felt-tip markers, all of which he'd found in the top drawer of my hutch. I grabbed a marker, scribbled *ring the doorbell* on a scrap of paper and showed it to Brad. He got up and left the room.

A few seconds later the doorbell rang.

"I better get that," I told Katie.

As I clicked off Brad returned to the breakfast nook and began clearing the clutter from the table. "Your sister?"

"Yeah, my mom had a heart episode last night. It's happened before. Her heartbeat gets all out of whack."

"I'm sorry," Brad said. "I hope it's nothing serious."

He picked up something from the table. "I made you a present." He handed me a small square package addressed *To Carrie, the Main Attraction.* It consisted of a single sheet of copier paper wrapped around something lumpy. He'd decorated the paper with stick figures of a blue-eyed boy and a girl with yellow curls. Between the two figures, purple lightning bolts showed the boy being drawn to the girl. Inside the package were two disk-shaped magnets, dull silver in color. I held them up. "Wow...magnets...from my own refrigerator."

The magnets, each the size of a chewable antacid tablet, had been on the refrigerator door when I'd moved into the house. I'd been using them to hold up my grocery list. Like all magnets, I guess, they either attracted or repelled each other depending on how the poles were aligned. Brad had aligned the magnets with the attracting surfaces snapped together.

"These magnets are special," he said. "They bear a secret message."

I pulled them apart. On the inside surface of each magnet Brad had printed a word in indelible marker. One said YOU. The other, ME.

I was unexpectedly touched. I handed him one of the magnets. I took the other and we brought them close. I felt the tug just before they clicked together.

I went to the refrigerator and used the magnets to attach Brad's artwork to the door. Brad came up behind me, wrapped his arms around my waist and said, "Just try pulling us apart."

Chapter 28

Looking back I believe our idyllic existence began to unravel the morning I asked Brad why he hadn't become an attorney like his dad. In all the years I'd known him he'd never once boasted that his father was a prominent Twin Cities trial attorney. I'd learned about it at the cabin from Marcy. In her bid to impress Larry the lawyer she'd drawn the juicy tidbit from her scabbard and wielded it like a sword.

On a Saturday morning toward the end of April Brad and I were lingering in bed with twenty minutes to spare before Brad's ten o'clock deadline would send him out the door. The weather had finally warmed and we were naked with just a sheet covering us.

The conversation had started out benignly enough. In answer to my question Brad told me he'd always planned to become an attorney. He described how he'd spent every summer during college working at the law firm where his dad was a senior partner. As a member of the litigation support staff Brad spent his time dealing with the minutia of the law: culling through boxes of files, redacting privileged information, copying pertinent documents and making sure exhibits were properly catalogued, numbered and organized so as to be at the attorney's fingertips in court.

"The summer before my senior year I helped my dad and his team of twenty lawyers prepare for a high-stakes trial. It was a class-action lawsuit worth billions of dollars. The atmosphere was intense. I watched the younger attorneys running themselves ragged, jockeying for position on the team. It had nothing to do with seeking justice for their clients. They were engaged in a mortal struggle to get my dad's attention. They all wanted to be the one to rack up the most billable hours."

He sighed. "I looked at that humorless bunch of men and women and thought, 'Why do I want to do this?' I'd never asked the question before. I'd never considered doing anything else. At that moment I knew I didn't want to be an attorney."

Brad sat up, leaned against the headboard and stared straight ahead as he spoke.

"I lived with that knowledge for months without telling anyone. I was afraid to disappoint my parents so I went ahead and applied for Yale law school. Unbeknownst to them I'd also applied to the business school. When I was accepted in both programs I had to decide what to do.

"I was still dithering when Marcy told me she was pregnant. Knowing I was going to be a father made my decision for me. If I became a lawyer I couldn't be the kind of father I wanted to be. My dad was a good dad, but he hadn't been around much when Greg and I were growing up. After working at his law firm, I understood why. He was too intent on trying to make partner to pay attention to his kids. I didn't want to raise my child that way."

I sat up and faced him, sitting crossed-legged on the mattress. "What did your parents say when you told them?"

"They were disappointed of course. They tried to talk sense into me. But in the end they respected my choice."

Brad gave me a humorless smile. "Marcy's parents were another story. Her mother accused me of pulling the old bait-and-switch on them. The high-power attorney she'd expected for a son-in-law had morphed overnight into a sales-man. Not only had I knocked up her only child I'd also con-demned her to a life of poverty."

"You're not poor."

Brad rubbed his face. "Carrie, I come from money and so does Marcy. Doing what I do I'll never make the kind of money I could have made as an attorney."

"But you have so much."

He shook his head. "It's a sham. I was doing okay in Cincinnati. But I took a pay cut when I left P&G." There was a long pause. I had the sense Brad was deciding how much information he wanted to share. Finally he said, "Marcy's parents bribed us to move back here. They gave us our house in Edina. They paid for our country club membership. They bought Marcy that fancy SUV you rode up to the cabin in. They pay her an obscene salary to work part time for their architectural firm. Marcy's mother calls all the shots. She—"

Brad clamped his mouth shut. I saw his jaw working. The air between us vibrated with his anger.

I had opened a can of worms. I didn't know what to say.

He stared at me. His look was hard. "I'm a kept man, Carrie. How does it feel to make love to a kept man?"

In truth I had never loved him more than I loved him at that moment. But it wouldn't do to say that.

The *ping* of Brad's watch announced his ten o'clock deadline. He broke off eye contact and like an automaton responding to its master's signal he tossed off the sheet, swung his legs over the side of the bed, reached for his cell phone and turned it on. Without a word he gathered his clothes and began to dress. I did the same. I wanted to say something soothing but I was afraid whatever I said would sound naïve. I was out of my depth with this man. He had been hurting and I hadn't had a clue.

When we were dressed Brad caught my eye and crooked his finger at me. He opened his arms and I walked into his embrace. "You didn't need to hear that, little girl. I'm sorry."

"I shouldn't have brought it up."

He took my face in his hands. "If you were a trial lawyer, or even his pauper son, you'd be aware you should never ask a question you don't already know the answer to." He kissed me on the forehead. "I propose we strike the preceding conversation from the record."

That episode marked the beginning of the end for us. Three weeks later I'd forgotten Brad's admonition not to ask a question you don't already know the answer to. Again we were in each other's arms in my bed. For the previous two weeks, ever since Chip had started playing baseball on Saturday mornings, Brad had been leaving before ten in order to catch the end of Chip's game. More to delay his departure than because I wanted to know I asked, "Do you feel guilty?"

"About what?"

"About us."

Brad looked annoyed. "Don't ask me that."

"Why not?"

"It's not something I want to discuss."

"Maybe we *should* discuss it."

"Don't talk to me about what we should do, Carrie." Brad slid his arm out from under me and rolled onto his back.

I was lying on my side looking at Brad. In his troubled expression I saw the answer to my question. I wanted to snatch back my words, make him forget what I'd said. I started to caress his chest, but he pushed my hand away.

Brad stared at the ceiling and spoke in a monotone. "I've never cheated on Marcy before. I worked with you five days a week for three years and managed to keep my hands off. That night in the parking lot at Luiggi's everything changed. When you moved here it seemed like the decision had already been made."

He huffed out a breath. "Until now I've managed to keep my life compartmentalized. This one hour on Saturday morning is my time with you. The rest is my time with Marcy and Chip. Now you want to have a big discussion about it?" He turned onto his side and looked at me. "Okay, Carrie, I'll answer your question. Yes, I feel guilty."

He stared at me unblinking. I couldn't bear to have him look at me like that. I reached for him again. He was stiff and unresponsive but he didn't push me away. "You can't kiss it and make it better," he said. "Kissing makes it worse."

He put his hand behind my head and pulled me into a crushing kiss. Then he released me, got up, collected his clothes and got dressed. At the bedroom door he turned and said, "Don't ask any more stupid questions."

Thanks to the miracle of birth control pills I had arranged a predictable twenty-eight day menstrual cycle with my period making its appearance on Sunday and bowing out on Thursday once every four weeks. However, that month—the lusty month of May—a perverse gnome had made me forget to take the last pill in the dispenser. Therefore the Saturday morning after my "do you feel guilty" discussion with Brad I woke to find I had started my period a day early.

"I wish I'd known that," Brad said when I gave him the news. He'd just come into the house from the garage.

"It started this morning. I didn't have a way to reach you since you don't want me to call you at work."

"After this I'll call you from the break room before I leave," Brad said.

I nodded, trying not to show how hurt I was. Until that moment I hadn't admitted that our arrangement was only about sex. Who knew an inconvenient flow of blood could be the kiss of death?

He looked at his watch. "You know what I might do if you don't mind. I might take in Chip's baseball game. I usually catch just the tail end of it."

I did mind, but said it sounded like a good idea. "I'd love to see him play," I said. "I bet he's good."

"He's amazing," Brad said. "He hit a home run last Saturday. I didn't get to see it." His wistful tone stabbed me with guilt. Brad had been missing his son's games because of me.

I had a vision of Chip in his uniform warming up on the baseball diamond. I pictured him glancing over to the sidelines and spotting his dad. His smile would be bright enough to light both their faces.

"You should go," I said.

My consolation prize was a hug and a fervent kiss on the lips. "Thanks," he said, and rushed into the garage without making plans for the following Saturday.

With a sinking sensation I watched his car pull out of the driveway. I pressed the button to close the overhead door. Then I shut the entry door and leaned my head against its chill surface. I had just run into the brick wall that was Brad's real life. The collision had stunned me.

I wandered from room to room like a zombie, not knowing what to do next. I found myself in the empty living room. Despite the freshly painted walls and ceiling the space was gloomy and uninviting.

My gaze strayed to the window. "Fucking bush," I muttered, filled with sudden loathing for the massive yew that blocked the light even on a sunny day. I headed to my bedroom to change into work clothes. That ugly shrub was about to get a serious haircut.

Henry Streator had amassed an impressive array of pruning implements, which hung from nails on one wall of the garage. I selected a hand pruner, approached the yew and started snipping. Half an hour later I had a two-foot high pile of sticks and greenery, scratches on my forearms, and a misshapen shrub that looked even worse than it had before.

While I was evaluating my less-than-stellar results Janet came across the street and stood next to me. Without even saying hello she said, "Get rid of it. Get rid of all these yews."

"Shouldn't I just prune them?"

She shook her head. "It's not murder, Carrie. Just yank 'em out. I have a back yard full of shade-loving plants. You can have as many as you want."

Janet's advice suited my ferocious mood right down to the ground. After she left I grabbed a long-handled lopper and waded in. This was war. Branches collected around my feet like hair around a barber's chair. When I had denuded the lower portion of the yew I dragged out the severed branches and attacked the trunk with a pruning saw. I quickly learned that a seven-inch pruning saw wielded by a hundred-and-five pound woman is no match for a mature yew. I was in the garage looking for more firepower when Greg Collins pulled into the driveway.

I emerged from the garage brushing the hair from my eyes. "Hi," I said, trying not to sound too friendly, although I had to admit it was nice seeing another human being. The yew had turned out not to be great company.

Greg got out and walked to the rear of his car. "I brought you something," he said.

Since I'd last seen him he'd trimmed his beard although he still wore his hair in a ponytail. He opened the trunk and lifted out a cardboard box. "I just helped a friend refinish his hardwood floors. I thought you could use the leftovers." He indicated the contents of the box with a nod of his head. "Stain. Polyurethane. It'll give you a start anyway."

I thanked him and reached for the box, but he carried it into the garage and placed it on the workbench. I led him into the yard and showed him what I was up to.

He surveyed the situation. "You need a chainsaw."

"There's one in the garage, but just firing it up is above my pay grade."

Greg tinkered around and got the chainsaw going. He made quick work not only of the one yew but all the yews that lined the front of the house. He cut them off close to the ground and helped me drag them to the curb to be collected by the city and turned into mulch. Then he offered to help me dig out the roots. I tried to tell him I didn't need help, but he looked skeptical. I was skeptical myself.

"Why don't we have some lunch first," I said. "I can't wait to go inside and see what my view looks like without the bushes."

The change was already apparent when Greg and I stepped into the house from the garage. Light from the liberated rooms spilled through the open doorways and into the hall.

While Greg went into the laundry room to wash up I slipped off my dirty shoes and headed for the living room. I liked what I saw. The room had been a dungeon, now it was an inviting light-filled space. My original vision for the room—gleaming hardwood floor, area rug and sleek furniture—was a step closer to reality.

I padded down the hall to the office and the guest room. The new carpeting, the freshly painted walls, the decorative touches I'd added—everything looked better without those forbidding shrubs at the windows.

Greg caught up with me.

"What an improvement," I told him. "Thanks."

He looked around, taking in the multiple changes I'd made since his last and only visit the day the carpet was installed. "You've been busy."

I'm sure he was wondering where I'd found the time, given the whirlwind social life I'd told him I was leading.

While I assembled sandwiches and heated leftover macaroni and cheese Greg wandered around inspecting the hardwood floors in the dining room, living room and hall. He returned to the kitchen by way of the breakfast nook. "The floors are going to finish up really nice."

He stopped in front of the refrigerator. I saw him studying the magnets Brad had inscribed for me. Thank goodness I'd stowed the incriminating artwork in the drawer of my nightstand. Surely Greg wouldn't intuit his brother's handiwork based on two printed words.

He took the magnets in his hands and tried them out. He snapped them together several times; to my overheated brain it looked suspiciously like sexual intercourse.

"My brother and I were fascinated by magnets when we were kids," Greg said, sending a shiver of fear down my spine. "One year Brad got a magnetic sculpture for Christmas. He was probably about ten. I would have been six. It had a black magnetic base with dozens of hex nuts on top that you could arrange in different ways. It was really cool." He laughed. "Brad used to lock it in his closet to keep me from playing with it."

"I remember that sculpture," I said. "He had it on his desk at P&G."

"Does he have it at TrueMark?"

"I don't know. We're on different sides of the building."

He returned the magnets to the refrigerator. "Kind of interesting how you both ended up working at the same company."

"It's turned out to be a pretty good job for me," I said. I handed him the plate of sandwiches and took the mac and cheese from the microwave. "Let's eat."

I was next to useless excavating the shrubs. Greg had at least seventy pounds on me, plus an impressive set of muscles—some of which I got to see when he stripped off his shirt—and even he had to employ every tool in Henry's arsenal to get the job done.

Greg was the surgeon. I was his assistant. Shovel. Pry bar. Lopper. Saw. Axe. I dragged them out of the garage and slapped them into his hands as he called for them. The day was cool, but sweat dripped from Greg's face and glistened on the aforementioned muscles.

There's something alluring about the odor of a man exerting himself on a woman's behalf. Greg's jeans had slipped low on his hips; his muscles rippled as he swung the axe; he grunted when the blade bit into the root. *Jesus.* This was Brad's brother. Watching him work felt a tad incestuous.

"Here, Carrie, grab the lopper and cut this root while I hold the trunk out of the way," Greg said. He was on his knees in the dirt, breathing hard.

I did as I was told and the entire root system finally gave up its hold on the earth. "I did it," I shouted, holding the lopper aloft. Still on his knees, Greg muscled the awkward root system out of its hole and onto the lawn. I extended my hand and pulled Greg to his feet.

He grinned at me. "You did it."

Before letting go of his hand I gave it a solemn shake. "That was one stubborn shrub."

It took the remainder of the afternoon to hack out the other stumps, load them into the wheelbarrow and wheel them to the back yard.

Some weeks earlier, by consulting a map and driving around the neighborhood, I'd discovered the land behind me was a wetland. The back of my lot where it joined the wetland grew wild with box elder trees and sumac bushes that gave way to tall grasses where the land turned marshy. That's where we dumped the stumps, having decided a few muddy root balls left to rot in that environment wouldn't hurt anything.

We returned the wheelbarrow to the garage. As we put away the pruners and loppers Greg noted the dullness of their blades and said, "I have a bench grinder up at the cabin. I could sharpen them and have them back in a week or two."

Generous offer, I thought, but all I need is to have Greg show up at my door when Brad is here.

"Maybe some other time," I said.

A trickling sensation between my legs reminded me it was my period and I hadn't been to the bathroom since lunch. I excused myself and hurried inside. When I came back out Greg was standing at the end of the driveway with Vic and Janet. Vic had a bottle of wine and Janet held four wine glasses.

Vic beckoned. "Come out here, Carrie, and don't turn around until I tell you."

Curious, I joined them near the street. I studiously avoided looking behind me.

Vic handed Greg the bottle, took me by the shoulders and told me to close my eyes. When I did, he turned me around to face the house.

"Okay, now you can look."

I opened my eyes and sucked in a breath. Here was a transformation akin to the first time Angie's sister had cut and styled my unruly mop of hair and spun me around in the chair to face the mirror. Before my eyes stood the house the architect must have envisioned, a structure whose clean lines and pleasing proportions attracted the eye and invited one inside. Here was another ugly duckling turned into a swan by means of a haircut.

"I'm stunned," I said. "I have a new house."

"I'd like to propose a toast," Janet said. She distributed the wine glasses and Vic took the bottle and poured a modest amount of cabernet into each.

Janet held her glass aloft. "To the demise of the yews."

We clinked our glasses. "The demise of the yews," we sang out.

After we'd downed our wine and the Lundgrens had departed, Greg and I stood in the driveway near his vehicle. Greg was barechested, his sweaty shirt thrown over one shoulder and his jeans and shoes caked with dirt. I couldn't very well send him away in that condition. I offered to wash and dry his clothes while he showered and had dinner. I wasn't quite sure what he would wear while he ate, but I guessed we'd figure something out.

"I wouldn't mind a shower," he said. "I have gym clothes in my trunk. Can I take a rain check on dinner?"

"Big date tonight?"

He shrugged. "Not sure how big, but yes." He didn't choose to amplify.

I don't know why I was surprised he had a date, but I was. And a little disappointed. Greg's presence had made me forget about Brad for a while. I wasn't sure I wanted to face the evening alone.

While Greg showered in the main bathroom I washed up in the laundry room, and then headed for the living room, drawn by the light. I went to the window and pondered the empty space where the yew had been. Greg emerged from the bathroom, clean and sparkling in a sleek gray warm-up suit with a black stripe and white piping on the sleeves and pants. When he joined me at the window I said, "I know what I'm doing tomorrow."

"Oh yeah?"

"Washing windows, cleaning gutters and begging Janet for plants."

He ran a hand through his damp hair. "I was thinking—like after you wash your windows and stuff—maybe you could come to my parents' house for dinner. It's Dad's birthday. It'll just be family, and you know most of them already."

Oh my god. The idea of me showing up at a Collins family celebration was downright scary. On the other hand it would almost be worth the price of admission to see Brad's expression when I walked in with Greg.

Those were the thoughts that flashed through my mind in the split second before I invented a competing invitation that would prevent me from accepting his offer.

I sensed he wasn't surprised to be turned down. He had another arrow in his quiver, however. He scuffed the tip of his shoe across the oak floorboards. "How about refinishing the floors next weekend? I'll drive my truck and we'll pick up a sander and whatever supplies we need. If we start early enough we should be able to sand all the floors in one day. I'll treat you to dinner."

"I'm the one who should treat you."

"Yeah, you should," Greg said with a grin, "but it ain't gonna happen. So what time do you want me to come next Saturday?"

I knew I was being railroaded. But being railroaded by Greg felt infinitely better than being dissed by Brad. Before I could change my mind I said, "Come as early as you want."

The next week at work I looked for an opportunity to tell Brad not to come on Saturday. I saw him a few times around the office but we didn't speak. On Thursday I stopped at the message center near the receptionist's desk and when no one was looking I slid a pink 'While You Were Out' slip into the slot labeled Brad Collins. I signed it with the initials ME. Even if he didn't get the magnet reference I knew he'd recognize my handwriting.

I was still miffed enough with Brad that scribbling "meeting cancelled" on the pink slip had felt like an act of defiance. I didn't stop to think it might be forever.

Chapter 29

"Hey, Carrie, come see what I discovered," Greg called.

It was the last Saturday in May and the first Saturday in a long while that Brad would not be walking through my door. His customary arrival time had come and gone. I'd told him not to come and now I didn't want him to come, not with Greg's truck parked in the driveway. Still, for the past half hour I'd been lingering in the living room glancing out the window every few seconds hoping to spot his silver Audi. My heart had sunk to the level of my shoes.

I found Greg on his hands and knees in the hall just inside the door to the garage. In preparation for sanding the floors he had pried up a metal strip where the oak floor of the living room met the vinyl tile of the hall.

Greg glanced at me. "Somebody slapped these vinyl tiles right on top of the hardwood." With a wide putty knife he lifted a corner of one tile. "See the wood under there?"

I squatted and looked. Sure enough I spotted an oak board. "I wonder how far it goes."

Greg stood and took in the expanse of dated and scuffed tile that continued down the hall into the breakfast nook and kitchen. "I'm guessing all these floors are hardwood. The only way to find out for sure is to remove the tiles. You were going to replace them anyway, right?"

I nodded. "The budget allows for new vinyl flooring, but if there's hardwood under there, that would be way better."

"Might as well find out now," Greg said. "We could toss the tile into my truck and haul it to the dump."

"Won't it mess up our timetable?"

Greg scratched his head. "We might not get as far as we hoped today, but I think we should do it. If the floor underneath is in decent shape we can refinish it along with the rest of the hardwood."

We decided to divide the labor. Before getting started we emptied the rooms of furniture. Then we sealed off the carpeted rooms with sheets of plastic at the doorways to keep down the dust. While Greg operated the sander in the living room I pulled up the tile. The mastic under the vinyl squares had dried, making removal relatively easy. I backed Greg's truck into the driveway and began dumping trash bags full of the brittle squares into its bed.

I am my mother's child. When I was growing up she always claimed the best approach to overcoming heartache was to get busy. Sure enough as I scraped my way down the hall into the breakfast nook, revealing ever-greater expanses of hardwood, my mood began to lift.

I'd worked my way into the kitchen, which also turned out to be hardwood, when Jill and Derek showed up and offered to help. I introduced them to Greg who introduced them to a piece of equipment. "One of you could take this small sander and go around the edges and into the corners where the big sander doesn't reach," he said. "It doesn't have a dust collector like the big one, so the other person should follow along with the vacuum cleaner."

Derek took the sander from Greg. "We'll trade off, okay, Jill?"

"Start with the coarse grit sandpaper," Greg said. "Then move to the medium grit and finish up with fine."

When Greg returned to sanding Jill wiggled her eyebrows at me as if to say, "Who's he?"

"Just a friend," I mouthed.

With the four of us working, all the floors—including the ones I'd uncovered—had received their first sanding by the time Jill and Derek departed for their real jobs. As always I was blown away by their generosity. I owed them big-time but they seemed to expect nothing.

Greg was generous too, but he did expect something. He wanted to spend time with me. Knowing this made me uncomfortable. I'd accepted his assistance under false pretenses. He was the brother of my lover. I could never become his girlfriend.

These were the thoughts tumbling through my head even as Greg and I worked side-by-side late Saturday afternoon to rid the house of the dust we'd been creating all day. After Jill and Derek had left we'd sanded the floors a second time with the medium grit paper. We'd made a trip to the dump and another trip to return the rented sanders. I'd hoped to keep the sanders overnight and do the final round of sanding on Sunday, but they'd already been rented out to someone else.

We were in the dining room brushing the sanding residue from the ceilings, walls and woodwork when Greg said, "I couldn't have helped you tomorrow anyway. I have something else going on."

I took a breath. Here was my opportunity to disentangle myself from him. "I can do the rest on my own, Greg. I appreciate everything you've done, but I can't keep asking you to give up your Saturdays to help me."

Greg continued to work. He had his back to me, wiping down the patio door. "I enjoy it," he said.

"I'm just saying, maybe I should strike out on my own and see how it goes."

I saw Greg's back stiffen. He stopped what he was doing and turned to me. The look on his face told me I'd hurt his feelings, but after a beat he made a wry face. "Are you being a feminist?"

I couldn't help but smile. "Maybe...a little."

"How are you planning to get that big sander in and out of your Corolla?"

I blinked. "Oh."

He pointed a finger at me. "You rent the sander for next Saturday. I'll pick it up and be here by seven-thirty."

I pursed my lips, went into the kitchen and started wiping dust off the counters and cabinets. That hadn't gone the way I'd intended.

For the second week in a row Greg showered at my house. Before he did we both went into the back yard and slapped ourselves silly trying to rid our clothes and bodies of as much dust as possible. My hair felt like sandpaper, my skin was gray and my eyes were scratchy. Although I'd worn a dust mask over my mouth and nose most of the day I still felt the need to cough my lungs out.

At my suggestion Greg removed his work clothes in the laundry room, dropped them into the washer, wrapped himself in a towel and headed for the bathroom. When he was safely out of the way I entered the laundry room, stripped down to my underwear and tossed my filthy clothes into the washer. Then I raced through the house to my bedroom and into the master bath.

There is nothing more welcome than a shower after a hard day's work. For a few moments I stood motionless in the steamy enclosure, simply letting the water sluice down my aching body. I set to work on my hair. Merely getting it wet was difficult, caked as it was with fine particles of wood dust and varnish. Three shampoos and one application of conditioner later it finally felt halfway normal.

I heard a thump from the other bathroom, which reminded me the two showers shared a wall. Right now my naked body is only three feet away from Greg's naked body, I thought. It was an odd intimacy that filled me with misgivings. What had I gotten myself into?

By the time I emerged from my room dressed in clean cargo pants, a tank top and a cardigan shrug, Greg—in a fresh shirt and pants he'd brought with him—had settled into a lawn chair on the deck. I started the washing machine, then snagged two beers from the refrigerator and joined him. I handed him one of the bottles, sank into a lawn chair and groaned with pleasure.

We sipped our beers in companionable silence. At half past seven the sky was clear, the sun still warming the deck.

A few weeks earlier, taking advantage of one of our first warm weekends, I'd spent hours crawling around on the deck hammering loose nails and scrubbing off the mildew. The next week, with the cedar boards thoroughly dry, I'd applied the sealer, a surprisingly easy job with a huge payoff. Like a home in the Hamptons whose cedar shakes only improved with age, my weathered deck with its silvery wood had become a thing of beauty. Adorned with patio furniture I'd hauled out from the three-season porch and spruced up, the space was down-right inviting.

When the washer was finished I transferred the clothes to the dryer and we drove in my car to an Italian restaurant in Burnsville. Over dinner I learned more about the Collins family than Brad had ever shared. Without my prompting Greg brought up Brad's decision not to go to law school. The story was even more dramatic than Brad had let on.

"Law is the family business," Greg said. "Both my great grandfather and my grandfather were attorneys. My dad's an attorney. My mom's a retired attorney. We were all expected to go into it. When Brad decided not to go to law school it was like the king of England renouncing his crown. Brad would have been a star. He has the brains, the looks, the personality. Well you know how he is.

"I was the one who would have failed," Greg said. "I had shitty grades in everything but math and computer science. Once Brad bucked the trend it took me off the hook too. My parents had no law school expectations for their less gifted son. I found my way into computer security, and it's turned out to be a good fit. I have so many clients I've had to hire people to work for me. I enjoy what I do and it pays well."

At the end of our meal I made a valiant effort to grab the check, but Greg was faster and ignored my protestations. As we left the restaurant, yawning and claiming to be weary to the bone, I turned down his offer to show me his townhome, which he said was nearby. Instead we returned to my house and I pulled into the garage. I was determined not to invite him inside so I got out of my car and headed outside to where his truck was parked.

Greg stood his ground. "I should get my clothes."

Damn. "Oh, that's right. They're in the dryer."

We went inside and Greg followed me into the laundry room.

To make a full load in the washer I'd thrown in additional laundry from the hamper. When I extracted the clothes from the dryer a tiny red thong—something I wore only on Saturday mornings for Brad—was plastered to the front of Greg's T-shirt.

Greg, who'd been standing beside me trying to make himself useful, cleared his throat. Trying to act nonchalant I took the T-shirt, peeled off the wisp of stretchy lace and dropped it on top of the dryer. Neither of us made a comment as I folded his clothes and handed them to him.

Instead of leaving like I wanted him to, he set his clean laundry on the washing machine. When he turned to me I knew what was about to happen. He was going to kiss me.

I snapped my fingers. "You know what? If you're planning to go up to your cabin would you mind sharpening my loppers and pruners? You were right. They really are dull."

That did the trick. By the time I'd loaded him up with an assortment of garden tools and hustled him to his truck the kissing opportunity had passed. Once he was safely behind the steering wheel he lowered his window and I handed him his clean laundry.

Something in his smile told me he knew exactly what I'd been up to.

Chapter 30

"What time is it?" Greg asked as I stepped onto the deck from my bedroom.

It was the first Saturday in June, a warm, sunny day with the humidity under forty percent—perfect weather for refinishing floors.

On Thursday I'd left a second cancellation message in Brad's inbox. Since I hadn't heard from him I could only assume he was relieved to be let off the hook. Watching Chip play baseball had become Brad's Saturday morning activity. Mine was refinishing floors.

After a morning spent sanding, clearing away the dust and wiping the floors with mineral spirits Greg and I had just put down the first coat of polyurethane. I'd done the living room and the hall that ran from the laundry room to the bedrooms; Greg had tackled the dining room, kitchen and breakfast nook.

He'd finished ahead of me and had come out onto the deck from the three-season porch. I'd come through the bedroom and out the French doors and found him sprawled in a lounge chair, glass of water in hand.

I consulted my watch. "It's almost two o'clock."

"Good timing," Greg said. "The first coat should take about two hours to dry. At four we'll start putting down the second coat and be done by six at the latest."

Hmm. What would we do for two hours while we waited to apply the second coat? We'd already eaten our lunch on the deck before applying the first coat of poly. Spending two hours with Greg, with nothing to do but wait, might be awkward.

I needn't have worried.

Greg drained his glass and got up from his chair. "I need to run some errands. I'll return the sanding equipment while I'm out. Plus I think we could use another gallon of poly."

He pulled out his keys and started walking toward the front yard.

I tagged along. "Shouldn't I go with you to pay for it?"

"You can pay me later. I'd like to do a few things on my own this afternoon. I'll be back by four."

I watched him leave. As he drove off I wondered if I could possibly be more contrary. A minute earlier I'd been worried about killing two hours alone with Greg. Now I didn't know what I'd do without him.

I returned to the back yard, washed and rinsed my brushes, tools and containers and arranged them on the deck to dry. That took all of twenty minutes. Now what? I thought.

I dragged a lounge chair to a sliver of shade on the deck, flopped onto it, pulled out my cell phone and proceeded to call my sister, my brother, Randy and Angie. One hour down.

I'd saved my mother for last. She could usually be counted on for fifteen minutes at least. I caught her in the basement working on a new quilt.

"I've never made a quilt like this before," she said, sounding excited. "It's called an impressionist quilt. If it turns out as good as I expect I'm going to enter it in a contest."

She explained that the history center in Cincinnati was mounting a new exhibit celebrating the domestic arts. A portion of the exhibit would feature quilts crafted by artisans from the Cincinnati area. Most of the quilts in the exhibit would be old, but the museum also planned to display a selection of contemporary quilts to show the tradition continuing and evolving. Both to call attention to the exhibit and to unearth the best contemporary quilts in the city, the Cincinnati *Enquirer* newspaper and one of the local television stations had teamed up to sponsor a contest.

"There's a cash prize and the winner gets the honor of having her quilt on display during the run of the exhibit," my mom said. She lowered her voice almost to a whisper. "Carrie, this is the prettiest quilt I've ever made. I haven't told anybody, not even your dad, but I think I can win this contest."

She laughed. "Can you believe how vain I've become in my old age?"

We gabbed for another twenty minutes. Not once did she ask about Brad. She never asked about Brad anymore. I always sensed the question on the tip of her tongue, but to her credit and my relief she never uttered it.

While we were talking I'd been wandering around the back yard. By the time we hung up I had wriggled between two head-high bushes and was standing on a patio that was so badly overgrown I hadn't known it was there. I slipped my phone into my pocket and started exploring. Aside from the mosquitoes, which were numerous and fierce, this fan-shaped wedge of earth occupying the southwest corner of the lot had the potential to be charming. When I spotted a weathered statue of Our Lady of Guadalupe nestled among the weeds in the very corner of the yard I suspected I'd stumbled upon Adriana's garden.

"Hey, Carrie."

Greg had come up behind me and was standing on the other side of the bushes. He would have startled me if his voice hadn't been so gentle.

"Look what I found," I said.

"Mosquitoes?"

I slapped at my arms and legs; the critters were beginning to swarm. "That, and Adriana's garden."

As I squeezed back through the bushes and we headed for the deck I described how Jill had found a handwritten copy of Henry Streator's will in the office. "She couldn't remember the exact wording, but it mentions Adriana's garden. When I asked my cousin Randy about it he strongly suggested I let sleeping dogs lie."

"Is that what you're going to do?"

I grinned. "What do you think?"

We climbed the two steps onto the deck and Greg went to the kitchen window and looked in. "If the clock on your stove is right it's three-thirty. Time enough for a beer before we hit the floors again." He started toward the cooler I'd stashed on the three-season porch. "You want one?"

I didn't often drink during the day. But, hey, I'd discovered Adriana's garden. "Sure, what the heck."

We went into the three-season porch and assembled a tray of snacks, then took our drinks and goodies onto the deck and settled into lawn chairs. Greg seemed preoccupied. I knew from experience he was mulling something over. Eventually he'd get around to making his point.

As I reached for a third pretzel he said, "Don't get too full."

"Why not?"

He cleared his throat. "I was wondering. Do you like steak?"

"I do."

He cleared his throat again. "I was just thinking. After we put down this second coat you won't be able to walk on the floors for two hours. While I was running errands I bought some steaks and stuff and I thought we could grill out at my place."

So that was the reason he'd gone off alone. He'd been planning this all along. He was so nervous and his machinations so transparent I almost laughed. But he was too sweet to laugh at.

"Sounds like fun," I said. And I meant it.

"There's something else. You don't have to do it if you don't want to. I have a client named Joe Rizzo. His son Danny is a comedian in New York. This weekend he's appearing at a comedy club in Bloomington. I promised I'd meet Joe and his wife there tonight. Show starts at nine. I could either drive you home after dinner or you could go with me."

I didn't even have to think about it. Here was my evening ready-made. "I'd like to go. I've never been to a comedy club."

Greg smiled, clearly pleased. "They can be a little raunchy," he warned.

I grinned. The beer was already having its effect on me. "I'm a big girl."

If I do say so myself alcohol makes me better at things. That second coat of polyurethane I applied went on as smooth as glass.

While I worked I decided what I'd wear to the comedy club. Some months earlier I'd purchased a mini-skirt—a skin-tight tube of spandex—that made me look like a tramp, especially when paired with the patterned tights and stiletto heels whose siren call I'd been unable to resist. For once I'd ignored Angie's dictum about never wearing black; all three items were that forbidden color. The article of clothing that would have redeemed me in Angie's eyes was the cranberry-toned Calvin Klein top, a silky, sleeveless confection with a drapey, low-cut neckline.

I'd worn the ensemble only once. That was the Saturday morning I'd waylaid Brad in the garage. I'd nearly frozen to death, but the lovemaking had been worth every goose bump on my body.

Time to give that outfit a second whirl, I decided. A raunchy getup for a raunchy nightclub. What could be more appropriate?

I wasn't sure Greg would approve. He seemed too wholesome to date a woman who dressed like a tramp. He might be ashamed to introduce me to his client. I'd play it safe by wearing something more conservative for dinner. Later I'd model the hooker outfit; if he didn't like it I wouldn't wear it.

Greg's townhome was spacious, private and expensive-looking. Like him, the furnishings were comfortable and not at all flashy. I already knew he was a good cook. For this meal, as at the cabin, he'd chosen simple fare—grilled steak, baked potatoes with sour cream, sautéed mushrooms with onions—but all were seasoned and done to perfection. The wine was so good it practically got on its knees and begged me to have a second glass.

For dessert Greg presented me with three exquisite, chocolate-dipped strawberries centered on a clear glass plate. An involuntary moan slipped from my mouth when I took the first bite.

Greg broke into a smile. "I thought you'd enjoy those."

While Greg was cleaning up the supper dishes I went into the bathroom and changed into "the outfit." His back was to me as I stepped into the kitchen. When he turned and saw me his eyes opened wide and he drew a sharp breath, which he disguised as a cough.

I raised my shoulders and gave him a doubtful look. "Is this okay? I mean, like, for your client?"

"Better than okay," he said.

We arrived at the club before nine. The room was crowded. People—mostly young folks like Greg and me—were packed in elbow-to-elbow like sardines, if sardines had elbows. Turned out my attire was appropriate; there were plenty of women displaying lots more flesh than I'd ever have the nerve to do.

Joe Rizzo and his wife were seated alone at a small round table directly in front of the raised platform that served as a stage. They'd been watching for Greg; when they spotted him they waved us over. We threaded our way toward them through the mass of humanity.

Joe jumped up and pumped my hand. "You must be Lisa."

Greg practically choked.

I laughed. "I'm the other Lisa. I'm Carrie."

Joe recovered quickly. "Good to meet you, Carrie. This is my wife, Anna."

"We saved you some seats," Anna said, and gestured for us to take the two empty seats on her left. The four of us arranged ourselves around the table in a semi-circle facing the stage. The microphone on its stand was no more than six feet in front of us. A server materialized, and Greg and I ordered draft beers.

Greg surveyed the room. "Impressive turnout."

Joe looked proud enough to bust the buttons on his shirt. "I hope you enjoy it. Three other comedians will come on before our Danny. He's the headliner."

The server brought our beers. I took a sip, then gave Greg a playful nudge with my elbow. "So who's Lisa?"

Joe sent Greg an apologetic look. "Hey, I'm sorry about that—"

"Not a problem," Greg said and turned to me. "She's one of my programmers. She's done some work for Joe, but they've only met on the phone."

"Yeah," Joe said, practically tripping over his words to explain, "the last time I talked to Lisa I told her about Danny coming to town and she seemed interested in seeing his show. I jumped to the conclusion you were her, although you don't look anything like she sounds."

My follow-up questions would have been, "How do I look and how does she sound?" but Greg seemed so uncomfortable I decided to give it a rest. I suspected there was more to the story than they were telling, but it wasn't my concern. I was there for the show and it was about to begin.

The house lights dimmed and a spotlight appeared on the stage. A master of ceremonies stepped into the spotlight and introduced the first funny man, a goofy-looking young guy high on drugs and obsessed with sex, if his ten-minute act was to be believed. The next two comedians, both young men, offered more of the same. All three were sporadically funny, but not often enough to be considered ready for prime time.

After the third comedian departed the emcee took the stage and warmed up the crowd for Danny Rizzo, the big name comedian from New York City. When the emcee had us all clapping Danny bounded from the back of the room and onto the platform. He was short, semi-attractive and as self-confident as a semi-attractive, short guy can be.

He wasted no time approaching our table. "My folks are here tonight," he told the crowd. "They have front-row seats." Looking diffident and respectful he bowed his head toward Anna. "For you, Ma, I'm gonna keep it clean." He backed away from the table and winked at the audience. "Not," he roared into the microphone. The crowd roared back.

Then Danny Rizzo proceeded to go about as low as you can go without being hauled off on obscenity charges. His act was consistently funny, but it was truly filthy.

He'd pick out couples seated in the front of the room and make knowing comments about their sex lives. When they blushed or blustered he would look at the audience and say, "Am I right?" He got a laugh every time. The harder Danny skewered his victims the more laughs he got. I found myself shrinking low in my seat, trying to make myself invisible.

The meat of Danny's act centered on his problems with women. His principal stumbling block was premature ejaculation. "Why do women complain about premature ejaculation?" he asked, sounding insulted. "I'm the one who should be sorry. It costs me dinner, theater tickets and four hours of my life to finally get a woman to go to bed with me. Then I'm done in, like, one minute. And *she* complains? She should feel flattered. The hotter she is, the faster I'm done."

He returned to our table. This time he was eyeing me. "What's your name?"

Almost without thinking I said, "Lisa."

"You're a beautiful girl, Lisa. Why are you sitting here with my parents?" In an indignant voice he said, "Ma, you been holding out on me?"

That garnered a laugh.

He pointed at Greg. "You with the ponytail. What's your name?"

What could Greg do? He gave Danny his name.

"You've got yourself a hot one there, Greg," Danny said. "With a girl like Lisa, how much time does it take *you*? I'm guessing forty-four and a half seconds between wham bam and thank you ma'am. Am I right?"

The crowd roared.

Poor Greg. He ducked his head and shielded his face with his hand.

Danny Rizzo nodded knowingly. Then he grinned and sprinted to the far side of the stage in search of another victim. Danny's act lasted another five minutes, after which he thanked the audience, hopped off the stage and disappeared into the back of the room.

The house lights came up—not too high, fortunately—since I was pretty sure there were pink cheeks all around our table. I caught Joe's eye. "Next time can we sit in the back?"

That broke the ice. We all laughed and Anna said, "Oh, Carrie, Greg, I'm so sorry."

Greg shrugged. "Hey, he was funny."

"We're meeting him in the bar across the lobby," Joe said. "Why don't you join us?"

Greg looked at me for permission. Anything that would keep the party going sounded good to me.

The bar was intimate and dimly lit. Our table was a row back from a minuscule dance floor. There was no music playing when we entered, but a grizzled deejay was setting up shop across the way.

We ordered drinks. I'd taken a few sips of my second beer of the night when Danny arrived, swaggering a bit and still wound up, flush with the success of his appearance. Heads turned as they recognized him.

He made his way to our table. There was no chair for him so he stood behind his parents. "Ma," he said, and bent to kiss Anna on the cheek. He clasped his dad's shoulder.

Joe patted his son's hand. "Good job, Danny."

"Thanks, Pop. I was nervous knowing you were there."

"Well we couldn't tell you were nervous," Anna said. "Not one bit."

Joe gestured toward Greg and me. "These are our friends, Greg and Carrie."

Danny leaned across the table and shook Greg's hand. "Thanks for coming." When he took my hand he said, "That's not the name you gave me."

I eyed him with a calculating smile and said, "I guess you're not the only one who's full of crap."

For a split second, during which I wondered if I'd over-stepped my bounds, the silence was deafening. I couldn't see Greg's face, but the elder Rizzos looked shocked, as did Danny. After a beat, though, Danny guffawed and waggled an index finger at me. "You should consider doing standup."

He borrowed an empty chair from another table and squeezed in between his parents. He was interested in getting our opinions of his act. He wanted to know what had worked and what hadn't worked so well. The subject matter may have been unconventional but the analysis was not. Analyzing his routine was no different from analyzing the effectiveness of a television commercial or a marketing campaign, a technique I'd studied in college and put into practice at P&G.

Once the music started it was too loud to talk. I made a run to the restroom and realized I was a bit tipsy when I had trouble pulling up my tights. The mirror over the sink told me I looked fine though. More than fine. I looked—and felt—hot.

When I returned to the room ZZ Top had just begun blast-ing everyone's eardrums. Instead of taking my seat I staked out a spot on the dance floor a short distance from the table and crooked my finger at Greg. I wiggled my hips to make sure he got the message.

He shook his head.

With a seductive smile on my face I slithered over to the table and bent over, aware I was sharing a generous helping of cleavage with anyone who cared to look. Affecting an exagger-ated pout I grabbed Greg's hand and tugged. "C'mon."

Greg gave me a sheepish grin. "Really, I don't know how to dance."

Danny nearly knocked his chair over in his hurry to get up. "I do."

Danny was not a bad dancer, maybe not as good as he thought he was, but he got the job done. Maybe I wasn't as good as I thought I was either, but he seemed to enjoy watching me. So did Greg.

Why do deejays always play a ballad just when you're ready for more rock and roll? In my book, "Natural Woman" should never follow "Gimme All Your Lovin'" on the playlist. But that's what this birdbrained deejay did.

As soon as I heard the first chords of "Natural Woman," I started to return to the table, but Danny took my hand and pulled me toward him. Before I knew it we were slow dancing and I was revising my opinion of the deejay and his choice. This was fun. Despite the fact that in my heels I was two inches taller than Danny he led me well. It was obvious he'd done this before.

By the time Aretha's soul was in the lost-and-found Danny Rizzo's hand was on my butt. I reached behind me and returned it to my waist.

A second later Greg was standing beside us gripping Danny by the shoulder. "My turn," he said with some authority. He towered over Danny.

Mister Chuckles backed off and Greg took me in his arms.

I wrapped my arms around his neck and tilted my head up to look at him. "I thought you didn't dance."

He gave me a testosterone-fueled smile. "I can do what he was doing."

He pulled me tight against him, at which point I realized my handyman was more than a little turned on. We swayed together in silence. When Greg's hand crept to my butt, I left it there.

The song ended, but Greg seemed reluctant to let me go. He put his mouth to my ear. "Let's get out of here."

We said our goodbyes and walked to the car with our arms around each other. Before he let me in on the passenger side he backed me against the door. A week earlier I'd gone to great lengths to avoid letting him kiss me. That night, however, when his mouth found mine I welcomed the exchange of bodily fluids. While we kissed his hands roved first to my breasts and then between my legs. When he ran up against the barrier of my tights he groaned. He gave me a look that left no doubt what he had in mind. "Do you happen to be wearing that red thong?"

I laughed, remembering how embarrassed I'd been when I'd peeled the lacy wisp of lingerie from his shirt. "No."

"I haven't been able to get that thing out of my mind all week."

I licked my lips. "Maybe I can arrange a private showing."

Ideas conceived deep in the loins are not renowned for their logic. In the twenty minutes it took Greg to drive from the comedy club to my house it crossed my mind what a mistake I was making. Still, it had been three long weeks since Brad had been in my bed. He wasn't monogamous. How could he expect that of me?

Greg and I bypassed the newly varnished floors by letting ourselves into my bedroom the same way I'd left, through the French doors on the deck. While Greg used the bathroom I found the red thong in a drawer, turned down the bedspread, dimmed the lights and closed the blinds.

When Greg emerged from the bathroom I went in and shut the door. I slipped out of my clothes and into the thong. I stood before the mirror and stared into my eyes; they were barely focusing, which signaled a satisfactory state of intoxication for what I had in mind. I put my skirt and top back on without the bra or tights and stepped into the bedroom.

Greg was standing there fully clothed, waiting. He seemed almost shy, like he couldn't believe what was happening. I wanted to get on with it. If I took time to think I'd lose my nerve.

I sidled up to him and smiled a naughty smile. I ran my hand down the front of his pants. He moaned and reached for my breasts. I struggled to undo his fly. He helped me, then lifted my top over my head. I unbuttoned his shirt and played with his nipples. They were hard. He hiked up my skirt in the back, caressed my bottom and slid his fingers down the thong to where it disappeared between my buttocks.

"Oh god," he breathed.

My skirt slid right off. I tugged his pants down. As my fingers wrapped around an impressive chunk of Greg's anatomy it was my turn to take the lord's name in vain.

Moments later I was coaxing him onto the bed and he was reaching for the condom he'd placed on the nightstand. I started to ease out of my thong but he held my hand. "Leave it on," he said, his voice husky.

If Brad hadn't done and said the same thing the last time I'd worn the thong for him I might have been okay. But he had. And I wasn't okay. I wanted to shove Greg off me, but I didn't have the nerve. He finished fast—just as Danny Rizzo had predicted—and collapsed onto the bed with a gasp. Although I tried to act fulfilled, he knew better. Neither of us said a word.

After a while he withdrew and turned onto his side, facing me. I was lying on my back. He gave me a tender look. "You didn't get satisfied."

"That's okay. I enjoyed it. I just didn't...you know..." I shrugged.

In a smoky voice he said, "I can help you with that." He leaned forward to kiss me and began to slide his hand between my legs.

"No!" I stopped his hand and turned away to avoid his lips. Greg froze. I could sense his shock and hurt. I clamped my mouth shut to keep from crying.

For a long moment we lay there in a state of suspended animation. My back was to Greg; I could hear him drawing heavy breaths. Neither of us spoke. Eventually Greg rolled to the opposite side of the bed, got up and went into the bathroom. After he closed the door I padded to the closet, found my robe and put it on. I sat on the edge of the bed until Greg came out and started dressing. He avoided looking at me.

"I'm sorry, Greg. I don't know what came over me."

He didn't respond. I saw his jaw working. He had that in common with Brad.

He dressed in silence. When he was about to leave I said, "Do you want to see the floors?"

He shot me a cold glance, opened the French doors, stepped onto the deck and disappeared into the night.

Greg called Sunday morning and asked if he could stop by. Without hesitation I said yes. He'd been so hurt when he'd walked out the night before I'd been afraid he wouldn't give me a chance to apologize. I knew if we could talk I could straighten things out and we would be friends again. I'd show him the floors. He could help me move the furniture back into the rooms. He could stay for lunch. We'd return to normal.

When he arrived I was sitting cross-legged on the driveway in front of my open garage door, sanding the rungs of a dining room chair.

Greg parked his car on the street in front of the house. When he approached I put down my sandpaper and stood. I could tell from his demeanor this wasn't a social call.

"Do you want to go inside?" I said.

Unsmiling he gestured to the dining room table and chairs, which were in the garage for refinishing. "Let's sit here."

I entered the garage and took a seat at the table. I was wearing shorts and a sleeveless top. The garage was chilly; I sat there hugging myself.

Greg sat across from me with his hands on his thighs. He said, "I feel bad about what happened last night. I thought you and I were on the same page. If I forced myself on you, I'm sorry."

I shook my head. "You didn't force yourself on me."

"I'm attracted to you, Carrie. In fact I'm—" He stopped short and swallowed. "I'm attracted to you, but I'm pretty sure the feeling isn't mutual."

"That's not true—"

He held up a hand. "Let me finish. When I think back I realize you've been trying to get rid of me since the beginning. You've never once asked for my help. You accepted it, but you were reluctant. I kept telling myself you just wanted to prove you could do everything yourself."

He blinked, then fixed his eyes on mine. "But last night I saw something in your face when I tried to kiss you after we...when we were in bed. You turned your head away like you found me repulsive."

I bit my lip to keep it from trembling.

"Were you just paying off a debt last night? Did you feel obligated to me because I helped you refinish your floors? If you thought I expected that form of payment you were wrong."

"It wasn't that way," I said. "I just—"

Again he stopped me with an upraised hand. "On second thought, don't try to explain. It won't change anything. I may be dense, but I finally got the message."

He stood and looked down at me. "I like being with you. I like helping you. But I can't bear to think I repulse you. I won't force myself on you again, Carrie. Enjoy your house. Enjoy your life."

With that, he turned on his heel and left.

Chapter 31

I woke Monday morning still feeling heartsick. I knew what I needed to do and I wasn't going to wait until the weekend to do it. When the time for my afternoon break rolled around I walked to the lobby and inserted a third "meeting cancelled" slip into Brad's box.

Late in the afternoon Brad reached me on my cell phone. I'd already left work and had just pulled into the garage. When he learned I was at home he said, "I'm coming over. I'll be there in fifteen minutes."

I'd half expected this and already had a plan. I didn't trust myself to be alone with Brad at my house. "I was about to take a walk," I said. "Meet me at the school."

I walked the few blocks to the elementary school. Soon after I arrived Brad's silver Audi turned into the deserted lot. I waited while he parked. I didn't dare get into the car with him. The Audi held too many temptations.

I started across the blacktop toward the playground. Brad caught up with me.

"Have you been to the doctor?" he asked. His tone was playful.

"What are you talking about?"

"All these cancelled meetings. You must be having the longest period in history," he said. "You need to see a doctor."

"Ha," I said.

"Oh, so maybe those pink slips you've been sending mean something else. Are you firing me?"

I took a deep breath. "You could put it that way."

He stopped, took my arm and turned me toward him. When I avoided looking into his eyes, he bent down and placed his face in my line of vision. His smile was heart melting. "You really don't want to see me anymore?"

I looked away. "It's not about what I want. It's about what's right."

Brad gave an exasperated sigh. "Who knows what's right anymore?"

"My mother. She warned me people could get hurt." I started walking again.

Brad fell in beside me. "Your mother knows about us?"

"She warned me not to get involved with a married man. You said yourself you felt guilty."

"You caught me at a bad time."

We had reached the deserted playground. I sat on one of the swings, a black rubber sling suspended from two chains. Brad took the swing next to mine. I stared down and rocked back and forth with my feet on the ground.

For a while neither of us spoke. Then Brad said, "Remember when we went to dinner with Clayton Shaw?"

"I do."

"Remember what you ordered?"

"Lobster."

"I've never seen anyone enjoy a meal as much as you enjoyed the lobster that night. Just watching you eat was an erotic experience."

Brad reached over and stopped my swing. He held the chain until I looked at him. His smile was as delectable as drawn butter.

"When we make love on Saturday mornings isn't it even better than lobster? Maybe you wouldn't want it every day, but my god, Carrie, isn't it the best thing you've ever tasted?"

I couldn't look at him and lie. "Yes." Tears sprang to my eyes. I longed to lean forward and press my lips to his.

Brad examined my face. "Here's the thing, Carrie. I only have this one life. It's a meat and potatoes kind of life. That's fine. I like meat and potatoes. But does every meal have to be meat and potatoes? Maybe I do feel guilty sometimes. But that's *my* problem, not yours. As long as I'm not hurting anybody else why can't I have lobster for breakfast once in a while?"

I considered that and said, "Because by choosing lobster your loyalties are divided. You don't give a hundred percent of yourself to Marcy and Chip."

"It's one hour a week. There are lots of other hours. Maybe I'm a better husband and father because I enjoy lobster on Saturday morning."

"What cheating husband hasn't used that line?"

A smile played on his lips. "That exact line? Zero to none."

I permitted myself a chuckle. "You know what I mean."

He sighed. "This isn't just any married man and his bimbo girlfriend, Carrie. This is you and me."

To look into his eyes for any length of time was to see my resolve crumble. I tore my gaze away and focused on his perfect shoes, the tips of which were coated with dust from the playground. "You say you're not hurting anybody else," I said, "but what about me? I can't live like this anymore. I need my life back."

"I thought you were happy."

"For one hour a week I'm happy. The rest of the time I don't function very well."

"Carrie, I've told you before. You're free to live the rest of your life the way you please. I don't ask who you're seeing or what you're doing because it's not my business. I admit I don't like to think you're having a relationship with someone else, but I can't ask you not to."

I dragged the toe of my sandal in the dirt under the swing until I caught myself drawing the letter B over and over. B for Brad. I rubbed it out. "That's just it. I can't have a relationship with someone else. I can't make love with you on Saturday morning and then go out with somebody else on Saturday night."

Brad sighed. "What do you want me to do? I can't change the way things are."

"We can stop seeing each other."

"How can we give this up? We have something special—"

"We *had* something special. In Cincinnati we were part of a team. We sparked each other's creativity. We accomplished things together. All of that is gone now. In Minnesota I'm just the girl who opens her legs for you once a week."

"That's disgusting, Carrie. It's not the way I feel about you."

I made my voice deliberately cold. "Nothing will change the fact that you're a married man getting a little something on the side."

"So you *are* telling me to get lost."

I swallowed hard and nodded. "That's what I'm saying."

I gave him one long look, then pushed off with my feet and started to swing. As I picked up speed Brad stood and grabbed at the chain. I kept pumping.

"Carrie, stop. If you would just let me take you back to the house we could have a conversation about this. We could work something out."

I pumped harder, fearing I'd lose my nerve if I slowed down.

Brad gave up trying to catch the chain. He put his hands on his hips and watched me swing higher and higher, my hair blowing into my face, then streaming out behind.

An eternity went by. Finally he smiled up at me. "I'm going to miss you."

Hearing his words, sounding so final, I almost sobbed. If I was getting my way it didn't feel like it.

Brad said, "Do you want me to drive you home? I promise not to grovel anymore."

"No. I'm going to stay here. I might just send this swing over the top."

He watched for a moment longer, then gave a little wave and turned away. I squeezed my eyes shut and pumped for all I was worth. When I felt the chains slacken at the height of my arc I stopped pumping and opened my eyes. Brad was gone.

Chapter 32

Tuesday I dragged myself to work. On a day when all I wanted to do was slink into my cubbyhole and lick my wounds I arrived to find all business office employees had been summoned to a nine o'clock meeting in the lunchroom.

"It must be good news," Amanda whispered as she, Tracy, Dawn and I filed into the lunchroom. "See the bagel boxes?"

Sure enough half a dozen boxes of bagels and a dozen tubs of flavored cream cheese were lined up along the counter near the microwave ovens. Presumably, good news was accompanied by bagels. I didn't know what bad news came with.

The lunch tables had been replaced by rows of folding chairs, before which a microphone on a stand had been placed. We customer service reps filed into the fifth row. I spotted Brad in the front row with Lindsey, CEO Laura Nichols, and some other big shots.

When the room had filled to standing room capacity the CEO took the microphone. "Before people begin heading out on their summer vacations we want to take this opportunity to thank you all for another terrific year." She ran down a list of the fiscal year's accomplishments. The upshot was: we made money, we renewed contracts, the money will keep on flowing.

The big news was the signing of the Mississippi contract. That's where Brad came in. The CEO asked him to flesh out the details. He stood and took the microphone.

It would have been gratifying to see a gaunt expression on Brad's face and dark circles under his eyes, evidence of a night spent tossing and turning. But no. In his impeccably-tailored suit, with his confident manner and infectious smile, he looked as good as he ever had—so good, in fact, that Dawn leaned toward me with her hand shielding her mouth and panted into my ear, "Huh-huh-huh-hot." Amanda and Tracy heard her and grinned. At that moment Brad's eyes flicked to us and just as quickly flicked away.

How ironic. My affair with Brad had begun the same snowy week in February when members of the Mississippi Department of Education had arrived in Minnesota to consider signing a contract with TrueMark. Four months later, just as Mississippi and TrueMark were getting into bed together, Brad and I were calling it quits. From now on, I realized, Brad and Meryl would be the ones spending time together.

In the following weeks the absence of the Audi in the parking lot at work told me Brad was doing his share of traveling. With schools on summer break I guessed it was his opportunity to travel around the country making sales pitches to relatively idle state departments of education. This was mere speculation on my part since Brad no longer placed late-night calls from his hotel room to my cell phone.

By mid-June, when my loneliness for Brad had settled in like a dull ache, my promotion came through.

Months earlier, in putting together the job description I'd sent to Lindsey, I'd realized that working with Michael to develop marketing tools and Web content for Brad's department would not take forty hours a week. With that in mind I'd designed a position that would not only perform those functions for Sales and Marketing but would continue to maintain the customer service data base and relieve Lindsey of some of the more mundane sales support functions she performed. In effect whoever got the job would become Lindsey's administrative assistant.

Lindsey had obviously liked the idea and been able to sell it to upper management. The job had been posted internally toward the end of May. I'd applied immediately. The third Friday in June, at the end of the day, Lindsey called me to her office and offered me the promotion, to take effect the first of July.

She outlined my new duties. "You and I are the facilitators, Carrie. Brad and his team make the promises to the clients. Our job is to make the promises come true. To keep the lines of communication open I'd like you to be a liaison between Sales and me. At the same time you'll work with Michael to supply Web content." She smiled. "How does that sound?"

I returned to my cubicle beaming. It was late enough that Tracy, Amanda and Dawn had left for the day, as had nearly everyone else in the building. At five o'clock I walked out the door into a glorious summer afternoon. It was the first time in weeks my heart didn't feel like a thudding lump of clay.

As I drove home I told myself it was the excitement of stepping into a challenging position that had me all tingly inside. Finally I'd have a chance to strut my stuff. I'd improve the website and make a difference at the company. I'd attract the attention of important people who could advance my career. The fact that I'd be interacting with Brad again was irrelevant and had nothing to do with my soaring spirits. That's what I told myself and that's the version of reality I chose to believe.

No sooner had I pulled into the garage than Jill pulled into the driveway behind me and got out of her car.

"What?" I said. "No Derek on a Friday night?

"He's out with friends," she said and followed me into the house shouldering a tote bag, which she deposited in the family room. I headed for the kitchen with my empty lunch sack.

Jill joined me. She said, "If you don't have other plans for tonight I thought maybe we could go through the keepsake box."

"Excellent timing," I said and crooked a finger at her. "Come with me."

We went out onto the deck and into the back yard. I led her to the fan-shaped patio I'd found the day Greg and I had refinished the floors.

"How come I never noticed this before?" Jill said.

"It was completely overgrown. See these shrubs?" I indicated the dozen foot-high mounds that curved along the outer edge of the fan. "These were almost over my head. I thought they were part of the wetland until I squeezed through and found the pavers and the statue. I've been pruning and pulling weeds like crazy."

It was true. In the lonely weeks since I'd stumbled upon what I was calling Adriana's garden it had become therapeutic for me to come out every night after work slathered with insect repellant and try to return the area to its original condition. I'd pruned the overgrown shrubs almost to the ground, trimmed the hedges and sprayed herbicide on the weeds and grasses growing between the pavers and around the statue. The previous few evenings I'd been raking up the now-dead vegetation.

"It's more of a patio than a garden," I said, "but don't you think it must be Adriana's garden?"

"For sure," Jill said. She headed for the clear focal point of the garden: a statue of a blue-robed woman standing on a cloud, arms spread, with golden rays emanating from her body. The figure was three feet tall and mounted on a concrete pedestal which itself was a foot high. "Our Lady of Guadalupe, right?"

I nodded. "I found this exact statue on the Web. She's kind of gaudy, but somehow she belongs here."

"Set designers would kill to have something like this," Jill said. "My teacher calls it authentic kitsch." Her gaze shifted from the statue to the surface of the patio. "Hey, check out the tiles."

She'd noticed what I considered the patio's most interesting feature. Although composed mostly of tan pavers, the patio floor was dotted in random fashion with an eclectic selection of tiles in various sizes and shapes.

We wandered around pointing out the more interesting ones. There were mosaic tiles, tiles made of thick glass, and colorful clay tiles that appeared to be hand-painted and fired. I assumed many were Latin American in origin. Others might have been from Europe and Asia.

"I'm guessing they picked them up on their travels," I said. I told Jill what Janet had told me about Henry and Adriana flying free on standby because Henry was an airline pilot. "When they returned from a trip they probably pried up the plain pavers and replaced them with their new finds."

Jill pointed the tip of her sandal at one of the larger tiles. It was slate gray and a foot square with a figure carved into its face. "This looks like Chinese writing."

"Yeah, I've come across four tiles like that. Each one is carved with a different character."

By then the mosquitos had found us so we hustled back to the house. I retrieved the keepsake box from the office shelf and placed it on the dining room table. While I heated canned soup and assembled a tossed salad topped with chunks of leftover chicken breast Jill rooted through the box.

After a while she said, "Okay, Carrie, here's the handwritten will I told you about." She came into the kitchen and waved a single sheet of white paper.

"What's it say?"

Jill read aloud. It was a simple will. Basically Henry had given all of his possessions to my aunt Cora.

"Now here's the part I told you about," Jill said. "Quote. 'The bounty of Adriana's garden belongs to the one who understands. Happiness is the key.' Unquote. Isn't that curious?"

I had her read it again. She wrote it on the back of an envelope and we pondered its meaning while we ate our dinner in the breakfast nook.

"The bounty of Adriana's garden," Jill mused. "What does he mean by bounty?"

I grabbed the dictionary I kept on the shelf above the hutch and opened it on the table between us. I found the word and scanned the definitions. "'Generosity, liberality, yield, especially of a crop.'"

I pictured the garden, which was mostly patio. "There's no real crop out there. Just that planting area around the statue."

Jill slid the dictionary closer to her. "How about this? 'A reward, a premium.' Maybe there's something valuable in the garden."

I scratched my head. "I don't know. Nothing strikes me as all that valuable, not in a monetary sense anyway."

"How about the tiles?" Jill suggested.

"Possibly. We'd have to do some research."

"Is the statue valuable?"

I shrugged. "According to the Internet resin statues like that are a dime a dozen. Unless there's a fortune sealed inside it."

Jill rejected that. "It doesn't seem like Henry would expect you to destroy the statue to discover the secret. Could the base be hollow?"

"I tried lifting it. It's solid concrete and weighs a ton."

"I wonder if it's more of a philosophical statement." Jill said. "What if the bounty of the garden *is* happiness. The garden itself makes you happy. Kind of a Zen thing, you know?"

"I do feel happy—well, content at least—when I'm out there." We ate in silence for a while.

"On the other hand," Jill said, "would Henry complicate the will just to make a philosophical statement?"

I laughed. "You're holding out for buried treasure, aren't you."

After dinner Jill and I sat across from each other at the dining room table extracting the contents of the box and spreading them out before us. In the photos, ticket stubs, menus and programs, one could reconstruct the blissful life of Henry and Adriana. Adriana was indeed beautiful and heartbreakingly young, too young to die. Henry was older, craggy faced and serious. In one of the few pictures where they appeared together they were posing before a fountain in what looked like the plaza of an old city. Henry towered over Adriana. He was staring straight into the camera, a protective arm around her shoulder. She was smiling up into his face.

"Not sure what she saw in him," I said, "but judging from her expression there was something she liked."

Jill unearthed another photo. "Aha, here's the garden."

She laid it on the table in front of me. It was a shot of the entire patio, probably taken just after it had been constructed. No special tiles interrupted the solid field of brown pavers. The shrubs were small and neatly spaced; they appeared fresh from the nursery. Adriana, wearing gardening gloves and holding a hand trowel, was on her knees planting flowers at the foot of the statue. Plastic flats of colorful blooms surrounded her.

"This is great," I said. "I'm going to plant the same flowers she did."

"Notice anything different about the statue?" Jill said.

I studied the photo. "She's not on her concrete pedestal. I wonder when that got added." My eye drifted to the photo's foreground. "There's the wrought iron bench I found in the garage. I was guessing it belonged on the patio."

"We could take it out there tomorrow morning," Jill said.

"Are you staying over?"

Jill gave me a shy smile. "Maybe...if you invite me. I brought some overnight stuff."

"You can be my first guest. Come look at the guest room. I fixed it up." I coaxed her out of her chair and we headed down the hall. "I bought a new mattress for the master bedroom and put the other mattress back in the guest room."

As we walked into the freshly appointed room I noticed that Jill was flushing to the roots of her tie-dyed hair.

"What?" I said.

"I have a confession to make. You know that time you went skiing up north?"

"And you had a key to the house?"

"Yep." She looked like the cat that swallowed the canary.

"Let me guess. You've already slept in this bed."

She plopped down on the mattress. "Technically speaking there was no sleeping involved."

I laughed. "No wonder you like it here."

She grinned. "Now that I've done it I like it anywhere."

"Who doesn't?"

"You won't tell my mom will you?"

I thought for a minute. "That's between the two of you. What I care about is that you're being careful."

Jill hesitated, then fixed me with her kohl-rimmed eyes and said, "Can I ask you something?"

"Maybe," I said, instantly wary. I had a feeling my nosy friend was about to enter forbidden territory.

"I know why you're so worried about me getting pregnant," Jill said. "My mom made me promise never to bring it up, but I know you got pregnant a few years ago. I thought now that we're friends you might want to talk about it."

"Why should I?"

"Why not? It's part of your life, Carrie. You had a baby and it died. Why keep it a deep dark secret? There's nothing to be ashamed of."

"You wouldn't say that if you knew the whole story."

"I'd like to know the whole story."

I shook my head. "I've never told anybody what happened."

"You can tell me."

My first instinct was to shut her out. I wasn't one to confide in other women. Only Kevin knew the shameful secret of that night in New London—what I'd said, what I'd done. But I looked at Jill sitting there on the bed, her eyes all big and sympathetic, and something stirred inside me. I took her hand and pulled her to her feet. "I'll tell you, but you probably won't like me when I'm finished."

I led the way to the family room and deposited Jill on the sofa along with a box of tissues. I grabbed a couple of Cokes from the refrigerator and set them on the coffee table. Then I sat down next to Jill, took a deep breath and started at the beginning. I told her about Kevin: how I'd had a crush on him growing up, how I'd encountered him as a sailor home on leave and lost my virginity to him a week later. I told her about the five-minute quickie that had gotten me pregnant.

"The irony is I'd been planning to break up with him that weekend. When my period didn't come I saw my whole future going down the drain. I didn't want to be a mother, but I couldn't bring myself to have an abortion. I knew I'd have to join Kevin in Connecticut eventually, but I kept postponing it. I was almost six months pregnant when I finally went with him. It was a miserable trip. We drove all day and got there late at night."

I closed my eyes and the memories flooded back with startling clarity. I saw the furnished apartment that Kevin had fixed up. I saw the crib he'd already bought and squeezed in beside the bed. I saw the brown teddy bear propped in one corner of the crib. It was wearing Kevin's baseball cap with the bill turned to the back.

"What happened then?" Jill prompted, and I realized I'd gone silent, lost in my own thoughts.

I swallowed hard and continued. "We were wiped out from all the driving, but we had sex anyway. Early the next morning I went into labor and Kevin rushed me to the hospital. They'd barely rolled me into the delivery room before the baby was born. I tried to sit up and look when it came out, but the nurse pushed me down onto the table and blocked my view. It was a boy. It lived eight hours. I never saw it even once."

Jill was listening with rapt attention. Tears glimmered in her eyes.

I told her about naming the baby, about the burial, how sad Kevin had been, how unmoved I'd felt. "After a couple of days I started wondering what I was doing in Connecticut. One morning I was talking to my mom on the phone and she asked if I wanted to come home and I said yes. Just like that I decided. I made a bus reservation, packed up my stuff and waited for Kevin to return from work."

I had reached the part of the story I'd never shared with anyone. I felt all quivery inside but I took a breath and plunged on. "As soon as Kevin came through the door he knew I was leaving. He was carrying a bag of groceries. He kind of threw the bag onto the kitchen table and it fell over. A jar of spaghetti sauce smashed onto the floor. We started to argue. He was trying to talk me into staying and I didn't want to. We got louder and louder. And then I said a terrible thing."

Jill's eyes were huge. "What did you say?"

I looked at Jill. This was the moment I'd been dreading. "I told him I was happy the baby died."

"Oh Carrie, you didn't," she breathed.

A sob welled up inside me. I pressed my fingers to my lips and gave a tiny nod. "I did. I said it." I squeezed my eyes shut and saw Kevin, white with anger, his fists clenched, broken glass and spaghetti sauce splashed across the floor. "We were yelling at each other. And I screamed it out. I yelled, 'I'm glad the baby died so I can get the fuck out of here.'"

Jill stared at me in horror.

Seeing her reaction opened the floodgates for me. "It's the worst thing I've ever done in my life. And I can't take it back. Oh, Jill, I hurt him so bad. If you could have seen how he looked at me. It was like all the love in the world had turned to pure hate."

I bent my head and wept. Jill put her arms around me and tipped her head to touch mine. I let her hold me until I'd cried myself out. She pressed a tissue into my hand and I blew my nose.

I took a tremulous breath and said, "You must hate me."

She didn't answer right away. Finally she gave me a frank look. "I can't pretend I'm not shocked. I hate what you said to

Kevin. But I don't hate you, Carrie. I feel sorry for you. For you and Kevin. And your baby."

I stifled a sob.

"Have you apologized to Kevin?"

"I haven't seen or talked to him since I left Connecticut. I don't know if I can face him."

"Do you ever think about your baby?"

I shook my head. "Until recently I never thought of it as a baby at all. At first it was just something growing inside me, something I had to deal with. Then after it was gone I looked at it as a sad episode in my life that I needed to forget. But this Mother's Day something happened. Do you remember it was a rainy, nasty day?"

"I remember."

"When I called my mom I was feeling homesick. I tried to keep it light but she picked up on my mood and said all the right things to make me feel better. Even though it was her day she was thinking of me. Annoyed as we can get with each other there's this bond between us that's stronger than the connection I have with anybody else. I guess that's what they mean by motherly love.

"Later that day when I took a package of ground beef out of the refrigerator to make dinner I noticed the weight on the label. It was just over a pound. That's how much the baby weighed when he was born. One pound, two ounces. I stood there at the sink holding that cold lump of meat, thinking, 'Oh my god, this was the size of my baby.' I tried to picture a little boy that small, with eyes, a nose and a mouth. With arms and legs...

"It's hard to imagine a human being so tiny. But somehow he lived for eight hours. For the first time ever I started thinking about his will to live...how he must have struggled..."

Tears rolled down my cheeks and dripped onto my lap. My voice had fallen to a whisper.

Jill leaned toward me straining to hear.

I forced myself to look directly into her eyes. "I wasn't there for him, Jill. I hardly thought about him during those eight hours while he was fighting for his life. I only thought about myself and what I wanted." I gulped back a sob. "It's so unfair. With all the love I've received from my mother over the years that little boy came and went from this world without ever being loved by his mother."

I stared down at my lap.

After a moment Jill covered my hand with hers. When I looked up her cheeks were shiny with tears. She said, "Maybe it's not too late to love him."

I nodded but I knew better. I'd already failed that test.

Jill's cell phone sounded, startling us both. Hastily wiping her eyes she stood and dug the phone out of her pocket. She cleared her throat. "It's Derek," she said, and started walking out of the room. I heard the murmur of her voice as she headed down the hall.

I leaned back and stared at the ceiling. The air in the room still trembled with the aftershocks of my revelations. I had just confessed my most heinous act and my friend had come close to forgiving me. I wondered if I'd ever forgive myself.

Jill returned and sat on the sofa. "How are you doing?"

"I'm okay. What did Derek want?"

"To come over." She dipped her head and looked contrite. "Since we're telling the truth tonight can I make another confession?"

I gestured. "Your turn."

"I had an ulterior motive when I came here this afternoon. I thought if I was staying overnight you might let Derek stay too."

"God, Jill, that sounds like something I would do." I couldn't help but smile. "So looking through the box was just an excuse to sleep with your boyfriend in my house?"

She wrinkled her nose. "Kind of. But I told him not to come."

"Why?"

"For one thing I never got around to asking you if it was okay, but besides that it didn't seem right after what you've been through tonight. You must be drained."

I thought for a minute. "I'm drained, but in a good way. It's like when you're sick and you just barfed your guts out. Then all of a sudden you're not sick anymore. You're completely emptied out and you feel so much better."

"Not to mention ten pounds lighter."

"That's how I feel, ten pounds lighter. Thanks to you."

She squeezed my hand. Then she held up her cell phone and gave me a pleading look.

I rolled my eyes. "Call him. Tell him the coast is clear. Your mom better not find out though. I'd be on her shit list for sure."

After rounding up extra towels and a toothbrush for Derek I said, "I'm going to give you guys your privacy. I'll grab some of those notebooks from the keepsake box and hide out in my bedroom. Just knock if you need anything."

I went into my room knowing a long night awaited me. Despite telling Jill I felt cleansed I'm not a person who can put herself through an emotional wringer then hop into bed and fall right to sleep. It had been a long time since I'd let myself think about Kevin. I hadn't seen him for almost three years. Where was he? What was he doing? Had he gotten over what I'd done to him? Just telling a friend about it didn't resolve the unfinished business between Kevin and me.

I heard Jill go to the front door and let Derek in. I heard the two of them talking but I couldn't make out what they were saying. Soon the house was silent; I assumed they'd gone to bed. If my guests were making love in the other room—was there any doubt?—they were being quiet about it. I reached for one of Henry's notebooks.

I woke the next morning to the sound of laughter. Jill and Derek were sitting at the table on the deck consuming celebratory bowls of cereal. They looked disgustingly sated.

When I joined them Jill and I told Derek about Henry's will and our hope of finding something valuable in Adriana's garden. After breakfast Jill used her cell phone to take pictures of the most promising patio tiles so she could research them on the Web.

Jill gave me a pointed look. "I'll have to do the research at my house since somebody I know doesn't have an Internet connection."

"Just think of all the money I'm saving," I said.

Derek shook his head. "What do you do for entertainment, Carrie?"

"Scrub grout in the bathroom. Doesn't everybody?"

Chapter 33

Sunday the ninth of August was one of those delicious fresh-washed mornings that often follows an overnight storm. I was sitting at the kitchen table eating breakfast in front of an open window. The previous day I'd hosted the annual neighborhood picnic in my yard. Every family on the street had shown up with lawn chairs, tables, games and tons of food. The weather had cooperated until the very end, when a sudden shower had sent folks hurrying home.

Before I'd volunteered to host the picnic I'd been debating about whether to renovate the kitchen on my own or hire a contractor to replace everything but the refrigerator, which was in good condition. There's nothing like a deadline to simplify a decision. I already knew what I wanted and the money was in the account. I hired a contractor and the new kitchen was installed a week before the party. The result was worth every penny I'd spent.

I sipped my coffee and gave myself a figurative pat on the back. I'd done so much of my own work on the house there was still money in the account Randy had set up. All the rooms were painted. I'd replaced all the woodwork in the rooms with varnished floors. I'd applied a fresh coat of exterior stain to the cedar siding and the yard was manicured to perfection. Aside from updating the bathrooms there wasn't a whole lot more to do.

I heard voices and looked out the window. Neighbors were wandering around in the back yard. Good thing I'd dressed for breakfast.

I spent much of Sunday morning visiting with my neighbors as they came to reclaim the lawn furniture they'd abandoned when the storm hit. Vic and Janet were the last to show up. It was almost noon so I asked them to stay for leftovers.

We sat on the deck eating pulled pork sandwiches and drinking draft beer, trying to empty the keg we'd purchased for the picnic. None of us made a habit of imbibing that early in the day, so we were feeling decadent and daring, swigging great gulps of the foamy brew from plastic cups. It wasn't long before Janet's nose and cheeks were pink.

She gazed into the back yard. "Carrie, everybody raved about the fantastic job you did restoring the patio. It looks so pretty with the flowers around the statue."

I'd planted the area around the base of the statue just as Adriana had planted it the first year, with waves of white and pastel petunias accented with golden poppies, bright blue delphiniums and purple spikes of astilbe. It had turned out well.

Vic scratched his head. "Considering that Henry had no idea what he was doing when he installed it, that patio's held up for quite a while."

"I think he built it the summer he married Adriana," Janet said.

"Probably," I said. "In the will he referred to it as Adriana's garden."

Vic looked surprised. "It was in the will?"

I put down my sandwich. "I'll show you." I went into the house and brought back a photocopy of the single sheet of paper Jill had found in the keepsake box.

Vic and Janet pored over it while they ate.

Vic shook his head. "Leave it to Henry to have a handwritten will."

"This part about Adriana's garden is fascinating," Janet said. "I wonder what it means."

"It means he didn't want Cora to have any claim on the patio," Vic said.

"Why is that?" I asked.

Janet said, "Do you remember the first day we were over here and you guessed we had some stories to tell about your aunt?"

I nodded. "You never did tell me any though."

"Well here's one, and it has to do with Adriana's garden." She sipped her beer and looked out at the garden. "Cora hated that statue. She tried to get rid of it I don't know how many times. Vic and I thought it was a joke at first. She'd haul it out to the curb on trash day and a little bit later we'd see Henry pick it up and haul it back. We thought they were playing a game. But then, maybe the fourth time this happened, Cora put the statue out on a day Henry wasn't home. The weather was warm and she planted herself in a lawn chair in front of the garage. She was in her bathrobe, smoking one cigarette after another and dropping the butts on the driveway. She sat there for the longest time, just waiting and watching for the garbage collector.

"Vic and I couldn't tear ourselves away from the front window. Then we heard the truck rumbling down the street, and there was that statue sitting on the curb. I was feeling kind of desperate, thinking we should intervene, when Henry pulls up in his car. He jumps out and snatches up the statue.

"Henry was not one to show his temper but you could tell he was angry. Cora shot up from her chair. She stood there with her hands on her hips, looking positively defiant. He ignored her and stomped to the back yard with the statue in his arms. All the while Cora's shrieking, 'It's hideous. I won't have it in this yard.'"

It wasn't a pretty picture Janet had painted and it made me ashamed of my aunt. My heart went out to Henry; he'd become dearer to me than Aunt Cora had ever been.

I remembered something. "I bet that's when he attached the statue to the concrete base." I told Vic and Janet about Henry's journals, the perusal of which had become a bedtime ritual for me. "He wrote almost every day. Sometimes it was just the date and the weather. Other times he'd add a few lines. An entry I read the other night said something like, 'Cemented the Lady to a chunk of concrete. She's not going anywhere.'"

Vic had gotten up to dispense another round of the too-warm beer. He stood at the railing and raised his cup. "And there she still stands."

I hoisted my cup. "Hail Mary."

Chapter 34

At the beginning of July I'd taken on my new role in sales support. My cubicle was located across from Lindsey's office and ten paces away from Brad and his sales team. The three of them—Brad, Eric and Sandy—spent a fair amount of time out of town. The same did not hold true for Michael. His computer duties, including his role as Web master for the company website, kept him at his desk five days a week.

Michael and I shared a wall. As I was getting settled that first day he'd poked his head around the corner to say hi. It had occurred to me that he might be sensitive about Lindsey's decision to have me develop marketing content for the website. Would he consider it a slap at his abilities?

His friendly welcome had dispelled that worry. He'd been eager to get started. With Lindsey's nod I'd begun my first day sitting beside Michael in front of his computer. We'd hit it off instantly. His skills and mine were complementary, with enough overlap where we could find common ground. Within a month we'd improved the website so dramatically we'd attracted the notice of the company brass. Lindsey and Brad couldn't stop congratulating each other for putting together such a winning combination.

Michael and I had been getting along so well I'd invited him to the neighborhood picnic. He'd turned me down though. Seems he'd acquired a girlfriend since I'd met him at Brad's cabin. Just as well, I rationalized. I can do without any more sexual complications at work.

I already had one major complication to contend with. Brad. The fact that I couldn't pass his office without experiencing a *frisson* of excitement told me I wasn't exactly over him. There was no way to avoid him since I sat in on most Sales and Marketing Department meetings. After a few weeks I was doing more than just sitting in. When Michael realized I articulated ideas as well as he did he encouraged me to do a fair amount of talking and presenting. By August I was contributing to the conversation like a member of the team, much as I had at P&G.

Brad scheduled regular staff meetings for Friday afternoons. At one such meeting he shared what for me was surprising but welcome news. It was late in the day toward the end of August. The five of us—Brad, Eric, Sandy, Michael and I—were sitting around a conference table. We'd wrapped up our business and were discussing our weekend plans.

I'd just told them about my cousin Randy, who was about to pay me a visit on Saturday, when Brad began slipping his papers into his briefcase. "We're throwing my brother an engagement party this evening," he said. "Marcy's idea, not mine."

Sandy grinned. "So nature boy's getting married."

"So it seems," Brad said.

"You sound skeptical," Eric said.

Brad shrugged. "The announcement came out of the blue. Greg's worked with this girl—Lisa—for three years but he's never brought her around to meet the family. The only way I know her at all is because Marcy and I ran into them once at a restaurant. I think the party's premature. I hope I'm wrong."

I hoped he was wrong too. I still felt awful about what had happened between Greg and me. More than once I'd been tempted to contact him to restate my apology. I had an excuse for calling because one of my hand pruners had gone missing. I was relatively sure he'd taken it with him to sharpen and had neglected to return it when he'd returned the other tools. I could have called him, but not anymore. Now that he was engaged the best thing for me to do would be to stay out of his life.

When I entered the house my gleaming hardwood floors made me sad. I never would have accomplished the job so fast or so well if it hadn't been for Greg. No doubt about it he was a prize catch. I hoped Brad was wrong and that Lisa had reeled him in for good.

I spent Friday evening preparing for my guests. Randy had scored a last-minute deal on a pair of round-trip tickets for himself and his realtor girlfriend Lori. They would arrive Saturday morning and leave on Tuesday afternoon.

I wanted to impress my cousin. I adored the place and couldn't picture myself moving out when my year was up. I hoped Randy would appreciate my efforts enough that he'd cut me a deal on buying it.

Then there was the matter of Adriana's garden. Jill had taken photos of the prettiest tiles and had been researching them on the Internet to see if any of them might be valuable. So far she'd found nothing. But if she did discover something of value she deserved to reap the benefits, not Aunt Cora. I needed to discuss the issue with Randy to be sure we were on the same page.

Early Saturday morning Randy and Lori pulled into the driveway in their rental car. The first thing Randy said when he stepped into the house was, "My god, Carrie, you're a miracle worker." He proceeded to exclaim over everything he saw as I led him and his girlfriend from room to room.

When we got to the master bedroom and I took them through the French doors onto the deck Randy threw an arm around his girlfriend's shoulder and squeezed. "What do you think, Lori? Is it ready to sell?"

"The house looks fantastic," she said. "I'm not familiar with the market up here but I'm guessing it'll sell fast."

"There's still stuff to do," I said. "The bathrooms need—"

Randy gave my arm a friendly jab. "Don't worry, cousin, I won't pull it out from under you, not without fair warning anyway. I do plan to get an appraisal while I'm here though, just so we have an idea what kind of money we're looking at."

From my own research I already knew we were looking at about two hundred grand, but I'd let him find that out for himself.

We crossed the deck and descended the steps into the back yard. I led them to the southwest corner. "This is Adriana's garden."

"What a lovely spot," Lori said.

My cousin wrinkled his brow. "What did Henry's will say about it?"

I recited from memory, "The bounty of Adriana's garden belongs to the one who understands. Happiness is the key."

Randy shook his head. "Inscrutable. Well, the probate judge decided to ignore it, so I guess we will too."

I didn't tell him Jill and I had been puzzling over the riddle for months. I'd save that discussion for later.

The Lundgrens were in their yard when we came around to the front of the house. I'd told them Randy was coming. With a wave I invited them across the street. Randy thanked them for keeping an eye on his mom and for taking care of the house once she left.

"Where's your mother living now?" Janet asked.

"She's with my sister Debbie and her family in Louisville." He hesitated a moment, then continued, "Mom's finally being treated for clinical depression. It's made a huge difference."

"Show them the picture you took," Lori said.

Randy produced his cell phone. "Lori and I drove to Louisville a month ago. I got a good picture of Mom." He pressed a few buttons and handed the phone to me. "Here she is with my sister's kids. She was happier than I've ever seen her."

I didn't even recognize my aunt. The pretty woman in the picture bore scant resemblance to the scary woman I remembered. She was sitting on a sofa with her arms wrapped around two little boys. The three of them were smiling into the camera.

I showed the picture to Vic, who did a double take. "I never noticed how much she resembles Adriana."

Janet took the phone and studied the photo. "They could have been sisters." She returned the phone to Randy. "What a nice picture. Give her our regards."

"What do you think of the house?" Vic asked Randy.

He and Lori both raved about what they'd seen.

"A lot of the credit goes to these two people," I said, gesturing toward Vic and Janet.

"We didn't do anything," Janet said.

"Are you kidding?" I pointed at the house. "*Your* flowers, *your* furniture, *your* advice. You helped resurrect the place."

"I have to tell you," Randy said, "when I took on the job of selling the house for my mom, my goal was to fix it up halfway decent and unload it as soon as possible. Now, though, with the improvements you've all made? If I lived closer I'd buy it myself."

The rest of the weekend I played tour guide for Randy and Lisa. On Monday I went to work and returned home to a gourmet dinner prepared by my guests. Over dinner Randy told me about the estimate he'd gotten on the house. It matched what I already knew.

It was time for me to lay my cards on the table. As we were eating our dessert I said, "I'd like to buy the house. I have a good job and a fair amount in savings. I'm pretty sure I'd qualify for a loan. I was thinking since you wouldn't need to hire a realtor maybe you could give me a good deal on it."

Randy waggled a finger at Lori. "You told me she had this up her sleeve."

"Educated guess," Lori said, and gave me a wink.

Randy looked doubtful. "I don't know, Carrie. Don't your parents expect you home by the end of the year? Your mother will kill me if I sell you the house."

"They won't be completely surprised," I said. "I started dropping hints when I got the promotion in July. They know how much I love it here."

Randy thought for a moment then said, "Okay, Carrie, we'll consider it when the time comes. Let's give it a couple more months. You need to make sure it's what you want."

Lori offered to clean up in the kitchen while Randy and I took a last walk around the yard. As we wandered onto the patio I brought up the matter of the will. "I realize the judge decided to ignore the part about Adriana's garden," I said, "but what does that mean? What if there *is* something valuable in the garden? Who would it belong to?"

"What's the will say again?"

I repeated the words from the will.

"Then it belongs to the one who understands," Randy said. "If you're worried about my mother, I know she wouldn't consider making a claim on it. Now that she's feeling better, she admits coming here was a mistake."

"Why *did* she come?"

Randy wagged his head. "There's no logical explanation. From what I can gather, Henry showed up at the bingo parlor where my mom went every Thursday night. He sat down next to her and offered to take her to a place where she could play bingo seven days a week. He might have been making it up, but that's what he told her."

"He was probably talking about the casino at Mystic Lake. They have lots of bingo."

Randy shrugged. "I don't think she ever made it to the casino. I only know she left with him that night without telling anyone. Lucky for her he was a decent guy."

"Just lonely and unhappy," I said.

"Which didn't change after Mom came here. She and Henry didn't hit it off. They slept in separate bedrooms. In the four years they lived together, they were never intimate. Out of the goodness of his heart, or maybe just inertia, he didn't send her back. Now that she feels better she thinks he was generous to give her the house and the car and what he had in savings when he died. She doesn't want anything more out of him."

Tuesday morning when we hugged goodbye Randy said, "I'll have Mom write a letter relinquishing all claim to the garden. If you do find something don't even tell us."

I laughed, thinking he was joking, but he took me by the shoulders and said, "I'm serious. Don't tell us and don't feel guilty about it. Just enjoy it, Carrie. You deserve it."

It's Jill who deserves it, I thought, as I drove to work. She's the persistent one.

As if to prove me correct, when I arrived home that after-noon Jill's car was in the driveway. I let myself into the house and headed for the kitchen. Through the window I spotted my friend on the patio staring down and taking photos with her cell phone.

I walked out to join her. "Still at it, huh?"

"I researched the tiles I thought were the most likely to be valuable. They were worth zilch so I'm moving on to the other ones. Did you have a nice visit with your cousin?"

"It was great. I talked to him about buying the house."

Jill squealed. "That's awesome. What did he say?"

"He likes the idea. I just have to be sure it's what I want."

Jill snapped another picture. "This place is perfect for you, Carrie."

"I know. I'll mull it over for a month or so for Randy's sake but I'm going to buy it. I can't imagine what could happen that would change my mind."

Chapter 35

TrueMark was branching out. The company that had made its reputation shipping and scoring standardized tests developed by other companies was in the process of creating its own testing materials for state boards of education to use in their assessment programs. This venture was a cut above anything they'd ever done before.

Writing test questions that accurately measure the knowledge and ability of the student population of an entire state is no easy task. It requires the expertise of people trained in a field of study called psychometrics. TrueMark had assembled a team of psychometricians who worked off-site. They'd been at it for a couple of years and were on the cusp of launching their first product.

In order for Sales and Marketing to promote the new service in an effective way we had to know more about it. Accordingly, Brad had scheduled a training session to take the place of our regularly scheduled staff meeting.

It was the last Friday in September. When Sandy, Eric, Michael and I entered the conference room Brad was already sitting at the table talking with a woman I hadn't met before.

She was gorgeous, and she was looking at Brad like he was a god. I was instantly jealous.

Her name was Danielle and she headed TrueMark's department of psychometrics. The title was impressive for someone so young, but my animus toward her was too virulent to give her much credit. I sat through the entire training session picturing Danielle making a move on Brad, and Brad succumbing to her charms. I imagined them taking a business trip together. When I pictured him spending the night in her room it felt like someone was plunging an icy hand into my chest and squeezing my heart.

I seethed most of the way home. Four months had passed since that day on the playground when I'd told Brad I needed to take my life back. I'd tried. I'd dated other men. I'd even attempted to get something going with Michael. Nothing had worked. I still thought of Brad a hundred times a day; I still longed for him every Saturday morning. My irrational pique over Danielle proved just how far I was from getting over him.

I was almost home, idling at a stoplight, when I admitted defeat. Either I needed to rekindle the affair or—

Or what?

All of a sudden I knew the answer.

The light changed. I drove the next few blocks trying to banish the thought. You can't un-think a thought however, especially when it makes sense. And this one made perfect sense.

If I truly wanted to take my life back I had to leave, not just my job, but Minnesota.

When I got home I called Randy and told him I'd changed my mind about buying the house. I said I'd have it ready to sell in another month.

The next morning I went out to mow the lawn for the final time.

Chapter 36

I felt my phone vibrating. I stopped the mower and dug it out from the pocket of my jeans. The name on the caller ID set loose a swarm of butterflies in my stomach. It was Greg Collins. I answered, not knowing how to act or what to expect.

Sounding nervous he identified himself and asked if I was missing a pruner.

"Does it have green handles?" I said.

"Yeah. I just found it in my truck. I apologize."

"No big deal," I said. "I've been using the orange one."

"You're kidding. That's not even a bypass pruner. I'd be surprised if you can cut butter with that thing."

"Oh, it's supposed to cut? I've been gnawing stuff to death with it."

Greg guffawed. For an unguarded second he sounded like the old Greg. Then he cleared his throat. "I'll drop it off this morning. Are you at home?"

I hesitated, wary about seeing him again. Why would either one of us want to dredge up painful memories? On the other hand it might be an opportunity to clear the air. Now that he was engaged maybe we could put the bad feelings behind us.

When I told him I was out back mowing the lawn he said, "I'll be there in ten minutes," and disconnected before I had a chance to reply.

I abandoned the mower and went inside to comb my hair and put on a clean T-shirt.

I was on the front stoop when Greg's car pulled into the driveway. He climbed out and came up the sidewalk. He'd lost weight. He was clean-shaven and his ponytail was gone; he was wearing his hair more like Brad's. I guessed Lisa was getting him in shape for the wedding. He looked good.

Greg handed me the pruner. "Better late than never I guess."

I turned the tool over in my hands. "Thanks." I didn't know what else to say. I'd already decided not to invite him in, where the first thing we would encounter would be the hardwood floors he'd helped me refinish.

We stood there for what seemed like an eternity. Greg made no move to leave.

I clicked the jaws of the pruner open and shut several times. "Looks nice and sharp."

"You should try it. Got anything to prune?"

I led the way to the back yard and clipped a twig from the first shrub I encountered. Holding it up to show Greg I said, "So this is how a pruner works."

What a relief to see him smile. He had a great smile; it lit his face.

"How about if I make it up to you?" he said. "Will you be using your chainsaw in the next two weeks?"

"Not bloody likely."

"I have a nifty new gadget for sharpening chainsaws up at the cabin. I'm going up there later today. I'll sharpen the chain and return it when I get back in a week or two."

I shook my head. "Thanks, but I won't be using it again."

"I thought you wanted to thin out those trees." He pointed at the grove of scruffy-looking box elders in the southeast corner of the yard. "I could give you a hand."

"I'm not going to mess with it. I'll let the next people decide what they want to do."

"What next people?"

"Whoever buys the house. My cousin's planning to sell it soon."

Greg looked like someone had socked him in the stomach. "Already?"

I forced a shrug. "That was the agreement. I'd fix it up and Randy would sell it."

"But you love this house. You belong here."

I started snipping branches off a poor, defenseless spirea growing next to the deck. "I'm ready to move on."

"Where will you go?"

"I'll find something." I wasn't about to tell him I was leaving town; nobody knew that yet.

"What if I bought the house—as an investment," Greg said. "We could work out a rent-to-own arrangement."

The kindness of this sweet, impulsive man was bringing me to tears. I set the pruner on the deck railing and turned to face him. For the first time that morning I looked into his eyes. What I saw there gave me pause. He might have been engaged to marry Lisa but his eyes told me what would happen if I took even one step in his direction.

I edged away. "I should finish mowing."

I could feel Greg watching me as I walked across the yard to where I'd left the mower.

"Okay if I take the chainsaw?" Greg called. "I might as well sharpen it."

I gave a dismissive wave. "Whatever." I bent down and started the mower.

I received another call that day. This one lifted my spirits. It was from my mother.

"Are you sitting down?" she asked.

I was on my knees in Adriana's garden clearing out the petunias from around the foot of the statue. We'd had a killing frost earlier in the week and the annuals were shot.

I sat back on my haunches. "I am now."

"Carrie, I won the contest. My quilt took first place."

"Oh my god, that is so great."

She went on to tell me she would be the guest of honor at an award ceremony at the history center on the opening night of the exhibit.

"I bet you'll be in the newspaper."

She laughed. "If I am we'll send you the clipping."

As it turned out no one needed to send me the clipping because I was there.

Chapter 37

I decided to postpone giving my notice at work until the house was ready to be placed on the market. I wasn't sure what I'd do next. I guessed I would move back home and live with my parents. Beyond that my plans were murky.

It's remarkably easy to hide one's private turmoil from coworkers. If you do your job and pretend to be interested and enthusiastic no one gives you a second look.

Following our training in the science of psychometrics Michael and I set about developing Web material to highlight TrueMark's test development services. In the process I found myself consulting with Danielle, the psychometrician who had incurred my wrath. She turned out to be approachable and informative. I still hated her.

After Danielle and her test development staff approved our work Michael and I showed Brad and Lindsey the Web pages we'd created. Having received their blessing the final step before we put it online was to present the proposed pages to the company president and the board of directors.

The presentation was scheduled for the second Friday in October. Instead of addressing a handful of colleagues in a minuscule conference room we'd be presenting our work to a dozen decision-makers—including top execs and the board of directors—in the much larger boardroom.

The presentation was set for the end of the day. The plan was for me to lead the presentation until the question and answer session, where Michael always shined. Brad introduced us and we were off and running. Michael cued the images and I found all the right words to go with them. The Q&A was lively and enthusiastic. Although the board would hold off giving the go-ahead until they voted in closed session it was clear they loved what they saw.

Michael and I practically hugged each other when we got out of there. We were standing in the hall just outside the closed door of the conference room.

"We were awesome," Michael whispered.

"I have to pee," I whispered back.

"Me too," Michael said.

We headed to our respective restrooms, then met back in Michael's cubicle. His face was alight, which I supposed was the black man's equivalent of flushing. I should be so lucky. I had just seen my face in the mirror; it was as pink as a ripe peach.

It was nearly five o'clock. Eric and Sandy had gone for the day and Brad and Lindsey were still in the meeting. Michael and I had just started rehashing our greatest moments when out of my mouth came the words, "You want to go have a drink or something?"

Michael looked pained. "I'm taking care of my landlord's dog this weekend. I need to let it out. I'm sorry—"

I held up a hand. "Say no more. I should probably go home too." For what reason, I didn't know.

Feeling foolish I excused myself and went back to my cubicle to gather my things. This was the second time Michael had turned down an invitation from me. I hadn't been asking him for a date, but he must have interpreted it that way.

We left the building together. Michael turned his face to the sun, which was still a good distance above the horizon. "Wow, what a day."

Our cars were parked a few spaces away from each other in the nearly vacant lot. I had just opened my door when Michael called, "Hey, Carrie, how about going with me to the Dakota tonight."

"Really?" What about your girlfriend, I wanted to say, but I didn't.

"Yeah, the Scott Miller trio goes on at nine. I could pick you up."

"That's out of your way," I said. "Why don't I drive to your place and we'll go together from there?"

He loped to my car. I scrounged a slip of paper and a pen from my purse and he drew me a map to his apartment in Minneapolis. He talked me through the directions and suggested I get there at half past eight. He sounded pleased, from which I concluded he really did have a dog that needed letting out.

At home I changed my clothes and went outside to rake leaves. An hour later I was standing in front of the open refrigerator deciding what to have for supper when the doorbell rang. I cringed. What neighbor kid is selling magazine subscriptions this time? I headed for the front of the house rehearsing a friendly but firm "no thanks."

When I opened the door Brad was standing on the stoop. He held up a plastic sack bearing the name of a Chinese restaurant. "Pity a poor bachelor?"

My planned response stuck in my throat. Ignoring the alarm bells going off in my head I stood back and ushered him in. "Since when are you a bachelor?"

"Since about an hour ago. Marcy's at a trade show in Chicago and won't be home until tomorrow afternoon. Chip's staying overnight with Greg."

I took the sack from him and headed for the kitchen. Brad followed me.

"I thought you were going pheasant hunting with some people from work," I said.

"That was the plan. But I think I might be coming down with something. Cough, cough. So I cancelled."

"Poor you."

He grinned. "Lucky pheasant."

I put the sack on the counter and extracted two grease-stained paper bags. "You haven't lost your appetite."

I was reaching into the cupboard for plates when Brad stopped my hand. He turned me toward him. "I couldn't take my eyes off you this afternoon, Carrie."

Trapped between Brad and the counter I pretended to weigh my options, but in truth it was already too late. My carefully constructed argument against the reunion of Brad and Carrie had collapsed like a house of cards the minute I'd spotted him on the doorstep. His arms slipped around my waist and his lips found mine. Like the magnets on my refrigerator our bodies snapped together, opposite poles aligned.

I led him down the hall to my bedroom and closed the door. With exquisite care we undressed each other. Our clothes slithered down around our feet. I removed Brad's watch and dropped it onto the pile; for once we would not be governed by the clock.

When my bikini briefs were the only item of clothing that hadn't found its way to the floor Brad scooped me into his arms and placed me on the bed. He sat beside me and fanned out my hair on the pillow. The late afternoon sun slanted across the room, burnishing our bodies in amber.

Brad's fingertips circled my breasts, coaxed my nipples and scampered across my stomach. In tantalizing slow motion he eased my panties over my hips, down my thighs and calves, and over my feet. His tongue trailed up between my legs. I closed my eyes and gave myself over to pure pleasure.

When I could hold out no longer I tugged him on top of me. I watched his face and he watched mine. His expression said, "I'm giving you this...and this...and this...and this..."

Even as the passion built he held my gaze. When at last his eyes lost their focus and I arched my back and cried out he responded with a deep thrust. I clamped my legs around his thighs and ground myself against him. I needed him to touch the deepest part of me. When he did I sobbed.

"You look like an angel when you make love," Brad said. He was lying beside me, his head propped on one hand.

I touched his lips with a forefinger. "How do angels look when they make love?"

"Their smiles are unearthly. They're lit by inner joy."

"Do angels cry when they come?"

He laughed. "They do now."

"I hope it wasn't too weird."

"It was a privilege. I felt like I touched your soul." Brad splayed his fingers on my chest. "Did I touch your soul, Carrie?"

I swallowed hard and nodded.

"Kiss me," Brad said.

What a post-coital kiss lacks in passion it makes up for in unguarded affection. When I kissed Brad that afternoon I came as close to saying I love you as I had ever dared go. I felt him respond with what could have passed for love, but I didn't presume to make that leap. He was someone else's husband after all.

Although my tears had dried, my unexpected sobs still echoed in the air and tinged the moment with melancholy. We clung to each other until the room began to darken.

I reheated our chicken teriyaki and fried rice in the microwave. We ate at the kitchen table and discussed the afternoon's presentation.

"You're a natural up there," Brad said. "You're poised and self-assured. You covered all the bases and answered every question without hesitation."

"Michael was good too, don't you think?"

"He doesn't have your rapport with an audience, but he knows his stuff. You make a great team."

It was nearly seven-thirty when we finished eating. I'd intended to leave the house by eight.

"You're fidgety," Brad said.

I was rinsing dishes at the kitchen sink. "I have plans for tonight."

He came up behind me and wrapped his arms around my waist. "But you don't want to go."

"I don't know what to do. I promised to meet some people at the Dakota."

"That's where Michael's going tonight."

"I know."

Brad moved away and leaned against the counter so he could see my face. "So—you and Michael. I didn't think he was your type."

"What is my type?"

"Me."

"Maybe I like more than one type of man."

"Explain."

"Okay, you're the star quarterback all the girls are hot for. Michael's the captain of the debate team. I like that too."

"Hey, I was captain of my debate team," Brad said.

I sighed. "You probably won every debate."

"Am I winning this one?"

I dried my hands and pointed at my cell phone, lying on the counter at Brad's elbow. He handed it to me and I scanned the directory for Michael's number. I wasn't looking forward to making the call. Turning my back on Brad I walked into the dining room and pressed send.

When Michael answered I fed him a lame excuse about a prior engagement that had slipped my mind. While I was talking Brad came up behind me and attempted to fondle my breasts. I fended him off. "Let's do something next weekend," I told Michael.

"Sure," he said, without conviction.

I clicked off as quickly as I could without seeming rude. Still standing with my back to Brad I gave his hands free reign.

"It's hard to concentrate when you do that," I said. "How would you like me to play with your private parts when you're trying to concentrate?"

"I'd hate it. But go ahead, I deserve it."

I laughed. "First things first. How about pulling your car into the garage? I'll open the garage door."

He headed for the living room, slipped into his shoes and found his keys in his jacket pocket. He started out the front door, but came right back in. "Four of your neighbors are having a gabfest across the street. Should we wait?"

"Probably," I said. "Let's watch a movie. I borrowed some DVDs from the library."

As we entered the family room Brad looked around and said, "I feel right at home here."

I made a mental calculation. "Not counting today you've probably spent less than twelve hours in this house."

"I'll double that tonight if you want me to stay," he said.

I stood on my tiptoes and kissed him. "Now that I've blown my other plans don't even think of leaving."

Brad stiffened and held me at arm's length. "If it wasn't me here tonight would it have been Michael?"

"No, we're just friends."

"Good. Or I might have to kill him."

"Please don't let this change the way you treat him," I said.

Brad chucked me under the chin. "I shouldn't have said anything. Just do me a favor. Don't mess him up as bad as you did me."

"You're not messed up."

"You're wrong about that, Carrie. Tonight's a prime example. Usually when somebody tells me to get lost I get lost. When you told me to get lost I came back—on my knees—with Chinese."

"You knew I couldn't turn you away."

"I did not know that. You turned me away that time on the playground. How could I know you wouldn't turn me away this time too?"

"And waste all that fried rice?"

He cupped my face in his hands. "I'm serious, little girl. Please don't send me away again." He put his arms around me and held me in an embrace so tender it made my heart ache.

I love you was on the tip of my tongue, but I managed not to say it.

Brad kissed the top of my head. "Let's watch a movie."

It was after ten on Saturday morning. I was making break-fast when Brad came into the kitchen and said, "Guess what's sitting in your driveway?"

I cringed. "Your car. Do you still want to pull it into the garage?"

"Too late now. I should leave after breakfast anyway. This hunting trip wasn't supposed to last very long. I told my brother I'd get Chip by noon at the latest." He poured himself a cup of coffee. "Not that Greg has anything better to do."

"What do you mean?"

"Oh that's right. You didn't hear the news. Greg broke off his engagement."

The fried egg I was turning slipped off the spatula, breaking the yolk and splattering butter across the cook top.

"What happened?" I asked.

"All I know is he went up to the cabin with Lisa and when he returned he was no longer engaged."

I was gripped by a sense of unease. "When did he get back?"

"Yesterday." Brad shrugged. "The whole engagement thing never felt right to me anyway. I don't know what was going on with him, but it sure wasn't love. Marcy will have a fit when she finds out. She threw that big party—"

He broke off abruptly and popped up the lever on the toaster. Black smoke was rising out of the slots. "Ah, burnt toast. My favorite."

I do my best thinking while performing physical labor. As soon as Brad left—with a promise to return the next Saturday—I went outside and started raking leaves. While I worked I turned things over in my mind. Just because Greg was no longer engaged to Lisa did it have anything to do with me?

Recalling how he'd looked at me the day he'd returned the pruner I knew the answer. He thought he had a chance with me. Whatever I said or did was going to hurt him. Again.

Before the day was over I expected Greg would return the chainsaw. When he did, I'd tell him about Dylan, a guy I'd met planting oak saplings one Saturday with an environmental group. That part was true. What I wouldn't tell him is that I'd dated the excessively earnest Dylan one time and he'd made my eyes glaze over. Instead I'd tell Greg we'd hit it off so well I was planning to move in with him. That should ensure Greg would never again show up at my house.

By two o'clock I'd raked and bagged the leaves in the front yard. I had just cleared the dead hosta leaves from around the front porch stoop and was about to pile them into the wheelbarrow when I remembered it was my dad's birthday.

I dropped my work gloves into the wheelbarrow and pulled my cell phone from my pocket. I sat on the stoop and started punching in my parents' phone number. Hearing the sound of a car slowing down I looked up. Greg was turning into the driveway.

I clicked off my phone and waved, but Greg didn't respond. He got out of his car, went to the trunk and pulled out the chainsaw. Without casting so much as a glance my way he carried it to the garage. I was beginning to think he hadn't noticed me sitting there when he emerged from the garage and headed toward me up the sidewalk. He was unsmiling. "I returned your saw. It's sharpened." His voice was cold.

I pocketed my cell phone and patted the concrete beside me. "Have a seat."

He stayed where he was. "I'd rather go inside."

With a sense of dread I got up and led him into the house through the garage. While I removed my shoes in the laundry room Greg walked toward the kitchen.

I found him staring out the window over the sink. His back was rigid, his profile steely. I stood facing him in the narrow kitchen. With the refrigerator on my right and the microwave oven on my left I felt hemmed in.

Greg turned and fixed me with a look that chilled me to the bone. "I came by here this morning to return the chainsaw. My brother's car was in the driveway."

I sucked in a breath. "He was just...he was picking up some work I did for him." It sounded feeble and I knew it. It didn't matter anyway; the heat rising in my face gave me away.

"You've been screwing him all along haven't you."

"He's never been here before. I swear nothing happened."

"Bullshit. Fixing up this house was just an excuse. You followed my brother here for one reason. These floors? The shrubs? The yard? You didn't care about any of it. You just wanted a place to—"

He clamped his mouth shut and stared at me with such intensity I couldn't help but flinch. Huffing out a breath he stalked toward me, gripped my chin in his hand and forced me to look at him. He said, "Tell me, Carrie, were you doing us both at the same time?"

"No," I whimpered. My lower lip had started to tremble. I clenched my teeth to bite back a sob.

For a long moment he held my gaze. Then he released my chin and said, "Chip was in the car with me this morning."

My hands flew to my mouth. I felt the color drain from my face. "What did he say when he saw Brad's car? What did you tell him?"

Greg watched me squirm. Finally he said, "You got lucky. He didn't know we were coming here. He was in the back seat playing a video game. When I spotted Brad's car, I drove on by. He didn't see anything."

Relief flooded over me. "Thank god."

Greg's laugh was mirthless. "You think god is watching over you? You think he'll fix things when you fuck up? Well he isn't and he won't."

His eyes wandered past me to the refrigerator. His jaw tightened and he reached over my shoulder, snatched the YOU and ME magnets off the door and shoved them in my face. When I cowered he muttered "fuck" and slammed them onto the counter.

"This shit's got to stop right now," Greg said. "Brad's coming to my place after Marcy gets home. I'm going to tell him what I know. He needs to realize how close he came to blowing everything."

"You won't tell him about us will you?"

His single bark of laughter cut like a knife. "You couldn't bear to have him know about our little episode could you? Don't worry. Your dirty secret is safe with me. I'm not proud of it either."

He narrowed his eyes. "Don't try to contact my brother. If you want to talk you call me. Understand?"

I nodded, too numb to speak.

"I'll be in touch," he said. He pushed past me and stormed out of the house.

Like a cripple I hobbled into the breakfast nook, sat on the edge of a kitchen chair and clamped my hands between my thighs to keep them from shaking. I pictured Brad getting the news. Did I dare call his house to warn him? What if his wife was already home? What if she answered? We'd been so careful until now; I couldn't risk another blunder. Brad would have to fend for himself.

Brad. A sudden vision of him leaning over me, lifting a tendril of hair from my face and smoothing it onto the pillow nearly brought me to my knees. I buried my head in my hands, but I was too scared to cry. I drew a ragged breath, got up from the chair and dragged myself outside to finish my yard work. I piled the hosta leaves in the wheelbarrow and rolled them to the back-yard compost pile. I put away the wheelbarrow, rake and gloves and went into the house.

I still hadn't called my dad. I took my cell phone into the bathroom and stood smiling into the mirror while I dialed. It was a phony smile but I hoped it would make me sound upbeat.

Dad answered and I went into my happy birthday routine. He thanked me for the card and the birthday check I'd sent. "Dinner's on you tonight, Carrie."

"You must be going to McDonalds."

Dad laughed. "We'll supplement it a bit."

We talked a while longer. Before we hung up my mom took the phone. "I only have a minute," she said. "Katie and the girls are stopping by to see Grandpa before we go out. But I wanted to tell you, Katie helped me find the prettiest dress for the award ceremony Monday night."

"What's it like?" I tried to sound enthusiastic but my mom must have heard something in my voice because she changed her tone and said, "Carrie, what's wrong?"

How long do umbilical cords stretch? Even from eight hundred miles away the maternal connection was so strong I couldn't resist its tug. I wanted to tell my mother everything and have her make it all better.

"Mom, remember when you warned me about people get-ting hurt?"

"Oh, Carrie, no..."

I held onto the phone for dear life and saw my reflection in the mirror turn watery. "I'm hurt, Mom. It's really bad. I love him so much and now I can never be with him again."

I'd started blubbering. My mother had the grace to be quiet and wait. I plucked a tissue from the box on the counter and blew my nose.

In a small voice I said, "And I hurt someone else."

I heard a sharp intake of breath. "Not his wife."

"No, thank god." I sniffed and dabbed at my eyes. "But his brother found out. He cared about me and I hurt him."

"Do you want to tell me what happened?"

"Won't Katie be there any minute?"

"She can visit with Dad."

"Mom, don't tell Katie."

"I won't, honey. Oh, here they come. They're just pulling into the driveway."

"You should go then. I'll call you tomorrow."

"Are you going to be all right?"

"What is all right, Mom? I don't think I'll ever be all right."

"Carrie, come home. We'll work it out together."

Greg called late in the afternoon to tell me Brad had agreed never to see me again. I wanted details but Greg informed me his brother wasn't my business anymore.

"What will you do now?" he asked. It wasn't out of concern for me that he was asking. He wanted me out of Brad's life. When I told him I was returning to Cincinnati he said, "Good. Maybe you can get rehired at Procter & Gamble."

That's when I hung up on him. I didn't want him to hear me cry.

Chapter 38

Just after midnight I was startled out of a troubled sleep by the ringing of my cell phone. *Brad*, I thought, and grabbed the phone off the nightstand.

"Hello," I said, breathless and disoriented.

The caller identified herself as Katie, but the voice was all wrong.

I was instantly alert, seized by a sense of dread. I sat up and pushed the hair out of my eyes.

"Carrie, I have bad news. Mom..." She faltered. "Mom had a heart attack."

"What do you mean?" I heard the panic in my own voice. "I was talking to her this afternoon. She was fine."

"It was a massive heart attack," Katie said and started to cry. "She didn't make it, Carrie."

"You're lying," I screamed into the phone, furious at this person who claimed to be my sister. "You can't be right. I just talked to her. We weren't finished."

Katie didn't answer. I heard her sobbing.

My brother came on the line. "I was there when it happened," he said. "I stopped at the house after Mom and Dad got back from dinner. It was still early but Mom was tired and went to bed. Dad and I were watching the news when she came into the room clutching her chest. Dad jumped up and went to call 9-1-1. Her knees started to buckle. I caught her and she collapsed onto the floor. She was in my arms. She looked at me and said, 'It's all right.' That's all she said and then she was gone."

"Oh god," I moaned.

"They took her to the hospital in the ambulance, but it was too late."

"Where's Dad?"

"We're both here at Katie's. We're going to stay overnight."

"I'll fly down tomorrow," I said.

When I arrived in Cincinnati, Dad and Tommy met me at the airport and we cried in each other's arms. The three of us spent the afternoon at Katie and Dean's house. Being reunited with my family again under those circumstances was surreal. One minute I'd be chattering with Megan and Becca, who couldn't quite take in the gravity of the situation. The next minute I'd be sitting on the sofa with my dad, the two of us staring into the void created by my mother's absence. I had never in my life felt so hollowed out.

After dinner Tommy drove Dad and me home. I moved back into my old bedroom.

The word bereft could have been coined to describe my dad. Sunday night into the wee hours I heard him shuffling from room to room in the darkened house. The next morning he sat bleary-eyed at the kitchen table. Although he knew Tommy was taking us to the funeral home to make arrangements for Wednesday morning's funeral I had to keep reminding him to get ready. Over and over Dad repeated the story my brother had told me about Mom's last moments.

On our way to the funeral home Dad told the story again. This time he looked at Tommy and asked, "What was it she told you?"

"She told me, 'It's all right.'"

"It's all right," Dad repeated.

When we returned home I gave Dad some lunch and persuaded him to lie down. I closed his bedroom door and went in search of my mother's new dress. At the funeral home Katie had suggested Mom be laid out in the dress they'd purchased for the award ceremony. I'd agreed to deliver it to the funeral home later in the day, but I hadn't found it in her closet. That left just a few other places it could be.

It was mid-October and the house was full of Mom. The place smelled of cinnamon and ginger from the cookies and breads she always baked in the fall. Just inside the kitchen door was a wicker basket she'd filled with dried leaves and bittersweet collected from the yard. An artfully arranged tumble of gourds and squash spilled across a living room table. A big orange pumpkin squatted on the front stoop.

Mom had been working on a quilt. Her basement sewing room was full of pieced and stacked swatches of fabric in shades of moss green and brown. These were my colors. I picked up one of the finished squares and crushed it to my chest.

My father, obviously unable to sleep, came up behind me and squeezed my shoulders. "She was making this for you."

"Will you keep it for me, Dad? I want to see if I can finish it somehow."

"It'll be right here." He walked to a garment rack that stood against the wall near the ironing board. "Here's the dress she was going to wear tonight."

I looked at it and swallowed hard. It was lovely.

Monday evening Tommy drove Dad and me to the award ceremony at the history center. Katie, Dean and my nieces were already there when we arrived.

I cried when I saw the quilt.

We walked into the exhibition hall and there it was: my mother's quilt, expertly displayed and hanging in the company of quilts that represented three centuries of women's labor. Mom's quilt was stunning, a work of art, an impressionist painting in cloth. To think my mother had made it took my breath away. If I ever became an actor and needed to cry on cue, the thought of my mother crafting that quilt would bring me to tears. Knowing she would not be there to see it or to receive the accolades she deserved would make me weep.

I had informed the award committee of our tragic news. Out of respect for us they'd temporarily closed off the hall to visitors. When we'd arrived they'd ushered us into the room and left us alone. After we'd regained our composure they seated us in the front row and opened the doors to the media and other invited guests.

The family had elected me to accept the award. When my mother's name was announced I walked on unsteady legs to the podium. My hands shook as I received a check and a framed certificate. To my relief I didn't have to speak. Later however the reporters covering the event wanted to interview the family. Because it was a school night Katie and her family had left as soon as the ceremony was over. My dad didn't want to be interviewed and my shy brother had made himself scarce. Thus it fell to me to handle the press.

I liked the newspaper reporter. She was sympathetic and asked good questions. She engaged me so thoroughly I barely noticed the photographer clicking away.

Tuesday morning a color photograph of my mother's quilt appeared on the front page of the Cincinnati *Enquirer's* Community Section. A smaller photo of me accompanied a thoughtful and mostly accurate story. My father stared at the photo of the quilt. He must have read the story five times.

All day Tuesday Dad and I took phone calls and received a steady stream of visitors bearing gifts of food. The florist delivered a bouquet of fall blooms sent by the Weikels. I put the flowers on the kitchen table where we could see them at every meal. Sharon called after dinner. She and Dad talked for twenty minutes. When he hung up he was wiping his eyes.

The two of us spent Tuesday evening alone. The funeral was the next morning. Neither Dad nor I felt like going to bed. From a shelf in his bedroom closet he took down a shoebox full of letters that Mom had forbidden us kids ever to read. We sat at the kitchen table and began pulling letters from the box at random and reading them. The correspondence was between Mom and Dad during the time he had been stationed in Viet Nam. Mom had been in her mid-twenties, a few years older than me. While not quite X-rated, the content opened my eyes.

"I didn't know you and Mom had such a hot relationship," I said, after reading several letters.

"What do you mean?"

"Like here, where Mom says, 'I can't wait for you to kiss me all over—and I do mean *all over*.' She underlines 'all over.' That's pretty hot, Dad."

He shrugged, unfazed. "We were in love." He took the letter from me and smiled as he read it to himself.

"I used to think Mom was a prude," I said, "but she wasn't all that different from me."

Dad put down the letter. He looked solemn. "The difference was we were married. To each other."

I winced. The arrow had found its mark. "Did Mom tell you?"

"She told me at dinner Saturday night."

I pressed a hand to my mouth. My lips were trembling. "Oh Dad, was it my fault? Did I cause her heart attack? I've been so afraid."

My dad's momentary hesitation told me the thought had crossed his mind too. But a heartbeat later he shook his head. "Don't blame yourself, Carrie. Who knows why these things happen?"

I grabbed a tissue—we'd stationed tissue boxes all over the house—and blew my nose. "Was she upset after she talked to me Saturday afternoon? How did she sound when she told you?"

He thought a minute. "She was sorry you were suffering. But no, in general I would say she was more hopeful than upset. She thought it was your opportunity to put this thing behind you and get on with your life. She was hoping you'd come home."

I nodded. That sounded like her and not like my dad sugar-coating a bitter pill so I'd swallow it. I said, "I'd like to come home, Dad."

"I'd like that too," he said.

Chapter 39

The morning of the funeral was appropriately cold and overcast. I woke early and slipped into sweats and sneakers, thinking I would take a walk before my dad got up.

I went into the living room and opened the front door. The pumpkin was gone from the porch stoop. Someone had snatched it during the night and smashed it in the street. A neighbor drove by on his way to work. The tires of his vehicle slogged through the remains.

Dad shouldn't see this, I thought. I found a plastic grocery bag in the kitchen, threw on a jacket and hurried to the end of the driveway. I collected the broken chunks of pumpkin and tossed them into the bag along with as much of the fibrous material as I could scrape up with my bare hands. I took the bag into the back yard and emptied it into the compost pile. When I let myself in through the front door Dad was standing at the window in the still-dark room. He'd been watching.

"Those bastards," he said. He looked so slumped and beaten it broke my heart. We put our arms around each other and sobbed.

For me the tears had a cathartic effect, enabling me to keep my emotions in check most of the morning. Even when I saw my mother's body in the casket for the first time, clothed in the new dress, I managed not to come completely unglued.

Randy and Lori were among the first to arrive at the funeral parlor. Without saying a word my cousin gathered me into his arms and held me for a long while. When he released me, tears glinted in his eyes. As other people began arriving he and Lori became our greeters, leading mourners forward to where Katie, Tommy, Dad and I had formed a sort of reception line.

I'm always surprised at how fast the news of a tragedy spreads. I'd been out of touch with my high school friends, yet several of them came to pay their respects. Angie called in tears from New York. Among the sprays and vases of flowers surrounding the casket I spotted an arrangement sent by TrueMark.

With twenty minutes to go until the end of the viewing I had hugged so many people and absorbed so many words of sympathy that I needed a break. I'd slipped away from the reception line in search of a glass of water when I heard a familiar voice say my name. I turned and there was Kevin. My former boyfriend was as handsome as when I'd left him in Connecticut three years earlier. But he was no longer a boy; he was a grown man, not so much in looks as in demeanor.

I was so stunned to see him I could barely stammer out his name.

He put his arms around me and murmured, "I'm sorry."

It was only an embrace. Embracing is what people do at funerals. It's what I'd been doing all morning. Yet Kevin's presence was so unexpected and triggered such powerful emotions that I found myself clinging to him as I had clung to no one else.

"Oh, Kevin," I gushed and started weeping.

For a few moments Kevin held me. When my crying showed no signs of letting up he steered me into a private room and onto a chair. He handed me a box of tissues from a table, then brought over another chair and sat facing me.

I blew my nose and wiped my eyes. I must have looked frightful. I said, "I guess you weren't expecting that reaction."

"I didn't know what to expect. I just wanted you to know I'm sorry about your mother."

"Thank you," I said. "I know you two didn't always see eye to eye."

He waved a dismissive hand. "All forgiven now."

An awkward silence fell. I watched myself fold and unfold a tissue on my lap. Finally I made myself look up. "Kevin, there's something I've been wanting to tell you if I ever saw you again. I'm sorry about what happened in Connecticut. I said horrible things to you. You would have been a good husband. You would have been a great father. Everything was my fault."

Kevin sat there stony-faced. In his eyes I saw sadness. In the hard line of his mouth I saw a more powerful emotion struggling for release.

I looked at this man, my first lover, and felt a rush of emotion that swept away the years. Without thinking I said, "I almost came back that day."

Kevin stiffened. He bolted up and backed away from me. "I don't want to hear what you *almost* did." Anger suffused his face. "What you *did*—"

He clamped his mouth shut; a tear slid down his cheek. He drew a ragged breath. "That was the worst week of my life." His dark eyes bored into mine. "I'm telling you all is forgiven. That doesn't mean I'll ever forget."

I felt my color rise as if I'd been slapped on both cheeks. I couldn't hold his gaze. The full depth of my treachery finally hit me. How could I have thought an apology would wipe it away?

Kevin stalked to the door. I expected him to leave but he halted just inside the doorway. He stood there with his back to me. Eventually I saw his shoulders heave and straighten. When he returned and sat down the anger was gone from his face. In a quiet voice he said, "This summer I visited the cemetery where we buried the baby."

"You did?"

He nodded. "A few months after you left I was transferred to Norfolk, Virginia. That's where I completed my service. I've been back in Cincinnati for about a year. This summer I drove to Connecticut. I went to St. Mary's cemetery and found the section where the babies are buried. There were a lot of numbered markers, one for each child. I didn't know the number for—for Kevin, but I'm sure it was nearby. I recognized that crooked tree."

I was stabbed by a pang of guilt. It never would have occurred to me to return to the cemetery. I tried to picture the scene but I couldn't. I didn't remember the crooked tree.

Kevin cleared his throat. "My wife was with me. We said a prayer."

"Your wife?"

"Jenna. I met her in Norfolk. We've been married over a year. We have a little girl, Emily." He pulled his wallet out of his back pocket and flipped it open to a photo of a raven-haired woman with a dazzling smile. Cradled in her arms was a beautiful sleeping infant.

I took the wallet and stared at the picture. "Wow."

"I know. I got lucky."

I touched the photo. "Emily. You always loved that name."

Kevin smiled, a smile of pure pride and joy.

I said, "You look happy when you talk about them."

"I am."

I handed him the wallet. As he returned it to his pocket he said, "So Carrie, are you happy? Did you do all the things you set out to do?"

I shook my head. "I've pretty much messed things up."

I stared at my lap until Kevin touched my hand and said, "I should go."

After he left I sat for a long time thinking about Kevin and the baby we'd created together on a bed in his parent's basement, the baby that had lived eight hours outside my body, the baby I had failed to love. I remembered it all now: the tiny Styrofoam casket, the priest, the funeral service at the gravesite. I thought I even remembered the crooked tree.

Katie came in. "We have to leave for the church soon."

I went into the restroom and repaired my face and hair. Then I returned to the main parlor and knelt before the open casket. *Mom*, I prayed, *if there's a heaven I know you're there. Please find that little boy and tell him his mother loves him.*

Chapter 40

It was Thursday evening, the day after my mother's funeral. My brother had returned to his job. Katie, Dad and I had spent most of the day reading sympathy cards and writing thank you notes. While we worked the house had filled with the comforting aroma of pot roast, which my sister had put on to cook in my mother's slow cooker. Late in the afternoon, after Katie had gone home to her family and Dad had arisen from a nap, he and I discussed my future. It had been a somber discussion, interrupted by the arrival of Tommy, who had stayed for dinner.

It was a relief to have my brother there. I was only too happy to clean up the supper dishes while Dad and Tommy retreated to the TV room. Men have a different way of communicating, with almost no talk necessary. Tommy had brought a stack of DVDs. They selected a movie and settled in for the evening.

I'd finished in the kitchen and was about to join my dad and brother when I heard the unmistakable closing of a car door. I looked out the living room window. The car in the driveway was unfamiliar but the man coming up the sidewalk was not.

Brad. Here was the answer to a prayer I didn't know I'd prayed. I rushed out the door and into his arms. He held me close and whispered his condolences.

"I can't believe you're here," I said.

"I was in Indianapolis. I finished my business a day early and drove down in my rental car. I'll fly home tomorrow afternoon."

He caressed my face with his fingertips. "Carrie, I have so much to say to you. Can we go somewhere to talk?" Before I could answer he said, "What I mean is would you stay with me tonight?"

I'd like to say I hesitated, but I didn't. "Let me run in and get a few things. I'll tell my dad I'm leaving."

A shadow crossed Brad's face. "I hate taking you away from him. I promise to have you home by noon tomorrow."

Brad and I drove to a high-rise hotel near downtown. We checked in, stowed our bags in the room and returned to the first floor restaurant. I sipped a glass of wine while Brad ate dinner. I told him about my mother's death, starting with my sister's phone call early Sunday morning. I told him about the award my mother had received, the unfinished quilt in the sewing room, my parents' love letters, the pumpkin smashed in the street. I was talking too much but I couldn't shut up. Brad did a credible job of appearing to be engrossed.

Eventually the wine worked its magic on my nerves. The tight spool that was me wound itself out as Brad finished his meal. He was signing for the check when I said, "Kevin came to the funeral home."

Brad looked up, surprised.

I said, "I hadn't seen him since I left Connecticut. All of a sudden he was standing there and I lost it. I threw myself into his arms, sobbing like a crazy person. He had to take me to another room."

"Will you be seeing him again?"

I shook my head. "He's married now. He has a baby."

"Do you still love him?"

I fingered the stem of my empty wine glass. "I never loved Kevin."

"Why not?"

I chewed my lip for a second and then I just said it. "Because I was in love with you."

The next thing I knew Brad was leading me to our room. At the door he kissed me and drew me inside. He turned the lights on low. Without a word he undressed me, lowered me onto the bed and made love to me. It was sweet and tender and exactly what I needed. I fell asleep in his arms.

A half-hour later Brad was still lying beside me. I nuzzled his neck. "That's the first decent sleep I've had in a week. Thanks."

He smiled. "My pleasure."

I sat up. "You said we needed to talk. I'm ready now."

We took turns in the bathroom and Brad opened a bottle of wine from the mini-bar in the room and poured us each a cup. We climbed back into bed and leaned side-by-side against the headboard. I was wearing Brad's dress shirt unbuttoned. Brad was in a T-shirt and boxer shorts.

We tapped our plastic cups together and sipped in silence. Eventually we'd have to talk about Greg. I sensed Brad was as reluctant to broach the subject as I was.

Finally Brad said, "Hard to believe it was only last Friday I spent the night at your house."

"I know. So much has happened."

Brad set his cup on the nightstand. He scooted away from the headboard and sat cross-legged on the bed facing me. "Carrie, I have to ask you. Why was my brother driving by your house on Saturday morning? How did he know where you live?"

As I explained how Greg had wormed his way into my life I could sense Brad's agitation. When I finished he said, "You should have told me."

"I'm sorry. I thought I could handle it."

Brad heaved a sigh. "Was my brother in love with you?"

"I don't know."

"I'm guessing he wanted to be more than your handyman."

"I guess."

Brad sat there looking at me. I prayed he wouldn't ask the next logical question: *Did he get what he wanted?*

If he'd asked I would have lied. Greg didn't want him to know. I didn't want him to know. And Brad only wanted to know if the answer was negative.

Brad considered me for a while. Then his expression softened, he crawled to me on his hands and knees and kissed me. When he sat back on his haunches he said, "I'm finally realizing what this affair has put you through, Carrie. All the secrets you've had to keep, how constricted your life has been." He took my hand. "I'm not going to ask any more questions about Greg or Kevin or anybody else. You already told me at dinner what I needed to know."

"What did I tell you?"

"You said you loved me. You haven't changed your mind, have you?"

I shook my head. "I've never changed my mind. Why did you need to know that?"

"Can't you guess?" He raked the hair back from my temples and gave me a steady look. "I love you, Carrie. It took this crisis to make me realize how much."

There they were, the words I thought I'd never hear. His eyes were on my face, his lips slightly parted. I leaned forward and kissed him. He enveloped me in his arms and I never felt safer.

When I sat back he said, "My brother told me you're planning to leave Minnesota." He ran a finger between my breasts and down to my navel. "I don't want you to leave. Will you stay?"

"What about Greg? He knows everything."

"That doesn't matter anymore. I'm going to ask Marcy for a divorce."

My mouth went dry. This was more than I'd bargained for. I said, "If it weren't for me, would you even be considering divorce?"

Brad looked thoughtful. "I'm going to tell you something I've never told anyone before." He refilled our wine cups then leaned beside me against the headboard. He said, "You already know Marcy and I had a shotgun wedding. What you don't know is how it came about."

He took a sip of wine and replaced the cup on the nightstand. "Marcy and I attended the same high school. We started dating when we were seniors. After graduation I left for New Haven and she stayed in Minnesota for college. We dated other people—at least I did—but we spent our summers and holidays together. Everybody assumed we'd get married. But in my senior year at Yale I met somebody else, somebody who gave me second thoughts about marrying Marcy.

"I should have told Marcy the truth when I went home for Christmas, but I held off. She must have guessed, though, because that February she paid an unexpected visit to New Haven. A month later she told me she was pregnant. Now this is the part I've never told anybody. Marcy claimed she'd messed up on her pills, but I don't believe it. I think she tried to get pregnant so I would marry her."

I made a face. "Do women still do that?"

"Like I said it's just a guess."

"You didn't ask her about it?"

"No. Remember what I told you when you got pregnant? You made a choice that put you in that situation. It was the same for me. I'd fathered a child. Marcy was dead set against having an abortion, so what good would it have done to make accusations? The die was already cast."

Brad sighed. "It's not an ideal marriage. There's a basic element of mistrust between Marcy and me that prevents us from being honest with each other. What's even worse she's turning into her mother. Ever since we moved back home she's all about status—where to be, what to say, who to know. It's so goddam calculated and superficial. The only thing we have in common any more is Chip."

Brad took my hand, placed it on my thigh and started tracing its outline. "In answer to your question, if you hadn't come along I'd probably still be toughing it out with Marcy. She's been through a lot. The miscarriages and the hysterectomy sent her into an emotional tailspin. She's pretty fragile and I care about her. I want her to be happy. But the way things stand neither one of us is happy. I don't see the situation improving."

Brad slid down in bed until he was lying with his head on the pillow. He tugged me down beside him, rolled me onto my back and trailed his fingers across my abdomen. "You make me happy, Carrie. You're everything I could have wanted in a woman. It may be selfish of me but you're the one I want to spend my life with."

He kissed me—a long, savoring kiss—then pulled me on top of him.

"You didn't answer my question last night," Brad said.

We were sitting across from each other at a round drop-leaf table in our hotel room. A continental breakfast of pastry, fruit, coffee and yogurt—assembled in the first floor breakfast room and schlepped back upstairs—was arrayed before us like a buffet.

Brad eased back in his chair and flashed his dimples at me. "Have I persuaded you to make the North Star State your home?"

The expression on my face must have spoken volumes. Brad straightened up. His smile was gone.

I put down my half-finished croissant and pushed my plate aside. "I've been awake half the night trying to picture how it would play out if I said yes. I don't like the ending."

"Play it out for me," he said.

"Okay. Let's say I stay in Minnesota. What happens next?"

"I'll ask Marcy for a divorce."

"How do you break that kind of news to somebody you've been married to for twelve years?"

Brad looked uncomfortable. "I'll just say it, I guess."

"Will you tell her about us?"

"God, no."

"You'll have to give her a reason."

"I'll say we're incompatible."

"Will you tell her you don't love her?"

Brad ran his fingers through his hair. "Oh, Carrie, I don't know. I don't want to hurt her more than I have to."

"Will you tell her you felt trapped into marrying her because of Chip?"

"I'm not going to bring Chip into it."

"Brad, if you get a divorce you'll be bringing Chip into it. His whole world is going to collapse. I've seen you and Chip together. I've heard you talk about him. Your every instinct is to protect him, to make sure he's safe and happy. The biggest threat to his happiness right now is you. And me. How are you going to protect him from us?"

"He likes you, Carrie. Maybe it won't be so bad."

"If you divorce his mother and I'm the cause he won't like me. Nobody will. Not your brother. Not your parents. Nobody. Even at work. Once this comes out we might lose our jobs."

"We'll move away. We'll come back here."

"What about Chip? If Marcy gets custody and you move away you'll hardly ever get to see him. Do you want Marcy to be the one who raises him? If she remarries do you want another man to—"

His hand shot up. "You made your point," he said. He shoved back his chair, got to his feet and disappeared into the bathroom. When he didn't return after several minutes I went to the door and tapped.

"Come in," Brad said.

He was leaning on stiff arms over the sink. It was obvious he'd been splashing his face with water. I handed him a towel. He dried himself and we looked at each other in the mirror.

"It's not going to work, is it," he said.

I swallowed hard. "No."

He turned and gave me a rueful smile. "You're getting good at this."

"At what?"

"Breaking my heart."

Brad drove the rental car out of the parking garage. As we headed for the west side of town I recounted the conversation I'd had earlier in the week with my dad. "He told me I'm welcome to move back home. I'll give my two-week notice at work on Monday. Then I'll start packing. Randy can sell the house after I leave."

"Seems so sudden," Brad said.

"No use prolonging it." I hesitated a moment then said, "Maybe with me out of the picture you and Marcy can make a new start."

His laugh was humorless. "So now you're my marriage counselor."

"If I were your marriage counselor I'd tell you to get as far away as possible from Marcy's mother."

"Good advice but Marcy wouldn't go for it."

"If she had to choose between you and her mother, who would she pick?"

"I honestly don't know."

"I'd put my money on you. I saw the way she looked at you at the cabin. She loves you, Brad. And I think you love her. I didn't want to admit it at the time, but there was a spark between the two of you."

Brad shrugged. "We'll see."

We were nearing my dad's house. As we approached the neighborhood park Brad said, "We have a few minutes," and pulled into the lot. He shut off the engine and turned to me. "Thanks for caring about my future but I'm not ready for that discussion yet." Tiny dimples creased his cheeks. "Let me drown myself in my sorrows for a day or two."

We climbed out of the car. Brad took my hand and we strolled down a pathway of shredded bark into a wooded area. The fall colors were at their peak. The sky was azure and the sunlight streaming through the foliage turned the trail to gold.

"I have business trips scheduled for the next two weeks," Brad said. "I won't be around much while you're getting ready to leave."

"Probably just as well. I'd rather say goodbye here than in an office full of people."

We paused on the leaf-strewn path and put our arms around each other. We kissed, and already it felt different. Already we had changed. The road not taken—the one we would have embarked upon together—had vanished the moment we'd stepped out the door of our hotel room. I couldn't even imagine it anymore.

At my dad's house Brad took my overnight bag from the trunk and handed it to me. I walked him to the driver's side and we stood looking at each other.

I pressed my hand to his chest and said, "Ouch."

He smiled and nodded. A moment later he slid behind the wheel.

Fallen leaves crunched beneath his tires as he drove off.

Chapter 41

On Saturday morning my dad and I were heading out the kitchen door on the way to the airport when the phone rang. It was Dad's landline.

I ran and snatched up the receiver. "Hi. This is Carrie."

There was a pause on the other end of the line, then a deep voice, like expensive chocolate melting on the tongue, said, "You're a hard woman to get ahold of."

It was Clayton Shaw, no introductions necessary. I couldn't help but smile.

"Tracking you down was not merely a self-serving quest," he intoned. "All summer I was hoping you'd lend your considerable charm to helping Troy Grove get re-elected in November, but the only thing I found out for sure is you're not at P&G anymore. Then this morning I was sitting here eating breakfast and flipping through a week's worth of neglected newspapers, and there you were on the front page of Section B."

He paused. When he spoke again the jocularity was gone from his voice. "Carrie, I'm sorry about your mother. It must have been a terrible shock. If I'd known sooner I would have come to the funeral."

I thanked him and asked how he'd gotten my dad's phone number.

He pitched his voice low. "We have our ways." Then he laughed. "Actually, once I had your father's name even a Luddite like me could figure out how to look up the number." I heard the rattle of newspaper on Clay's end of the line. "I see you haven't gotten any uglier."

"Thank god for that. How about you?"

"Ugly as ever. But you shouldn't take my word for it. A good reporter checks these things out for herself."

"I'm not a reporter."

"Could have fooled me. You know, Carrie, I thought maybe you'd call me when our mutual friend left town. But I haven't heard a peep out of you."

"I've been busy."

"Where are you working now?"

"I'm between jobs." Almost the truth.

"In school?"

"No."

"Not campaigning, not working, not in school. How busy can you be?" He paused for a beat. "Have you been avoiding me?"

"Let's just say I'm swearing off men for a while."

He made a sniffing sound like a hound when it when it picks up an intriguing scent. "Do I smell a woman on the rebound from a failed relationship? Carrie, women on the rebound are my specialty."

I laughed. "Thanks for the warning."

"So do you have a phone of your own? Or do I have to keep bugging your dad?"

While I recited my cell phone number my dad stood at the door jangling his car keys.

I said, "I have to leave for the airport now. I'll be out of town for a couple of weeks."

"I'll call you after the election," he said.

Jill and Derek collected me outside baggage claim at the Minneapolis airport. On the way to my house I asked Jill about her research on the patio tiles.

"Nothing yet," Jill said, "but I have a few more tiles to check out."

"Hope springs eternal," I said, but I didn't really expect her to find anything.

Sunday it rained. The dreariness of the day matched my mood as I started packing to leave town. Late in the morning Jill called, sounding excited. "I discovered something about one of the tiles. I'll come over after I get off work."

By the time Jill arrived darkness had fallen. With the rain still teaming down I had her park in the garage. In the kitchen she opened a tote bag, pulled out a photograph and laid it on the counter. It was a print of a snapshot she'd taken with her cell phone.

"That's one of the Chinese tiles," I said.

"Right. Now look at this." She brought out a sheet of printer paper with the bottom three inches folded under. On the upper portion of the paper was a computer printout of a Chinese character. She laid it next to the photo.

"It's the same character," I said.

Jill nodded. "Now look at what it means." She unfolded the sheet and smoothed it on the counter. Printed in big block letters beneath the Chinese character was the word HAPPINESS.

A chill ran down my spine. "Oh my god, Jill."

"The bounty of Adriana's garden belongs to the one who understands," Jill recited.

"Happiness is the key," we both chanted. We threw our arms around each other and jumped up and down like we'd just won the World Series.

"Do you think there's something buried under that tile?" I said.

Jill grinned. "One way to find out."

She'd come prepared with rubber boots. I pulled my own boots out of the closet and found a large umbrella in the garage. I took a flashlight from my car, gathered some hand tools and a pair of work gloves and dropped them into an empty five-gallon paint bucket. We suited up. I turned on the floodlights, Jill opened the umbrella and we set out for Adriana's garden.

With the help of the flashlight we located the tile. I knelt on the wet patio. Jill squatted and positioned the umbrella over both our heads. In her other hand she held the flashlight with the beam trained on the tile. I pried up the slate. Beneath it was a layer of sand and gravel, which I scooped out with a hand trowel. Five inches down the trowel scraped against something that felt and sounded like plastic. I excavated around it. It was a kitchen storage container. I pulled it from the hole and felt below it for something else but found nothing but dirt.

"I think that's all there is," I said.

"It's not very big," Jill said.

It wasn't. It was a Tupperware sandwich container, about five inches square and an inch deep. I brushed off the sand. "Let's go in and see what we've got."

We shed our wet outerwear on the floor of the screened-in porch and took our find to the kitchen. Good old Tupperware. The inside of the container was completely dry. It held a zip-lock bag, inside of which were two sheets of folded paper. The pages were in perfect condition. When I unfolded them a small white envelope fell onto the counter. Jill picked it up and lifted the flap. There was a key inside.

We looked at the papers. One was a typed letter on official-looking stationery. The other was a note written in Henry's recognizable scrawl, which read:

> If you found this key I'm probably dead. I don't know how you came to possess it. My hope is that you read the will and your curiosity and persistence brought you to the place where it rested. Perhaps you were tearing up the patio and stumbled upon the key by accident. So be it. The fate of Adriana's garden is beyond my control.
>
> My one request is that you'll look kindly upon this piece of land. It isn't a shrine. It never was. Adriana called it a place to be alone with your thoughts. That's what it was for me. I was happy here. The accompanying letter will tell you what to do next.
>
> Henry Streator

The typed letter was even briefer than Henry's note. It said: *I am an attorney representing the interests of Henry Streator. Please contact me at the law firm named above.* It was signed: Milton Edgerton. The name of the firm was Edgerton and Trent.

"This is amazing," Jill said. "What do you think the key is for?"

"I'm guessing a safe deposit box."

I remembered Randy being surprised that Henry's estate hadn't included any mention of a retirement account. Could this be what had happened to it?

"You should call the attorney tomorrow," Jill said.

"Maybe you should call him," I said. "If it weren't for you we wouldn't have found it."

"But it's your house."

"Actually it's my aunt's house."

"You're buying it though, right?"

"Not anymore. Randy's going to put it on the market soon."

"Why?" she said, sounding disappointed.

I hesitated. I'd have to break the news sooner or later. "Jill, I'm moving back to Cincinnati."

She pressed prayer-folded hands to her lips. "Your dad needs you, doesn't he."

"That's not it. I have to get out of Minnesota."

"Something happened with that guy."

"What guy?"

Jill cleared her throat. "I wasn't going to say anything but last winter Derek and I got here early one Saturday morning. We were coming down the street when we saw a silver convertible pulling out of your garage. There was a hot-looking guy behind the wheel. I saw him when he drove past." She gave me a probing look. "You didn't really have a yoga class on Saturday mornings, did you?"

I shook my head. "He was my boss at P&G. He was married. Last week he came to Cincinnati and offered to divorce his wife for me. I have to leave, Jill. I can't break up his marriage."

Jill gave me a steady look. "You're doing the right thing."

"I know," I said, and surprised myself by believing it.

My plan when I got to work Monday morning was to hand Lindsey my notice. I didn't allow for the fact that so many people would want to offer their condolences on the loss of my mother. With such an outpouring of support from the CEO on down, tendering my resignation at that moment didn't seem appropriate. I decided to postpone my announcement.

On my morning break I called the attorney whose name was on the cryptic letter included with the key. I told him what I'd found and we set up an appointment to meet at his office. The earliest he could see me was Thursday afternoon.

Milton Edgerton was an older man, probably in his sixties. He had a storefront law office on the main street in downtown Lakeville. When I arrived he led me into a small conference room. Rather than staring at each other across a desk we sat side-by-side at an oval table.

Once I'd shown him the key and the two letters, he told me about the arrangement Henry Streator had made with him. "The key is for a safe deposit box at the Wells Fargo bank across the street. The box belongs to Mr. Streator, who gave me a sum of money and hired me to rent the box. We set up an account from which the bank makes an automatic withdrawal every year to keep the rental current."

He asked if I knew how safe deposit boxes worked. When I confessed my ignorance he explained that it takes two keys to open the door that allows access to the safe deposit box: the master key owned by the bank and the key of the person renting the box, whose signature must match the signature on file at the bank.

"The renter receives two identical keys," he said. "The second key allows another person access to the box as long as his or her signature is on file. When Mr. Streator rented the box he had me sign my name to the signature card. But he kept both keys."

"So you couldn't open the box."

"Right."

"But now you can," I said.

"Now *you* can," he said.

"But my name isn't on the signature card."

"Not yet, but it will be." He tapped a manila folder. "These are Mr. Streator's instructions."

He opened the folder and picked up what looked like a legal document. I recognized Henry's signature at the bottom. "Here are the instructions. When someone comes to me with the key and the two letters you provided today I'm to take that person to the bank and turn over to him or her the safe deposit box and its contents."

He looked at me. "You're that person, Ms. Matthews. Since you may not want me to see what's in the box I'll have it switched over to your name. At that point it'll be your box and you alone will have access to it."

"What about the other key?"

"I believe you'll find it in the box. Henry's intention was to put it there." He stood. "We have an appointment with a banker at three-thirty. Why don't you drive your car over to the bank parking lot. I'll walk over and meet you."

I had butterflies in my stomach by the time we sat down in front of the banker, a youngish woman named Beth. She'd been briefed and the paperwork was ready, so the process didn't take long. Within ten minutes I was standing in the bank lobby saying good-bye to Milton Edgerton.

"It's all yours," he said, shaking my hand. "I wish you the best of luck."

I thanked him and he walked across the lobby and out the door. I marveled at his restraint; he had to have been curious about what the box contained but he'd never once asked to have a look.

I followed Beth into the vault. She unlocked the door to a caged area and led me to a wall of safe deposit boxes. We located the correct box number and used our keys to open it. The banker stood aside while I extracted the sturdy metal container from its cubbyhole. It was almost two feet in length, but only about five inches wide and three inches high. The lid was long and hinged toward the back. The box was heavy, with the lion's share of the weight in the front.

"This thing weighs more than my bowling ball," I said.

Beth located a trolley cart for the box and stayed with me as I rolled it into a private room containing a table and two chairs. After giving me instructions on what to do when I was done she stepped out of the room and shut the door behind her, leaving me alone with my new possession. I transferred the box from the cart to the table, surprised again by its weight.

I released the clasp and laid back the lid. When I realized what I was seeing I drew in a sharp breath and sat down hard on one of the chairs. The front third of the box was stacked with gold coins.

My hands flew to my mouth and tears started in my eyes. I could feel my lips quivering as I did the mental arithmetic. I was looking at fourteen columns of gold coins, arranged two columns per row and extending seven rows back into the drawer. Thirteen of the columns were identical: thirteen tall stacks of coins, each stack sleeved in plastic. At the front of the drawer was a partial stack where the plastic had been cut open and some of the coins were missing. Two wedding bands, a large one encircling a small one, had been placed on top of the short stack of coins.

I picked up the plain gold bands, laid them side-by-side in my palm and thought about the two people who had worn them. I recalled the photo of Adriana kneeling at the foot of Our Lady of Guadalupe and planting flowers, her dark hair falling into her face. I saw Henry and Adriana standing in front of a fountain in some foreign land with their arms around each other. By all accounts he'd been an odd duck, but she had loved him.

Through reading his journals, sifting through his mementos and living in his house I'd come to know Henry Streator. In

Adriana he'd found the love of his life. When he'd lost her he'd lost everything. In my aunt Cora he'd been seeking a substitute, but she'd become a burden. As the end approached he'd needed to shield his most precious possessions from her.

I set the rings aside and removed one sleeve of plastic-wrapped coins from the box. The label indicated it contained twenty gold coins, each coin weighing one ounce. The partial stack contained fifteen coins. That made a total of two hundred seventy-five coins. I returned all but one coin to the box. I cradled the rings in my palm once more before putting them back where I'd found them.

Toward the rear of the safe deposit box was a sheaf of papers, folded in half lengthwise. They appeared to be records of financial transactions. The only other item in the box was the duplicate key the lawyer had promised would be there. It was attached to a key ring.

I put the two keys together on the ring and slipped the papers into a tote bag I'd brought with me. I wrapped the coin in a facial tissue and buried it deep in a zippered compartment of my purse so I wouldn't lose or damage it.

I shut the lid of the safe deposit box, transferred it to the cart and opened the door. Beth had been keeping an eye out for me. She watched me return the box to its niche and showed me out of the vault.

I called the Lundgrens from the bank parking lot. Months earlier my neighbors had offered me the use of their computer and its Internet connection if the need ever arose. For once I'd take them up on their offer. Vic sounded pleased to grant my request. "Janet's out, but there's a pot of decaf brewing," he said. "I'll have the computer booted up and ready to go."

When I arrived at the Lundgrens Vic showed me into the office. He brought me a cup of coffee, then left me alone. I sat in front of the computer, called up Google, typed *gold prices* into the search box and clicked on a likely link. When the site came up I scanned the page and sucked in a breath. If I was reading it right, an ounce of gold was selling for eleven hundred thirty-six dollars.

"Oh my god," I said and clapped a hand to my mouth.

Vic came to the open door. "Everything okay?"

"Do you have a calculator?"

"There's one on the computer," he said. He approached the monitor and pointed to an icon at the bottom of the screen. I clicked on the icon and a calculator appeared. With trembling fingers I keyed in 1136 and multiplied it by 275.

Vic read the number that came up. "Three-hundred-twelve thousand, four hundred what?"

"Dollars," I whispered.

I hadn't told him anything. He didn't know we'd found the treasure or where I'd been that day. But he knew awe when he heard it in someone's voice.

I reached for my purse and found the tissue-wrapped package. When I opened it and produced the gold coin he ran a shaky hand through his hair. "You found Henry's treasure." He sank into a chair and I began telling him the whole story. Janet arrived home halfway through the telling, so I started over.

When I finished Janet shook her head in disbelief. "He must have invested a good chunk of his savings in gold."

Vic chuckled. "That Henry. He was crazy like a fox."

I pulled the sheaf of papers from my tote bag. "These were in the box with the coins."

Janet was a retired accountant. I handed her the pages and she leafed through them. "This is pretty straightforward. At age sixty-five Henry took his pension as a lump sum distribution. He paid off his house and car and invested a hundred thousand in gold. He acquired the coins over a period of about two years and he never paid more than three-hundred-seventy dollars an ounce."

I turned back to the screen and clicked on the gold prices website I'd been using. "Am I reading this number right?"

Janet and Vic looked too and verified I wasn't seeing things.

"It could go up or down tomorrow, but right now that's what it's worth," Janet said.

Vic grinned. "So Carrie, what are you going to do with your newfound wealth?"

I didn't want to tip my hand just yet, so I told him I needed time to think about it. I thanked them, then rushed home and called Jill, who agreed to go with me to the bank on Saturday morning. I didn't let on about the magnitude of the find.

That evening I contacted Randy and reopened my inquiry into buying the house.

Brad had been out of town on business all week. On Friday I would be seeing him for the first time since we'd parted in Cincinnati. I steeled myself for the encounter, only to arrive at work to find he'd taken a day of vacation to whisk Marcy off on a weekend getaway to San Francisco.

"Doesn't that sound romantic?" Sandy said when she told me. I had to agree it did.

On my lunch break I visited a local jewelry store, showed them the coin and asked if it was real. It was. When the jeweler offered to buy it from me at a price considerably lower than the price posted on the Internet I discovered I'd have to shop around to get the best price. Ah, the perils of being rich, the perils of staying rich.

Since Brad was away the sales department skipped its Friday afternoon staff meeting. I sneaked out early. I still hadn't tendered my resignation.

Jill picked me up Saturday morning and I directed her to the Wells Fargo in downtown Lakeville. The process of registering her signature went smoothly. Fifteen minutes after arriving we'd been ushered into the vault. This time Jill inserted her key into the lock. But I was the one who slid the narrow box out of its slot and onto the cart; I didn't want her to feel how heavy it was.

We entered the same room I'd been in the day before and I transferred the box to the table. "Go ahead—open it," I said.

Jill lifted the lid and stared. "It looks like gold," she breathed. "Is it real?"

"It's real. I already checked."

"Oh look," she said, and I could tell by her tender expression she'd noticed the rings. She picked up the wedding bands and pressed them to her lips. There were tears in her eyes as she returned them to the box.

I held up the gold piece I'd taken home with me. "This one coin is worth over eleven hundred dollars. There are two hundred seventy-four others just like it." I showed her the sheet upon which I'd written the calculations.

She sputtered and shook her head. "I can't believe it. What are we going to do?"

"I have an idea," I said and asked her to come back to the house so we could talk.

On the drive home I told her what Janet had gleaned from the sheaf of papers Henry had placed in the box. I explained how the skyrocketing price of gold had turned a one hundred thousand dollar investment ten years earlier into the fortune we'd seen in the box.

"Minus a few coins he must have cashed in," I added.

Jill laughed. "How dare he spend our money."

At the house I went into the kitchen to put on a pot of coffee. Jill headed for the dining room, where she stood before the patio door gazing out at Adriana's garden.

"How do you like this house?" I called.

"You know I love it," Jill said.

I pressed the brew button on the coffeemaker and joined her at the door.

"How would you like to own it?" I said.

She looked at me, her eyes wide. "I couldn't."

"You could, Jill. You could pay cash for this house."

"What about you, Carrie?"

"I'm leaving, remember?"

"But what about the money? I'd need over half of it to buy the house. We agreed to split whatever we found."

"We didn't agree to split it evenly. Jill, if it hadn't been for you we never would have found the money. You're the one who saved the keepsake box. You're the one who stuck with it and solved the riddle. I'd like to be reimbursed for the things I bought that I won't be taking with me. Like the bed, for instance. But the rest of it should go to you."

Jill looked doubtful. "I don't know," she said, but I detected her resolve crumbling.

"I'm not trying to railroad you into a decision, but I did tell my cousin you might be interested. He liked the idea. He said you could stay here as caretaker even before the sale goes through."

My friend shook her head as if to clear it. "I can't quite take it all in."

"Think it over," I said. "You know there's nobody I'd rather have live in this house."

On Monday, a week later than I'd planned, I resigned my job at TrueMark. My colleagues were stunned and disappointed. As the word spread through the office I let everyone believe my mother's death had prompted my decision to move back to Cincinnati.

I spent my final two weeks at TrueMark tying up loose ends and saying goodbye. It's funny how when you're planning to leave a place of employment your attitude changes. I did my job but I didn't really care anymore.

I was more interested in the phone call I received from Clayton Shaw. The first thing he said was, "Are you home yet?"

"I'm running late," I said. "I'll be back next week."

"Oh yeah? And what excuse are you going to give me next week?"

I giggled like a teenager. "No, seriously, I'll be back by then."

"Still between jobs?" he said.

"I am."

"Well here's an opportunity for you, Carrie. As you probably know, Troy Grove was re-elected last Tuesday. He's looking to add a staffer here in Cincinnati. It's part-time for now, but positions like that have a way of evolving. It might be right up your alley. Interested?"

I grinned. "It's the best thing I've heard in a long time." I gave him my work email address so he could send me a link to the Grove website.

"Check out the job description," Clay said. "If you decide to apply, be sure to put down my name as a reference. Let me know if you'd like me to call Troy and give you a plug."

I'd taken Clay's call in the break room. By the time I returned to my desk, his email was in my inbox. I followed the link to the website. The job was a good, even exciting, fit: mostly public relations with a dollop of website work on top. And the part-time nature of it appealed to me since I'd be returning to school in January.

For the first time ever I could afford to go to college without working. Despite my protests that I didn't deserve nearly so much, Jill—who'd decided to buy the house—had insisted I keep three sleeves of gold coins. Sixty ounces of pure gold. With the value of gold on the rise my share was already worth seventy thousand dollars. I had another thirty thousand in savings, thanks to being frugal and not having to pay rent.

How ironic. My high school dream of attending college full-time was finally within easy reach. The dream had lost its appeal however. I was a big girl now and I couldn't imagine not working if an interesting position was available. I applied for the job and offered Clayton Shaw as a reference, along with Brad, Lindsey and Michael.

By return email I asked Clay to put in a good word for me. With some hesitation I attached my résumé. In milliseconds my secret would be out: Clayton Shaw would know where I'd been for the past year and with whom I'd been working. I pictured the sly smile that would steal across his face when he started connecting the dots.

Chapter 42

On Saturday morning, my last day in Minnesota, I found out why I'd delayed my departure for a week. When I opened my eyes at eight the bedroom seemed unnaturally bright even with the blinds closed. I padded into the bathroom. It was bright in there too.

I pushed aside the curtain and beheld the first snowfall of the year, a thick blanket that weighed down tree branches and mounded three inches high on the deck railings. It had crept in during the night and descended like a blessing. Now the clouds were rolling off to the east and the sky above was clear. The sunlight bouncing off the snow filled the rooms with light.

There was snow on the ground when I'd arrived in Minnesota. That it would return in mid-November to bid me farewell seemed appropriate. I turned from the window and saw my face in the mirror. I was smiling. Not broadly, but enough to get me through the day.

I dressed quickly. I would be handing the house over to Jill that morning. I suspected she and Derek would arrive early, so I postponed breakfast and hurried outside to clear the driveway and sidewalk.

The weather was surprisingly warm. Mid-twenties, I guessed, with no wind. Toward the end of the previous winter I'd bought a new snow blower on clearance. I fired it up and accomplished the job in fifteen minutes flat. I was about to go inside when the city snowplow came by and deposited a mountain of snow at the driveway entrance. My trusty machine made quick work of that too.

While I'd been outside Jill had called and left a message on my cell phone. She and Derek were on their way and would be there by nine. Jill had confessed to her mother that she and Derek were sleeping together, so it came as no surprise that Derek would also be moving in.

They arrived in two packed cars. I had left the garage door open and was shoehorning some things into my own overstuffed vehicle when they pulled into the driveway.

Jill emerged from her car grinning. I called, "Welcome home," and she rushed forward and hugged me. When she let go her eyes were wet.

Derek joined us. "The roads are slippery, Carrie. Don't feel like you have to leave today."

"You could stay for the celebration," Jill said. "My mom and dad are coming down for dinner tonight. Mom's bringing her famous chili."

Happy as I was for Jill and Derek, I wasn't sure I could handle a celebration. "Sounds tempting, but I'm just about packed. I should go."

"Why don't you hold off for a few hours at least," Derek said. "The roads should be clear by noon."

"That'll work. I was planning on a two-day trip anyway."

While I ate breakfast Jill and Derek began transferring the contents of their cars to a temporary staging area in the vacant living room. I finished my cereal and went outside to help Jill empty her car. We were chatting across the car roof when she looked past me and stiffened. "Carrie," she said, her eyes locking on mine, "you have company."

I didn't need to look. The Pavlovian lurch of my heart told me who it was.

I turned around and saw the silver Audi parked on the street. The driver's door was opening and Brad was getting out. Then the passenger door swung open and there appeared a blond head and the face of an angel attached to a slim body two inches taller than when I'd last seen it.

Chip slammed the car door and gave me a wicked grin. Without a word he bent and picked up a handful of snow.

"Duck!" I yelled to Jill. I bolted for the edge of the driveway and started scooping snow into my hands. There followed a mad flurry of snowballs flying through the air. Brad, Jill and Derek got in on the action, which only ended when I managed to tackle Chip and pull him down with me onto the ground. Our faces were about three inches from each other. He was flushed, his hair and eyelashes caked with snow. For the first time I saw not just Brad but Marcy in his looks.

"Hey, Chip," I said.

"Hey, Carrie."

We got to our feet. I introduced Brad and Chip to Jill and Derek.

Brad ruffled his son's hair. "Chip, tell Carrie what you said when you saw the snow this morning."

"I was wondering if you could go up to the cabin again. But Dad said you were leaving."

I cleared my throat, which had suddenly closed on me. "I'm moving back to Cincinnati."

"We decided we couldn't let you go without saying goodbye," Brad said.

I gave Chip a playful punch. "You were just looking for another excuse to clobber me."

He smiled and ducked his head. "I guess."

"Now that you folks are soaked from head to foot, we should let you get back to work," Brad said. He put a hand on his son's shoulder. "Say, Chip, how about waiting in the car. I need to talk to Carrie for a few minutes."

Jill gave me a look that asked if I was okay with that. When I nodded she said, "I have an idea, Chip. Do you know what the front yard needs on a day like this?"

Chip screwed up his face and looked around. "A snowman?"

"Exactly. Wanna help?"

"Sure."

As Jill, Derek and Chip set to work building their snowman Brad and I headed up the street. When we were out of earshot of the others Brad said, "I knew this might be awkward, but when Chip mentioned you first thing this morning I took it as a sign. It didn't seem right not to see you off."

"It's perfect. I'm glad I was still here."

He fixed me with a probing look. "How are you doing, Carrie?"

"Well let's see." I held up my hand and began ticking off items on my fingers. "I'm giving up my house. I miss you. I miss my mom. I'm worried about my dad. I feel like crap most of the time." I laughed. "The good news is that things are shaping up in Cincinnati. I might even have a job when I get back."

"So I heard."

"Did Clayton Shaw call you already?"

"Of course. And he was annoyingly smug."

I cringed. "I'm afraid he knows about us. I hope that doesn't cause you any problems."

"He'll be the soul of discretion. Just remember I warned you about him."

"Eyes wide open," I said. "Anyway, I hope I get the job."

"You'll get the job. And not because of Clay Shaw."

"What do you mean?"

"Carrie, I'm not sure you realize how talented you are. I wouldn't be surprised if you end up in Troy Grove's Washington office. The sky's the limit for you."

We sloshed our way single file around a parked car. When we returned to the side of the road and fell into step beside each other Brad gave me a wry smile. "If that job doesn't work out you might consider becoming a marriage counselor."

"You took my advice after all?"

"I did. When I got back from Cincinnati I told Marcy I wasn't happy with the way things were. I asked her to choose between her mother and me."

"Let me guess. She chose you."

"You're more sure of it than I was. But yes she chose me. The next weekend we flew to San Francisco, just the two of us." He caught my eye. "Remember what I told you that night in the hotel room? The suspicion I had about Marcy?"

"You thought she'd tricked you into marrying her."

He nodded. "I was right, she'd planned the whole thing. But it didn't work out the way she'd imagined."

"She got you to marry her."

"True. But put yourself in her shoes. All these years she's had to live with that lie, knowing I married her not because I wanted to but because I had to. Think what something like that does to a person's self-esteem. She was terrified if she told me the truth I'd leave her. In San Francisco when she finally admitted it and I told her I loved her and wasn't going anywhere, she...I don't know, Carrie, it was like the suit of armor she'd been wearing melted away. She blossomed like a flower."

I looked at Brad. It was clear from his expression something special had happened in San Francisco. I nudged him with my elbow. "I don't suppose you'll give me credit for the save."

"Not publicly. But I'll be forever grateful."

I smiled. "Somebody had to be the grownup."

We'd arrived at the corner. Brad took my arm and we stepped back to dodge a rooster tail of slush kicked up by a passing car. He turned to me. "Well, little girl, our paths are diverging. Pretty soon we'll have changed so much we'll no longer recognize each other."

"I suppose," I said, but I didn't believe it. Even if I spotted him fifty years later across a crowded room I was sure the sight would jolt me like a pacemaker going off in my chest.

Brad's eyes scanned my face. "Three weeks ago when you told me you were leaving I didn't want to let you go. But you were right. My future is here with my family. Your future is somewhere else, Carrie, somewhere exciting."

I couldn't hold his gaze without crying. I bowed my head and leaned into his chest. When I'd harnessed my emotions and looked up he traced the angle of my jaw with the back of his hand. Without another word we turned and headed for the house.

We were nearly there when Brad said, "I talked to my brother this morning. For Marcy and Chip's sake I had to pretend not to know where you lived, so I called Greg and went through the charade of getting your address. Just before we hung up he said, 'Tell her I'm sorry for the way I treated her that day.'"

A pang of guilt twisted my insides. I said, "I'm the one who should apologize. I hurt him, not the other way around."

Brad sighed. "We both hurt him."

Hearing the tone of regret in his voice, I said, "How wide is the rift between you?"

"Yawning chasm would be an exaggeration, but not much. Right now he's only pretending to like me." He caught my eye and smiled. "No offense, but now that you're leaving, things should improve."

My throat tightened. "I'd give anything to change what happened."

"There's nothing you can do, Carrie. It's up to Greg and me to close the gap. It'll be a long haul and I suspect there'll be scars. But we're brothers and best friends. We'll ride off into the sunset together if it kills us."

I squeezed Brad's hand. "When the time feels right please tell him how sorry I am. Thank him for everything he did for me."

Brad nodded. "I will."

We'd arrived at the house. In the front yard Derek, Jill and Chip were putting the finishing touches on a whimsical snow creature that could only have sprung from the combined imaginations of a graphic artist, a set designer and an eleven-year-old boy.

"Take a picture, Dad," Chip called out when he saw us. "I wanna show Mom."

"Are you all right?" Jill said.

She, Derek and I were standing in front of the house watching Brad's silver Audi drive off into a future that didn't include me. I'd just hugged Brad and Chip goodbye. Although I'd challenged Chip to a revenge snowball fight if I ever returned to Minnesota, I knew I'd be unlikely to see either of them again.

I inclined my head toward the house. "Do I still have a bedroom?"

Jill's smile was sympathetic. "It's all yours."

I went inside, removed my jacket, shoes and socks in the laundry room and headed down the hall to the master bedroom.

I closed the door, stripped off my wet jeans and top, threw myself onto the bed and cried.

I cried for everything I'd lost and everything I was leaving behind. Most of all, I cried for the passing of an era. For more than four years, ever since I'd first stepped into his office and he'd rocked my world with his smile, Brad Collins had been the center of my universe. Without a backward glance I'd abandoned my high school dreams and poured my energy and passion into gaining his notice, his approval and his love. He'd given me all those things and more: he'd wanted to spend his life with me.

I rolled onto my back and let my gaze travel around the room. There were the mini-blinds I'd salvaged, the dresser I'd refinished, the moss green walls and brown carpet I'd selected to harmonize with the out of doors. Sunlight poured through the conservatory windows onto the bed. Brad had been right— it was like making love outside. I'd become a woman in this room. He'd touched something deep inside me and I'd sobbed in his arms.

A knock on the door drew me out of my reverie. "Sorry to bother you," Jill said, "but I was wondering if you'd like me to throw your wet clothes in the dryer."

I went to the door and handed her my jeans and top. "I'm finished feeling sorry for myself. Mind if I take a shower?"

"Go for it. I'll put your dry things by the door."

By the time I emerged from the bathroom—having showered, styled my hair, collected my few remaining possessions in an overnight bag and scoured the shower, toilet and sink—the house had changed ownership. There was a new comforter on the master bed and different placemats on the dining room table. Unfamiliar dishes had invaded the kitchen. The wall above the mantle in the family room was no longer bare. Everything looked wonderful, but it was Jill-wonderful, not Carrie-wonderful.

I didn't belong there anymore.

Jill and I cleared up after lunch. Then we put on boots and trudged out to Adriana's garden. With the temperature near forty and the sun bright in the sky, the snow had shrunk back to reveal the tiles and pavers.

We stared down at the slate tile that bore the Chinese character for happiness.

"Derek suggested I give it to you," Jill said, "but I was pretty sure you'd want it to stay in the garden."

"It belongs here," I said. I caught Jill's eye. "Quite an adventure, wasn't it?"

"The best," Jill said, and I heard the catch in her voice.

I held out my arms and we embraced.

"I wish you happiness, Carrie."

I squeezed her tight. "I wish you happiness, Jill."

She stepped back. "I'll be inside."

I watched her return to the house. She'd sensed I needed a few minutes by myself. Only I knew why.

The previous Wednesday evening, preparing for a Thursday morning trash pickup, I'd been emptying the bedroom drawers, packing the must-haves into bags and boxes and tossing the discards into a plastic trash bag. My last task of the evening was to empty the nightstand. I was sitting on the edge of the bed going through the top drawer when I unearthed two wrinkled sheets of paper. One was the colored-marker drawing Brad had made for me one Saturday morning and dedicated *To Carrie, the Main Attraction*. The other was the Word of the Day calendar page with my cell phone number scribbled beneath the definition for propinquity.

I smoothed the papers on my lap, one on top of the other, and fished in the drawer for the magnets. My fingers closed on them: two cool disks nestled together in one corner. I took them out, pulled them apart and read the words one last time: YOU. ME.

With grim resolve I centered the magnets on my lap and folded the papers around them. Cradling the bundle in both hands I pressed it to my heart. A moment later I dropped it into the trash bag. Without giving myself time to reconsider I cinched the bag closed and dragged it to the curb.

I was on my way to work the next morning when I saw the trash hauler turning down my street. At that instant I knew I'd made a mistake. It was the same mistake I'd made ten months earlier. That time Jill had saved me by rescuing the keepsake box. This time I would do the saving. I made a U-turn and beat the garbage truck back to the house.

After work that evening I'd buried the mementos in Adriana's garden under the happiness tile. My first impulse had been to enclose them in the same Tupperware container in which we'd found the key, but in the end I'd placed them in the ground unprotected.

That had been two days earlier. My heart had ached as I'd lowered the small bundle into the hole and packed dirt and sand on top of it. Since then, however, like the snow that had fallen during the night, a certain peace had descended upon me.

I knelt and flattened my hand on the sun-warmed tile. With a finger I traced the Chinese character for happiness and imagined the melted snow percolating down through the soil toward the parcel hidden below. Soon the water would work its magic and the buried pages would begin to disintegrate. Eventually, inexorably, they would become part of the earth.

The magnets would last longer. It could be decades before the elements would reclaim them. Would they remain undiscovered all that time? Maybe not. Maybe ten years from now, a child—Jill's daughter perhaps—her imagination fired by the tale of hidden treasure, would dig them up and run to the kitchen to show her mother.

I sat back on my haunches and looked toward the house. I pictured Jill taking the magnets from her daughter and turning them over in her hand. The metal might be rusted. The words might have washed away. But Jill would remember having seen those magnets holding up a grocery list on the refrigerator. She'd put two and two together and when she did she'd smile and reach for the phone.

I wondered where the call would find me. Where would I be living? What would I be doing? In high school I'd dreamed of setting the world on fire. I'd promised my mother I was going to do something important. At the time I didn't know what it would be. I still didn't know, but now I had an inkling it might take me to the nation's capitol.

I had a vision of myself striding down a marble hall, briefcase in hand, credentials dangling from a cord around my neck. I'd be on my way to a press conference or perhaps to a hearing. My phone would sound and I'd put it to my ear.

The voice of a young girl would say, "Aunt Carrie, guess what I found in Adriana's garden."

Remembering those magnets and what they had meant to me would I still feel a pang? Probably. But nothing I couldn't handle.

I trailed my fingers across the happiness tile one final time. Then I stood and brushed the dirt from my jeans.

My gaze swept the patio. Above the steam rising off the pavers the Lady looked serene. I closed my eyes and inhaled the moist, earthy scent of Adriana's garden. My lungs expanded and my heart lifted in my chest.

A chapter of my life was coming to an end. In a few minutes I'd climb into my car, turn the key, and the next chapter would begin.

Your future is somewhere else, Carrie. Somewhere exciting.

Brad had predicted it and he was usually right.